MISSISSIPPI
RECKONING

MISSISSIPPI
RECKONING

MITCHELL
ZIMMERMAN

Hunts Point Press
Palo Alto

ISBN: 978-0-9600107-0-7

Designed by Anna Thompson

For Richard Neuhoff

Devoted friend,
wise mentor, brilliant advocate

PART ONE

I

At ten minutes before midnight, the prisoner sat in the last holding cell, at the end of the Row. He was wearing brand new denim trousers and the brand new work shirt they had given him twenty minutes earlier, pursuant to the official protocol.

The years and months and weeks, and the final days and hours in which others had struggled for him were ending.

The prisoner heard the clanking of the iron gate at the other end of the Row, and the sounds a group of men make even when none are talking. *A stay?*

His final meeting with his attorney.

I killed, Gideon, so I got to pay the price. Maybe it ain't fair I got to die. But that's the way life is. Let it go, my man.

From the mattress on the floor of the cell where he sat, he looked up. The warden, with several guards, stood close to the door.

Gideon's last embrace. Knowing that, over so many years, Gideon was someone he had come to trust. That he had become capable of trusting.

"It is time," said the warden.

He rose, his heart pounding, as a guard with handcuffs came forward and took out a key ring. For the last time, he turned around and put his hands behind him, to the opening in the cell door designed for this purpose, so they could handcuff him behind his back before opening the door.

For a moment an impulse to fight gripped him. He could hit one of these white motherfuckers before they took him away. Why should he go quietly? The impulse faded.

I understand now. I'm not going to end hurting anyone again.

Just get it over with.

He was six. Running wild in the kitchen late at night, knocking an open bottle of whiskey over onto the table. The smell of the spreading booze, his father's hands jerking out to right the bottle, then seizing him and shaking,

– *Look what the fuck you done, you little bastard you!*

– *Jason, baby, he was just . . .*

The door to his cell swung open and two large guards took him firmly by his shoulders as he emerged. They went toward a riveted iron door, and a man in a gray suit opened the door and they all went through.

Helpless in his father's grip. His heart thumping, the ribs of the radiator against his back, the sharp place on one of them cutting, then the searing heat, his scream –

The room they'd entered seemed to be made entirely of metal, painted light green up to the level of the top of the door. Like a hospital. On the wall to the right was a bank of three phones. One of them had a label that said "GOVERNOR'S OFFICE," and another, "SUPREME COURT." Both were silent. The warden lifted the third phone, which had no label, and spoke to someone to confirm that the witnesses and observers were ready. The hands of a clock on the wall pointed to two minutes before midnight.

Momma's arm swinging, the crunch of the bottle shattering and dad slumping and blood flowing onto his own face and screams that seemed to be coming from somewhere else.

Just ahead was the small octagonal room, built right into the wall, with a pyramidal roof. On top was a pipe that disappeared through the ceiling of the room. A guard had told him that the pipe was to carry the gas away afterward. On this side of the chamber was a panel with rows of buttons and switches. A large metal lever, painted red, was in the up position. Near the lever was a window covered by Venetian blinds, the same color green as the walls.

The door to the chamber was oval shaped, and there was a rubber ring where it would close, to ensure a good seal. A large wheel was mounted on the door, with spokes and handles at the ends like the wheel for steering a pirate ship, so they could cinch the door tight.

The sparkle of light off the waves at Manhattan Beach, his mother's gasp as she pulled her face up from the water.

Through the door he could see the windows in the front of the chamber, four big rectangular windows, each with a line of rivets and rubber gaskets around the rim. The windows faced where he would sit, so everyone on the other side would have a good view. He could see the bank of seats out there, and the people in them. He felt embarrassed and looked down.

Panic seized him and his heart sped. *You white bastards, you got me where you want me again.* They stepped into the chamber. In the center there was a chair with heavy leather straps and buckles.

A metal panel ran around the part of the chair below the seat, with a grillwork of holes for the gas to come through. Now they unlocked the cuffs and sat him in the seat, and buckled straps around him. Two straps for his chest. Another around his waist. Straps to hold his arms down. There were metal stirrups along where the backs of his legs rested, and two straps held each leg in place against the metal. The guard was getting the straps tight, but not so tight as to hurt him.

"Try to move," the guard said, stepping back.

You goddamn . . .

He calmed himself and did as he was told. He tested the straps around his chest and the ones that held his arms against the chair. They were tight. The leg ones too. But not so tight as to cut off his circulation. They were satisfied.

"Any final words?" the warden asked.

He shook his head.

"I'm sorry," he heard himself say softly. "I'm sorry for . . . "

It was too complicated to explain.

They left without another word. The wheel on the door screeched, as they sealed the room tight. Through the windows, he saw dozens of people, looking in at him, their faces vacant. Waiting. Someone from the victims' family must be there.

There was one face he knew. He looked into his lawyer's eyes, saw the pain in them, mouthed "Thank you" to him. Then he heard the clank of the lever, and the quiet little splash as sodium cyanide pellets dropped into the vat of sulfuric acid under the chair. His eyes dropped.

They had told him if he breathed deeply, it would be over fast. The gas burned his lungs, and he gasped. He saw the interest in the eyes of the witnesses. Immediately there were sharp pains in his shoulders and chest, as though he were being squeezed by a great hand. *Like when Dad . . .* A crushing pain across the top of his chest. *No.* The pain was intense, *No,* and he tried to rise up, *please,* strained against the straps. But the buckles held, and then he couldn't feel his arms and legs. He could no longer see, there was nothing but the agony at the center. In his heart, the pain so intense, then –

✳ ✳ ✳

12:09 a.m. December 20, 1996. Charles Joshua Jackson, aka Kareem Jackson, was dead.

2

Gideon Roth lurched into the cold night outside the prison buildings. He passed through the gate in the high chain-link fence that secured the main prison complex, and, for the very last time, Gideon walked down the long path that ended at the heavy iron gates guarding the outer perimeter of San Quentin State Prison.

The guards he passed nodded respectfully, appearing content with the orderly achievement of the prison's mission that night. Gideon did not notice them. Before him were only images of the death chamber and Kareem's last moments.

He stumbled through the outer gate, pushing past thirty or forty prison guards and state police, massed by the gate as though they expected to have to repel an attack by the death penalty opponents who were still conducting their silent vigil.

Perhaps a dozen of the demonstrators remained, holding flickering candles, the flames shielded against the wind by little wax paper cups. Their leader was trying to speak. But a group of young men with signs celebrating the execution were taunting him, chanting, "Inhale, Jackson, inhale!"

For a moment Gideon considered punching one of them, he thought how surprised the man would be when Gideon's fist smashed into the side of his head. But Gideon was too dazed to stay focused on these punks.

Gideon knew the organizer of the vigil, who beckoned to him, hoping he would have uplifting words for the demonstrators. He shook his head. As he advanced, a television reporter, a dazzling figure in a circle of klieg-light illumination, approached and asked Gideon to talk to the television audience.

"Mr. Roth, the Attorney General says the long wait of the victims' family for justice is finally over. Do you have any . . ."

Gideon seemed not to notice her and plodded obliviously past the camera crew and back into the darkness. They got him back in their lights, following his retreat as the reporter smoothly continued. "That was Gideon Roth, lawyer for Dark Nines killer Kareem Jackson, just now coming out of San Quentin. Some say that Mr. Roth was a callous advocate for his vilified client, others say he delayed justice for fourteen years with a series of frivolous appeals based on legal technicalities. But tonight Mr. Roth looks grim, understandably grim, after personally watching his client put to death in the gas chamber. Mr. Roth refused . . ."

Her voice faded as the cameramen abandoned their pursuit. Gideon was at last left alone.

He shambled down the street mechanically, passing under the freeway that ran toward the bridge to the East Bay. He reached a nearby parking area, now nearly empty, where he had left his car.

Gideon sat in the driver's seat with his keys in hand, exhausted from several nights without sleep.

He saw the gas chamber, Kareem mouthing the words, "Thank you," and responding, "I love you," before the gas hit. He saw Kareem contorted in pain. Kareem straining at the straps, convulsing, then slumping.

Afterward, Gideon had remained, frozen, in his seat. As the witnesses to the execution left, he heard the fan come on to carry the gas away. Some of the others turned to take a last look at the body. Finally, the guards returned to the chamber. One shoved a broomstick against Kareem's chest to expel the remaining gas from his body. Then they noticed Gideon, and someone pulled the curtain across the windows, and they made him go.

Gideon wanted to strike out, but there was no target for his anger and despair. The long years he had struggled for Kareem Jackson were over. He had proven inadequate to the task.

Gideon took his cellphone from the glove compartment and opened it. He looked out into the night. Then he closed the phone. The other members of the defense team knew how it had ended. He had nothing more to say. Not for him to comfort them, nor to thank them for their efforts. Useless, like his own.

His wife Helen also knew—so many times over the years, she had warned him it would end this way.

He should go home to Atherton. But the drive was long, and what was at home for him? He closed his eyes.

Gideon woke twenty minutes later. His car was being rocked. The raucous pro-death group was celebrating, and one of them had recognized the graying, middle-aged man asleep inside the car as Kareem Jackson's lawyer. Several young men were pushing down on the hood together, then releasing it, then pushing down again, making the front of Gideon's car bob up and down. Now they ridiculed, "Inhale, Roth, inhale!"

Gideon opened the door, banging it into one of them, and he stepped out.

"Shut your idiot faces and get the fuck away from my car."

Laughing, they ignored him.

"I'm not going to tell you again," Gideon said.

"What are you going to do about it, you old fart?"

Gideon stepped up to the closest one, grabbed him by the back of his jacket collar and whirled him away from the hood and into a lamp post. The man gasped, lost his balance and tumbled to the ground.

He rose to his feet, slowly took off his coat, and handed it to a friend.

"Hey, mister," another said. "Maybe you should get out of here now. You don't want to fuck with Richie."

"Fuck you and fuck Richie."

Richie, a small but heavy-set man in his twenties, charged Gideon. Gideon tried to meet him with a punch, but the little man rushed through it, hitting Gideon in the mouth and knocking him down. It hurt, and Gideon tasted blood. "You and your fucking killers," Richie swore drunkenly as he closed to stomp on Gideon's legs. "They should all die. You too, you fucking lawyer."

Richie swung his leg back to kick Gideon in the stomach but lost his footing. While he staggered, Gideon rolled away and scrambled to his feet. Before Richie regained his balance, Gideon waded into him, punching him savagely in the face. He took Richie's return blow without flinching, moved in close and stamped hard on Richie's foot. Richie cried out, and Gideon kneed him between the legs. Richie wilted, sliding to his knees. "Whoa!" someone said.

But Gideon did not stop. A slam to the side of Richie's head knocked him to the ground. Gideon dropped onto him, and raked the fallen man's injured nose and eye with more blows.

Two men tried to drag Gideon off Richie, but Gideon sprung at them ferociously. Suddenly a siren screamed.

A police cruiser was beside them, lights flashing. Two cops jumped out to break up the fight. One of them held Gideon's forearm in a tight grip. The second cop pushed the others back by the car.

"This bastard beat up our friend," one of the young men protested.

"You telling me he attacked someone half his age?" the cop asked. "With all you guys around?"

"Hey, just look at Richie. This guy's an animal."

"This guy in the classy suit and the nice tie, he jumped out of his BMW to mug Richie? For no reason. Maybe he wanted to take Richie's three-buck watch? I don't think so. Maybe you guys was trying to mug him and it didn't turn out so good?"

He looked toward Gideon, questioningly. Gideon shook his head. Disappointed, the cop let out a big breath, then looked back toward the young men.

"All right, getta the fuck outta here before I give you trouble."

Still holding Gideon, he waved the young men away.

"Come over here," he said to Gideon, firmly moving him toward the patrol car. He opened the back door.

"Siddown for a minute."

Gideon sat on the edge of the seat with the door open. The other cop took out their first aid kit and gave Gideon something to wipe his cuts with.

"Aw, you messed up your expensive suit," said the first cop with mock sympathy, staring fixedly at Gideon. He waited, but Gideon said nothing. "I don't know what happened here, but looks to me like you know how to take care of yourself, buddy. You know how to play a little rough, huh? Maybe you got a little out of control?"

Gideon still did not respond.

"Looks like it," says the other cop. "Looks to me like this Richie started something and got more than he bargained for." He chuckled softly.

They looked at Gideon, but Gideon remained silent. He winced as he tried to get dirt out of the abrasions on his cheek. He thought how he appeared to the cops—a gaunt, older man in a disheveled suit that now had a tear in the trouser leg. Smeared with grime from the parking lot, his face bruised, his salt-and-pepper hair and trim beard now grungy, his scraped knuckles bearing smudges of the younger man's blood. Not the image of the distinguished 52-year-old attorney Gideon Roth was usually at pains to project.

The first cop asked, "You was the lawyer for Jackson, right?"

Gideon nodded.

"A rough night for you, buddy."

He patted Gideon on the shoulder. "Jackson got what he deserved, but you was just doin' your job."

The cops turned away to talk. Then the first came back.

"We got to make a report whenever there's a fight, but we're not going to book you. You can go. See if you can stay out of trouble until morning. Or at least 'til you get out of Marin County."

3

Gideon drove over the Golden Gate Bridge. Across the water, ahead and to the left, he saw the lights of San Francisco. On the right, the never-ending blackness of the Pacific. His cellphone rang. He did not answer.

Kareem was dead. Killed before his eyes.

He remembered the years in which he thought he could save Kareem. He had pictured finding in the mail a large envelope with the return address, United States District Court, 312 N. Spring Street, Los Angeles, CA 90012. Almost against his will, because he had been afraid to hope, he had imagined opening the envelope and reading: "Order Granting Writ of Habeas Corpus," overturning the death sentence.

Writ granted! He had seen himself standing at the podium, speaking at a conference of death penalty lawyers, explaining how he'd done it.

When reality began to sink in, the grim reality against which Helen had so often warned him, the writ fantasies had turned into escape dreams. In some of his dreams, Gideon found Kareem standing beside him when he reached his car in the San Quentin parking lot, and Gideon had to figure out how to hide Kareem and where to take him. Once, in another dream, he saw Kareem sitting on a swing in the playground in Gideon's old neighborhood in the South Bronx, and he thought, *I've got to get him out of here!*

But Gideon had never had an execution dream in all those years.

He had tried to force himself to imagine opening the envelope and seeing, "Order Denying Writ of Habeas Corpus." So he would be ready for the worst. Yet over the long years, he had never been able to encompass the thought that his efforts would end in failure. Would end with the death of the man he had, over the years, grown close to.

Notwithstanding all his cynicism—notwithstanding his conviction that the politics of the death penalty had made it impossible to find fair judges in capital cases, or for fair judges to decide justly—he had never really believed Kareem would be executed.

Now he hated himself for having clung so long to the illusion that he could halt the machinery of death. Kareem's life had been in Gideon's keeping. Now Kareem was gone. They had killed him. There was no way for Gideon to make it right.

Drained, Gideon drove through the city and into the lonely darkness of the freeway that ran above the Peninsula.

He drove slowly, scarcely focusing on the road. From time to time a car passed, the red glow of its rear lights swiftly shrinking into the distance. He slowed further and moved to the right lane. He needed a few more minutes of silence before he reached home and had to face Helen's sympathy.

He turned into a rest area. It looked over a narrow lake, a reservoir in the dark hills that shone in the quarter moon. But his mind was too turbulent to be stilled by a vista.

He thought of his life and saw a trail of failure. A former civil rights worker, anti-war activist and student radical, Gideon had watched with disgust as the country had become ever more conservative over the decades, and he felt responsible for not having done more to fight it. Instead of becoming a civil rights lawyer, as he had once intended, he had somehow turned into a copyright and trademark litigator at a high-powered and prosperous Silicon Valley law firm.

Kareem's case and the other pro bono cases he had handled over the years had helped him deal with these contradictions. Gideon's long struggle for Kareem spanned half of Gideon's adult life.

But now it was over.

4

When Gideon reached home, the bruises on the side of his mouth had darkened, and his left eye and lips were swollen. Traces of blood still streaked his cheek, and he moved stiffly as he walked to the front door. Helen opened it and he entered.

"Good God, Gideon. What happened to you? Where have you been?"

"It's a long story, Helen. And it's not what's on my mind right now."

She moved toward him, but he stiffened, and she halted.

"Gideon, I haven't seen you in a week. And you look like you've been mugged."

"No, just brawling."

"Brawling. I don't understand."

"Drop it, Helen."

"I'm not supposed to notice or care?"

She followed as he went into the living room.

The mantle was adorned with Christmas greenery, amidst which stood sleigh and reindeer decorations, a small wooden Saint Nick, and red candles in heavy silver candlesticks. But the fireplace was cold and the room was dim.

Helen watched as Gideon threw his suit jacket onto a chair, and poured himself a large whiskey.

"Gideon, I am sorry. So sorry for how this ended. How it had to end. It must have been horrible." She rested a hand gently against his back and spoke softly. "Kareem had the best lawyer in the world."

"Kareem had a lawyer who lost his edge," Gideon snapped. "A lawyer who failed. A lawyer whose last service was watching his client gassed to death."

He dropped himself onto the sofa, sloshing some of his drink onto his pants.

"A lawyer who lost," Gideon said. "Nothing else matters in the end."

"No, that's wrong, Gideon. You kept him alive for fourteen years—in the face of a system rigged for death." She sat by him.

"Someone needs to pay," he said, "for all the suffering and pain the system inflicts. For all the injustice. For the things Kareem suffered when he was just a child. But no one will."

He swirled his drink round and round. He took a large sip, then limply rested the hand with his glass on his lap. A little more spilled.

"One of the losers," Gideon said. "That's all I was."

"There's more than one kind of winning in this kind of fight. You told me that yourself, years ago."

"Tell that to Kareem."

Helen recoiled.

Why am I doing this? he thought. He put his drink on the coffee table, stretched out a tentative hand to her.

"I'm sorry," he said.

"Oh, Gideon. It's gone on so long."

And are you relieved, now it's finally over?

Helen wrapped her arms around him and put her face against his chest. He tried to soften himself to receive her comfort, but could not let go his rigidity.

"Poor Kareem," she said. "Poor Gideon. Poor all of us. So long and so horrible. To do that to a human being, in cold blood." Her voice choked up. He looked down and saw tears on her cheek. Tears that ought to have been his.

5

Gideon lay next to Helen, sleepless despite his exhaustion. He thought of his first meeting with Kareem. *So long ago.*

He had known only the bare outline of the case when he accepted the California Supreme Court's appointment to represent Kareem Jackson. The crime was a hideous double kidnapping and rape and murder – the victims, a young mother and her small daughter. And the killer had nearly slain someone else with a shotgun in the robbery spree that had led up to it. One of those cases notorious enough to get a nickname in the press, the Dark Nines Murder, after the Compton motel where the crime took place.

Gideon remembered the headlines:

NINE-YEAR-OLD AND MOM KIDNAPPED,
MOTHER BUTCHERED IN DARK NINES HORROR

TERROR IN DARK NINES MOTEL:
MOTHER RAPED AND SLAIN,
DAUGHTER ASSAULTED

DA SEEKS GAS CHAMBER
FOR DARK NINES KILLER-RAPIST

JURY TO
DARK NINES KILLER:
D I E

A friend who had handled several death penalty appeals told Gideon there was nothing wrong with choosing a case where you had a chance of winning. Where the crime was not so shocking that you were bound to lose. But Gideon had been confident in his lawyering in those days, and he wanted to rescue someone from death row in a seemingly hopeless case.

Gideon did accept his friend's advice that it might be easier if he got to know the defendant as a person before he read the record, viewed the crime scene photos, held the murder weapon in his hand, handled the victims' blood-stained clothing. So, two days after he received the order appointing him as Jackson's counsel, Gideon wrote to introduce himself and to tell Jackson he would visit him at San Quentin the following week.

Gideon admitted to himself he was uneasy about meeting Jackson. Is a killer a person so different from ordinary humans that we won't speak the same language? he asked himself. Would he feel the same awkwardness, talking to Jackson, that people usually feel when they are forced to talk to someone who's had a death in the family?

Gideon was uneasy, but he found the rituals of entry into San Quentin State Prison exotic and intriguing. Driving up one foggy summer morning, he first saw the great iron outer gates, set in their stone pillars. Behind them, two hundred yards further away, stood the mist-shrouded prison itself.

Visitors did not pass directly through the main gates, but turned left down a short driveway that flanked the Visitor Processing building. Gideon parked in the lot below, picturesquely located along the water. From there he could see the yellow-brick prison, sitting atop a low bluff. On clear days, if you turned away from the prison, you'd enjoy a striking view of the northern part of San Francisco Bay.

Pursuant to prison regulations, he carried only two keys, his driver's license and attorney identification, a file folder containing a yellow pad and some papers, a pen, and one twenty dollar bill. Also a pocket full of change for the food-and-drink machines. He had left his wallet and briefcase at the office, along with credit cards and other forbidden items.

Gideon had been told to go straight to the head of the line in the hallway of the entry building. Attorney visitors came before families and others, before the mostly black and Hispanic women with their children, who waited for hours to visit their incarcerated men.

The door into the visitor processing room was flanked by windows nearly entirely obscured with notices.

> AN INMATE AND THEIR VISITOR MAY EMBRACE, INCLUDING
> A KISS, AT THE BEGINNING AND END OF EACH VISIT.
> NO OTHER PERSONAL PHYSICAL CONTACT IS PERMITTED.

Another notice set out clothing standards for visitors:

PROHIBITED ATTIRE:

- Clothing which exposes the breast/chest area, genitals or buttocks
- Tank tops, halter tops, slingshot shirts or sleeveless garments
- Sheer or transparent garments
- Clothing exposing the midriff area

Some of the signs presumably had to do with jailors' fears that prisoners might be given something that could help in an escape attempt:

> "NO WIGS
>
> "NO HAIRPIECES
>
> "NO EXCEPTIONS"

Another sign confirmed:

> ATTORNEYS TO HEAD OF LINE.

A small, makeshift cardboard box that was taped to the wall held blank Visitor Passes. It bore another instruction, "Fill Out Before Ringing Bell." Gideon wrote down Kareem's actual full name, Charles Joshua Jackson, and copied Kareem's California Department of Corrections ("CDC") number from his pad. He filled in his own name and business address. He signed an acknowledgment he would abide by CDC regulations.

Gideon pressed the bell only one time, as another sign commanded. The door buzzed. Gideon pulled it open and entered

He was in a large, mostly empty room with lockers along the wall near him. A chubby black woman in a khaki uniform sat on a tall stool at the far end, behind a narrow counter on which rested a computer monitor.

Crossing the room, Gideon thought for a moment of the "power offices" he visited, in which a generous distance from door to executive's desk served to remind you that you were in the presence of the mighty. In this shabby room, the effect was parody.

The computer monitor was grungy with dust and grease from being handled for years. The walls bore the detritus of myriad Scotch-taped CDC notices. The shallow wooden box that sat on the counter was dull with the nicks and dents of thousands of keys, glasses, pens and shoes having been dropped into it for inspection over the years. The only plainly new items were the airport-style metal detectors next to the guard.

"Gideon Roth, here to see Kareem . . . Charles Jackson."

"Let me see your driver's license and bar card."

He handed them to the guard, and she checked them against the list on her clipboard.

"First time here?" she demanded.

"Yes." He tried to adopt a bright and friendly tone.

She showed her boredom in response.

"Put everything from your pockets, and everything metal, in the box. Shoes too. And let me see your jacket and the pad."

She squeezed his jacket and peered into the folder, only enough to see that it contained nothing but papers. Meanwhile Gideon emptied his pockets into the wooden box that sat on the metal detector's conveyer belt. He took off his shoes and balanced them on everything else. The guard pressed a button and the box moved through. No problem.

Then she instructed Gideon to walk through the gateway metal detector. The gate buzzed.

"Take off your belt and your glasses."

Gideon took them off and walked through again.

The gate buzzed again.

This time he removed a pen. Still the gate buzzed. Gideon pulled his pockets inside out and patted himself here and there.

"The only metal left is my wedding ring. The ring hasn't been off in decades, and I don't think I can get it off my finger."

This had evidently come up before: "Try wrapping your other hand around the ring finger like this and stepping through." Gideon followed the instructions and this time he passed through the gate without triggering the alarm.

The guard stamped Gideon's Visitor Pass and handed it to him with his license and bar card. Gideon put on his shoes and jacket and refilled his pockets. The guard pointed him to the other door, into the prison grounds, and up the long walk toward the inner gate. Ahead he saw a five-story gun tower, which looked like traffic control at a small town airport, just past the nine-foot chain link fence.

At the end of the walk, at the gate, was a small booth, a sign-in sheet and another metal detector. A guard took Gideon's papers and examined them against the list on his clipboard. Gideon emptied his pockets again, put his watch and glasses into another old wooden box, and stepped through the second metal detector. This time, after it pinged, the guard just ran a hand-held detector along Gideon's body, satisfying himself that the beeps came only from Gideon's belt and ring. He stamped the back of Gideon's hand with yellow ultraviolet-light-sensitive ink.

The guard pointed Gideon toward the visitors' building, and Gideon crossed a small road bordered by well-tended grass next to the gun tower. He stood quietly before a door made of iron bars covered on each side with plexiglass. Abruptly, the door rumbled along its track to the right, and Gideon stepped into a small entryway. The door rumbled shut behind him, and Gideon found himself in a kind of visitors' air lock, with a similar door on a track in front of him. The sallyport.

To his left was a glass window into another guard's station. The window had a small opening along the bottom—like the ticket booth at the movies—for visitors to present their papers. The guard inspected Gideon's pass, compared Gideon to his driver's license photo, and held onto the papers.

"You'll be in cell number 4, Mr. Roth," the guard said with easy courtesy, for which Gideon was grateful. "Mr. Jackson will be down in a few minutes." The guard pressed a button, and the inner gate clanged open. Gideon walked through, and the gate closed behind him.

Twelve visitors cells were grouped together, six on each side, with a corridor running between them wide enough for two people. Each visiting cell was a small cage of metal bars, with plexiglass sheets affixed to both sides of the bars, so you could see into all of the cells from any side, but discussions could be private. While he waited for Jackson, Gideon bought cans of soda and juice, a cup of hot tea, and candy bars from the vending machine area outside the group of cells.

Visitor cell number 4 had an outside window with a view of the north bay and the Richmond – San Rafael Bridge. Gideon rested a hand on the many-times-painted-over window ledge and looked out. It had the aged feeling of his high school in the Bronx. Then he turned from the window and saw Kareem Jackson for the first time.

In years to come, Gideon must have been asked a hundred times whether he had met the condemned prisoner he represented. He had thought it peculiar anyone would imagine that Gideon could represent someone for a decade or more without meeting him. He realized, finally, that they were titillated by the same concerns that had, unarticulated, pre-occupied Gideon before his first visit: whether this was like meeting with a monster—or with a dead man.

Kareem Jackson was a disappointingly ordinary looking black man of average height, perhaps a couple of inches shorter than Gideon's six feet, in his early twenties, with muscular arms and chest. He was looking down, and the top of his shaven, slightly beaten-up looking skull, shiny and very black, was prominent. His face was broad and his nose flat, and his jaw was square and solid. There were small scars near his eyes on one side. But his mouth was immobile, and a lack of expression robbed his face of any presence. His eyes, remote, flickered up toward Gideon for a moment.

Two enormous guards stood at Jackson's sides, men much larger than Jackson or Gideon, and he shambled because his steps were constricted by leg irons. His hands were cuffed behind his back, and the guards held his upper arms lightly. Gideon had no feeling that Jackson was a menacing person, but the two guards were clearly in control of him.

Gideon said "Hello," then fell silent. He was suddenly aware that ordinary social conventions could not apply here. For Gideon to introduce himself while Jackson was chained and handcuffed, while his jailors handled him like an object, was to become complicit in the definition of Kareem Jackson as something less than a person. Jackson may have been the perpetrator of horrible crimes. But he was still not an object. Gideon knew he must merely stand, he must say nothing until Jackson was unbound, and they were alone together.

Jackson stepped into the cell. A guard slid the heavy barred door closed with a clang, placed a massive padlock into the hasp, and snapped it shut.

The door had an opening to allow the guards to unlock an inmate's handcuffs after he had been secured with his visitor. The opening was about twelve inches wide and six inches high, and was covered by a metal flap with its own hasp and its own heavy padlock. The guard un-hooked that padlock and dropped the flap. Jackson backed up and put his cuffed hands to the opening. The guard reached in, unlocked and removed Kareem Jackson's handcuffs, and closed and padlocked the flap. He and the other guard departed. Jackson and Gideon were locked in together.

Jackson's leg irons were still on, but that didn't matter in this small space. Gideon and Jackson looked at each other. Gideon reached out his hand, and Jackson took it weakly.

"I'm Gideon Roth. I'm the lawyer the court appointed to represent you in your appeals. Call me Gideon. How are you doing?"

"Fine." Jackson spoke slowly, in a low voice. "I'm doin' just fine."

Gideon gestured to the sodas and the candy, as they sat down. "I wasn't sure what you might want to eat or drink."

"That's fine."

Gideon had prepared some chatter to keep things going until they could become more comfortable with each other. He hoped he had enough. Jackson looked at Gideon.

"I haven't received the record of the trial yet," Gideon said, "so I don't know all that much about the case or the trial, and I'm not in a position to talk to you right now about what kinds of issues we might be able to raise to challenge your conviction or the death sentence. But I thought it would be a good idea if we got together for a bit anyway. How are things going here?"

"No one's hassling me."

"How long have you been here?"

"'Bout a month. Right after the judge sentenced me, they rush me here. Didn't have no chance to get my goods out of my cell in county jail."

"That's too bad." Gideon thought quickly about whether he should say he'd look into it, decided this was one of those things he probably could do nothing about. He let some silence accumulate, waiting to see whether Jackson would fill it. He didn't.

"I'll tell you about myself. I've been a lawyer for ten years. I've done quite a few appeals in federal and state court, though this is the first death penalty case I've had. I'll be pulling together a team of lawyers from my firm to work on your case. We're a fair sized firm, about a hundred lawyers, and some very good people are going to be fighting for you. There's a resource center called the California Capital Project we're also going to be working with—"

He could see Jackson's eyes drifting off. What did "resource center" mean to Jackson? Gideon was losing connection with him, but wasn't sure what to do, so he rattled on.

"—they're really experts in death penalty law, and they'll be working with us, to help us spot all the issues."

Okay, start again. I'm being too abstract.

"Anyway. What can I tell you? Do you have any questions for me about all this, about what's going to happen?"

"How long is it gonna take?"

Gideon had been told this was one of the questions they always asked.

"Well, it's hard to say, depends on a lot of things, but I'll try to give you an idea. First thing, the record has to be certified and corrected. That means that the court reporter and the clerk in the trial court, the court where you were tried, are going to write up the transcript of what everyone said during the trial . . ."

Gideon explained what that was about, and started drawing a time line on his pad as he spoke, making the time and the process visible by drawing a vertical line next to the word "record," writing "6 - 9 mos" next to the line. He went on to talk about the perhaps-200-pages-long appeal brief ("1 yr," "Brief").

Gideon extended the line and jotted down more numbers as he described what was going to happen. Was Jackson following all this? He seemed to be trying hard to understand.

"That all adds up to, let's see, around four, four and half years. Might be less, could easily be more.

"What happens next depends on what they decide. Things can go different ways. There are different possible branches. If they reversed both your death penalty and your murder conviction, you would be entitled to a new trial on everything.

"If they said the murder conviction, for first degree murder, was right, but they overturned the death penalty, the state could decide whether to have a new trial, a new trial just on whether or not you should get the death penalty. Maybe we would negotiate with them over whether we would agree not to appeal the conviction further if they agreed not to pursue the death penalty."

"I'm not going to make any deal," Jackson said. "I'm not gonna spend the rest of my life here."

"Well, obviously, we're going to fight as hard as we can for you. At this point, I don't even know what the issues are going to be, and I just don't have any idea at all what our chances are."

"My chances, not your chances. You're not the one they're going to strap into the chair in the gas chamber. After I'm dead, you'll be heading out for a weekend in Vegas on the money you get for defending me. I'd rather be dead than spend the rest of my life here."

Gideon was taken aback, but he responded, displaying only a little indignation.

"You think I'm in this for the money? I get $60 an hour for the time I spend on this case. My usual billing rate is $135 an hour."

Jackson snorted. "Sixty dollars? For one hour?"

"I didn't take this case for the money. I took this case because I don't think you should be put to death and I mean to put everything I've got into keeping the state from killing you.

"As for life in prison, we're a long way from having to make a decision one way or another on that. Don't be in a hurry to give the state what it wants."

Gideon wasn't sure if he should have confronted Jackson's challenge more forcefully. He didn't know Jackson. He didn't feel entitled to have Jackson view him one way or the other before he had given Jackson reason to trust him.

"Let me go on telling you about what we expect to happen as the case unfolds."

Gideon saw Jackson wasn't looking at him, but he went on.

"If we lose in the California Supreme Court, that's not the end of the road, not at all. Then we're ready for federal court." He outlined getting a stay of execution from a federal judge, filing a federal habeas corpus petition, and the investigation, and the briefing and the appeals in the federal courts. Jackson looked back at the time line.

"You need to understand," Gideon said, "that nothing we do could end with a judge just saying, okay, Kareem Jackson goes free. All they can say, at best, is there were mistakes, big mistakes, in the way the case was handled below, so you're entitled to a new trial.

"There are a lot of moving parts here, but all of that could take at least another three, four years. Maybe more. Maybe a lot more. If this all went badly, in the end we'd have a shot at asking the Governor to grant clemency. For what that's worth.

"Putting all this together, adds up to eight years, probably more, before you could be executed. No guarantee. But that's what it looks like."

While Jackson was thinking this over, Gideon was reflecting again that when he had decided to take on a death penalty case, he had made a decision—like getting married—that was destined to go on for quite a while. Except this would last longer than many marriages.

He'd done a lot of talking so far, and Jackson had done a lot of listening. Or maybe just sitting there, letting Gideon's words wash over him. Gideon wasn't getting to know Jackson this way. He wasn't doing this very well.

"Tell me, Kareem, did you feel that anything that happened at the trial seemed unfair to you? I mean, I'll read over everything when I get the transcripts, and we'll decide what the legal issues are. But it might be helpful if I knew there were some things to look for. Did anything about how the trial went bother you? Other than them deciding to kill you."

Jackson smiled briefly, then responded. "The jury was all white. There were no blacks on the jury."

"Do you remember . . . before they picked the jury, there was a bigger group of people who were possible jurors, who were called into the courtroom. The panel they were picking the jury from, they call it. Were there any blacks in that group?"

"Not many. The DA got rid of all of them"

"Did your lawyer say anything about it?

"Don't remember."

Batson challenge? Ineffective assistance of counsel? Gideon wondered, but only to himself. It wasn't time to take sides against the trial lawyer, before he knew anything about what had happened. But neither did he want to dismiss Jackson's concern.

"Okay, that's something I'll look out for. Sometimes it's just the luck of the draw. The panel they draw happens to have only a few black people on it. Just like you shuffled a deck of cards, and your hand doesn't happen to have any spades in it." Lord, what had he said? "So to speak. But it could be that something else is going on. Maybe the system is rigged in some way, and the DA had no good reason for excluding the blacks from the jury. That would violate your constitutional rights. We'll take a hard look at that. Anything else?"

"He called me a jungle animal," Jackson said, but without any passionate concern.

"Your own attorney?"

"No, the DA."

"The DA. You know, the prosecutor's got a lot of leeway in this kind of thing—you were charged with rape and murder and armed robbery—but that may be going too far. Seems to have a little racist edge to it, doesn't it?"

"Thank you."

Gideon made notes on his pad about the issues Jackson had raised.

"Anything else?"

"Can't think of anything else."

"Well, let me know if you have any more ideas. Here are some envelopes with my address on them. Just write to me any time you want, about anything at all.

"There are going to be long times when there's nothing happening in the case, but I'll try to keep in touch with you anyway. I'll write to you at least once a month, and I'll come up whenever I can. Is there anyone else who comes up to visit you, by the way?"

"No."

"No family or anything?"

"Haven't seen no family in ten years."

Gideon mulled that one over, and decided to put off exploring it.

"One other thing. It's important to try to avoid any trouble while you're up here. This case is going to go on for years, and the day may come when there's a hearing, or you might have a new trial. It would be great to be able to say you were a model prisoner for six years or whatever. That you didn't hurt anyone, and didn't get into trouble or anything."

Jackson listened to this homily without reacting. Gideon knew that the kind of people who ended up on death row were not models of self-control, but he hoped for the best. He got up and waved to one of the large guards, signaling he was ready to leave. A few minutes later, one of them put the handcuffs back on Jackson through the port in the cell door, then unlocked the door. Gideon became conscious again of the shackles around Kareem Jackson's waist and legs. Jackson was led away and the visit ended. Jackson would be strip searched, Gideon had been told, to make sure he had received no contraband from Gideon.

Gideon left the now open cell, dropping the empty soda and juice cans into a recycling barrel near the entrance to the visiting room. But Gideon couldn't leave yet, not until Jackson had been cleared. Walking across a white line painted onto the floor ("No Prisoners Past This Point"), Gideon went into the visitors' men's room.

Well, that was interesting, he thought. I wasn't great, but it wasn't that bad. I've started connecting with a condemned man.

6

Christmas came five days after the execution. It was an empty gesture. In the days before the holiday, Helen tried to get Gideon to talk about what he was going through, but their conversations had been forced and abortive.

Gideon's effort to be cheerful on Christmas morning had foundered against his bitterness and exhaustion, and Helen was left wondering whether he saw celebrating the holiday as an insult to Kareem's memory.

A week later, they went to a large New Year's Eve party. Determined to have a festive evening, Gideon knocked back two large Scotches right away. Someone he didn't know began talking to Gideon about how horrible all the shopping had been in mid-December, and asked Gideon whether he was one of those well-organized people who got all their Christmas shopping done early.

"I was too busy working on a case to do any shopping until Christmas eve," Gideon said, instantly regretting it.

"I'm an attorney, too," his new friend said. "What kind of case?"

"A death penalty case."

"Whew! Those go on forever, don't they?"

"Not this one," said Gideon. "Let's talk about something else."

Gideon saw the man's expression turn from cheery to appalled, as he suddenly realized which case Gideon was referring to.

Many of the guests knew Gideon and knew how the Kareem Jackson case had ended. They offered regrets, awkwardly. Instead of relaxing, Gideon felt he was tiptoeing through a field of social landmines.

Helen and Gideon were relieved when the winter festivities ended.

A week into the new year Gideon returned to his office on Sand Hill Road, in Menlo Park. Things were not going well for Gideon at the firm. While working nonstop on the death penalty case, he had pushed onto the back burner several cases for the firm's business clients. An associate missed a deadline in a case Gideon was supposedly supervising, nearly leading to a malpractice claim. Nor was this the only problem.

"You know we support pro bono work to the utmost," the chairman of the firm had told him yesterday afternoon. "And we all sympathize with you over the bad outcome we had in Jackson. But we're running a business, Gideon, and you can't keep dropping the ball. We had to report your little problem in the Kingston Memory case to the firm's insurance carrier. I'm concerned about your work, Gideon."

Bad outcome? Concerned? What if I punched you out right now, Gideon thought. I could make you "concerned" about whether your face would look the same. I could make you look like Richie. Can't you try to understand what it's like when your client's facing death?

Gideon controlled his anger. "The death penalty case was a mite distracting, Wendell," he responded. "But it's over now."

"I understand. But you win some cases and you lose some cases. You can't get over-involved. Why do I have to tell you this, Gideon? I'm worrying about how you're managing your caseload. Get your act together, Gideon."

Three days after the execution, and on her own initiative, his secretary had sent off to storage two dozen boxes of Jackson case materials that had been in Gideon's office. She had left a small photograph of Kareem as a child, the only one Gideon's team had ever located, which he had had framed. It sat on a low bookcase. All else relating to the case had been cleared away.

Everyone was ready to move on.

Gideon sat in his office, trying to get himself to work on something. He swiveled his chair so it faced the large window that looked out at the grassy hills of Santa Clara County. The rains of winter had greened the grasses, and the hillsides were dotted with oak trees crouching here and there.

Gideon had once taken satisfaction from the thought that in sight of these hills, in these suburban, near rural surroundings, world-changing technologies were being born that would transform how we do everything. Silicon Valley was the birthplace of a renaissance much as Venice and Florence had been, and attorneys like Gideon were as integral to it as the merchants and ship-captains who had revolutionized trade and fueled a cultural rebirth in the fifteenth century.

But Gideon's sense of wonder at being part of it had always been at war with his feeling this wasn't what he was meant to do. That The Cause really mattered more than The Next New Thing. And now, he was finding it hard to care about the firm's work. He felt no desire to reengage with the cases he had delegated to senior associates or more junior partners.

Maybe he should just get out of the office for a while, go for a run or something. But though he knew this would do him good, he couldn't summon the energy to move himself.

"Gideon."

He turned as Amy Koznowski and Lisa Maldonado came in and sat down. Amy was a second-year litigation associate, inexperienced but eager and enthusiastic. Lisa was a senior associate, close to partnership. They were here to talk about Petfood Solutions versus KibbleSoft, a software copyright dispute.

At the outset of the lawsuit ten months earlier, Gideon's team had failed to obtain a preliminary injunction to stop KibbleSoft from selling its re-tail management software for pet food distributors—a program that was a rip-off of their client Petfood Solutions' flagship product. But, unlike many intellectual property disputes, which settled soon after the judge either issued or declined to issue a preliminary injunction, this lawsuit had dragged on bitterly.

They had been pursuing the case for months, and, like hunters long on the trail of wounded prey, they now saw the opportunity to bring down their quarry. Lisa's determined investigation had established that the declarations KibbleSoft had submitted to fend off a preliminary injunction were filled with falsehoods. If they could prove this, the judge might grant judgment against KibbleSoft as a sanction.

Now they were pressing KibbleSoft in discovery, the pre-trial procedures that allowed each side to obtain information from the other side before a case went to trial. They wanted to force their opponent to either own up to the earlier lies or dig themselves in deeper. Of course, KibbleSoft was trying with all its might to avoid both alternatives, mostly by not answering the questions Gideon's people asked in discovery.

The sensitive antennae of KibbleSoft's lawyers were exquisitely tuned to ambiguities too subtle for ordinary mortals to detect, and they had (in place of real answers) gravely explained why, confronted with questions "so poorly framed," it was impossible for KibbleSoft to respond even though they were eager to provide the information Petfood Solutions needed to fairly present its side of the dispute.

The usual polite legalese that meant: "Piss off."

Of course, Gideon would have done the same thing in their position.

KibbleSoft's evasions had been skillful, but they had failed in the first round. When Petfood Solutions brought its motion to compel answers from KibbleSoft, Judge Temple told KibbleSoft he thought they could probably make a wild stab at understanding what Petfood Solutions' questions were getting at, since he got the point immediately. He ordered them to provide answers "promptly, directly and honestly." But now that Gideon's young colleagues had looked at the KibbleSoft responses, they concluded that "promptly" was all they had gotten.

"I've done the analysis of the interrogatory responses from KibbleSoft,"

Amy started before she even reached a chair, "and they're still a bunch of crap. They didn't tell us squat. We should go back to Judge Temple if they won't roll over."

"Tell me all about it," Gideon said.

Amy began a well-organized account of the defects of KibbleSoft's "Further Responses to Plaintiff Petfood Solutions' Fourth Set of Interrogatories." The responses could not be squared with the documents in the case. "First, you will recall, we asked them for all the facts they had at the time they filed their response . . . "

— Gideon sat in a hard folding chair in the front row as they brought Kareem into the chamber. A man kneeled next to Kareem, adjusting the straps that held Kareem's legs—

"Gary's original affidavit," Amy was saying, "denied that he'd had any access to the procurement engine when he worked for Petfood Solutions . . ."

— He saw the fear in Kareem's eyes, as Kareem found Gideon's face among the witnesses—

". . . but the email record shows that he himself sent four messages to the senior programmers . . ."

— They looked into each other's eyes, mouthing words of farewell, as the door to the gas chamber was sealed, and the lever clanked down —

He shivered, and shook his head slightly. Amy paused.

"Sorry. I drifted off a bit there. Go on. You were saying about Gary's emails while he was still at Petfood Solutions," Gideon prompted.

Memories of the gas chamber scene, increasingly tinged with anger at his impotence, were becoming more frequent. They impaired Gideon's ability to focus on the great world of intellectual property litigation. He made himself think harder about KibbleSoft, and he called up some in-dignation about KibbleSoft's outrageous deeds.

"Yes. Point two," Amy said. "We can show that Gary lied about what he took with him when he left Petfood Solutions because . . ." She resumed her exposition of KibbleSoft's wrongs.

Gideon was only a little outraged, and not shocked. He knew that oth-erwise law-abiding businessmen often find the temptation to commit perjury in civil litigation as irresistible as some inner city youths found the impulse to lift tape decks from cars on dark streets at night. And there was a fine line between framing what happened a little more favorably to one's side, and lying under oath. Sometimes Gideon has not been sure which he had been encouraging witnesses to do.

Amy's report showed that—notwithstanding KibbleSoft's nonresponsiveness—they basically had KibbleSoft cold. KibbleSoft was not going to escape. Gideon's only question was whether they should bother with one more, final discovery effort or go directly to a motion to reconsider the preliminary injunction and for sanctions.

"What do you think we should do next, Amy?" As he had gotten older, Gideon found it helpful to get the measure of the younger attorneys by seeing what they came up with on their own. It was more revealing than telling them what to do. Amy and Lisa had been unfolding this one just right.

In the final months of Charles Joshua Jackson, aka Kareem Jackson vs. Arthur Calderon, Warden of San Quentin State Prison, Gideon and the death penalty team had been engulfed by the case. Against the misgivings of some of his partners, Gideon had allowed Lisa Maldonado to manage the KibbleSoft matter on her own. So at least one of Gideon's cases has been handled properly. Lisa had a fine sense for the jugular, and Gideon had been comfortable letting her run the case.

Amy, too, was getting better at thinking more than a step or two ahead, an important skill in law. She was also good on her feet. She proposed, now, to show a little more "patience" with the other side.

"OK, Amy. I agree you should push them just the way you suggest. This time you can make the call to him and do the meet-and-confer, with Lisa on the line. But be firm. Don't give up anything nontrivial to reach an agreement with them. If they won't yield, place a call to Judge Temple's clerk and set up a hearing on the discovery dispute. Lisa should do that hearing I don't think I need to be involved. But keep me posted." They grabbed their papers and ran off.

Gideon's temporary engagement in the dispute faded. Why should he give a good god damn about KibbleSoft?

Once he would have taken real pleasure at how Amy and Lisa were developing as lawyers, at how effectively ruthless they were becoming. But he didn't care about that either.

Then what am I doing here? he thought.

7

The phone's message light was flashing.

"Hello, Gideon. Abe here. Just givin' a holler. Let's get together for lunch and a jaw-jaw."

Abraham Rutledge Sanford frequently adopted this mock folksy tone, but nothing could obscure his patrician manner or commanding presence. Head of the California Capital Project, the legal resource center that advised the California Supreme Court on appointing death penalty attorneys, and then assisted them, Abe had recruited Gideon to represent Kareem 14 years ago.

Gideon had sought his guidance from time to time and Abe had become a friend. Now, Gideon knew, Abe wanted to see how Gideon was doing after the execution. In the wake of his failure.

He wondered if Abe regretted recruiting him for the case. But Gideon had enough regrets for both of them.

They'd met the first time at the Capital Project's offices in San Francisco's seedy Mission District. Sanford's physical appearance—the abundant white hair, the bushy eyebrows, the strong features—enhanced the impact of his personality, and his six foot four frame could be daunting. Most of the time, though, he simply radiated authoritative good will and the confident expectation that things would go as he suggested.

Men of Gideon's size, six feet, didn't often meet people who towered over them, and it created a psychological dynamic that most had not encountered since adolescence—the just-below-the-surface feeling you were looking up at a grownup. And the feeling that if you did not accede to Abe Sanford's "requests," you were being rebellious.

But Gideon had been eager to handle a capital appeal, so their first meeting had largely been a matter of persuading Sanford that he was capable enough and did not have quirky motives.

"I've been against the death penalty since I was a kid," Gideon had told him. "In fact, when I was in high school, my idea of flirting with a girl I had a crush on in Sophomore English was to ask her what she thought of the death penalty."

"And why do you need to do this now?"

"I think the death penalty is barbaric—the knowledge sickens me that we live in a society in which there are executioners. Angers me, actually. And I know how arbitrary it is, and how easy for the criminal justice system to get the wrong person. Even when the defendant is guilty, more killing isn't the answer . . . isn't what's needed. The lust for revenge obscures the root causes, where these horrible crimes come from."

Sanford nodded, but didn't say anything. Gideon swirled the remaining coffee in his cup round and round, allowing a quiet moment. He looked at the beat-up desk Sanford was sitting at. It might have come from Goodwill. But Sanford had a real oil painting on the wall behind him, a portrait. Of an ancestor, maybe. Someone who'd come over on the Mayflower?

"On the personal level," Gideon went on, "I suppose it's a couple of things. Something in my childhood or upbringing left me with a passion for fighting injustice. When I was a college student, I was in the civil rights movement in the South. For a while. And though I love the intellectual property cases I do, I feel it's not enough . . . I want to be doing something about racism, and the death penalty is certainly applied in a discriminatory way.

"I'm not sure I can explain any better without a few rounds of psychoanalysis."

"I don't think we need go that far," Sanford said. "Tell me this. Do you think you'd enjoy doing this? If that's the right word. How do you feel about the notoriety?"

"Isn't it our duty, as attorneys, to represent those who are despised? But the truth of the matter is that in the circles I run in, there aren't a lot of death penalty enthusiasts. So, frankly, I expect a little secondary gain, maybe a chance to show how noble I am for doing this.

"But actually, I think I will enjoy handling a case, a long, hard fight with a lot of challenges. I can do the job."

That had been good enough. When Abe Sanford asked Gideon to take on Kareem Jackson's case, Gideon agreed. And with the Capital Project's recommendation, the California Supreme Court had appointed him.

It was clear from the outset this wasn't going to be one of those cases where the defendant would be proven innocent. The issue was simply whether Jackson's life could be saved. Gideon had thought he was up to the task.

And now Abe wanted to jaw-jaw about the outcome. Of course, if they got together, Abe would be too polite to say that Gideon hadn't been up to it.

Gideon didn't think anyone's sympathy would do any good. He didn't want any sympathy. Actually, he wanted to hurt someone, but there was no one to get back at.

He did not return Abe's call.

8

Gideon's secretary Mindy brought in his mail. As usual, the envelopes were neatly slit open, and papers containing motions or notices from opposing parties were stamped "docketed," to indicate that any deadlines they triggered had been placed on the firm's calendar.

Among the docketed items was a document from the State Bar of California.

To Attorney Gideon Roth:

This letter places you on notice that the Attorney Ethics Division of the State Bar of California has initiated an investigation of your conduct at San Quentin, California on the night of December 20-21, 1996.

A Report filed in the Sheriff's Department of Marin County (a true copy of which is attached hereto as Exhibit 'A') shows probable cause to conclude that you may have committed an uncharged crime, to wit, misdemeanor assault, against an individual or individuals unknown. Such conduct, if proven, would be inconsistent with the high ethical standards demanded of members of the California Bar, and could subject you to attorney discipline.

You may reply to these charges, if you so choose, by filing a written response, at the address shown below, no later than fifteen calendar days from the date of this letter. Please include the case number set forth . . .

They are investigating my conduct on the night of the execution, Gideon thought. Not the fact that the State of California killed a man that night, and that I failed to save him. No, they are investigating a few punches I exchanged with a young thug. Idiots. They will look like idiots when I am through with them . . .

Gideon knew this would not end in disciplinary action. But it had been docketed, and an entry was now in the firm's system: State Bar Ethics Investigation of Gideon Roth, last day for written response: January 23, 1997. It would appear on the firm's Master Calendar, reviewed by the firm's management.

There would be a commotion.

Above a table across from his desk were shelves with photos and various objects, souvenirs of pro bono cases he has handled, awards he did not deserve for public spirited activities. On the table, stacks of briefs and case materials waited for Gideon, a pile for each pending case. Gideon thought about getting up, leaving the building and never returning. He didn't have the energy to do that, either.

Gideon walked down the hall to the office of Greg Evans, head of the litigation group. Greg, a thick bodied, dark haired man in his late forties, was one of Gideon's last friends in the firm. They had often worked together when they had been associates, though collaborations of that kind had become less frequent in recent years.

Greg held two phones, one against his ear, and the other pressed firmly against his chest, but managed a come-in gesture with his eyebrows. "You don't really imagine my client would accept that, do you?" Greg said coldly to someone on phone number one. Then he twisted the handset up so he could listen to the response with one ear while whispering to his client on the other phone. The calls were wrapped up in a few minutes, and after bellowing instructions to his secretary, Greg turned to Gideon.

"What's up, Giddy?"

Gideon handed him the notice from the State Bar. Greg read it rapidly, looked up at Gideon, then looked down and read the second page with the Sheriff's Department Report again.

"What's this about?"

Gideon told him about the fight the night of the execution.

Greg opened his mouth to say something, then closed it. He fiddled with his coffee cup, then slowly drummed his fingers in the way that tended to frighten young associates.

"Okay, I understand. That was a bad time. Nothing to do about it now. But you haven't exactly been endearing yourself to anyone around here for a while. Wendell came in my office this morning to complain about your hours and your attitude, and to tell me what he thinks of you. Not much. This isn't going to make it any easier. We'll have to hire outside counsel to represent you and hope that this doesn't generate publicity."

"Whatever you have to do."

Greg frowned.

"Gideon, you seem a little disengaged about this problem . . . about all your problems at the firm. Maybe you need to take time off?"

"What would I do?"

"Rest, travel, forget about it all. Come back afterward, get back into it, and take up another struggle. Sorry. I'm not saying, 'Pick up a new puppy at the pound' after your dog died. Bad analogy. You know what I mean. But not another death penalty case. None of us can bear that again."

"You think I would ever again believe I was qualified to handle another capital case?"

"No . . . 'Qualified'? Are you trying to tell me, after all the years you worked on it, that you didn't do everything anyone could possibly have done for Jackson? Anyway . . . Look, you know this is your real life, Giddy."

"Is it?"

"You just have to get into it again, after you've had a rest."

Gideon did not respond.

"Giddy, I'm on your side, but I'm wondering myself what's going on with you. The firm does expect fire in the belly, and not just for the pro bono cases."

"Do whatever you have to do, Greg."

"Don't you want to give me anything to work with, Gideon? We've got a nontrivial problem here."

Gideon walked out.

He returned to his office. Just after 5 p.m., Greg came in to see him and closed the door.

"Here's the way it is, Gideon. Wendell and some of the others actually wanted to shit-can you outright. He said you hadn't been pulling your weight for months, things weren't getting any better, and now you're a serious embarrassment. They wanted to call an executive committee meeting to terminate your membership in the firm. Best I could do to divert them, they've suspended you until the State Bar investigation is over. The firm will pay for counsel for you. We'll see what happens after that."

Greg waited for a reaction, but Gideon offered none.

"Gideon, I've got to say this, because I'm wondering too. If you want to have a future in this firm, you need to turn your attitude around, and fast."

"Fuck it," Gideon said. "Good night, Greg, and thanks for nothing."

9

Gideon Roth's legal career collapsed swiftly.

The State Bar investigation would end, eventually, in a mild reprimand. But the story of the lawyer for the Dark Nines killer slugging it out with death penalty supporters on the night of the execution occasioned a frenzy of media coverage, coverage that was considered very much at odds with the dignity of Harkin & Lessman.

Big corporate clients quietly called to convey their concern. Heavy hitters among the partners warned that Gideon's tabloid activities could mark the firm as an unsuitable business platform. And younger partners considered Gideon expendable.

At the partnership meeting, Gideon expressed no regret for what had happened nor did he communicate any enthusiasm for doing his part in the firm's mission. He had had a couple of drinks in his office before the meeting, and displayed little fervor in his own defense. His friend Greg Evans was silent, and when Wendell Dale and the heads of the corporate and tax groups said that they would resign if Gideon did not, virtually all of the other partners joined in a "sense-of-the-partnership" resolution, urging Gideon to amicably end his relationship with the firm on reasonable terms.

Gideon returned to his office. He had another drink. He was confused about what was happening to him, and wondered why he wasn't angrier. What was he actually going to do next? He was too depressed to care.

He took out his pen and wrote a one-line letter of resignation. He addressed the letter to Wendell Dale and placed it in his outbox.

Gideon looked at his phone. Soon, he knew, a new message would answer calls to his number, advising that "Mr. Roth is no longer associated with Harkin & Lessman. Please press pound, zero to be connected with someone who will assist you." He played his own message one last time, listening to the part that said, "Operator, we accept collect calls from San Quentin." Then he erased it.

Gideon looked around. What did he need to take with him from here? He slipped the small framed portrait of Kareem Jackson into a pocket of his suit jacket, and walked out the door without his briefcase for the first time in twenty-five years.

10

Two weeks later, Helen left him.

Gideon was stunned when she told him she was moving out. Over the years, their growing preoccupation with their individual careers had pulled them further apart. But it never occurred to Gideon that Helen might leave him.

Now Gideon realized she had stayed the last year only because she foresaw Kareem's execution. She had felt she needed to be there to help him survive the pain and what he would perceive as the shame of defeat. But it was as she had said just before she left: No one could live with him now.

He had rejected the comfort she offered in the weeks since Kareem's death, for reasons neither she nor Gideon could understand.

He remembered their last real conversation. They had been sitting at the round wicker dining table on the glassed-in porch of their house in Atherton, a house too large for their childless life. It was a weekend morning, but—unusually for Gideon and Helen in recent years—no briefs, case notes or memos littered Gideon's side of the table, none of Helen's company financial reports or printouts of an upcoming software release, tabbed with post-its in her purple fountain pen ink, marked with comments in her small, exact handwriting, were on her side.

Helen, who stood only five foot four, was thin near to gauntness. A relentless exercise regimen had hardened her limbs, and her once black hair, which she now wore very short, was mostly silver. Gideon's, by now, was salt and pepper. Like his neat beard. At least he was not bulging too noticeably, though he had been putting on weight recently, and his beard wasn't looking so neat since he had stopped trimming it. And some days Helen had to remind him he needed to take a shower.

As Gideon made a desultory attempt to interest himself in the Sunday Times, Helen tried once more to talk to him. She had grown increasingly acerbic, as Gideon's remoteness since the execution had proven impenetrable. Now, there was little sympathy or warmth in her observations.

"You don't want to talk about it," she said, "because you feel you should be punished even though you can't say just why it was your fault. You continue to hold onto the guilt so you can be a martyr to your failure."

"I understand what you're saying. But knowing that it wasn't all my fault isn't helping. It's not exactly that I want the hurt. . . . I can't explain."

"You're not trying. I think you want to hang onto your misery because part of you wants the punishment. You like it and you are also ashamed of it. But either way you're satisfied."

"No, that's not—."

"Let me finish, Gideon. Don't interrupt me. You're wallowing in how inadequate you must have been, re-thinking everything you should have done differently, but that's just another form of pride. Pride and contempt for everyone else. It's your Gideon way of telling everyone that if their standards were as high as yours, they would never forgive you."

Gideon saw it might look that way. But that wasn't the way it was. His tangled thoughts no longer unraveled into sentences when he tried to talk to Helen. And his thoughts were always being interrupted by memories of the execution. So their conversations were filled with long silences, punctuated by brief, unilluminating exchanges.

In the end, he wasn't sure whether he couldn't explain it, even to himself, or whether he was holding out, as Helen thought, and did not want to subject his self-hatred to Helen's critical view.

But the fight for Kareem had been important, and he could not simply "move on." He had struggled to save a man's life. This had been his true passion, his real work, for most of his professional life. None of his partners had given a damn, and Gideon had often made clear his fuck you in response.

Now they had kicked him out. But what did that matter?

His job had been to hold the line, in this one case, against the momentum of generations of racism. To save Kareem from being swept away and destroyed. He had failed his trust. What could he do to right the balance? Nothing. He longed to take action. But there was nothing to do. Why should he go on?

"Say something."

He looked up, startled. He had forgotten Helen was still there, waiting, wondering just how long Gideon would linger in never-never land before he spoke.

"Helen . . . ," he started. But again he had no sentence to attach to her name. It was only after long silence that he asked, "How can you think that I want to exclude you, to shut you out?"

She looked at him and he saw she was appalled. "That's exactly what you are doing, Gideon. You've been doing it month after month after month. And for the last ten minutes."

He rehearsed further sentences in the emptiness that followed. *You can't understand this if you haven't lived through it.* Before he could say this aloud, though, he could hear what she would say:

I did live through it with you, Gideon, as much as you would let me. Why do you want to hold onto this?

There's no 'wanting' about it. This is the way I am now. I can't stop thinking about Kareem and his life and his death and how I failed him, and . . .

And this has nothing to do with me? Because you keep it separate—apart from us. It's your precious possession. You need nothing from me.

Pieces of conversations they had had, or maybe they had had, over the months. The impetus to say anything faded, and he drifted off. Actually, he wished she would leave him alone. After a time she walked quietly out of the room.

Later that morning, Helen came back out onto the porch, where he stood watching the rain.

"Gideon, sit down, I need to talk to you." When he joined her at the table, he noticed she was holding herself very straight, in a way Gideon recognized—she was uneasy but about to assert herself. She paused.

"This is very hard for me to say, though I've been thinking about it for a long time." She hesitated, then spoke quickly, in sentences he thought she must have composed in her head earlier. "Gideon, I'm going to leave you. There hasn't been much between us for years, but neither of us has let ourselves think about it, and we certainly haven't talked about it. But it's become clear to me since Kareem's execution that you don't need me any longer. I'm not doing you any good, and you're definitely not doing me any good.

"I can't even tell how much you'll really care, or even notice, once I'm gone. Actually, I don't think I matter to you all that much anymore."

"Helen, how can you say that? You mean the world to me."

"No I don't, Gideon. You know that's not true. Kareem meant the world to you, fighting to save him was your world. I thought when that ended maybe you and I could rebuild something . . . find our world together again. But you've kept me out. Now I'm not sure I want in anymore." She looked down and straightened the doilies on the arms of the wicker chair. Then she looked at him.

"There's something else. I've been seeing Tony Alcala. I'm not moving in with him right now. But he has helped me to remember what a real relationship can be."

"Tony Alcala! That smarmy little dickhead! You yourself told me what an unctuous jerk he was."

She blushed.

"That was years ago. I've come to see there's more to him than that. And he was there when you weren't."

"I am sure he was. You mean when I was wasting my time with my pointless efforts to save Kareem, when I was up around the clock writing emergency petitions to keep the state from gassing Kareem Jackson to death, when I wasn't home to share a nice warm supper with you, Tony was there for you all right, there in your pants."

"When it comes to it, Gideon, it's been a long time since you showed any interest in that either."

He sat up stiffly. He searched for an angry reply, but before he could speak, she reached across and touched his arm.

"Gideon, I didn't mean to say that. But your indifference to sex has just been part of how disconnected you've become from anything to do with me."

"All right. But . . . Tony Alcala. Look, let's talk about it some more. You can't just make a decision like this on your own, you can't leave just like this. We need to talk."

"We need to talk? You haven't needed to talk to me for months! Whenever I tried to talk to you for the last three months . . . When I worried about what was happening to you, when I tried to keep you from going off the deep end, all you . . . all you . . ."

She broke into sobs. Then calmed herself.

"All you did was ignore me. All you did was creep into your stupid little mind so you could be by yourself. All you . . . Now it's too late. You need to talk to me? I don't need to talk to you anymore."

She cried. Gideon stood next to her, and hugged her to him. Her tears wrenched him. But he found nothing to say.

After a time Helen went on.

"You've pushed me out of your life, Gideon. Now it's too late. I hate you . . . I love you. But there's nothing left. And I'm not going to be dragged down into your craziness. Not anymore."

She held him tightly against herself, and wept bitterly. She kissed his neck and put her hand on his chest, then began tugging on his shirt. "One last time. It won't make any difference. I need a life with someone who cares about me, but one last time."

"I care, Helen," he said softly, but his words seemed unheard.

She dragged the big cushion off the wicker chaise, and they lay on it, on the floor of the porch, their lower clothing now off, touching each other.

The emotional turmoil had engendered a sexual tension that Gideon responded to even as he thought to resist. For many months he had turned away from making love with Helen. Now, part of him wanted to do whatever she asked, her desire must mean she could not really want to leave. But he felt too near to tears, the tears that would not come, for sex. And he felt that if he made love to her, he would be agreeing to her demand he accept that their relationship was over. Nonetheless, Helen's desire provoked a response.

At the same time, he felt as though he were watching it all from outside his body. Moving remotely, he fell into her rhythm, entered her when she opened to him, soon felt her shudder and gasp, then slow down. How can you do this to us? he thought, Why won't you give me a chance? But no words came out, and as she lay still, he felt himself reaching all the way into her, reaching, reaching, faster, angrily, and then it was over.

She stroked his head. "Gideon, Gideon," she said softly, and he didn't know what to make of her tone. Nor could he think what to ask. His dismay was beginning to fade, *Another thing is happening I can't do anything about,* he thought.

After a time she said, "I've got an apartment in Sunnyvale, and I'm going to move there. We can still talk, even after I leave. But I need to move on. I can't be with you any more."

Helen packed some clothes, and twenty minutes later Gideon heard the door open and quietly close. He heard her car back into the street, then fade away.

She returned the next day for a few boxes of possessions, and again a week later for more things. She didn't remove everything. But any implication that her departure might be provisional was belied by the excision of a host of small personal items, things that had over the years acquired their own homey places on bureaus, counters, window sills, bookcases, shelves.

The disappearance of these items—tiny wooden boxes and other funny stuff, small treasures that had engaged or amused Helen, little cacti and succulents in odd-shaped pots, little clay animal sculptures made by a niece, occupational curios, old photos of her grandparents, strange sea shells, candles in queer shapes too nice to burn, index cards with faded poetry she'd once copied—the flotsam of life that comforted and encompassed you—the departure of these things left craters in the landscape of their home, their life together. These things had been his, too, because they had been hers, and Gideon felt his life had been looted.

II

Get out now, Gideon.

Kareem's voice seemed remote, hoarse. His lungs must have been burned by the gas. But this was before the gas came.

Gideon was in the chamber, kneeling beside Kareem, struggling with the straps when he heard the sound of the wheel tightening, sealing the room. Go away, Gideon, Kareem croaked again.

Gideon wanted to open the straps around Kareem's arms first, so Kareem could help with the other straps. But Gideon did not seem to know how the buckles worked, and each time he tried, his fingers slipped.

He was running out of time, and he could not get the prong out of the hole in the first leather belt. He yanked in frustration, but that only tightened the belt.

He heard the cyanide drop.

Make them let you out, Kareem whispered. *Don't stay here with me . . .*

Gideon tried to get up, but he slipped and fell. Tried again, fell again, then he smelled the acrid gas seeping from under the chair. He was holding his breath, the way he had the first time they killed Kareem, but he couldn't hold it any longer. Through the glass, Gideon saw a guard smile as, involuntarily, Gideon began to inhale . . .

He woke. He was shuddering.

Gideon was afraid to return to sleep. He got out of bed and sat on the stairs, and listened to the rain. He realized his body was damp and that he smelled funny. He took a shower—when had he last showered?—then put the same pajamas back on. It was easier than seeing whether he'd put a pair in the wash that he'd never taken out of the drier.

Gideon went downstairs and made a cup of tea.

It was a month since Helen had moved out, and Gideon was alone with his fears and his depression. He missed her. Even when they had, without noticing it, lost the ability to talk about anything that had to do with themselves as a couple, home was still for him the place where she was. There was an irritating strangeness, now, to night time in a bed by himself at home. If it could be called home anymore without her.

On the other hand, now there was no one to tell him to stop fulminating when he thrashed noisily about, raging over the morning newspaper, over unknowable technical difficulties with his computer, over being unable to find things he had just put down, over the many things that angered Gideon in between feeling nothing mattered any more.

There was also no one to hold him when the gas chamber nightmares woke him, the nightmares that had begun after the execution. He hated most the one where he found himself in the gas chamber with Kareem. He was ashamed that each time, at the end, he wanted to get out more than he wanted to save Kareem.

Gideon sat in the porch, looking at the rain. After a while he calmed and the dream faded. But it didn't matter anymore whether he slept or was up all night. He had no job to go to, nothing to work on during the daytime. Nothing he cared about. Nothing but memories of his failures.

And memories of his life with Helen.

It was thirty years this spring that we met. In May, we would have been together thirty years.

It was the spring of 1967, nearly the end of the school year. He had graduated from college the year before and since then had been embroiled in anti-Vietnam-war organizing in Boston area colleges. Now he was back on his own campus. The images of the university that day were still bright in his mind. Hundreds of students in front of an ROTC building in a demonstration he had helped organize, holding signs, chanting and singing, flashing V-for-victory fingers every now and then. "Hey, hey, LBJ, how many kids did you kill today?"

Over a bullhorn, the simple speeches of clear moral purpose reverberated, one of them his own. But still brighter, the feelings of that time, the feeling of righteous purity. Could he ever recapture that? What wouldn't he give to feel that again! Yes, rage that another people were being destroyed, literally burned alive in the napalm fires of the U.S. war machine. But also gladness at being part of the struggle against it, the exhilaration of fighting for what was right, the special joy of youth, of youth in motion. We did not admit it to ourselves, but we were having a blast.

Police had gathered and formed a line. Gideon could hear the garbled, ragged-edged braying of their bullhorns, though not their words. But he knew. They were going to clear the courtyard. "You've made your point," they were saying, "Now go home." Gideon and his compatriots were not ready to fight them hand to hand. But they also felt it would be cowardice to run before the cops charged. They weren't going to be cowards. And joined with their fear was excitement at the prospect of being chased.

Suddenly, there was a swirl of confusion and screams. A wedge of police had emerged from between two buildings. They were driving toward the students around Gideon, yelling and swinging their clubs. Firing tear gas, too. Pigs. The students fled, not many steps ahead of the cops. Gideon darted away, tripping on picket signs, bumping into people. Cutting through a flower bed, Gideon deliberately trampled a petunia.

Behind him, he could hear people crying out as they were clubbed. But Gideon was not running in panic, and he was monitoring what was going on around him.

Gideon saw a small, thin girl with long black hair slip and fall. People were dodging around her, but she wasn't coming right to her feet again. Nice legs, he thought. He pushed someone out of the way, and ran across to her. He crouched, quickly put his arms under hers and yanked her upright. He remembered that moment so clearly, remembered enjoying his own self-confidence, being conscious of his fearlessness.

She wasn't very heavy. Putting his arm across her back and pulling her against him, he dragged her in motion, out of the tear gas, away from the swinging clubs. They were part of the fleeing mass again, being dispersed by the police into smaller groups. Then they were alone in the entryway of Marley Hall. The cops were rampaging outside. But for Gideon and this girl, for now, it was over.

He was still holding her, or perhaps he had taken the opportunity to hold her again. "You're trembling," he said, and kept her close. While they both knew that was true, that she was shaken, they were not blind to the drama and romance of the moment.

One of Gideon's hands rested gently between her shoulder blades. The other stretched around her waist or perhaps a little lower, seemingly accidentally. Suddenly but inevitably, she lifted her face and kissed him. He remembered this first kiss of Helen's so well. It was soft and not very long, though not hurried. Then they both laughed a little laugh.

She reached up and touched his cheek with her hand, then kissed him again, longer this time. Gideon cupped her head, and their tongues touched, and through the memory of fear came a rush of desire, and he pressed against her body.

She rested her cheek against his neck.

"I'm Gideon," he said. "Gideon Roth."

"I know. I heard you speak. I'm Helen Samuels."

He let go of her shoulders, and they headed toward another exit from the building.

"Let's go to a coffee shop," Gideon said, taking her hand.

Over coffee and a Danish which they split, they talked about what they majored in, where they were from, their parents' reactions to the war, his civil rights experiences, the war, love, the revolution.

"Come to my room with me," he said at last.

"Yes. I want to."

His arm around her, her shoulder under his, they walked two blocks to the flat Gideon shared with two other members of the Boston Committee to Stop the War. He took her hand as they climbed to the third floor. He unlocked the door with one hand, then led her to his room.

On one wall, a poster of a Vietnamese family tearfully fleeing the U.S.

bombing, and the words, *This is the Enemy*. On another wall, a civil rights poster, a photo of an elderly black man in overalls, with the words, *One Man One Vote*. His brick and board bookcases, with books on Vietnam, pacifism and revolution. Stacks of anti-war posters and leaflets, a mimeograph machine. An old desk with a big Underwood manual typewriter. And a window overlooking a playground where trees were at last blossoming.

They stood and kissed. Slowly, he undressed her. He turned her back toward him when she was naked, so he could unbraid her hair, and then they made love on his narrow bed. Afterward Helen lay on top of him, her hair on his face, covering his neck and shoulders with little kisses.

"Giddy, Giddy, Giddy, I'm giddy, too," she said. "You're so sweet." Gideon was thinking it was too soon to say it, but the words came to him: I love you. And wondering, Are you thinking the same thing?

Within two years, the Viet Cong's Tet Offensive had shattered the long-repeated U.S. claims that victory was around the corner. Lyndon Baines Johnson decided not to run for re-election. Martin Luther King and Bobby Kennedy were dead.

Nixon defeated Hubert Humphrey for the presidency. And still the agony of the war persisted. From morning to night, for years on end, Gideon had been consumed by the anti-war struggle. And even as the war was supposedly winding down, the bombing and strafing and civilian deaths mounted. Hundreds of thousands more died while Nixon and Kissinger sought their face-saving exit.

After all the meetings, the sit-ins and protests, all the writing and leafleting, all the confrontations and arrests, Gideon Roth was finally burned out.

Helen and Gideon were still together, and they married in June 1969, to the relief of Gideon's father and Helen's parents. That month Helen received her master's in mathematics, and was hired by a Massachusetts company called Digital Equipment Corporation to do something called computer programming. In the fall, Gideon began law school.

12

Helen and Gideon owned a small cottage east of Portland, Oregon, in the woods a few miles from the Columbia River Gorge, on the Washington State side. A few weeks after Helen's departure, Gideon summoned the energy to book a flight to Portland, and by 8 o'clock he was at the cottage.

Helen's things were all about. Clothes that she kept at the cottage, on a shelf in the closet, neatly folded. An orderly stack of CDs she played the last time they were here, squared on the table next to the little music machine. A novel Helen thought she had mislaid at home.

Helen and Gideon had thought they'd come up to the cottage at least once a month, as a get-away, though they generally brought work along. But as their careers moved into overdrive—Helen, a software engineer, had become one of the founders of a startup; and Gideon, maturing as a high tech litigator, had become a partner in his firm—the trips became less frequent.

Gideon went into the kitchen, found an old beer in the fridge and drank it. He drifted from room to room, imagining Helen's presence. Everything bore her mark, and in her absence the house felt emptier, as though it were awaiting her arrival.

He remembered the good times they'd had here. Sitting in a soft chair in the living room, reading, he would look up from time to time and see Helen in the other armchair, working away on her laptop. He would feel a surge of love for her, a feeling of absolute connection as he took in her concentration, the occasional furrowing of her brow, her beauty.

At dinner, which was often just sandwiches they'd bought on the way up, sandwiches and chips and the local beer, she would try to explain the elegant programming solution she had devised for a troubling software bug she was working on. He didn't grasp most of it, and Helen knew it, but she was lit with her bursting excitement, and he basked in it. After she had chattered on for a while, she paused and laughed. "This is a little too technical for you, isn't it?"

"Only for the last five minutes," he said, smiling.

He recalled their familiar private jokes, "We'll always have Marley

Hall." The humorous-to-them turns of phrase jointly used to ridicule lame politicians, pop lyrics, clichés in the evening news, friends' foibles.

Now, Marley is dead, he thought, but wasn't able to smile at what she would have called his leettle joke.

Gideon went into the bedroom on the first floor that had served as an office. Under a small table was a pile of papers, discarded drafts of briefs filed long ago in Kareem's case. He sat down. Abruptly, he stood and kicked viciously at the stack of papers. They flew across the floor. "What fucking good...," he yelled. Then he kicked the table. A leg snapped off, and a small lamp crashed to the floor. He moved to stomp it, then stopped himself.

His heart was pounding and his hands were trembling. He put his hands over his face and breathed heavily. What would Helen think of this little scene? But she would likely never see this place again. Nor would she be sharing her judgments about his behavior any longer.

He collected himself, and looked down at the scattered pages. He thought of the legal arguments he had so carefully crafted, and how pointless they turned out. His entire career had been pointless, a mistake. A wrong turn. He had made a wrong turn when he decided to become a corporate lawyer.

I started out on the right foot, in the Sixties. Why didn't I stay on that path?

∗　∗　∗

Spring 1964. It was the summer before his junior year in college, and he was swept into an audacious movement of young people who were changing the world.

Ten years earlier, the federal courts had declared segregation unconstitutional. But day-to-day life in the South remained unchanged. Then, starting in 1960, in Greensboro, North Carolina, young black students launched a nonviolent movement of sits-ins and mass resistance to segregation that swept across the South. Eventually some of them turned to the rural countryside, where they tried to organize local Negro people to fight for the right to vote. And they inspired some young whites like Gideon to join the struggle.

Gideon's was the first generation to come of age after two decades of economic depression and war. Their parents had shared in the prosperity of the 1950s, and Gideon and his classmates had gone to college in the 1960s as a matter of course, often the first in their families to do so. They believed that all of the good things in life were theirs for the taking, and that nothing really bad could happen to them. They believed in justice and the American Way.

They were also ripe for adventure.

In the spring of 1964, a coalition of civil rights groups called for a thousand young people to come to Mississippi for a summer of voter registration, organizing and education—Mississippi Freedom Summer. The goal was to draw the nation's attention to the heart of racist resistance, to the most violently segregationist state in the Union. Gideon was determined to join them.

Before spring break, he called home.

"Dad, there's something I need to talk to you about. I'm thinking about not doing the internship with Representative Foley's office this summer. I think I want to go to Mississippi to join a big civil rights project."

'I think'? 'I want to'? I was going to say *'I'm going to Mississippi . . .'*

"Are you crazy?" his father yelled. "You're going to throw away your career for a bunch of shvartzers? This is what we sacrificed to send you to college for? For this, we worked all those years?

"First in your class at Stuyvesant High School. Headed for Phi Beta Kappa at an Ivy League college. Interning for a Congressman, going to a great law school. You could be a Senator some day. Now you're going to throw it all away?"

"What's he saying?" His mother's voice in the background.

"He says he's going to throw away his future, forget the summer job with the Congressman and go to Mississippi."

"Mississippi?" Gideon heard the querulous voice of his mother. "Mississippi?"

"Giddy, this is no game. They're killers, they're Nazis down there. You're a Jew, they'll murder you."

"Dad . . ."

"How can you do this to your mother? To me?"

"Please, Dad. It's my life and I've got to decide what to do with it."

"It's your life? You owe us nothing? You can throw your life away? The future we've planned?"

"Dad, of course I owe you everything. But that doesn't mean that I don't have to make my own decisions. Do you want me to be one of the good Germans? You want me to watch while they oppress other people and do nothing?"

"You don't know what you're talking about, Germans," his father said. "If you want to do something for the coloreds, stay in New York for the summer. Volunteer in a summer school. Don't get yourself killed."

"Dad, I'm not going to be murdered."

"This is the kind of summer vacation you want for us, to worry about you and wait until we hear about them murdering you?"

"That's not fair."

"It's fair that you should kill your mother? You know she has a weak heart."

"Max," he heard his mother's voice in the background. "I'll throw myself out the window. Tell him I'll throw myself out the window."

"Did you hear? Your mother's going to throw herself out the window if you go. Don't do this to us."

"Let me talk to her . . . "

"Giddy, I can't stand it. If you tell me you're going to go, I'm going to throw myself out the window. I'll end it right away. I'm telling you, my heart can't stand worrying about you until they kill you in Mississippi."

"Look, I'll think about it. This isn't absolutely decided. But I want to go."

"Don't do this to us, Giddy."

"Mom, I've got to get back to a paper I'm writing. We'll talk about this some more."

Gideon was sure his mother would not throw herself out the window. But she did have a heart condition. He knew, too, that their fears were not crazy. As for his father's ambitions for him, Gideon had let that metronome beat time for him all his life. He tamped down the small, familiar surge of anger at his father's endless efforts to dominate, first his mother, and now him.

Afterward, he wasn't sure how he found the strength to wear them down so they accepted that he was going. Part of it had to do with his need to prove himself.

As a child, Gideon had obeyed his parents' demands that he be a "good boy," and he had tried to avoid fighting. On the streets and in the school-yards of the South Bronx of his childhood, though, there had often been no choice. And when someone else started it, Gideon had experienced a secret glee at letting himself go and trying to pulverize another boy.

Now, he wondered, could he face danger bravely if striking back were not an option? When the opportunity came to go to Mississippi, in the cause of something he believed in, Gideon could not turn aside.

13

June 7, 1964. Gideon's first evening in Mississippi. After orientation in Oxford, Ohio, the students were assigned to different county projects. Gideon and several of the other northern students had been driven down to Hokes Landing, Mississippi, on the edge of the Delta, by the county project leader Brian Butler. Brian was a wiry young black man who was himself from the North.

The Summer Project was sponsored by a coalition of civil rights groups known as "COFO," the Council of Federated Organizations. But like most of the full-time civil rights organizers in the state, Butler and the others in the Crenshaw County Project were from SNCC—or "Snick," as everyone said it— the Student Nonviolent Coordinating Committee.

The Freedom House, the Project's headquarters and main housing for the summer volunteers, was in a dormitory of a small Negro college that was closed for the summer. It would ultimately house about twenty volunteers, along with a half dozen SNCC staff members who had been work-ing in the county for nearly a year. Gideon had a bunk in a room with two other beds. For now he had the room to himself.

After getting settled (which just meant parking his suitcase next to the bed, putting a book on the pillow, and leaving his toilet kit on a small dresser), Gideon went downstairs.

He felt awkward about having nothing to do, about being the "other" here—a useless white person among a larger group of Negroes who knew what they were doing and were paying no attention to him.

He read over the Security Handbook he had been given in Oxford.

```
Travel
    a. When persons leave their project, they must call
their project person-to-person for themselves on arrival
at destination point. Should they be missing, project
personnel will notify the Jackson office.
    b. Doors of cars should be locked at all times. At
night, windows should be rolled up as much as possible.
Gas tanks must have locks. Hoods should also be locked.
    c. No one should go anywhere alone, but certainly not
in an automobile, and certainly not at night.
    d. Travel at night should be avoided unless absolutely
necessary.


Living in Homes or in Freedom Houses
    a. If it can be avoided, try not to sleep near open
windows. Try to sleep at the back of the house, i.e.,
the part farthest from a road or street.
    b. Do not stand in doorways at night with the light at
your back.
```

"Anything I can help with?" Gideon asked Butler.

"Nope. Not right now. You want to come to a mass meeting tonight?"

Gideon did. A few hours later, he and four other newly arrived white students piled into two old cars with Brian and several other blacks who had been organizing in nearby Panola County. Brian was driving an old Studebaker, and he worried about the tires. So before they set out, he rearranged how the white students were sitting in back, to distribute the weight better.

Security Handbook notwithstanding, they were heading into the Mississippi countryside and it would be night before they returned. The cars raced between fields and shacks and neat farm houses, the windows down, the hot wind blowing in, bearing the not unpleasant odor of southern vegetation mixed with the smell of dust from the car ahead, as it tore down a long, straight dirt road before them, raising an enormous tan plume.

After a while, the car swerved, and they stopped. A flat. The other car would continue on its own, and they would catch up later. Gideon felt very much exposed. They were a small integrated group ("black and white together, we shall not be moved"—he heard the song in his head) on a public road, even if it was just a dirt road without much traffic. He thought that separating the two cars was not the safe thing to do. But then nothing here was safe, and what did he know? He hated to think about how afraid he was.

Everyone got out while Brian and the other black organizer, Fred, swiftly put on the spare. Fred told the white volunteers to hide in the bushes by the side of the road.

In the awkward silence, Gideon looked over a leaflet that had been on the floor of the car.

GIVE THEM A FUTURE IN MISSISSIPPI

Below the headline was a photograph of seven or eight half-clad Negro children, on the porch of a small, unpainted wooden shack without a railing. The photograph was not particularly artistic, and depicted a condition familiar but unchanged since Walker Evans and Dorothea Lange had documented such scenes of dirt poverty during the Great Depression. Beneath the photo were a few simple words:

ONE MAN - ONE VOTE
FOR FREEDOM

The other side of the leaflet conveyed a message that would scarcely have been deemed subversive anywhere outside the Black Belt South:

```
* YOU ARE A CITIZEN *

* YOU HAVE A RIGHT TO VOTE *

Only when government officials are elected by

all the people and for all the people,

will there be freedom in Mississippi.


YOU CANNOT HAVE

— FAIR JOB PRACTICES

— GOOD EDUCATION

— FREEDOM FROM INTIMIDATION OR

  BRUTALITY BY POLICE

— A FAIR AND JUST TRIAL

— GOOD LAWS THAT PROTECT ALL CITIZENS


UNLESS YOU HAVE THE RIGHT TO VOTE!


COME TO A

MASS MEETING

MISSIONARY BAPTIST CHURCH

BATESVILLE

* JUNE 7, 1964 * 7:00 P.M. *


JOIN THE

MISSISSIPPI FREEDOM DEMOCRATIC PARTY
```

This was where they were headed.

"Careful about handing that to anyone," Brian joked when he noticed Gideon holding the leaflet as he got back into the car. "Panola County has an ordinance against distributing leaflets without a permit."

"A permit? For handing out leaflets? That can't be constitutional."

"Something to what you say," Brian said. "I bet you also think American citizens are entitled to demonstrate peacefully in front of government buildings."

"Umm. . . Something I seem to recall about the right to assemble peaceably, to petition for redress of grievances."

"Very good, Gideon. The First Amendment. But that's just the United States Constitution. Here, we have Mississippi law. Peaceably assembling to petition the government is called disturbing the peace when we do it. Maybe when black people vote, we'll have different laws."

"So what is the voter registration picture in Panola County?" Gideon asked.

"Panola is one of the black-majority counties of Mississippi," Brian said. "Fifty-six percent Negro. But less than two tenths of one percent are registered to vote. So much for democracy in the Mississippi Delta."

Klan and police terrorism, and fear of economic reprisals, kept most Negroes from even trying to register to vote, Brian explained. For those bold enough to apply, the task of disenfranchisement was completed by discriminatory "qualification" tests or by simply putting Negroes' voter registration forms in the trash. Or by telling them to go away.

They drove the better part of an hour before they reached their destination, a church on a back road a few miles west of Batesville.

The church was a small building, large enough for only about eighty people, and appealing in its white paint and diminutive steeple. Three Negro men were standing outside, waiting for them. Two were in their thirties; the third, apparently the pastor, was a good deal older. After some brief greetings, they went inside. One of the men stayed outside to keep the lookout for night riders. Gideon noticed a shotgun leaning against a pillar of the porch.

Scattered in the pews toward the front half of the church were a dozen people. The heat was still intense, and they were all trying to cool themselves with the paper fans at each place. The fans had pictures of Jesus on them.

Brian had hoped they would draw as many as twenty-five or thirty local people, but he did not look disappointed at the smaller group. As he had explained earlier, they counted it a success in many places when four or five brave people attended the first "mass meeting." That was how the freedom movement began in a place: with a handful of courageous Negro men and women willing to put their lives on the line.

These people were there because Brian and the other organizers, Fred and Ruby and Hank, had spent weeks going from farm to farm in the company of a few such brave souls, talking to Negroes about voting, about the Movement, about what it would take to make life better for black people.

Now Brian and Ruby stood up front, along with the pastor and some local people. The volunteers and the other SNCC staff sat in the first few rows, next to other local people. Gideon noticed how intensely black was the skin color of these people. Growing up in the South Bronx, he had of course seen Negroes in other parts of town. But their skin was rarely much darker than the color of dark chocolate. Most of the Mississippians in this room, Gideon observed, were really black, not dark brown.

"Lord, help us to fight this battle," he heard the preacher begin, in an earnest, beseeching voice. "Give us the courage to start right here. Don't let us stop until the victory have been won. In Jesus' name we ask these blessings, and for his sake's, Amen."

"Amen," many voices responded.

One of the men near the pastor began a hymn.

Lord, hold my hand

The roomful of black voices responded immediately:

While I run this race,
Lord, hold my hand
While I run this race
Lord, hold my hand
While I run this race
'Cause I don't want to run this race in vain

This sounded like no choir Gideon had ever heard. Separate voices, filled with emotion, interjected *Hold my hand*, slightly out of time with the rest, but not clashing. "Ev'ry body git in it," the pastor urged.

The caller began another line: *Lord speak for me*, and the congregation responded immediately, *While I run this race.*

Lord, speak for me
While I run this race
Lord, speak for me
while I run this race
For I don't want to run this race in vain

More verses followed,

Lord, search my heart
Lord, guide my hand

"Lord Jesus, amen, bless this gathering," the preacher took up again. "Make us strong enough. We thank you for your blessings, Jesus. We been struggling long, Lord, by ourselves. We have been struggling to get by."

"Amen," some voices responded.

"We been patient, Lord, but we have suffered. Help us to stand together, Jesus, amen."

"Amen."

"Help us stand up for ourselves and for our childrens, Lord Jesus, amen. The white men says we are contented. They says we are satisfied. They says without these outside agitators"—he put his arm around Brian—"everything be fine. But we all know that is not truth. No one can honestly say Negroes are satisfied with injustice."

"No, suh," said a very small elderly woman.

"No one can honestly say Negroes are satisfied with gettin' cheated, with gettin' beaten, with gettin' killed. We are sick and tired, and it's time for us to be free. Free at last, Lord, free at last!"

"Speak the truth!"

"We been tired all our lives here in Mississippi. Now these Freedom Riders have come to help us, Jesus. But you know, Lord, we got to work with them. No one's going to give our freedom to us, Lord. We got to take it for ourselves. Make us strong enough, Lord. Amen."

"Amen."

"Bless these Freedom Riders, Lord Jesus, amen. They have come down to Mississippi to help us, and to lead us too. Now listen to Brother Butler," the pastor concluded.

Brian moved into the aisle between the rows of pews, so he was closer to the small group of people who had come to this meeting. He spoke in a larger voice than Gideon had heard him use before, large enough to command attention, but not so loud as to distance him from those around him. His voice was not so big or his manner so noble as to turn them into an audience.

"Thank you, Reverend Henry. Most of you all know us. We have spoken to you in your homes, and we thank you again for welcoming us. Thank you, Reverend Henry for letting us use this house of God for God's purpose—to move our people to Freedom. Like the people of Israel, we got to have freedom. But when we run away to Chicago, to Detroit, to New York, we still have not found freedom. So we are going to start bringing freedom here, right here to Panola County.

"Some people say you gonna have trouble for having to do with these here Freedom Riders, with this freedom movement. But is there anyone here ain't got trouble already, livin' in Mississippi? Anyone here who ain't been treated unfairly all by theyselves? Is there?" Brian waited for a response, and there was a silence.

"No suh," another old black woman responded at last.

"The trouble of living in Mississippi somehow miss anyone here up to now?"

There was chuckling, and "No," a number of voices responded. "Speak the truth, Brother Butler."

"Anyone here who never been treated unfair by a white po-lice? Anyone here who works for the white man never had the white man cheat him?"

"Amen. Tell it."

"Anyone here who ain't worried some time about havin' enough to feed his kids during the winter?"

"No suh." "Tell it like it is."

"Anyone here ain't had to teach they children how to be careful 'round white folks, so they can live to grow up?

"And they tell us 'bout trouble! Black people got trouble already! But a change be coming. We used to have our trouble by ourselves. Now our troubles be together, because we gettin together to fight back."

"Yes sir, tell it, Brother Butler."

"Across the South, across Georgia and Alabama, across Mississippi, and now here in Batesville, as Reverend Henry say, we are sick and tired, and we are sick and tired of being sick and tired. The trouble don't end because you wish by yourself it would. The trouble we got as Negro people will end when we stand together to make it end. We gonna end it by coming together and stayin together and fighting together for the freedom God promised."

"Amen, amen."

"Freedom is coming to Panola County! Freedom is coming! It ain't gonna be easy, but it's coming, and we gonna welcome it. And we gonna fight for it."

"Yes sir."

"There ain't been no life without trouble for Negro people in Mississippi. But we gonna face the trouble together now. And we will overcome. We gonna build our freedom movement in Panola County. We ain't gonna be turned round until we gets our freedom!"

From behind Brian Butler, the strong baritone voice of Fred broke out in song, joined right away by the others who were standing at the front.

Ain't gonna let nobody turn me round,
Turn me round,
Turn me round,

Ain't gonna let nobody turn me round,
Gonna keep on a walkin, keep on a talkin,

Marching up to freedom land.

Ain't gonna let Sheriff Benson turn me round,
Gonna keep on a walkin, keep on a talkin,
Marching up to freedom land.

The freedom song followed the melody, and adapted the words, of an old Negro spiritual known to everyone in the room, and everyone joined in after the first mention of Sheriff Benson. There had been a few chuckles. Gideon sang along haltingly, at first, but then he caught on. Brian struck up the next stanzas:

Ain't gonna let Ku Kluxers turn me round . . .

Ain't gonna let police dogs turn me round . . .

Ain't gonna let segregation turn me round,
Gonna keep on a walkin', keep on a talkin',
Marching up to freedom land.

At the end of the first song, Ruby immediately started another, to a faster, livelier tune, that the entire assembly joined in:

If you don't see me in the back of the bus,
You can't find me no where, oh-oh-oh
Come on over to the front of the bus,
I'll be ridin' up there.

I'll be riding up there,
I'll be riding up there,
Come on over to the front of the bus,
I'll be riding up there.

If you don't see me in the cotton field,

You can't find me no where,
Come on over to the courthouse,
I'll be votin' right there . . .

"It's been a hundred years since Emancipation, and we still bein' beaten and shot at," Brian said. "Crosses are still bein' burnt, we're still bein' kilt for trying to stand up straight, like men and like women. Now's the time to change that. And it's gonna start this summer. It is not going to change all at once. But it is going to change. We are going to make it change.

"To change Mississippi, we got to vote. Everyone in this room is a citizen, and you have a right to register and vote." (Brian actually said "radish and vote," and it had taken Gideon a while to figure out what he meant.)

"It is against the law for anyone to stop you from voting on account of your race. It is a federal crime, just like robbing a bank is a federal crime. But robbing you of your right to vote matters more than robbing your pocketbook. The man who robs your vote keeps you a slave. We ain't gonna be slaves no more."

"No, suh," a voice echoed.

"No more!

"Everyone is watching Mississippi this summer. The newspapers and the TV from up North are here, and they are watching. The Federal Government is here and they are watching. President Johnson is watching. They don't usually watch, so the white people can do anything they want to you without the world knowing. But right now, the whole world be watching.

"Governor Barnett is telling the President that Negroes don't vote in Mississippi because we don't want to. That's a lie! You know it and I know it. You are Mississippians, and you are American citizens. Now is the time for you to tell them you want to vote. If you want the rest of America to know you're not happy with the way things are, the way Governor Barnett says, you got to stand up and let them know. Now is the time!"

Brian paused, then turned, half facing the preacher who had opened the 'mass' meeting.

"You know, Reverend Henry, you are a good man and a brave man. But I am afraid I got to disagree with one thing you said. Reverend Henry say we come to lead you. No . . . you, the Negro people of Panola County are going to lead yourselves. No one knows better than you the lives you lead in this County, and the problems you have. So no one is more qualified than you to lead. We will be here to help you. But you are going to be the leaders! Some of you right here in this room!

"Sister Marks, tell about the voting classes and about the MFDP."

Sister Marks (Gideon later learned) had been a sharecropper before being turned off the land for civil rights activity, and was emerging as a leader of the Movement in this area. She explained there would be classes three nights a week, to teach how to fill out the voting forms and how to interpret the sections of the Mississippi Constitution the registrars would ask about when they went to register to vote.

"The old Democratic Party in Mississippi won't let Negroes in," Sister Marks explained, "so we have formed a new party, our own party, the Mississippi Freedom Democratic Party—the 'Em-Eff-Dee-Pee,' we calls it. The Freedom Party is open to people of all races and colors, and we even got some white folks in it. The MFDP is the only party in Mississippi that is for freedom and democracy. We the majority in Panola County. If we got democracy here, we could elect one of our own people as sheriff, 'stead of Sheriff Benson.

"But to be a real party, we got to have chapters and members in every county. So right here, right now, we are going to form a section for Panola County."

Sister Marks urged and cajoled, and an older black woman and a middle-aged black man volunteered to lead the section.

"Anyone else want to run for the position?" Sister Marks asked. Then the two were unanimously voted the heads of the Panola County Freedom Democratic Party.

Brian talked about how each person who had come to this meeting must recruit more people to come to the next meeting.

Finally, they all held hands and they sang:

We shall overcome,
We shall overcome,
We shall overcome some day,
Deep in my heart, I do believe
We shall overcome some day.

It was after 10 o'clock when the meeting broke up, late for farmers whose day started around four in the morning. After some further talk, they got into the cars and started back, with Hank Jones's vehicle again in the lead.

Now it was completely dark. Gideon was excited about the meeting and almost calm about the drive back to the safety of the Freedom House. As they started, Brian and Fred were talking to each other about plans for the morning.

They were just a mile down the road toward Batesville when they saw Hank's tail light glow red. Someone had waved him down. Hank had pulled off the road. Brian slowed down and stopped a little way behind Hank's car.

"It's the Man," Fred said. "Batesville deputies."

"Shee-it."

14

Shortly after Gideon's first visit with Kareem Jackson at San Quentin, he received the transcript of the trial. He also got the trial attorney's files on the case, a copy of the prosecutor's records of interviews with witnesses, and the tapes of Jackson's confession and that of his accomplice. Next he went to the courthouse where the case had been tried. He looked at the trial exhibits, the color photos of the motel crime scene, the pictures of the victim's body, dumped on the floor. While a courthouse clerk watched, he unwound the string that closed a heavy manila envelope, and removed a knife that bore rust-colored stains he knew were not rust. He unfolded a beach wrap, a blouse and bra, and a little swimsuit top, all soiled with blood. He saw the frayed slits where the knife had gone through the blouse.

*   *   *

On Sunday afternoon, June 14, 1981, through fatal happenstance, Luisa Flores and her nine-year-old daughter Marisol crossed paths with 22-year-old Kareem Jackson, a drug addict from South Central Los Angeles, and Jackson's friend Dave Hollister.

Jackson and Hollister had been drinking and doing meth for four days and nights, and now they were starting to come down. Most of that time, they had been lying about the Dark Nines Motor Lodge, a seedy motel in Compton where there was a dealer on the second floor. But when they ran out of money on Sunday afternoon, they were not ready to stop. So they ventured out with their sawed off shotguns to get cash.

They began in Torrance around three thirty in the afternoon, at the Seven-Eleven at Sepulveda and Crenshaw. The only customers were four high school students, who were chatting and joking near the frozen yogurt machine. When Kareem Jackson and Dave Hollister entered, two young employees, a male cashier and a female clerk, were behind the counter, arranging the racks of things for sale near the register.

Jackson fired two shotgun blasts into the ceiling. He sensed a special brightness in the smell of cordite, the unending echoes of the blasts, and the click of the new shells he pumped into his double-barreled.

Hollister stood by the door, guarding the exit and scanning the outside, where their car stood with the engine running. He slowly swung his shotgun from side to side, pointing it for a moment now at one, now at another of the young customers. They tried not to move, but couldn't help cringing. Hollister was jittery and his eyes darted back and forth at high speed. One of the high school students pissed in her pants, and the smell of urine filled the room. The clerk and cashier had raised their hands right after the two blasts.

Kareem Jackson pointed his shotgun at the cashier's chest, and spoke in a confident voice, loud and fast. "No one make a fucking move and nobody be brave or your guts will be all over this room. Everyone else's guts, too." Jackson advanced toward the cashier, and gestured with the shotgun. "Open the register. Put the money onto the counter. Every fucking last bill. Anyone fucks with us, we'll kill every motherfucking one of you."

The cashier emptied the till and put the money on the counter. He backed away a little, holding his hands out, trembling.

Less than four hundred dollars lay on the counter.

"What about the rest?" Jackson asked, in a dangerously quiet voice.

The cashier spoke hoarsely.

"In the two-key safe in back. We drop the money in at noon and four and ten o'clock. Can't open it unless someone from Brinks is here. . . Sunday afternoons are slow round here."

Kareem Jackson's hand tightened on the shotgun grip. Then he nodded.

"Put the money in a bag."

Jackson took the Seven-Eleven sack. He and Hollister backed toward the door, then turned and walked briskly to the car and drove off. Less than two minutes had elapsed from the two shotgun blasts to the squeal of their tires.

None of the witnesses would remember much of anything about the robbers and what they looked like, except that they had been black and that each had had a shotgun. But that didn't matter. The entire event had been caught by the video camera over the cashier area.

The cops got there ten minutes later, and shortly called in the details of the crime, including a pedestrian's report on the robbers' vehicle: a purple Pontiac, license number 2 CCM something.

After Jackson and Hollister had raced four blocks north on Crenshaw Boulevard, they concluded they were not being followed. Hollister, who was driving, slowed down.

"That was cool," Hollister said. "Smooth."

"We didn't get much, though," Jackson said. He thought for a moment. "That wasn't worth going out for. Let's try the In-and-Out-Burger on Torrance. We can hit it just as fast."

Again, two shotgun blasts brought fast cooperation, and Jackson made the same threats. This time, though, more customers were inside. While Kareem Jackson dealt with the cashier, Hollister herded the customers into a back corner of the store and made them toss their wallets onto the floor in front of him. Between the wallets and the till, they had around $800. It took less than five minutes. Again, no one was hurt. But when word reached police headquarters—another fast food place, another shotgun-blast robbery—the cops thought, "crime spree," and broadcast an emergency alert. The information on Hollister's car was also broadcast. Police cars from Torrance and neighboring cities began to converge on the area.

"We are rollin', my man, rollin'," Jackson said.

"Those fools want to make us rich," Hollister said. "You see how fast that punk moved with the money this time?"

"Let's do one more," Jackson said, "then we go back."

Luisa Flores was a thirty-two-year-old accounts receivable manager for a downtown law firm who was raising a nine year old on her own. She was the kind of woman who said, "I'm no feminist," but had ended her brief marriage to Carlos Flores when she concluded he was not going to be the right kind of father for Marisol.

Marisol had been two years old then, darling in the little dresses Luisa bought even though money was short. Carlos, a roofer, had been out of work for a while, and Luisa was working and going to school at the same time. She had tried to be supportive of Carlos—she knew a man's feeling of dignity is tried when he can't get a job. So even when her feelings were hurt by his scornful remarks about "your important job" and her becoming a "big deal college graduate," she tried to joke him out of it.

But she didn't know why he had to be snotty about taking care of Marisol at home, so they could save on childcare expenses when he wasn't spending much time looking for work anymore. And she didn't see why he couldn't have supper ready some of the time, even if it was just grilling some hamburger meat, so she had more time with Marisol when she got home tired from the office and would be going out to class right after dinner. Or why he couldn't tackle the dishes every other night. That would be fair. Or why he thought he had the right to be demanding about sex, when he just sat around doing nothing all day, and she was tired and didn't feel like it.

Carlos had never actually slapped Luisa, and she didn't really think he would have. But he abused her with words, and as time went by, she started to feel menaced.

She would have put up with it if it had just been herself. But when he started to aim sarcastic remarks at little Marisol ("Your precious baby doesn't need you right now"), she realized she could not count on him to put Marisol first. If he wasn't going to do that, what was it they were in this together for? So she left with Marisol.

Some people thought it had been tough for her, working and bringing up Marisol on her own. Actually it was a lot easier, not having to manage Carlos at the same time. Not having to balance what was right for Marisol against whatever Carlos wanted. Not having to be tense about Carlos all the time. Not having to deal with his temper. She hadn't realized how much energy that took until she didn't have to do it anymore.

Luisa and Marisol were on the way back from the beach—Marisol's skinny little body still shiny from the sun block Luisa had slathered her with—when they decided to pick up a bucket of chicken for supper.

Things had gone poorly for Jackson and Hollister at the Kentucky Fried Chicken they hit for the third robbery. The double shotgun blasts had quieted down most of the dozen employees and customers, but a couple of women were crying hysterically, and Hollister couldn't make them shut up. When one of the clerks seemed to reach for something under the counter, Kareem Jackson yelled, "Stop," and fired on him. The man fell, badly wounded, and Jackson jumped over the counter to get to the cash register. A tall man in the corner pulled out a hand gun. Hollister blew him away with a blast to the chest, splattering the woman next to him with blood, and the others ran for the back of the store, where there was another exit.

Hollister wasn't up for killing everyone in the room, whatever Jackson's rap had been. He just stood there, dazed, while the customers ran away.

Then they heard sirens.

"Fuck," said Jackson. "Let's rumble."

They burst from the front doors, shotguns waving. But an SUV had double parked, blocking their car. There was no one in it. The sirens sounded closer.

"We don't have time for this shit," said Hollister. "We got to get out of here."

Luisa Flores pulled into the parking lot. Jackson stepped in front of her minivan, and pointed a shotgun at her. She braked sharply.

"Open the door and get out," Jackson ordered. "Fast." She undid her seat belt, telling Marisol quietly, "Come over here and stay right by me." Luisa opened the door and got out, as Marisol scooted across the front seats, close to her.

Jackson hesitated, as Luisa tried to sidle away with Marisol.

"No, both of you get back in, get in back."

This time Jackson took the wheel. Hollister leaned back over the other seat, pointing his gun toward Luisa and Marisol to make them be still, as the vehicle shot out of the parking lot. Leaning on the horn, Jackson drove around the cars stopped at the intersection, darting into the oncoming traffic. As cars braked and dodged out of their way, Jackson wove in and out of traffic.

Heading toward them half a block away was a squad car, sirens screaming, responding to the robbery. Jackson hesitated only a moment, then aimed the minivan at the cop car and punched the accelerator. "Get the fuck out of my way or die, you fucker!" he yelled.

The police car swerved, smashing into parked vehicles, as Jackson side-swiped the car and bounced away. He zoomed forward, screeching round a corner, turned again at the next block, then blazed ahead. No one appeared to be following, and he slowed down and made another quick turn.

Twenty minutes later they were back at the Dark Nines.

"Please let us go," Luisa said. "We don't know where we are, and you'll have plenty of time to get away."

"Shut up, Mex bitch," said Hollister, hustling Luisa and Marisol into the motel room with them.

Luisa and Marisol huddled quietly on the floor, in a corner of the room, and Luisa tried to listen for clues that might help her get them out of this. She was keeping calm because she knew she had to, so she could act at the right moment.

"What the fuck now, Kareem?" asked Hollister.

"Go upstairs and buy some crystal," said Jackson.

A few minutes later, Hollister returned with the meth, also with a bottle of tequila.

"Come over here, bitch," Jackson said to Luisa.

Luisa came over. Maybe if she handled this right, they would not hurt Marisol.

"You can do anything you want to me," Luisa said softly, "and I won't fight with you, but please leave my girl alone."

"You're fucking right we'll do anything we fucking want."

Jackson wrapped electrical tape around Luisa's wrists, over and over, and pushed her into the corner of one of the beds against the wall. She called quietly to Marisol, "Come over here, honey. It'll be okay." Marisol sidled up to her, but Luisa couldn't put her arm around Marisol because of the tape. Jackson and Hollister sat on the other bed, putting something into a glass pipe. Soon they were smoking and drinking, and they seemed to calm down. Hollister laughed softly, and she could hear both men breathing heavily. They looked dazed, but they were conscious.

Luisa could see no way to escape. *Can I at least get Marisol out of here? If they nod off, maybe Marisol could run out the door before they can stop her.* But they'd thrown the bolt and put the chain on the door. She didn't see how a scared nine year old could get past them. *Maybe we shouldn't do anything risky. If we just stay calm and quiet, maybe we'll be rescued before anything happens. You can't just kidnap someone and drive off without anybody noticing.*

"Honey," she whispered to Marisol, "if I tell you to . . ."

"Shut up. No talking," Jackson said. He walked over and put a piece of tape over Luisa's mouth.

"What are we going to do?" Hollister asked a few minutes later. "Their fucking van's outside, and the cops probably figured out who we are from my car."

"Let's just chill before we do anything."

They drank some more tequila.

"We have to take them with us and dump them somewhere," Jackson said. "We just got to take a chance on the van for a while."

He walked over to Luisa, and yanked the tape off her mouth. She gasped, and Marisol whimpered.

"Anyone expecting you any time soon?"

Luisa was silent for a moment, trying to calculate whether some lie would be safer then the truth. But there was no time for calculating. Jackson swung his palm hard across her face, knocking her into the wall.

"Answer me, bitch."

"There are just the two of us. I'm divorced. No one is expecting us until work and school tomorrow." Jackson nodded and walked away.

Luisa tasted blood in her mouth, but she tried to sooth Marisol, who'd begun crying.

"Shhh, honey," she said softly. "Mommy's not hurt. You be as quiet as you can, and stay by me, and do exactly what I tell you." She couldn't talk clearly because her tongue had been cut. Marisol huddled against her mother. *This wouldn't be happening if I'd stayed with Carlos,* Luisa thought.

"Okay," Jackson said to Hollister. "We got a while, let's smoke some more and relax. We'll go somewhere after it gets dark."

Hollister inhaled a long, deep drag of the drugged smoke. "Let's fuck mommy while we're waiting," he said, giggling.

Hollister reached across and grabbed Marisol's arm, and pulled her away from Luisa, as Jackson moved toward the bed. Luisa had tried to make herself think that cooperating might save her and Marisol. Though she had known from the start that this moment might come, it came too abruptly for her to think. She knew in her head that no matter what they did to her, she had to be calm and quiet, for Marisol's sake. But when Jackson violated her, she could not keep from crying in pain, as Jackson's thrusts tore at her.

"Mama, mama! Don't hurt my mama!" she heard Marisol crying. Luisa tried to talk to her. "Mari, don't look," she gasped. "It's . . ." But she could not talk, and now the child was screaming.

"Shut her up, Dave," said Jackson. "Shut her the fuck up." But Jackson could hear her gasping cries even as Hollister tried to put his hand over her mouth. Jackson flashed on Mom's boyfriend Lenny doing it to him when he was nearly the girl's age. Lenny made him be quiet, too; Lenny hurt him more if he yelled. But he remembered crying, trying to cry quietly.

"God damn it, shut up you little bitch. I'll give you something to cry about."

Jackson withdrew from Luisa, and shoved her head into the wall, knocking her half-unconscious. Turning to the child, he paused as he reached, everything seemed to be happening in slow motion. He saw Lenny touching him the first time, *No! Let me be*, he felt a weak, sick feeling in his bowels. He grasped the girl, holding her down with one hand.

"No, no, mama," Marisol cried, as Jackson slowly pulled at the small swimsuit. He felt the rage, *You bastard, Lenny, I'll* . . . but he couldn't take her. The sick feeling welled up again and his vision dimmed. He saw the fear in the girl's face, and he hit her, "Don't look at me that way!"

Marisol's screams had pierced the thin walls of the Dark Nines. They were recognizably a child's cries, cries of such dread that even one of the jaded clientele of the Dark Nines had decided to call 911. ("Hey, man, I'm calling you from the Dark Nines motel, on Compton Avenue? Some very bad shit goin down in the room below us. We're in 205. Sounds like a kid, a little kid being hurt bad. I mean killed or something. I'm not shitting you, man, send a cop right away.")

Jackson leaned back on his heels by the girl, not moving, staring at her, his face a mask. Luisa rose from her concussion and tried to throw herself at him, tried to gouge his eyes, to put herself between Jackson and Marisol, to pry him away from the girl, anything, scratching him as Hollister tried to pull her away.

Jackson emerged from his daze.

"This is fucking over, you bitch," he said. He grabbed Luisa by her hair, yanked her to the side, and punched her in the face, breaking her nose. Drawing a blade from the pants around his knees, he snapped it open and knifed Luisa in the stomach. As she sagged, he yanked her head back, then slashed her throat deeply. Blood poured out of her, and she collapsed onto the floor next to the bed, dying.

Jackson turned to the child, wide-eyed with horror, screaming. He drew back his knife . . . then let it fall. He put his hands over his ears and squeezed his eyes shut.

"Jesus Christ," Hollister said. Then the police burst into Room 105.

✶ ✶ ✶

Gideon Roth sat in the evidence room of the Superior Court of Los Angeles County, holding the knife and touching the blood-stained cloth-ing of Luisa and Marisol Flores. He tried to make himself objective and calm, so he could do his job. His hands trembled as he looked at the knife again. *Why did this happen? What kind of human being could do such things? How had Kareem Jackson become such a person?*

There were answers to these questions, answers that the jury had never heard. But it would take a long time to find them.

15

June 7, 1964, 10:15 p.m. The two cars were alone in the heat and darkness of the rural Mississippi night, alone and in the grip of the local police. Gideon felt an emptiness in the pit of his stomach and the thudding of his own heart, as their headlights illuminated a deputy leaning into the car ahead of them, saying something to Hank.

After a minute the deputies waved both cars forward. The two SNCC cars drove at a sedate pace, scrupulously staying a few miles an hour be-low the speed limit. But as they approached the courthouse square, the police siren started up. Wheeling around both cars, the police forced them to the side of the street across from the square. A second police car pulled up at once.

Looking out the rear window, across the street, Gideon saw the stately white courthouse, surrounded by a wide lawn. Almost immediately, he saw four or five cars, filled with young white men, circling round and around the courthouse square. Not chance traffic for ten thirty on a Sunday night in Batesville, Mississippi, Gideon thought.

A raucous crowd of young whites gathered on the lawn across from the police cars and the two SNCC vehicles, soon growing to about a hundred people. Another crowd collected on a nearby corner. Before long, the number of cars cruising around the square increased to twenty or thirty. Ominously, some of the cars headed out of the square in the direction Gideon's group would have to take to get back to Hokes Landing. Gideon was more frightened than he had ever been in his life.

The heat was still intense, and they rolled the windows of the car part way down to breathe. More police came, and the licenses of the drivers were taken and examined. And they waited. Around 11:00 p.m., Sheriff Benson himself arrived. He was a tall and heavy man with a red face and, predictably, a very red neck and arms. This was the man they'd been defying in the song, singing he wouldn't turn them round. Benson leaned into the window by Gideon's side and said, "What the hell are you all doing here in my county?"

Gideon froze. After a moment the summer volunteer next to Gideon, a student from the University of Pennsylvania named Blake Townsend, spoke up. "We're exercising our constitutional rights. We're helping citizens to vote."

"What the hell you talking about?" the Sheriff yelled. "Our niggers don't want to vote, and no one needs your god damn help. Get out and let me see your identification." As the Sheriff went around the other side to examine Blake, Brian turned to Gideon and urged, in a sharp whisper, "You have to talk up. Don't sass them, but show you're not afraid." Gideon wasn't sure he could because he was so afraid.

"You a communist?" the Sheriff was asking Blake.

"No, sir."

"Yes, you are. You all are beatnik type communists. I can smell it—you never take baths, and you smell like niggers." The nearby crowd laughed. "You're not wanted down here, and we know what to do with trouble-makers."

"Sir, the Negro people who invited us down here think we're needed, and we've got a constitutional right to be here."

"Tell me the names of the niggers from Batesville who invited you," the Sheriff asked.

Blake remained silent.

"You a liar, then. We been followin' the Constitution jes fine without your help," the Sheriff added. "You disagree with that?" he asked, leaning over Blake.

"Yes sir. With all respect, sir, you don't let Negroes vote."

"You jes a damned liar when you say that." The Sheriff spoke in a great voice that carried across to the square, so the crowd could hear him. "You just lying. You communist trouble-makers are only going to make things worse for the coloreds. We treat them fair, and they know their place, and they got no need to vote, and they don't want to."

The Sheriff made a white girl from the other SNCC car get out next, and he looked at her identification. "What's a white girl doin' in Mississippi, livin' with niggers?" he asked.

"I have also come here to help those who asked me to come," she said firmly.

"Our Southern white ladies know how to help our Nigras without living with them. I know what you've come down here for, you slut. But our good colored folks won't have nothing to do with you." The crowd burst into applause.

The white girl responded. "Your white ladies only know how to preserve their own privileges. Colored people are about to take charge of their own destinies without the help of Southern white ladies, and nothing you do can stop them."

"Get back in the car, you damn nigger-loving whore."

"You are all a bunch of misfits," the Sheriff announced. The other student in the car with Gideon retorted: "I was president of the freshman class."

Finally, Gideon was called outside the car.

"And why have you come down to our great state of Mississippi?"

"To try to help people," Gideon said in a tentative voice.

"But I've already said that we don't want your god damn help!" the Sheriff thundered in Gideon's face. "Didn't you hear me?"

Gideon felt himself cringe.

"You hear me?"

"Yes sir." Then: "But this is the United States. We've got a right to be here."

"This is Mississippi, and this is my county. If you're acting suspicious, I've got a right to hold you for investigation until I'm satisfied you ain't about to commit a crime. I want you out of my county."

Gideon could feel how hard his heart was pounding. But he made himself speak as firmly as he could, even though his voice was shaking.

"We will come back anyway," Gideon said.

The Sheriff looked contemptuously at Gideon. Then he examined Gideon's driver's license. "'Roth.' You a Jew?"

Gideon thought better of going into atheism right now, or whether Jews were a religion or a people. "Yes sir."

"You a *Jew* communist bastard, then. We don't need your type here. We didn't have no problems in Mississippi before you all showed up. Our 'knee-grow' people," he said, "have made as much progress as niggers can, and they done it without you Jew agitators. You got nothing to offer them but trouble, and you and they are gonna get plenty of it if you don't crawl back to New York City." Another burst of applause from the drunken mob in the square, along with rebel yells.

The Sheriff loomed over Gideon and glared. Gideon took a deep breath. "Nonetheless," he said, "we are not going to leave Panola County, Mississippi, the United States of America."

The Sheriff wrenched the car door open and shoved Gideon inside, banging Gideon's head against the car. "I've heard enough of your Commie crap. Get the hell back in there and don't give me any more trouble." Gideon lurched back inside the car.

The Sheriff and the cops conferred, and the group in the other car began singing "God Bless America." Gideon's car joined in. They sat in the cars for another thirty minutes, singing and talking quietly. One of the cars was supposed to have a citizens band radio so they could communicate with the project headquarters in Hokes Landing. But it wasn't working. Gideon's heart was thumping so fast now, he felt out of breath, and found it hard to speak in full sentences without stopping. But he had stood up to the Sheriff.

Finally, a little past midnight, Sheriff Benson told them to get out of town. The two cars carefully backed up, then slowly turned toward Hokes Landing, with the Sheriff's car close behind.

"Hope you've got your running shoes on," Fred joked to the back seat. Then to Brian, "I'm worried about that spare tire." As the town receded, they reached a straight stretch of road, and Gideon looked back. Behind them was the police cruiser, and behind it, a long line of headlights, twenty or so cars. Gideon wondered if someone might be waiting a few miles ahead.

No one knows where we are, he thought. It wouldn't help if they did. As the cars reached the city limits, the Sheriff turned on his overhead red flasher, slowed down and stopped.

The SNCC cars continued. No one was behind them. Half a minute further along, the road turned and they were out of sight. Brian flicked his lights off and then on, and Hank pulled away. Brian stomped the accelerator, and in a moment the two old cars were up to seventy miles per hour, high speed for these roads. Wondering each moment whether they would be cut off by someone ahead or whether the line of cars behind the Sheriff would catch up and force them off the road, they barreled down the highway, screeching round turns, racing for Hokes Landing and safety.

Gideon saw that on the harder curves, Hank was pulling away from them. He realized Brian was favoring the bald rear spare tire, trying not to make the car skid sideways too much. But he caught up each time in the straight aways. Soon it appeared they were not being followed, but they were taking no chances.

Ten miles out of Hokes Landing they hit trouble. After a turn through what felt like a tunnel of kudzu, the cover-everything vine that draped itself over trees, abandoned cars, even old barns and houses, like a great green blanket, they broke out into a long stretch of road that must have been between some fields—it was hard to tell just what was in the distance off to the sides, in the darkness of the night. About a quarter mile ahead stood a pair of cars, probably one on each shoulder of the road, their high beams shining toward the SNCC cars. A third car sat crosswise between them, blocking the road, with a lantern before it.

Hank reacted first, jamming on his brakes, and Brian, closing too fast, hit his brakes harder than he wanted. Hank was turning around, but their headlights had already made it obvious to the men at the roadblock that they had been approaching, and were now about to flee back in the direction they had come from.

"The fucking Klan," said Fred.

"We're not going to hang around to ask," said Brian. "It's dark, and all they can see are our headlights, and they can't be entirely sure who we are—maybe we're bootleggers who don't want to be hijacked."

"Maybe they are just hijackers," Fred suggested.

"Count on it," Brian said.

Hank was now pointed south, and was already beginning to pull away as Brian finished his U turn. They could hear car doors being slammed in the cars that had blocked them.

"I surely wish we had better tires," said Brian. "But I know this car can move when it's got to. And it's got to now."

Brian raised his voice so Gideon and the others in back could hear him. "Just hold tight. These crackers will try to swing around us and force us off the road—when we're all going so fast, they'll be afraid to try to bump us. Hank and I went over alternative routes before we left, and we're gonna take another way home, over some dirt roads. Gideon, you turn around and look back and tell me what you can see. I've got to concentrate on the road ahead."

Gideon knelt on the seat and looked out the rear window. He could see two cars following. They did not seem to be gaining right now, and seemed some way off. When the road dipped between hills for a moment, they couldn't be seen. Then on the next rise, Gideon could see further.

"All three cars are following," he said. "Two of them are maybe two, three blocks behind us, and there's a third car, a ways further back."

A few very long minutes went by before Gideon reported the cars seemed to be getting a bit closer.

"OK, turn around and sit down. We gonna be rockin' and rollin.'"

Their high beams showed the road ahead, ditches alongside the road, fences beyond. From time to time, as the road turned, their lights swept across a barn or a house. But there were no lights and nothing broke the darkness but their headlights. As far as Gideon knew, there was no one to give them shelter, no law to protect them, no place of safety at hand.

As the road turned a corner to the left, all of the lights of Hank's car flicked off, then back on. Gideon felt their car immediately slow down, as Brian took his foot off the gas and began braking. Seconds later, they passed through a hamlet with a single light on a pole by a closed gas station. Suddenly, Hank's car went completely black. Brian immediately doused the lights on their car, and the two careened forward in complete blackness.

Gideon was blind in the sudden darkness. The vehicles giving chase no longer had tail lights to follow, but Gideon felt sure his own car and Hank's would veer off the road into a ditch or a tree at any moment. Abruptly, Brian yanked on the hand brake, to slow them without making the brake light go on. He was close behind Hank who was also braking violently. Leaning onto two wheels, the cars turned into a dirt side road, to their left, proceeded about fifty yards, then halted at the side of the road.

"Keep your heads down," Brian commanded, turning around to look back toward the highway they had just turned off. "Fred, hand me the heat." *I thought this was a nonviolence movement,* Gideon said to himself. They heard the approach, then the roar and whoosh, and then the distancing sound of the two cars rushing away down the highway. There was no sound of braking. A moment later, the third car flew past. Brian jumped out of the car, standing in the road, listening. A pistol was in his hand, at his side.

"Don't hear any sounds of them returning yet, but we've only got a couple of minutes before they realize we're no longer ahead of them and decide what to do."

Hank had run up to Brian from the other stopped car.

"This road or back to the highway?" Hank asked.

"The highway," Brian responded immediately. "They won't expect that—they'll either figure we took this road or stopped with someone in the town we just went through."

The lights went back on, the cars turned and resumed their northward race at top speed. Gideon was again told to look back. No one was following. After ten minutes, they began to feel hopeful their pursuers had given up or were too far behind to catch up. They passed the site of the roadblock, and no one was there. They continued on, dropping to the speed limit as they finally entered Hokes Landing. A few minutes later, well past midnight, they pulled up at the Freedom House, and stepped shakily out of the car.

As they walked toward the door, Gideon murmured to Brian, "You've got damn good night vision."

"You're fucking A," Brian responded lightly.

Hank explained to a dozen anxious people in the office why they were two hours late. Brenda, the young black woman who was on the phones, called the Jackson office immediately. "They're back; it's OK." Brenda listened quietly for a moment, then signed off. She was near tears. "Hey," Brian said, his arm around her. "Be cool. We just had a little adventure. We're all OK."

"Been too many damn adventures around here over the years, and it was damn late at night."

"We're gonna see a lot more scary stuff this summer, Brenda."

Brian held her for a moment, and the rest of them went to their rooms.

16

Young Gideon looked glumly out into the Mississippi darkness until he remembered about not being a back-lit target at a window and drew down the shade. But he was too troubled to sleep, and he lay on the bed staring at the ceiling. There was an elaborate pattern of cracks that looked like this or that, and his eyes traced and re-traced them obsessively as he ran over the events of the night. He was ashamed of his fear in the Batesville courthouse square—he knew everyone could tell how terrified he'd been.

Gideon thought, *We could be dead right now. But what choice do we have?* Then Gideon wondered again what he was doing here if he couldn't stop being afraid.

There was a knock at the door to Gideon's room. It was the girl in the other car at the courthouse. Gideon had met her briefly at orientation. Susan Channing, she went to Oberlin.

"Hi," she said. "You're Gideon, right? Can I come in for a while? I'm still scared."

"Not as scared as I was," Gideon replied glumly. "You were so brave in the Batesville square. I was awful, my voice was shaking the whole time and the sheriff could tell, I know he could."

"Tell me what you were feeling." Susan came over and sat at the foot of the bed. She was a tall girl with long, thick dark hair, now done in braids for the night. Neither thin nor fat, exactly. She was wearing a long cotton nightgown with a scoop neck, and over it a short light robe. Though this was not at all a sexy outfit, Gideon still interrupted his self-criticism to wonder whether they were supposed to act like brothers and sisters here.

The air in the room was close, and even after midnight the heat was oppressive. Gideon noticed little beads of perspiration on Susan's face and neck and on the skin around her collarbone, and he wanted to run his fingers along there and feel the dampness on her neck. Suddenly Gideon was aware that he wanted to hold her or to be held.

He pondered Susan's question, about what he had felt during his confrontation with the sheriff. He thought about how much to say about his fear in the face of the enemy. Meanwhile thoughts about sex flicked on and off. Even while he considered asking her to leave, he turned over in his mind the logistics: Would she come close enough so he might touch her casually? Was there an approach that would allow him to retreat without shame if she were not interested? Would she have come into his room if she were not?

But these thoughts were only a passing intrusion into his anxiety over the day. His body was stiff, on guard. He contrasted his plan to be a civil rights hero with the reality that, confronted with danger, he had been terrified and indecisive. He sat up in bed and wrapped his arms around his knees, his eyes downcast. He opened his mouth to speak, then closed it. He did not know what to say.

Gideon felt he was an inadequate person in a dangerous place. He didn't want to say that. Susan reached across and put her hand on his ankle. He spoke.

"You heard most of it. The sheriff was bellowing so loud. Everyone else was speaking up, showing you couldn't be bullied. You were incredible, what you said about the white ladies and all. But I was afraid of the mob and I was afraid of him. You heard the way my voice was shaking. I felt weak, and I know he sensed it. I thought, he's going to hit me in the face. I was afraid. I think everyone could hear my voice quiver," he ended with a whisper. "I know I didn't respond enough."

She thought for a moment. "You weren't so bad. I mean, you told him twice that we were going to come back; that was pretty defiant. I thought it was snappy, too, the part about Panola County, USA.

"I could tell you weren't feeling too bold. Maybe it was partly the surprise of it? We heard about all this in Oxford, but having a sheriff threaten you face to face is different. We've led privileged lives, and we don't expect it. Maybe you'll do better next time, if you can prepare yourself."

But I did prepare, Gideon said to himself. In my mind I rehearsed confrontations with Southern sheriffs a hundred times. But my fantasy defiance took place in broad daylight, where too many people would be around for them to kill us. Not at night, with a mob nearby.

"I had thought about it before," he said after a while. "But it didn't help. I didn't think what it would be like for someone that big to be menacing me. He was like the bigger guys in my neighborhood in the Bronx when I grew up. The ones I was always afraid to fight with.

"Actually, I feel like Jim in *Lord Jim*, after he jumped off the ship, abandoning the pilgrims. Now it's too late to go back and make it right. I jumped into cowardice, and everyone knows. I can never jump back."

"Gideon," she said. "No. No." She moved closer, her body upright, as she walked on her knees across the bed to be closer to him. She wrapped her arms around his shoulders. He rested his head against her, feeling the softness of her breasts next to his face.

"No. That's not at all what it's like," she said. "Don't be crazy. You didn't abandon the ship. You didn't leave anyone to drown and die. You didn't endanger anyone. That's melodramatic shit. And you didn't surrender to the Sheriff either. Maybe it wasn't even a good idea to respond the way we did, when I was being so brave. This is only the beginning, this is just the start of a long hot summer."

She stroked his head, and he could feel that his damp breath was going through her nightgown, touching her. His breath was touching her skin. Fear and embarrassment and anxiety were mixed up with desire, and Gideon did not know what was in his mind.

"Anyway, you told him you weren't giving in, even if he could tell you were afraid." She paused. "Maybe you weren't as brave as you wished. But you definitely weren't as cowardly as you think you were, and you defied him. Shit, that took bravery. We're all needed here. Just being here is being brave. Maybe it will be OK."

A wave of relief engulfed Gideon. He wrapped his arms around Susan.

"You know what one of the things is that we have to learn from the local people?" she went on. "How to be brave. Mississippi Negroes have always had to have courage of a kind we've never needed."

Gideon slowly stroked her back, but his arms felt as though they were being operated remotely, by poles, as though he were a kind of puppet. She reached across him to turn one of the lamps out, and then she wriggled out of her robe. She drew him down alongside her, and they lay side by side. *We are going to do it, then.* Susan looked at Gideon as she rested a hand on his chest. But he turned his gaze away from her face. She touched his cheek lightly. "Look at me. It's all right. Just be here now, in the moment."

He looked at her and noticed how gray her eyes were. *What astonishing clear, gray eyes you have.* Gideon touched her through the nightgown, and he could feel her nipple, hard and enticing. Their faces moved together and they kissed. He pressed his mouth down too hard, banging his teeth against hers. "Make your mouth soft," she said. As he did, and their lips and tongues yieldingly merged, a surge of unafraid lust coursed through him.

"You need to learn to be brave in this, too. Brave for yourself, not for anyone else." She rolled over on top of him, sat up a little, straddling him, and unbuttoned Gideon's pajama top. As she stroked his chest, Gideon tried to put his hand between her legs. Susan shook herself, and took his hands in hers for a moment. "Not yet."

He stroked her arms and her sides through her gown, moving more slowly, and he felt that place along her side where her breasts began to swell out. Susan began to breathe heavily, and Gideon was aroused. He pushed her nightgown up, and now he touched her skin itself, fighting to be patient. His hands felt awkward, and he squirmed into a more reasonable position.

At last she pressed herself against him, moving back and forth a little, as he pushed between her legs through his pajamas. She moved closer and hugged Gideon, so he couldn't bring his hands to bear the way he'd been trying. "Stop worrying about the goal post so much," she whispered right into his ear, and then she laughed a little and he did too.

He was suddenly aware of the sexiness of the skin near her armpits, it was so soft, and he kissed her neck lightly, then the place under her chin. Then she put her tongue into his ear, and he felt a madness taking him, and now he reached around and felt the damp softness between her legs.

She shuddered, and quickly drew her nightgown over her head and tossed it to the floor. Gideon slid his pajama bottom down, and Susan reached down to move him into her. "Now," she whispered, "now," moving her legs a little further apart, and he was altogether within her.

After a time in which their movements became faster and less voluntary, she stopped him again, this time all the way inside her.

"Start again as slow as you can," she said. "Torture me with slowness." As he tried to do so, he was conscious of her as well as of her body, of a deliciousness he later called her Susanness. But soon they both became frenzied again, and a throbbing took them, and Susan cried out quietly and she came, and Gideon did too.

Susan laid herself flat against his chest, gently rocking her hips every now and then. Then finally they lay together silently, in their moisture and sweat, and they were aware again of the cloying Mississippi heat.

"That was completely wonderful," he said. "Amazing."

"Dreamy," she agreed. "Don't go to sleep right away. Let's talk."

"You are amazing. You know what's right about everything, don't you? When to be afraid and when not. When to make love. When you need someone else."

"Are you trying to tease me?"

He shook his head.

"Then don't be silly. I don't know everything, even about making love. But I do know something about being open and direct."

Gideon was quiet a few moments. "I don't. I'm not even sure I know what you mean by that." His eyes flickered away and back.

"But you're starting to try right now, aren't you? Just with that question."

"Maybe. I hope so."

"Don't talk to me about it then, not yet. Not with words. But look at me, and stay with me."

Her eyes were relaxed and wide, and Gideon felt warmed by her smile. He wondered just what it actually meant for eyes to be open and inviting. *An eyeball's always the same shape, isn't it? But my eyes don't look so open to people. Now I'm thinking too much when I should be here in the moment. But how do I stop myself from thinking? What can I think about when I'm not thinking?*

"It's OK," Susan said. She reached over and gently touched the soft place next to the side of his eye, and slowly ran her finger along the skin under his lower eyelid. He was aware of the tension in his muscles there, and of its passing.

He grinned at her. "This has been quite a day, hasn't it?"

She leaned across in response, and kissed him on his eyes. "You are a very sweet young man." Then she started to laugh, a great open laugh, and Gideon knew she was not laughing at him. He did not entirely get what this laugh was about, or why Susan was laughing just then, but he knew it had to do with life in the face of danger and opportunity. Her laugh softened into a satisfied sigh. He nestled into her, and they fell asleep.

17

Gideon rattled around the Washington cottage, thinking how full of meaning his time in Mississippi had been. How alive he had felt. Now he could barely summon the energy to get out of bed.

Gideon forced himself to go for a walk. Climbing into the hills that would eventually offer a glorious view of the Columbia River Gorge, he picked his way through the stones in the path through the thick woods.

He saw again the satisfied look on Wendell Dale's face, at the partnership meeting, at the moment it had become clear that Gideon was going to be forced out. His stomach churned, and he clenched his fists unconsciously. *My career ended, my years of dedication to the firm, flushed away because of a farcical fight in a parking lot.* He relaxed his hands. He knew there was more to it than that. What was the use?

What had he accomplished in all that time? Some victories for the likes of Petfood Solutions. How had he gone from idealistic activist to Establishment gladiator?

When he started law school, Gideon imagined himself battling in courtrooms for the movement. But by the early 1970s the civil rights movement had stalled or been stymied. The Vietnam war was over. And the movement for which he had wanted to do battle was not so clearly discernible.

As a conservative backlash swept across America, Gideon grew demoralized about politics and starting thinking about a career. The ambition his father had tried so hard to instill played a role. Gideon wanted more than to have been a student firebrand. He wanted to make a name for himself.

Then, too, there was the sheer intellectual interest. The emerging technologies and the copyright law that protected them generated fascinating and subtle legal problems, problems that Gideon enjoyed thinking about while he was paid to fight with other people.

He and Helen had both realized big things were destined to happen in Silicon Valley, so they moved there. Now he looked back on the ruins of his career with disgust. He thought of all the injustices he had tried to address part time, as pro bono projects, on the side, with such dubious results. And he thought of all the injustices he had not had time for. How much more might he have accomplished?

Gideon knew he had a special talent for framing an issue in a way that people could respond to. He had often conjured political ads in his mind that, he thought, would have moved people in a way that would have changed the outcome on big issues. But his work for the law firm had come first, and he had made no effort to connect with any group that might have benefited from his involvement, his insights. His leadership.

He felt guilty about how little he had done. In fact, he felt that many of the bad things that had taken place in the country since the 1960s were his fault. That his failure to act was responsible, in part, for things like so-called "welfare reform," the destruction of the social safety net that the poorest Americans relied on.

Instead he had spent most of his time working for big businesses, fitting pro bono work in at the edges. But to what end? When he thought of the years he had fought for Kareem Jackson, one image supplanted all others: the gas chamber. Ending with death.

Gideon thought, too, of Helen.

18

Two years after Gideon became a partner at Harkin & Lessman, Helen became pregnant. They had been putting it off because of the pressures of work and all, but Helen was 35, and they thought they shouldn't wait any longer.

When they had the amniocentesis, to make sure there were no genetic abnormalities, they learned the baby's sex.

"It's Amanda who's on deck, Gideon, not Daniel."

"Ladies first . . . another time, Danny boy. We're ready for you, Mandy! You'll be as sweet and smart as your mother."

They planned how to have it all, with the benefit of flex time at work (she was one of the bosses, after all), and household help. By six months into the pregnancy, Amanda's room was ready for her, and they were wrapping their minds around parenthood. Spock's Baby and Child Care and Brazelton's Infants and Mothers were on the bedside tables. Was it a surrender to sexist role-typing to have so much pink clothing, identifying her as a female baby? They painted Amanda's room a creamy lavender, but filled a little white chest with mostly pink sleepers, sweaters and caps, courtesy of their parents.

At 26 weeks, Helen went in to the emergency room. She had begun having severe cramps and bleeding, and the baby didn't seem to be moving anymore. Amanda was stillborn. She never saw her room, her little outfits, her crib mobiles, the soft animals. She had died in the womb, apparently because of some problem with the placenta. Gideon flew back from San Diego, where he had been in trial. They induced labor to deliver the lifeless child.

After the birth, the nurses washed off the dead baby, and Helen and Gideon held her in turn. Amanda was as warm as if she were actually alive. It was hard to believe she was dead. You couldn't help counting the little fingers and toes, she looked perfect.

Helen's grief was accompanied by guilt—she felt her body had been inadequate, hadn't been good enough to sustain her baby's life. The doctors attempted to reassure her it was nothing she had done or could have done. She had abstained from alcohol throughout the pregnancy, and had never used tobacco or drugs. In fact, no one could say just why it had happened; a loss so late in a pregnancy was just a very rare misfortunate.

But it was more common with older first-time moms. Why did they wait?

The social worker talked to Helen and Gideon about pictures and other remembrances, and a volunteer photographer took photos of Amanda. The nursery at home now contained portraits of the baby, framed footprints, and a lock of her hair.

The top drawer of the little white chest held only the one piece of baby clothing they had put on Amanda when Helen had asked to see her a few days after the stillbirth. They gave the rest away.

Gideon was supposed to return to the trial after the weekend. But he couldn't.

The loss overwhelmed them for weeks, and never entirely left. Gideon felt defensive about his part in their decision to put off babies for so long, though Helen didn't say anything blaming him. Eventually, work helped keep his mind off it.

A year and half later Helen wanted to try again, but Gideon felt it would be coming at a bad time. The next inopportune time was Helen's, and then ... then she was 39 years old and afraid of another stillbirth. One Friday evening, when Gideon returned late, he found all of the baby furniture in the driveway, with a paper taped on the crib saying "Goodwill." Helen did not speak to him all weekend.

19

Two weeks after Gideon had arrived in Hokes Landing, Brian mentioned he was heading for Jackson, where Summer Project headquarters were located, with Ann Kravitz, a white physician from the Medical Committee for Human Rights. The group was supporting the Summer Project with medical services and was documenting the unmet medical needs of blacks in Mississippi. Because it would be provocative and dangerous for Brian, a black man, to drive alone with Ann, a white woman, he asked Gideon to come along for the ride. Ann sat in back.

Brian had meetings in Jackson, planning for the next wave of volunteers, and Gideon would make himself useful however he could.

Early on Sunday afternoon, Gideon was asked to man the WATS line—the flat-rate-for-calling-anywhere-in-the-state telephone service that was the civil rights coalition's life line to all the projects. Gideon was apprehensive about the responsibility, but this was the way SNCC worked—people jumped into responsibility, or were thrown in, and they saw how it worked out.

Billie Grant had been on the WATS line for fourteen hours and needed to be relieved. Before she went to the Freedom House to crash, Billie told Gideon what kind of matters would require urgent follow-up, and which only had to be recorded and monitored.

Billie showed Gideon the list of phone numbers for the FBI in

Mississippi and in Washington, as well as police agencies in the state, and other people who would need to be contacted in an emergency. One of the names on the list was Jim Forman, SNCC's executive director. Billie told Gideon that Forman and Bob Moses, the director of the Summer Project, were at the orientation session for the next wave of volunteers, in Oxford, Ohio.

At first Gideon was doing the usual stuff, taking reports of harassment, arrests and so on. The WATS LINE entries for the last week included these items:

Starkville. Shots fired into Freedom Center last night. No one hurt. Reported to local police, who said we did it ourselves to get attention.

Grenada. About 300 people attended the mass meeting that was held at Bell Flower Church. The people marched from the church to the downtown square. Bill Harris was hit in the face by a white guy; the police took the white man away. The marchers went back to the church and completed their meeting. 28 people in jail now in Grenada.

Harmony. Twelve black parents have signed a desegregation lawsuit.

Carthage. Two volunteers, an Iowa minister and a Harvard student, beaten by a mob inside a doctor's office where the student had gone to get medical treatment. Police arrested the two white volunteers.

Holly Springs. Summer volunteer threatened in a store. Two white men walked in, had this conversation: 'What do you think we should do about civil rights workers?' 'I think we should kill them.'

Holmes County. Night riders burned a SNCC car.

Hattiesburg. Freedom schools launched.

Philadelphia. Mt. Zion Church burned to ground. Was to be used for Freedom Schools.

<u>Drew.</u> Seven civil rights workers arrested for
distributing voter registration literature without a
permit.

<u>Canton.</u> Headquarters rocked when bomb bounced off wall,
exploded on side walk.

Gideon added similar items in the course of the afternoon.

Around four o'clock there was a call from the woman on the phones at
the COFO project in Meridian, saying they were worried about Mickey
Schwerner and James Earl Chaney. Mickey and J.E. had gone out to
Neshoba County with a volunteer that morning. They should have been
back by two o'clock, two thirty at the outside. But there had been no word.

Meridian said they had already phoned the State Police and the police
in Philadelphia to ask whether they had been arrested, and had learned
nothing. They also called the hospitals, to see whether the men had been
in an accident. Nothing.

Gideon spoke to the person who had been left in charge of the Jackson
office while Forman and Moses and most of the usual folks were in Ohio.
She said there were some people she would call, but he should call Jim
Forman in Ohio right away.

After he heard the news, Forman sounded grave, and told Gideon this
looked bad.

"The Klan burned a church near Philadelphia a few days ago," Forman
said. "Neshoba County's a bad place. Very bad. Anything could happen
there."

Forman gave Gideon instructions and some numbers to start calling, and said he would be calling people too, people in the North who
Washington might listen to.

Gideon started with the local FBI, in Meridian, and told them three
civil rights workers were missing. It was urgent, would they look into it?

"We're just an investigative agency. We're not a police force. We can't
intervene if there's no known crime."

"Look, just make an informal call, please. It could make all the difference."

"You guys knew the federal government wasn't going to protect you before you came here."

Around four thirty, Gideon got through to John Doar, the head of the civil rights division of the Justice Department in Washington, at home.

"Three young men from the project in Meridian are missing," Gideon explained. "They were visiting a burned out church near Philadelphia, in Neshoba County. Jim Forman says it's a really bad place. Maybe someone's holding them and they are still alive. But if they are, they won't be for long unless someone acts fast. You've got to tell the local FBI to get on it right away. They're telling me they won't do anything."

"That's nonsense," Doar said. "The FBI can make a few phone calls. Let me see what I can do."

Gideon called Forman back to tell him what had happened, and he called the people in the project in Meridian, to let them know what they'd been doing. Meridian still hadn't heard from Mickey.

By then it was six o'clock. Fears were mounting.

Gideon called the Neshoba County Sheriff's office, the local office of the State Police, State Police headquarters in Jackson, and the jail in Philadelphia, Mississippi, the town closest to the burned out church. The jailor's wife told him she didn't "know nothin about no civil rights workers" being held there. And, again, he called John Doar of the Justice Department.

While Gideon was going back and forth with the FBI and the Justice Department, other people in the office were calling Congressmen and other politicians in the North, civil rights supporters, newspaper and television reporters, liberal politicians, progressive clergymen around the country, trying to mobilize them to press Washington to act.

Gideon called the FBI office in Meridian again.

"I just spoke to John Doar in Washington. He told me he was going to call you and tell you to start looking for Chaney, Goodman and Schwerner."

"This isn't our job," an agent with a deep southern accent told Gideon. "We're not the police. I told you to call the local police."

"I did," Gideon said. "They claim they don't know anything."

"Probably because there's nothing to know," the FBI man said again. "You know, kid, we're not the Bureau of Missing Persons for the state of Mississippi. There's no indication a federal crime's been committed, so we can't do anything even if we wanted to. Probably these boys are just off somewhere, getting drunk or getting laid or something."

"You know that's not true. Not without telling anyone they're going to be five hours late. Not in Neshoba County. Not this summer. Come on, I'm begging you—please, just make a couple of calls to the Sheriff, to the Police Chief, to the jail. Let them know the FBI is interested in the case. It's going to be night soon. We don't want them missing in the dark of the night here."

"Kid, you want help, you call the police, not the FBI."

"Please," Gideon said. "I told you, I called the police a dozen times. You know the police are part of the problem. But maybe you are too."

"It's not our job to make the local police do nothin'," the FBI man said firmly in his Mississippi drawl. "They're not telling you anything because there's nothing to tell."

Gideon wasn't handling this right. He should have been able to cajole them into making a call. He'd antagonized them by saying they were part of the problem.

Gideon called John Doar back. "Look, the FBI in Meridian is saying they can't do anything. Haven't you called them yet?"

"'I spoke to the FBI in Jackson," Doar said. "They told me they would look into it, but they couldn't be starting a ruckus every time a few outside agitators were late for supper."

"Mr. Doar, this is an emergency. The Justice Department's in charge of the FBI. It could make all the difference if someone from the FBI, someone local, called or, hell, drove out there to the jail to talk to the sheriff and see what's going on. Why can't they do that when this is a matter of life and death?"

"I'll call again. But, unfortunately, I can't guarantee anything."

It was after seven o'clock. Gideon went back and forth between Doar and the FBI a few more times. Was there something else he could have done that would have worked, some avenue he was too inexperienced to know? Why couldn't he get Doar to do something? Should he have confronted Doar more forcefully? He'd wasted precious time being patient with the Justice Department. Maybe it was his fault they weren't doing anything.

Doar's last words to Gideon: "There's nothing we can do."

The night was endless.

After a while there was no one left for any of them to call. They just waited, waited to hear from someone, even though they knew the news could not be good.

Around eleven, Gideon finally reached Mickey's parents and then Andy's folks in New York, to tell them their sons were missing. Chaney's people, who lived near Meridian, already knew.

I'm placing the calls, Gideon thought, that Mom and Dad feared they might receive about me.

"Mr. Goodman? This is Gideon Roth. I am one of the civil rights workers with COFO, in Mississippi, calling you from Jackson. I've got bad news. Your son Andy is missing."

"Missing? He was only supposed to be arriving in Mississippi around now," Goodman said. "Maybe he's not there yet."

"No, I'm sorry. He is definitely missing. He arrived at the project in Meridian, Mississippi yesterday evening. This morning, he went with two of the leaders of the project there, Mickey Schwerner and James Chaney, to Neshoba County to look at a church the Klan burned down a few days ago and to talk to the local people.

"They were supposed to be back by early-afternoon. They weren't. They didn't call in, and they know the procedure. Schwerner and Chaney know the ropes—they always call if they're going to be late."

Gideon could hear a woman's voice in the background, *"What is it? Is Andy okay?"*

"Andy's missing," Gideon heard Mr. Goodman tell Andy's mother in a choked voice. *"He's in Mississippi and they don't know where he is."*

"How can he be missing so soon?" the father asked Gideon.

Gideon heard Mrs. Goodman pick up on an extension.

"This is Carolyn Goodman. What's happened to my son?"

The tension in her voice was terrible.

"I'm sorry, Mrs. Goodman. Andy's missing. He was with two veteran civil rights workers who drove out to investigate the burning of a church in Neshoba County this morning. They were supposed to be back by mid-afternoon. But they never got back to Meridian. They didn't call in, and no one knows where they are. We've been calling the police, the FBI, and everyone we can think of for hours."

There was a stunned silence.

Gideon told them of the unsuccessful efforts to get the FBI engaged. "I talked to John Doar myself, and I talked to the FBI in Mississippi many times. I can't get them to do anything."

Gideon hesitated, but he needed to make sure they understood the urgency—the desperation—of the situation.

"We think they are in terrible danger. We'd like you to call people in Washington, if you know anyone with any influence, to try to get the federal government to do something."

Gideon could feel the awful anxiety in their voices, as they repeated the names and phone numbers he gave them. Goodman's father said he would take the first plane to Washington in the morning.

The Schwerners were equally frantic. He wished he could say something to comfort them, but he feared the worst.

They had all known their sons were going into danger. Now it had happened. And if the three were already dead, the most they could achieve was a decision by the FBI to come into the crisis one day too late. Too late to save them.

The night wore on. Everyone in the office in Jackson felt more and more horror at what they now saw as inescapable: the three young men would never again be seen alive.

After a time, Brian spoke. "We knew this might happen. We've just got to keep going. We can't let them frighten us into stopping."

They formed a circle, standing hand in hand to sing. Gideon knew the melody from orientation in Oxford, and he picked up the chorus after a while.

We've been 'buked and we have been scorned
We've been talked about, sure's you're born
But we'll never turn back
No, we'll never turn back
Until we've all been freed
And we have equality

We have walked through the shadows of death
We're had to walk all by ourselves
But we'll never turn back
No, we'll never turn back

We have hung our heads and cried
For all those, like Lee, who died
Died for you, and he died for me
Died for the cause of equality

But we'll never turn back
No, we'll never turn back
Until we've all been freed
And we have equality.

The Lee of the song, Gideon had learned in orientation, was Herbert Lee, a black farmer and civil rights leader in Amite County who had been shot to death in broad daylight in Liberty, Mississippi by a white state legislator.

20

On Sunday night following his visit to the exhibit room at the courthouse where Kareem Jackson had been tried, Gideon stood at the sink at home, starting to wash the dishes after a late dinner. He stared down into the sink.

"Helen, I'm having trouble handling knives right now. Would you mind doing this part? I'll take care of everything else."

Helen stood behind Gideon, gave him a long hug.

"What's going to happen with this case, love?"

"I don't really know. The California Supreme Court's a sympathetic forum. But this was a particularly awful rape and murder. And the defense attorney didn't do much to try to humanize Kareem, to show that he was a person, not a monster."

"Did Jackson do it? Was he the killer?"

"No doubt about that," Gideon said. "There was a ton of evidence on guilt, including his own confession on tape. Scores of witnesses. Fingerprints. Blood. Semen. You don't want to know."

Helen stopped moving the dish brush and turned to Gideon.

"Maybe I need to know, if we're going to be living with this case for a long time. You think I'm too frail to hear about brutality? Or are you afraid I won't see the case the way you do?"

"No, no, that's not what I meant. It's just . . . I found it disturbing myself. Later I'll tell you everything you want to know.

"But just to wrap up, whatever flaws we find in the trial, it's going to be hard to argue anything would have made a difference in the guilt phase of the trial—because the evidence was overwhelming that Kareem Jackson kidnapped poor Luisa and Marisol Flores, raped and murdered Luisa, and brutalized Marisol. And he was guilty of first degree felony murder in his accomplice's murder at the KFC. So there's no way the murder convictions are going to be reversed. The only issue can be the death penalty. And the attorney general's going to argue that the crime was so horrific that the jury would have voted for death no matter what.

"But we just don't know. We'll investigate Kareem's background completely, look into whether he was abused as a child, insanity, the whole shtick. Go back more than one generation to complete the picture. I'm hopeful we'll uncover substantial evidence to mitigate this terrible crime against the victims."

Helen held still for a moment.

"Gideon."

"Yes."

"You know, when you talk about it the way you have been . . . you say the whole thing in that recounting way, you sound like you're practicing a speech, not talking to me. 'Kareem Jackson raped and murdered poor Luisa Flores,' and 'this terrible crime against the victims'; it's almost like you're reveling in how bad it was. Are you trying to provoke me?"

"No, of course not," Gideon said. "What do you mean?"

"Well, you've talked about the case a few times, and you've never asked me how I felt about it."

"Well, you're also against the death penalty; I assumed you supported me on this. Don't you?"

"That's different. I'm talking about how it feels to be involved in something this terrible. Gideon, he kidnapped and brutalized a little girl and her mother, and finally raped and killed the mother in front of the child. Suppose it had been me and Amanda. Do you ever think about that?"

"I hope if anything horrible like this happened to you, I'd have the character to stick to what I believe."

"That's the kind of thing a man would say. To avoid thinking. Or feeling. And only men commit crimes like these."

"What are you saying—"

Helen pulled the apron off and threw it down.

"You can finish up in here."

21

Kareem Jackson's jury had been instructed to choose between a sentence of death and a sentence of life imprisonment without the possibility of parole. The District Attorney offered much evidence in support of his plea for death. In addition to the crime spree, the rape and the murders, Kareem had a long history of crime, though little of his previous history involved serious crimes of violence.

What was on the other side, supporting a life-in-prison sentence?

The lawyer who had represented Kareem at trial wanted to make the jury feel sympathy for Jackson. He thought that meant looking for evidence of bad things that had happened to Kareem, like child abuse. But Kareem told him that he didn't want anyone bad-mouthing his mother. If he'd done wrong, it was his fault, not hers. And he didn't want no one saying he was crazy.

The trial attorney took this to mean he shouldn't delve into Kareem's family background. So he limited his investigation to the files on Kareem's youth that he had obtained from Children's Protective Services and from California Youth Authority.

These reports were all he put before the jury. He offered no live witnesses. No one told the jury what Kareem's childhood had been like. Instead—based on these paper records—the trial attorney argued that Kareem had been abandoned by his drug-abusing parents as a child, had grown up on his own, in poverty, and had himself in turn yielded to the lure of drugs. This had led to the crimes Kareem had committed.

The prosecutor was swift to point out that many people grew up in poverty without turning to crime. And how, he asked, could Jackson's supposed need to steal for drugs possibly justify the shooting of a convenience store clerk, the kidnapping of an innocent mother and her helpless little girl, and the rape and the ruthless murder of the mother?

The first young associate to work on the case with Gideon had had a similar reaction.

"I know we're not trying to argue it's okay what Jackson did," he said. "But the rape and all, it's hard to take. Just to get money for meth? And we're trying to get him off?"

"No, no, no," Gideon said. "There's no question of 'getting him off.' We just want to stop the state from killing him, so he'd been in prison for life, without parole."

Gideon thought, if one of our own team doesn't get it, what chance do we have?

"Look," he said. "Obviously, needing money for drugs doesn't justify Kareem's crimes. Nobody says it does. The point is to understand what happened. There's a reason he got the way he was. Perhaps he had been a victim, too."

"You don't really know that, though. You're just assuming it. And two wrongs don't make a right."

Gideon shook his head. *Two wrongs don't make a right? Does he still not get the point?*

"Yes, I am assuming we will learn that something twisted Kareem into what he became. Horrific deeds are not the result of Satan inserting evil into a person. They happen because things were done to human beings that deformed them, made them capable of doing terrible things. Usually when they were children."

Gideon did not know what had happened to Kareem. But he meant to find out.

✳ ✳ ✳

San Quentin. Six weeks after his first visit to the prison, Gideon returned. In the attorney visiting room, he bought two coffees and some packaged donuts from the vending machines, and waited for Kareem in visitor cell number six. He saw attorneys and prisoners in other cells, and he no longer felt entirely like a neophyte. He knew a little about what he was doing.

After five minutes, two guards approached with Kareem, and Gideon stood. Kareem seemed more at ease this time as he walked with the guards. Perhaps, Gideon thought, he's settled into life at San Quentin, whatever it might mean to settle into death row. Or maybe Kareem was glad to have his lawyer visit. Gideon was beginning to understand that in the bleakness and depression of life on death row, an attorney's visit was a link to the possibility of hope that even the most cynical of the condemned could not spurn.

Kareem entered the cell. A guard slid the barred door shut and snapped the big padlock that secured the door. Then he unlocked and dropped the flap that let him reach in and remove Kareem's handcuffs. This time, Gideon noticed, there were no ankle chains, maybe a sign Kareem was behaving.

Gideon clasped Kareem's hand in both of his, gave it a squeeze, then they sat down.

"So how's it going, Kareem?"

"Not so bad."

"Great, glad to hear it," said Gideon. "What's happening?"

"We were locked down in our cells for a week. No showers, no yard, no nuthin. There was a fight between two guys—from the Crips and the Bloods. It was in the next yard from the one we're in, but we could see it. A guard fired a warning shot from one of the towers. They didn't break it up fast enough, so he sent one of them a bullet."

"Holy shit," said Gideon. "There's no way they can stop a fight except shooting?"

"That's the way they do it here, Mr. Roth. I hear the guy survived. That's life in S Q."

Gideon stared back at Kareem. *Not what I would have thought of as things going "not so bad."*

"This is a frightening place," Gideon said.

"I can deal with it."

Gideon wanted to express more sympathy for what life was like for Kareem in here. But he didn't know what he could say in the face of the invulnerability Kareem was projecting. He sipped his coffee, then went on.

"I came up mainly to talk with you about what's happening with the case. The transcript of the trial arrived two weeks ago, and I've read it. Also been to the court house and seen the photos of the crime scene and the victims and the trial exhibits and all." Gideon waited to see whether Kareem would offer comments, but he didn't.

"You mentioned the all-white jury, which was obviously a serious problem. You're a black man and the victims were Hispanic. Studies have shown that made you many times as likely to get death as someone who murders a black person. White jurors are the key to that.

"As you mentioned last time, the prosecutor got rid of all the blacks from the jury. When they started picking jurors, two blacks were on the first group of twelve they put in the box for questioning. Their answers to the questions weren't that different from anyone else's, but the DA knocked out both of them. After more strikes by both sides, seven new jurors were put in the box, and one of them was black. The DA struck her too."

"Yeah, I remember that. She looked mad when he was making believe he was so polite about it."

"Right. 'The People thank and respectfully excuse Juror No. 15.' Doesn't change the facts. He wanted an all-white jury and he got it. Your attorney objected to striking the blacks, but the judge wouldn't even ask the DA why he was doing it."

Gideon turned to the mitigation investigation.

"Kareem, we are also going to need to look deeper into your background. The jury really didn't hear much about your life—the defense's part of the penalty trial was only an hour, including your lawyer's argument. We have to find out what else the jury could have heard that might have made them think about jail instead of a death sentence."

"I know where you're going," said Kareem. "I told my first lawyer and I'm telling you: You're not gonna go dragging my momma through the mud. She didn't do this, and I ain't gonna make her pay for it."

"Kareem, that's what you told your first attorney. Did you like the way it turned out?"

"You just try something else, Mr. Roth. The jury thing you just tole me about sounds okay. But you leave my momma and my pops out of this or I'll fire you. I'd rather give up the appeals and let them gas me than have you dissing my mother. You hear?"

"Calm down, Kareem . . ."

"Don't tell me to calm down, asshole. I know the things you lawyers do . . . I've been talking to other guys on the row. You'll want to make me look like a retard and you want to say my family were freaks."

Gideon pushed his chair back, and put both hands up, palms out. He waited until Kareem ran down.

"Kareem," Gideon said in a soft voice. "Kareem. I don't know a thing about your mother or anyone in your family. I don't have a sneaky plan to say anything bad about them. I am not going to do anything you don't want me to do."

Kareem folded his arms across his chest and tilted back on his chair.

"You heard me."

"Let's make a deal," Gideon said. "I've got to do an investigation. It's my duty as your lawyer to find out everything I can about your background. But before I say anything in court about whatever I learn about your family, I will talk to you first. Okay?"

"No, it's not okay. I know what you're gonna do."

"Kareem, I don't know what I am going to do myself because I don't know what we're gonna to find out."

Kareem didn't move.

"Kareem, we're going to be working together for a long time. I can't do that if you don't trust me. I understand you have to decide for yourself how far you can trust me. But cut me some slack while you're deciding."

He looked Kareem in the eye, and was conscious of his effort to appear sincere.

"I won't lie to you. I will never lie to you. I'm asking you to trust my promise. I won't use anything that reflects badly on your family without talking to you about it first."

"Not just talking. Without me saying it's okay."

"Right," said Gideon. "Okay. That's the deal. Without you saying it's okay to use it."

Kareem slowly let his chair down and looked Gideon in the eye. He gave a small nod.

✳   ✳   ✳

It took more than a year for Gideon and his team to uncover the story of Kareem and his family and to understand what it meant.

Kareem was not retarded and he was not insane. But he had suffered experiences that people with a normal upbringing could not imagine.

Born prematurely after his father had battered his seven-months' pregnant mother, Kareem had himself been beaten, neglected and abused since he was a baby. The emotional harm had left a Kareem who was unable to trust anyone and unable to empathize with others. The physical harm had left Kareem with frontal and temporal lobe brain damage. These are the parts of the brain, a psychiatrist was to explain to Gideon and the team, that enable normal people to exercise judgment and to control their anger and their violent impulses. Those parts of the brain just did not work very well for Kareem Jackson. His brain made him more prone to violence than ordinary people. But getting Kareem to agree they could put this evidence before the court was going to be a challenge.

22

"It's one of the things you just have to stop paying attention to." Helen had said this to Gideon time and again. The San Francisco Symphony was doing the first Shostakovich cello concerto with a celebrated Russian cellist. But Gideon was irritated and distracted by the coughing that erupted every few moments from the audience.

"People always cough at the symphony," she said during the intermission, "especially in winter when there are lots of colds going around. Be understanding, Gideon. They can't help it."

"They should stay home if they're too sick to keep quiet."

"It's not that rude, Gideon. You know, in the eighteenth century, people at concerts were nowhere as quiet as we are now – they would talk to the people around them, laugh aloud, eat, belch, fart."

"Well, that was then."

"Anyway, who is going to skip a concert in a series they paid a lot of money for just because their throat is scratchy?"

But Gideon knew that most of the people who coughed simply weren't trying hard enough. When he went to a concert with a cold, he made control of his cough an exercise of will.

At the beginning, a couple behind him had murmured to each other about the music. Go home and listen to concerts on the radio, he thought angrily. He turned slightly to convey that he would really be glaring at them if he weren't so polite. Helen pinched his leg, hard, to tell him to stop fidgeting. At least they're not talking any more, he thought.

His mind drifted to the deposition in Los Angeles earlier that week. That asshole Guttman, the opposing attorney, pretending to be marking up some papers while I was questioning his client, to show his contempt for me. Not that it made any difference. What would have happened if

I had reached across the conference table, grabbed Guttman's papers, ripped them in half and thrown them into the air. Then grabbed Guttman by the throat . . .

Gideon thought about the draft of the brief in Kareem Jackson's case. He'd reviewed it on the flight back from L.A. Really good brief. But with this judge, would it matter? His stomach started churning.

Gideon was tracing a pattern, over and over, on the back of his left hand with his right index finger. The pattern was a letter "C" drawn in bubble writing. Including a serif. When he noticed he was doing this, he wondered if it qualified as obsessive-compulsive behavior. He made himself stop.

What Gideon liked most about a concert was that you could see, through the bowing and movements of different groups of musicians, how different parts in the music were going back and forth. The musicians taking turns, exchanging thoughts, roles. Like attorneys, with our formalized exchanges. But we trade acts of aggression, socially permitted hostility under our role masks. Knowing that, in the end, it's just a case, an opportunity to display one's fighting skills. But a death penalty case, it's more than that.

Gideon closed his left eye and lined up the ear of the tall man sitting in front of him with one of the cellists. Then, by shifting his head slightly, lined up the ear with a violist. He noticed that the women musicians' outfits were all black, but did not match each other's, the way all the men's black concert dress did. Why was this okay?

Helen nudged him and he stopped moving his head.

Gideon listened to hear whether the people behind him were still murmuring. Actually, they had not done so since the first bars. Still, Gideon imagined them whispering distractingly, he imagined asking himself, Should I just let them go on spoiling the concert for everyone around them, or should I be the one to stop them?

He saw himself turning, saying in a firm but low voice, "You need to stop talking right now." He saw them looking at him out of the corner of their eyes, smiling disdainfully, even while they continued to whisper. Gideon imagined complaining to an usher during the break between movements. No, I couldn't get past all the people between me and the aisle in time.

As, in this imagined scene, he turned back to the concerto, he felt the man staring contemptuously at the back of his head. Maybe the man would softly kick Gideon's chair, to disturb him. Then what would Gideon do? Had anyone ever sued a fellow concert-goer for intentional infliction of emotional distress?

Perhaps the man would whisper into Gideon's ear, "Enjoying the concert?" As everyone got up for the intermission, Gideon would confront the man, he would . . .

Gideon closed his eyes, took a slow breath. *This is crazy. I don't need to do this.*

He tried to listen to the last movement. The conductor's motions reminded Gideon of a professor he'd had in college who flailed around energetically. *The guy had given him an unfair grade. Maybe Gideon should have been more assertive about it. If he'd had a higher GPA . . .*

The soloist and the orchestra were winding up for the finale. Gideon noticed that the cellist, who was relatively young, had an interesting hair style, with a subtle tint on top. *I wonder if I could try that. No, my clients would think it looked weird. Or the judges.*

As she applauded, Helen leaned toward Gideon, "That was amazing, that long section when it was just the cello."

"Oh," said Gideon, startled. "Oh, yes, it was great." Helen gave him a sharp look.

As they were driving back she launched into him.

"It's bad enough you can't stop yourself from wriggling and moving so. It's idiotic, in fact, that you keep being bothered by a little coughing when you're distracting everyone around you with all your jiggling about. And your mind's never on the music anyway. So why would you care?"

"Well, everyone drifts off during a concert, unless they were music majors."

"Not like you. It's bad enough you're in a perpetual daze about your death penalty case—it's all you ever think about. You have a glassy look whenever I try to talk to you because you're really thinking about Jackson."

"That's not fair. It's really not true!"

The concert had been almost half over before he'd thought about Jackson.

"Or about some other lawsuit. How would I know? You never talk to me anymore."

It's because you've lost all patience with me these days; you're always jumping on me about something or other.

"I'm sorry," he said, beating down his resentment. He knew that if he told her what he'd been thinking during the concert, she would say, "See, that's exactly what I was talking about."

The silence between them faded into emptiness. It was dark along the highway between the city and home, and there were few cars on the road. Gideon wondered if putting on more witnesses would help or hurt when the case went up for the inevitable appeal.

23

In the cottage in Washington, Gideon thought about the Mississippi Freedom Summer murders, and how the killers had gotten away with it.

Mickey Schwerner and his wife Rita were organizers for CORE, the Congress of Racial Equality, and had been working in Mississippi since January 1964. Long enough to make bitter enemies among local whites. Their civil rights office was in Meridian, but Schwerner often traveled to nearby Neshoba County, a frighteningly dangerous place. The danger to Schwerner and to anyone with him was even more extreme than he knew, for the White Knights of the Ku Klux Klan had marked "Jew-boy" for elimination.

On Memorial Day, Schwerner and a young local black man, James Chaney, had spoken at Mount Zion Methodist Church in Neshoba County. They had urged the Negro congregation to register to vote, and got permission to use the church for freedom schools during the Summer Project.

Two weeks later, during a meeting of the Neshoba County "Klavern" of the Klan, KKK members received word of "suspicious activity" at Mount Zion. They dispatched thirty armed men to the church in hopes of catching Schwerner. But Schwerner was in Oxford, Ohio at the training sessions for the summer volunteers. The Klan members acted anyway. When the Negro parishioners tried to leave the church that evening, a phalanx of white men assaulted them.

The Klan group returned to the interrupted Klavern meeting, disappointed about missing Schwerner but otherwise pleased with their work. The next night, they burned the church to the ground. The Klansmen correctly believed that destroying the church would lure Schwerner to visit the area so they could seize and kill him.

Dozens of churches used for civil rights meetings in Mississippi had been torched since 1962, to instill fear of involvement with civil rights, and it was to happen thirty-six more times that summer.

One evening a simple wooden church would be there, the meeting place for ten or fifteen or more Negroes who came together with a civil rights organizer to discuss the requirements for voting, or how they might secure their rights. The next morning, nothing remained of the beams and walls, of the white wooden pews, of the bibles and books of hymns, of the steeple and the cross, but a pile of charred, smoldering wood.

The remains of Mount Zion Methodist Church smoked and steamed in the morning mist, the bitter smell of blackened wood mixed with a whiff of gasoline. Some half-burned pages of prayers fluttered in the light wind.

Mickey Schwerner and Jim Chaney returned to Mississippi three days later. They had left Summer Project orientation early on the morning of June 20 so they would be sure to reach the safety of their base in Meridian before dark. One of the northern students, twenty-year-old Andrew Goodman, was with them. The next morning, the three drove to Neshoba County to inspect the burned church and meet with local movement leaders.

On their way back to Meridian, in the early afternoon, they were spotted by Deputy Sheriff Cecil Price, a member of the Neshoba County Klavern. Price arrested Chaney for "speeding," even though he had actually been by the side of the road changing a flat tire, and held Schwerner and Goodman for "investigation of church burning." But there was no investigation. Price did not ask the young men any questions while they were in custody. He simply held them in jail until his fellow Klansmen were ready.

Gideon thought of the fear they must have felt as the afternoon faded into night, alone in their cells in Neshoba County Jail, isolated from the world.

At 10:30 p.m., the three were asked to pay $20 bail, ejected from the jail, and told to "get out of Neshoba County."

They fled south on Highway 19 toward Meridian. But Deputy Sheriff Price and two cars of Klansmen followed. Price stopped their vehicle again, and this time forced them into the police car, taking them north—but not to the jail. Klan member Wayne Posey followed, driving Schwerner's station wagon, and the caravan of killers proceeded down a county road. There, they stopped.

As the confession of one of the conspirators later revealed, even at the last Schwerner had tried to reach out to them. "Sir, I know just how you feel," Mickey said, just as the man fired a bullet at close range into his heart. Goodman was swiftly slain by a second shot, and Chaney with three more. Their car was doused with gasoline and burned, and their bodies were driven to a remote place where another of the conspirators used a bulldozer to bury them under an earthen dam. Their bodies lay rotting for six weeks before an FBI reward elicited information on where they were buried.

Nothing special for Mississippi, really. Blacks had been openly lynched or quietly "disappeared" for decades with no special attention being paid. Indeed, no white person had ever been convicted of a crime of violence against a black in Mississippi. But this time the victims included two young white men. And this time the Summer Project had focused the nation's attention on the struggle for human rights in Mississippi. Too late to prevent the killings, the FBI swung into action.

Gideon had still been in Mississippi when the bodies were found. It was only later that the roles of the various killers had been revealed. And the killers—never charged with murder—were still at large, those who hadn't died peacefully of old age.

Why should they be alive and well, Gideon thought, when Kareem was dead?

Finding them proved ludicrously simple: you just looked on the Internet. After ten minutes of online searching, Gideon found a report that former Deputy Sheriff Cecil Rae Price, one of the killers, was alive and well, living not far from the scene of the triple murder he had organized. From there, the search was nearly instantaneous. In less than twenty seconds, Altavista's People Finder displayed Price's street address and phone number.

Gideon was bemused. It was the companies he had worked with every day as a lawyer that made it possible to locate anyone, anywhere, any time. But even though he was not entirely surprised, he was also angered that the killer's whereabouts would be so brazenly displayed:

Cecil R. Price (More Info)   map
444 Center Ave, Philadelphia, MS 39350   driving directions
(601) 656 - 5915   add to My Directory
                                                                           update or remove

Did you go to High School with Cecil R. Price?

Send Flowers   Visit this City Page!   Send a postcard   Send a Gift Certificate

Gideon clicked on "(More info)," and the computer screen displayed a street map of Price's neighborhood, with a star showing 444 Center Avenue.

A few more clicks and the Altavista web site generated a cross-country map—

Door to Door Directions

—with complete driving instructions. Twenty-four turn-by-turn directions showed the entire route from Gideon's office in Silicon Valley—from what used to be his office—to Cecil Price's home in Mississippi:

"1. Start out going West on SAND HILL RD by turning right."

And 2294.9 miles later:

"24. Turn LEFT onto MS-19/MS-21. There are 0.11 miles to 444 Center Ave. Use local roads to get to 444 Center Ave."

Gideon remembered the photograph of Deputy Sheriff Price and the other Klan killers snickering in court after they had finally been arraigned on federal civil rights charges. (Who would charge white men with murder for such a killing?) They were laughing and smirking, and Price's cheek was distended by a chunk of chewing tobacco.

Astonishingly, a Mississippi jury found that Price and the others had killed the three young men, and the jury convicted them of violating a Reconstruction Era federal law that prohibited "conspiring to violate the civil rights" of citizens "under color of state law."

The sentences, imposed by segregationist federal judge William Cox, were not severe. None of the convicted men served more than six years behind bars. Judge Cox explained, in sentencing them, that "They killed one nigger, one Jew, and a white man. I gave them what I thought they deserved."

Price was imprisoned for four years. None of the men were prosecuted for murder.

That image of the killers, defiant, confident they would emerge unpunished, was as vivid in Gideon's mind today as it had been thirty-three years earlier.

Kareem was executed before my eyes. But Price walks free. For killings I could have prevented if I only got the FBI to step in in time.

Cecil Price, and probably the other killers, too, were living normal lives near the scene of their crime. They felt no compunction, no fear, no uneasiness. Price saw no reason even to have an unlisted telephone number.

Anyone in America who still cared could pick up the phone and call Cecil Price, could tell him that he had no place among decent people. Did no one in the entire country have that much of a sense of responsibility?

It was two a.m. at Gideon's cottage in the State of Washington. Five a.m. in Philadelphia, Mississippi. Gideon stared at the computer screen. What the hell. He lifted the phone and dialed.

A double ring. Then another. And another. Then a sleepy male voice, in the slow accents of white rural Mississippi. Gideon had never heard this man's voice before, but he recognized the accent he had so long ago identified with hate.

"Hullo, who is this?"

It's a voice out of the past, you racist dog.

"Hullo? Hullo? God damn it, who the hell is this, callin' in the middle of the night?"

Your time is coming.

Slowly, quietly, Gideon put down the receiver. He was breathing heavily, and his mind was aflame. His stomach churned, but he was alert, alert and focused on that voice, on the voice that could not imagine, more than thirty years later, that there was anything to worry about, the voice of a man who had forgotten the summer of 1964.

Anyone in America who still cared, Gideon thought, could get computer-generated directions to the home of former Deputy Sheriff Cecil Rae Price. Anyone in America who cared could drive to 444 Center Ave., Philadelphia, MS, and blow Cecil Price's fucking brains out. But who would care enough to risk his life and liberty for the sake of justice, for justice so long denied?

Gideon stared at the phone, and he could still hear Price's voice. "Hullo? Hullo? Who the hell is this?"

Gideon printed out the driving instructions and the map showing the way, and he put them in a file folder. Thirty-eight hours, fifty-six minutes from Silicon Valley to 444 Center Ave., Philadelphia, Mississippi. Not so very long.

Gideon stared at the map for a long time, a map with a line that stretched across America, across time, across his own history. He thought about how someone might get to Philadelphia, Mississippi without being noticed or recognized. He thought about how easy it might be for someone to bring Cecil Price to justice.

24

A tree grew next to the cottage, and was framed by the small window in the bathroom. A dark branch with only a few leaves slanted across Gideon's view, behind the square of the four window panes, forming a composition that could have been a painting. But it was reality, and he wondered if he were abstracting himself from reality by thinking of it that way. His breathing slowed as he stared, eyes losing focus, at the window and the branch.

Then . . .

> *He could hear the door to the chamber being sealed. Kareem looked through one of the windows into Gideon's eyes. A lever clanked, to drop the cyanide, and he saw Kareem take a deep breath. Gideon was holding his own breath. Kareem's face filled with pain, and he strained against the straps . . .*

Gideon shuddered.

No, he was at the cottage. He would never see San Quentin again. It was over.

Gideon sat on the edge of the tub until he stopped shaking. He hadn't brushed his teeth in days, and his beard and hair were ragged. He used to have a haircut every third week, and clipped his beard each Sunday morning to maintain a trim appearance. It had been a few weeks since he'd done that. He made himself clean up a little.

The call to Price had wakened Gideon from his torpor, but only for a while, and he sank back into depression. He ate a little breakfast, then got dressed and decided to go for a drive.

He drifted along, off the main roads, not exactly getting lost but not quite in a place he knew. Suddenly he saw a large sign painted on the side of a barn: GUN SHOW! Images of hand guns and rifles flanked the three-foot high lettering, and, painted underneath, a heroic American Eagle, wings wide, arrows in its talons. A waving banner across the eagle's breast was emblazoned "Liberty!"

He slowed and pulled into a dusty parking lot. Leaving the car, he saw an array of a thirty or so tables with firearms on them. Other tables bore petitions in support of the right to bear arms, books on the Second Amendment, magazines titled Guns & Ammo, Handguns, Firearms Tactical, Shooters News, Soldier of Fortune. Gideon bought a beer out of a cooler and walked around, admiring the wares.

Guns. Once, Gideon had thought you needed a license or something to buy a gun, or that your identity would be checked and recorded. But that was only if you bought from a gun dealer. At gun shows you could buy firearms from private individuals on a completely unregulated, no-questions-asked, no-information-sought, cash-will-do-nicely basis.

Cecil Price's voice came back to him, and he wondered how someone might arm himself without leaving a trail, assassinate with little risk. If you cared about the risk.

Gideon looked at the guns again.

Firearms were not part of the upbringing of a nice Jewish boy from the South Bronx. But they were not so strange to Gideon. During his years as a student radical, he had owned a handgun and a rifle. In case the revolution came. Of course, he had never fired a weapon at anyone, but he'd enjoyed target practice. And he had learned how to assess the condition of a gun.

A dozen handguns rested on the table before him. Behind the table stood a man wearing sunglasses, with a big dark beard, and a large gut hanging over his belt. Gideon wondered if Price was still just as fat.

Gideon picked up a 9mm Beretta, felt the satisfying weight. He took it apart, examined it, smelled it. Stroked it. After a little bargaining, Gideon paid $210 for the gun, with some ammo thrown in. He was pleased with the transaction.

Whatever the weapon's original provenance, it had passed from the man with the gut to Gideon Roth with no record of the transfer. The seller had no idea who Gideon was or where he came from. He had seen Gideon for five minutes. The chances he might recall anything that could identify Gideon a month from now were nil. If a weapon like this were recovered after a crime, let's say without fingerprints on it, it would be impossible to trace the gun to its last owner.

Helen would think this is crazy, Gideon thought to himself. *Why on Earth do you want a gun, Gideon?* she might have asked. *This is a bit twisted, Gideon, don't you think?*

Just curious about whether it's still so easy, he answered in his mind. *Just thinking about it.*

When he got back to the cottage, Gideon placed the handgun on the small table by the sofa in the living room, opposite the fireplace. Next to the lamp. The table had a drawer, and he put the ammunition in that.

As he made himself lunch, Gideon was conscious of the presence of the gun in the next room. He thought of Chekhov's saying, if you put a shotgun on the mantle in the first act, it must go off by the third. He got up and put the gun in the drawer, and returned to his lunch.

Gun people claim they need them for self-defense, Gideon thought. But more often a gun in the house gets someone killed accidentally. Or it's used for suicide. Which will it be here? None of the above?

After lunch, Gideon sat on the swing on the porch, trying to read. The swing faced a grassy open space that once upon a time had been a lawn. A rusting barbeque sat there. Across the road was more open space, then the woods began, red alders.

Gideon put his book down and went inside. He took the Beretta out of the drawer, and felt its weight. He looked up as if to see whether he was still alone in the house. Looked down at the gun again.

He sat down and ejected the clip. It was empty, as he knew, and he slid it back into the gun. He opened the chamber and confirmed that there no round in the gun. Then he turned the safety to off. Gideon placed the barrel in his mouth. It had an unpleasant metallic taste. A bitter taste would be one of your last sensations. I wonder if people think about it for a long time before pulling the trigger. He maneuvered the gun, pointing upward toward the brain, then let the weight rest on his lower lip and teeth.

Gideon couldn't get himself to pull the trigger. No matter he'd checked moments ago, he could not entirely believe his own action making sure the gun was not loaded. Not ready for this, he told himself.

He took the gun out of his mouth and wiped off the saliva, on his shirt sleeve. He went upstairs and put the gun on a shelf in the closet.

It's just for a hobby, he told himself. Next day Gideon found a place in the woods, half a mile behind the cottage, butted up against a steep hillside, where he set up cans and hand-made paper bullseyes for target practice. His skills returned. It was satisfying to be shooting again.

25

Gideon bought a second handgun at another show one week later, a small, pocket-sized Glock 26. One week after that he placed a second call to Cecil Price. This time it was seven in the morning in Mississippi.

"Hullo, Cecil here."

Again, Gideon said nothing.

"Hullo, hullo. Wrong number?"

Price hung up noisily.

Gideon thought about the logistics of going to Mississippi and shooting Cecil Price. He told himself his interest might be, say, like that of Civil War buffs who sew their own uniforms and reenact battles. This wasn't for real. But his conviction that Price did not deserve to live was growing.

He had started to work out certain practical problems, as a sort of hobby. He was developing some of the skills and acquiring some of the arcane knowledge an assassin would require. Gideon had also collected most of the tools and now made a number of other arrangements that would be needed for such a job.

Preparatory activities fell into three categories. The first he called "Data Acquisition"—identifying and locating the surviving murderers. He had the little maps and printouts for the homes of Cecil Price and a number of the others. Jimmy Arledge, Alton Wayne Roberts, Jimmie Snowden, Billy Wayne Posey. The second was "Cold Trailing"—techniques for avoiding detection in going to and from the scene of the intended killing. Disguise, cover, creation of false identities, planning escape routes, finding hideouts. The third covered actual skills in violence. "Killer Application," he called this, in a Silicon Valley joke he shared with no one.

Behind all his compulsive planning, Gideon did not think it would really be all that difficult, once you accepted there was a certain level of unavoidable risk. Gideon knew that most crimes were never solved unless the criminal was caught in the act or recognized by an eyewitness, and that most eyewitnesses were too upset by seeing a real act of violence to accurately recall much of anything they'd seen. With a small amount of luck, the chances of being caught or recognized were miniscule. Nonetheless, Gideon's years as a litigator had taught him that the path to success was painstaking attention to detail. Nothing that could be anticipated should be left to chance.

Right now Gideon was mulling over a theoretical travel issue: How to get from the West Coast to the South without leaving a trail of data? Flying was out of the question. Paying cash for air travel made you look like a drug trafficker. Fake IDs would be scrutinized at the airport by people in the business of scrutinizing IDs, and how would Gideon get a fake ID anyway? And carrying firearms was basically impossible.

Plainly, it had to be ground travel. Eventually an assassin would need a car in Mississippi. But would it be safer for a killer to drive his own car all the way from the West, or to take a bus or train and then buy or steal a car in the South? He disliked the idea of bringing a vehicle that could be tied to him anywhere near the scene of the crime. But if the vehicle could not be linked to himself, there was no more anonymous and witness-free means of getting from here to there.

26

Gideon fiddled with the radio in the cottage. He picked up an oldies station in Portland.

Did you ever have to make up your mind? Gideon sang along. *Did you ever have to finally decide?*

Gideon imagined a dialogue, perhaps with his own lawyer after he was apprehended for killing Cecil Price. Or perhaps with himself.

I thought you were against killing people for punishment.

Well, actually, I have never said I opposed the death penalty in all circumstances. When I took on Kareem's case, I just thought that someone who's been condemned to death deserved the very best representation. I wanted to face the ultimate challenge for a litigator: going up against a system biased in favor of death, and saving someone's life. I thought I was up to it.

So you do not believe capital punishment is wrong?

Well, obviously, I'm generally against it. The death penalty doesn't deter the kind of dysfunctional people who commit the worst crimes. It's racist and unfair. And our criminal justice system is too unreliable to make irreversible judgments like death. All the same, there are people who deserve death.

I see. But not a ruthless killer who rapes a woman in front of her child and butchers the mother at the conclusion of a murderous crime spree?

I'm talking about Lyndon Johnson and Richard Nixon and Henry Kissinger—mass murderers—people who calmly decided, for reasons of state, to launch wars that killed millions of innocent people, not about individual criminals who were themselves twisted by circumstance beyond their control.

So we're into assassinations for political change? That's brought us to a nice place so far in America. John F. Kennedy. Malcolm X. Martin Luther King. Robert Kennedy.

Gideon did not bother to frame a riposte—he was not about assassination as a means of political change.

And was Cecil Price a mass murderer? He was a poor, pathetic, young loser when he was deputy sheriff of Neshoba County, and now he's a pathetic old loser whose life is nearly over. Not so different from the killers whose lives you explored with so much understanding and compassion at death penalty conferences.

He was no powerless loser when he organized the murder of Schwerner, Chaney and Goodman, and no one ever said that murderers should not be punished at all. Price's unpunished murders are still an aching sore. The memory of Schwerner, Chaney and Goodman deserves better. And Price's execution will at last honor their memories properly.

Oh please. You know that rhetoric is rubbish. What does that really mean, and what does it have to do with you?

The question is, what is justice, what does justice demand? What must be done when the system's failure to address certain crimes signifies more than the isolated wrong verdict? What is to be done when the equal protection of law is denied to an entire people? The balance must be restored by private action if the state cannot provide justice. Punishment is needed to affirm that the victims' lives had meaning—that you don't have the right to extinguish other peoples' lives by your private choice to defend a dying social order.

Did I just hear you say individuals don't have the right to extinguish others' lives by private choice?

Yes. I know.

But what I'm doing is different. Cecil Price and his lynch mob were murdering to stop a people from exercising their lawful rights, and—

But when you were in the Movement, you didn't think that "lawfulness" determined when direct action was necessary. Price could have said he had no choice but to protect the judgment of his people that race mixing was wrong. He could say that he and his friends knew they had to go outside the law to keep outsiders from destroying their way of life, to keep the powers in Washington from thwarting the social verdict of their people. Wrong, but not so hard to understand.

I do understand. But I don't care what he could say and I don't care about the social verdict of the white South. In the end, the difference is that we were right and they were wrong. We were good, and they were evil. And, finally, I'm going to do something about it. Something I've got to do.

So you just happened to have noticed this tear in the fabric of justice, and decided, in a completely disinterested way, after all these years, that Gideon Roth must be the one to stitch it together?

Well, actually, I was part of that struggle. I noticed injustice thirty years ago and I have never ceased noticing it. And now I'm going to act. This time, I'm not embarking on a futile fourteen-year legalistic struggle. This time I'm going to get it done right by myself.

*　*　*

When Gideon stopped thinking about the speeches he might give about why Cecil Price should be killed, he thought about why these things meant that he himself, Gideon Roth, should actually consider going to Mississippi to kill someone. Why didn't the irony weigh more heavily on his mind? A death penalty lawyer committing murder. But so what? Maybe he had finally realized something. Maybe he just needed to make it up to all those he had failed.

Gideon was tired inside. Tired of his life that had accomplished so little. Tired of what he had given to no avail.

Sometimes you just want a clean, simple result. Sometimes you need to cut through all the bullshit, all the waiting, all the maneuvering and compromising that you can't avoid when you use the law. Sometimes justice must be done, and you have to do it yourself, without having to persuade someone else it's the right thing to do. Sometimes you have to forget the rules and take charge and get even. Sometimes you have to go back and show that, at last, you do know how to do it right. Sometimes you don't want to fail someone you care about.

Maybe this doesn't make any sense, Gideon thought. It's Kareem I want to avenge. But there was no one he could strike at who was responsible for that—except himself.

27

At his office at the cottage, Gideon pulled up the testimony in the 1964 federal trial for conspiring to deny the three young men their civil rights. He printed copies and put them into dossiers he was keeping.

Now he read the confession of one of the participants, Horace Doyle Barnett. Barnett recounted that, after Deputy Sheriff Cecil Price had seized the young men and they had been driven to a remote place, Wayne Roberts and Jim Jordan had killed them. In a sworn statement, Barnett described the scene that night:

Wayne ran past my car to Price's car, opened the left rear door, and pulled Schwerner out of the car. He spun him around so that

Schwerner was standing on the left side of the road, with his back to the ditch. Wayne said "Are you that nigger lover?" Schwerner said, "Sir, I know just how you feel." Wayne had a pistol in his right hand, and without answering he shot Schwerner in the chest.

Wayne went back to Price's car and got Goodman, took him to the left side of the road with Goodman facing the road, and shot Goodman. Goodman spun around and fell back toward the bank in back.

Jim Jordan said "'Save one for me."

He got Chaney out of Price's car. I remember Chaney backing up, facing the road, and standing on the bank on the other side of the ditch. And Jordan stood in the middle of the road and shot him.

"You didn't leave me anything but a nigger," Jordan said, "but at least I killed me a nigger."

Seven of the defendants—Cecil Price, Wayne Roberts, Samuel Bowers, Horace Barnette, Jimmie Snowden, Billie Wayne Posey and Jimmie Arledge—had been convicted of conspiring to violate the federal civil rights of the three young men by murdering them.

Gideon decided he would not be entirely acting as a vigilante if he were to execute some or all of these men. They had had a fair trial, and a jury of their Mississippi peers had found they were the killers. His role was but to impose a real sentence in place of the trivial admonishment they had received. What was so extraordinary about that? He wished it were within his power to impose live imprisonment on them. But he couldn't. Should they continue to evade real punishment just because of that?

He would leave off his list those defendants, like Sheriff Lawrence Rainey, who must surely have been part of the murderous conspiracy, but had not been convicted by the white Mississippi jurors.

Calling the killers was an easy way to check whether the Internet information was accurate, and that they were still alive and well. So, after locating many of them on Altavista's People Finder, and printing out their contact information, and the little maps showing where they lived, and the directions on how to get to their homes, Gideon placed more silent calls like those to Price.

They had not been in the news for many years and he supposed they were now, in the main, considered law-abiding elderly men. Some of them could still be located in Mississippi.

Ringing up at different times of day or night, and never saying a word, Gideon listened to the voices of one murderer after another, to their sometimes sleepy, sometimes brusque, sometimes nonchalant, sometimes angry responses. Gideon formed the impression these men were satisfied with themselves.

Now Gideon needed to hear the voice of Wayne Roberts, the man who'd killed Schwerner and Goodman, in Barnette's account. Roberts had also been one of those who had attacked the parishioners at the Mount Zion Church before it was burned down. He'd returned to the Klan meeting with blood on his knuckles, and bragged he got this when he was "beating a nigger." "The niggers were well beaten and well stomped," he had reported.

Gideon pulled Wayne Roberts' page from his folder. It was around eleven at night in Mississippi. Gideon picked up the phone and dialed.

" 'Lo," a soft, drawling voice answered.

Gideon was silent. "Hullo, anybody there? This is Wayne here." The voice seemed cheerful—like someone who'd been drinking a little—and the man sounded old. Gideon opened his mouth, and considered speaking. Your time may be coming, Wayne. But he thought better. "Goodbye," Wayne said softly, and hung up. Gideon also put down the phone.

He had listened to the voices of many of them, now, men who were eking out unjustly quiet lives. Men who had ruthlessly plotted and murdered. Forgotten by them and the world, the agony of their victims, the pain of the families. Forgotten, the unsatisfied longing for justice. Justice that had been denied to Kareem Jackson, too.

Should these killers be allowed to escape justice?

Gideon thought of Chaney and Schwerner and Goodman's long, final day, as Cecil Price held them incommunicado, waiting to release them for the Klansmen's slaughter.

Was this really his business?

Gideon thought of the guards strapping Kareem into the chair, then leaving; he heard again the sound of the lever, he saw Kareem drawing the poison gas into his lungs, his agony. Because Gideon had failed him. As he had failed Schwerner and Chaney and Goodman.

Gideon decided. He would go to Mississippi. He would start with former Deputy Sheriff Cecil Rae Price. Then Wayne Roberts.

28

Gideon's search for an anonymous, untraceable means of getting to and from Mississippi had proven more difficult than getting guns. Obtaining a vehicle whose license plate led only to a false identity was doubtless child's play for CIA operatives. But it had posed a problem Gideon could not entirely solve.

His fix was imperfect, but good enough. He responded to a used car ad in a Portland newspaper and bought a beat-up 1990 Chevy pickup of indeterminate, mustard-like color, with a camper shell. The kind of vehicle so ubiquitous as to be invisible.

Introducing himself as Bob Heller, Gideon wore large, aviator-style, mirror sunglasses and a dramatic, black cowboy-type hat during his meeting with the seller, James Cargill. He had acquired these props for the occasion and discarded them afterward.

Gideon bought the pickup for cash—$3,800—without Cargill asking for any identification, got a hand-written bill of sale from Cargill, and promised to record the change in ownership.

He never did. The truck was still registered in Cargill's name. Gideon thought that even if the vehicle were identified and somehow traced to Cargill after he killed Price and Roberts, chances were small that Cargill would remember enough from their brief encounter to really identify Gideon.

Using the Cargill name at a garage, and again paying cash, Gideon had a more powerful, rebuilt engine installed, also a high-speed rear end. He replaced the tires, and had everything else checked and brought up to good condition. One night, he put the pickup in the garage next to the cottage.

Renting a sprayer at a local hardware store, and buying the paint at yet another place, he repainted the vehicle dark blue. His amateur paint job wouldn't hold up. But that did not matter.

Gideon's limited immersion in criminal law had taught him that eye-witnesses were extraordinarily unreliable, and he decided on simple means of personal disguise, changing his hair, eyewear, and clothing style. He began by shaving the top of his head, making a big circle of baldness in the center and over his forehead. Then he cut off the beard he had long worn, leaving a half-gray mustache. He would let his head and face gradually pick up some sun over a couple of weeks so as not to look newly white, and meanwhile he would let his mustache grow more prominent.

During this time, he would isolate himself nearly entirely in the cabin, keeping fit by hiking and exercise. He would shop at different markets each week and avoid anyone who might remember him or notice his appearance was changing.

By mid May, he was ready to complete his transformation. He dyed his now generous, droopy mustache and his eyebrows a dark reddish-brown, likewise the hair he'd left on his head, in back and on the sides. He replaced his narrow, tortoise-shell-framed eyeglasses with a pair of black, thick-framed prescription spectacles he bought at a walk-in, franchise eyeglass store in Portland, also paying cash. He put on his new Sears Roebuck ensemble, a cheap short-sleeved plaid shirt over a pair of chinos.

Gideon looked in the mirror on the back of the bathroom door. Gone was the distinguished, yuppified lawyer, the casually dressed, dignified professional with a close crop of salt-and-pepper hair and a neat beard. Instead, before him stood a working-class man of indeterminate age with a large and somewhat ragged dark moustache, and a prominent, shiny bald patch. He scarcely recognized himself.

As a man of no importance, he would effectively be invisible. The chances were miniscule that anyone who saw him in passing would recall anything about Gideon except, at most, those aspects of his appearance— the baldness, the moustache, the glasses—that were most dramatic and least permanent. If, after killing Price, he could escape immediate capture and remove himself from sight for a few weeks, until his hair began to grow out, he could be home free.

Or, if he felt that more slayings were an appropriate risk, he could return and take out Wayne Roberts, Jimmie Snowden and the others.

Gideon's office at the cabin included a computer, a scanner, and a high-quality color printer. He did not intend to rely on false papers if he could avoid it. But there might be circumstances in which he would be asked for identification, and he needed something other than his actual drivers license.

He had finally realized he could do something easier than trying to counterfeit a California drivers license, a hard plastic photo ID card embedded with holograms impossible for him to forge.

Gideon had made a quick trip back to California. He went to the DMV and reported his driver's license as lost. He was given a temporary license, good for two months. The temporary license had been printed on the spot, using simple black ink on paper with the DMV Logo and the seal of the state of California as a light blue background.

Gideon scanned the Interim Driver License into his computer. He manipulated the text, substituting "James Cargill" for "Gideon Roth," altering the street address, and changing the hair color and height to match his new image.

He printed a color copy of the temporary license that looked very much like the original. It was not perfect. But it would pass muster outside of California, and would certainly be good enough if a Cheapo-6 motel clerk in the middle of the country demanded identification. He carried it in the pocket with his keys for a few days so it would get beat up a little, then put it in his wallet.

Over the weeks, Gideon had gone to more gun shows. In addition to the 9mm Beretta and the Glock handgun, Gideon now owned a Browning Automatic Rifle with a telescopic sight, a small arsenal of ammunition and cartridge magazines, and a silencer.

In the cargo area of the pickup, an earlier owner had installed one of the long steel Delta Pro metal boxes people lock their tools in. Gideon put his guns and ammo into the box.

He placed an air mattress and sleeping bag, a tent, camping gear, and a cooler under the camper shell. A few bottles of good California chardonnay, too. What the hell.

He packed changes of clothing in a duffel bag. In a canvas satchel, a few books, tapes, his maps and photos of Price and Roberts. Nothing with his real name on it.

He put another $6,000 in cash—enough for a range of contingencies—in a tool kit under one of the seats, and headed out of town. In a few hours, he was on Interstate 84, heading east toward Idaho and Utah.

Gideon Roth was on his way to Mississippi.

PART TWO

29

Before he left, Gideon had called Helen. He left a message at her new apartment in Sunnyvale rather than calling her at work because he did not want to speak with her. "Helen, I'm at the cottage in Washington. I'm going to do some camping, and I'll be out of touch. I don't know how long it's going to be. Maybe weeks. Take care." He hesitated. "I love you."

Gideon began to settle into the rhythm of the long cross-country drive. This was the first time he had done this drive alone, and he was taking it slower than he ever had before, rarely doing more than ten over the speed limit. He wanted the time to think, to unwind, if that wasn't a crazy way to put it.

He got off I-84 at Pendleton, Oregon for gas. It was late morning, and he took the opportunity to place a silent call to Cecil Price, to make sure he was still alive and well, and in town. This time, Price expressed some exasperation.

"If you got a wrong number, it's only polite to say so, and say you're sorry!" Price said before he slammed the receiver down.

Gideon smiled.

* * *

Just before the end of the day, in Meridian, Mississippi, Sheriff Timmie Ray Phelps, a short, skinny man with thinning ginger hair, in his late thirties, removed the headset and left the wiretap interception room in the basement of the local office of Southeast Mississippi Telephone Co. The tape was still running. He walked slowly, distractedly, up the stairs and out the front door. He crossed the street to the County Courthouse.

He climbed the marble stairs, went inside, and, on the first floor, walked through the glass doors with the black-rimmed gold lettering that said,

OFFICE OF THE DISTRICT ATTORNEY
GERARD JEFFERS

"Mr. Jeffers," Timmie Ray began. " 'Bout the '64 Summer murder wiretaps. We're still not hitting pay dirt. None of them are calling each other, even though you told me your little talks with Price and Posey and Roberts spooked them real good. Well, didn't spook 'em real good enough to visit with each other on the phone. But there was another of them silent calls."

"You started to tell me last week," said Jeffers, "but I didn't have time to listen. Start over, would you?"

"Well, we started these phone taps when you decided we'd take a look at the old 1964 murders, to see whether you could make a murder case against Cecil and some of the others after all this time. I suppose you decided the coloreds would be glad to see those old farts sent up to Parchman to get the 'lectric chair, and maybe the whites wouldn't be too upset about it being raked up. Not sure you called that right, Mr. Jeffers . . ."

"Now, Timmie Ray. You know there's no statute of limitations on murder. They say justice delayed is justice denied, but they also say better late than never. I believe it would do this part of Mississippi a lot of good for the country to see that things have changed so much that, even decades later, we're determined to bring the killers to justice. That's why the Attorney General deputized me to investigate this matter."

"And it'll be good for you and him to be in the papers again. Not that anyone reads them. Well, I'm sure it's got nothin a'tall to do with votes, but anyway . . . Price and them have not been calling each other since we started listening, so we ain't getting what you were looking for. But there have been these calls from this person who don't say nothing."

"Did you get his number?"

"Nope. Like I told you, when we started the taps we didn't pay it no mind. We was listening for Price to talk to Wayne Roberts or Billy Wayne and for them to say something about the Yankee civil rights workers and the colored boy they killed. And mostly we're not right there listening when the calls are happening. I don't have enough men to sit around all day waiting for Cecil Price or Wayne Roberts to pick up the damn phone. So we've got a tape that starts recording whenever there is a call. There's no way we can trace who's placed the call when we're not there. We just hear it later.

"But we started noticing a few of them, where someone calls Price and don't say nothing. Then it was the same thing with the others. Started with Price, least as far as we know. Then Posey. Arledge. Now Wayne Roberts got one of these calls, too.

"They ain't wrong numbers. Never an apology, 'Oh, sorry, wrong number.' And he holds the line open for too long after they answer and they chatter away, getting cross. We didn't think on it much. Just a little strange. But I'm starting to worry. Maybe would be a mistake to ignore this."

Timmie Ray sat on the edge of a table in Jeffers' office. District Attorney Jeffers said nothing. For two or three minutes, he stared out his big windows through the blinds at the large trees in the courthouse square. This was a grand office, and he liked the view of the big old trees that had been here for a century. Some of them since the War between the States. This was a better office than any he'd ever seen, outside the views from the Governor's Mansion in Jackson.

"So what do you think about Mr. Quiet Caller, Timmie?"

"Leaves me with a bad feeling. Too many funny calls. This ain't no coincidence. I am thinking someone else is interested in the same old boys we are. Wants to hear what they sound like. No telling who or what for. Makes me uneasy. Up to no good."

"Could be a gal," Jeffers teased. "Miz Quiet Caller, they'd say nowadays." Timmie Ray did not dignify this with a response. Ladies didn't do this kind of thing.

From the credenza behind him, DA Jeffers picked up an eighteen inch, six pound, extra heavy bolt he had saved as a remembrance from a murder case, and fooled with it. The bolt still bore a trial exhibit tag. The defendant was the wife of a contractor, and she had walked into the office early one evening while hubby and a secretary were having intercourse on an old couch at the shop. The wife grabbed the first thing at hand—the six pound bolt—and brought it down on the woman's forehead. Though maybe her husband deserved it more.

The woman died a day later from intra-cranial bleeding. The wife got six years for manslaughter. Jeffers thought that was enough. Her husband visited her each month at the penitentiary in Pearl, Mississippi.

A super-sized nut fit the end of the bolt—Jeffers never did learn what you did with a bolt this size other than kill paramours—and he liked to rotate the nut back and forth while he was puzzling a problem.

"Whatever it is about," he said, finally, "it will come to nothing. I've learned there are funny curious people everywhere, and sometimes these funny curious people get a curious excitement out of calling people they've heard of but don't know. Some of them utter death threats, and that's the end of it. Satisfies whatever is in them. Some, I think, just want to hear a voice. They mostly also never do anything."

"Mostly," Timmie Ray said.

"Look, you're the sheriff. Talk to the phone company. See if you can have someone listening, say at night, whenever the silent calls mostly happen, and try to trace the calls."

30

Jennie Courtney, a middle-aged black woman, was the paralegal who spearheaded the Jackson life history investigation. Family history, physical and psychic trauma, possible hereditary conditions or influences—all were to become part of the picture. The goal of the investigation was to understand how Kareem Jackson came to be the kind of person who committed the horrific crimes for which he had been condemned.

The story—pieced together from medical and social service agency records, police and employment documents, interviews with family members, acquaintances and others—was intended to present an understanding of Jackson as himself a damaged human being, perhaps even a victimized person, for whom life imprisonment with no possibility of parole was sufficient punishment.

Four months after Gideon's San Quentin visit, Jennie entered Gideon's office to talk about what they had learned.

"Well, chief," Jennie said, "there is one helluva tale to tell about Kareem's family. His father Jason was one deeply messed-up dude who proceeded to mess up Kareem. But the story's very different when you go back another generation. That story helps you understand why Kareem's pappy Jason got to be the way he was.

"Kareem's grampa Joshua Jackson had been a hero in World War II. Had trouble getting back into the expected life for black folks in Mississippi, though, after the war. They weren't too big on black war heroes in Mississippi in 1946.

"I'm making light of it. Shouldn't." Her voice dropped. "There's more than one grisly crime in this case. Actually, the story's horrible. Horrible beyond what I imagined."

* * *

October 1946. More than a year after VE Day and VJ Day. Sgt. Joshua Jackson was finally going home. Home to Fannie Jo, home to the five-year-old son he had not seen since he was a baby. Home to Greenwood, Mississippi. Home to the Delta.

Jackson rode in a "Coloreds Only" car at the back of the Southern Railway train that was taking him from an Army camp in Alabama to Greenwood. The car's windows were trimmed with wood that had once, long ago, been a classy dark Mahogany. Here and there, if Jackson tried hard, he could see a tiny spot where the original varnish still clung to the wood, making a small shiny, dark patch. Nearly every other place was worn and nicked, tacky and sooty.

The bench seats were wicker. But it seemed as though the wicker had as many broken places as smooth ones. Each break in the wicker made a loose end that scratched or poked. But that was okay. In fact, it would have been seen as an insult to the dignity of white folks for niggers to have a car that was half as good as the Whites Only cars at the front of the train.

The cars at the back of the train were twenty to thirty years older than those reserved for white people. Back here, smoke and cinders from the engine flew in, too, so you had to keep the windows closed. Hardly any of the ventilating fans worked, and the air was unbearably stuffy.

Only after Jackson had gone off to war had he met a colored man from the North who told him that the segregated cars—like segregated everything in Mississippi—schools, parks, doctors' offices, entrances to the courthouse, buses, restaurants, drinking fountains, rest rooms, movie theatres, churches, morgues and cemeteries—were supposed to be "separate, *but equal.*" Jackson had been too incredulous even to smile. His jaw had actually dropped.

It had taken him a while to grasp that, in a distant place, in Washington, nine white judges in black robes had once had to grapple with the fact that the law had put colored people at the bottom of the heap in the South.

Jackson finally understood that the judges had been trying to square the "different" treatment of colored people with the idea that they were supposed to be treated equal under the law. The judges' clever fix was to say colored folks had equal rights even though the law kept them *separate* from whites. Separate, but equal. And that if colored people thought this meant that they were being treated as inferiors, well that was their problem.

Jackson was sure there was not one single person in the entire state of Mississippi, not one, white or colored, old or young, to whom the thought would have occurred that keeping the races apart in Mississippi meant anything but keeping colored people down.

Jackson had not exactly forgotten about his place in Mississippi, in his three years at war. But he had had other things to think about.

On this train, Jackson was reminded again how things were. It was crazy, he thought, that—coming home safe from war—he needed reminding that he was less a person here than he had been in Europe, where as a soldier he had faced drudgery, degradation or death nearly every day since the middle of 1944.

He had learned, in Europe, that he and the other Negro soldiers did not have to *yessuh* and *no suh* every white person they encountered. They were men, and they could stand up for themselves in front of the American whites and say what they thought, or even tell a white officer when they'd had enough. Quite a few Nazis had also learned that he was a man, not a "nigger," when Jackson ripped them with machine gun fire. He had been a man, too, to the French women he had sex with at the ports in Northern France. Not that white pussy turned out to be all that special.

At first, he, like most of the enlisted coloreds, had not been in a combat unit though he was eager to fight. But even in the Quartermaster Corps, he had seen action.

Because he knew how to drive, Jackson had become part of the famous "Red Ball Express," the chain of trucks running day and night, often bumper-to-bumper, that carried ammo, gasoline and food from the invasion beaches (and then the channel ports) to the front lines. The Nazis had put the French trains out of operation as they retreated after D-Day, so it was the mostly Negro truckers of the Red Ball Express who brought to General Patton's tanks and fighting men the supplies the Third Army needed for its drive through France and into Germany.

Strafed by German aircraft, shelled by German artillery, the truckers of the Red Ball Express had driven on, sometimes dodging off the roads into fields where more than one truck was blown apart by mines.

At the end of the trip from St. Lo, near the beaches, to the front, sometimes Jackson had had to pick up his rifle and shoot back when Germans fired on them. Jackson had seen trucks in his line blown up by bombs or ripped by Messerschmitt machine gun fire. But he was destined for more combat than that.

* * *

Fall 1944, Northern France. Excitement blazed through the ranks of the truckers when the 761st Tank Battalion landed on Omaha Beach on 10 October 1944. They were the first Negro tankers the drivers had seen, the first Negro tankers to reach foreign soil. Pride filled Jackson's chest, and envy, when he saw these black men, fearsome astride their Sherman tanks, rumbling down a road toward their bivouac at La Pieux. He had been within earshot, two weeks later, when General Patton himself had told the Negro tankers, "I don't care what color you are, so long as you go up there and kill the Kraut sons-of-bitches. Damn you, don't let me down." Jackson could see their determination.

Now it was November 9th. The 761st Tank Battalion had been launched into combat the day before in Athaniville, and Jackson's branch of the Red Ball Express was running from Cherbourg toward Morville, where the tankers were pushing the Germans back. Jackson's truck was at the head of three others, loaded with shells, machine gun bullets and material for the tanks. As ever, there was fear when they ventured out—they were never entirely sure where they were going and what might happen.

As they reached the thin woods around Jarville, they saw signs of fierce fighting—blasted trees, crushed fences, once-neat fields churned into muck by tank treads, and still the stench of exhaust fumes and of gunfire. Jackson heard the blast of cannon not far off.

He could not tell where they were supposed to rendezvous with the quartermasters at the front. Sometimes, finding the "front line" was dicey, and Jackson wasn't sure whether the Red Ball hadn't run past its terminus this time.

Soon things would get much clearer.

The road ran through some woods. It turned to the left and a large clearing seemed to be opening up on each side ahead. As Jackson came round the bend, heavy machine gun fire raked the side of the truck, knocking it right off the road into a ditch, tilted on its side.

Jackson grabbed his rifle and clambered out of the smoldering vehicle, wondering how long it would take the ordnance in the truck to explode. He was scrambling along, unseen, in a ditch by the side of the road when the Germans gave the truck another burst and it blew up. Pieces of metal rained around him, and a wheel rolled by. Jackson wasn't hurt, but was deafened by the blast.

He saw no sign of the other trucks and assumed they were quietly backing off to get the fuck out of there. He crept further from the remains of his truck, then lay still.

Jackson peeped over the edge of the ditch. In the field ahead, Jackson could see Germans. Two Panzers stood on a small rise to Jackson's right, a ways off. Rumbling in from the left, in the distance, were three Sherman tanks, from the 761st. Jackson saw that before the tank battle began, the American tanks would pass through the place before him, just ahead of the German machine gunners.

Three German soldiers were repositioning their machine gun, turning it away from the road. Their attention was back to the impending tank duel, and Jackson saw they were concealed behind bushes among a few trees, along the flank of the American tankers' line of advance. The machine gun was silent now. They were about fifty yards ahead of Jackson.

As the American tanks approached, Jackson could see the Negro machine gunners and commanders sitting up in the open hatches. They probably could not see the Kraut machine gun, and Jackson knew the Germans meant to pick off those men before the battle with the Panzers got started.

Between Jackson and the machine gun, there was only open ground, offering no opportunity for concealment. Jackson had just his rifle. The spare clip was in the ruins of the truck. *Fuck. I can't let these boys get knocked off like this. Maybe . . . But not from this far away.*

Jackson had been a hunter at home, and he knew how to move quietly. He put a round in the chamber. Crouching low, he slunk ahead swiftly. Meanwhile the tankers were coming on, faster than he thought those big old machines could go. When Jackson had gotten as close as he could, he lay down to make himself a small target.

Before he could take aim, the first two tanks came abreast of the machine guns, and the Germans opened fire, spraying bullets across both tanks. A machine gunner in the first tank fell forward, hit, and the second tank immediately turned. But the machine gun nest was not visible, and they weren't headed quite the right way.

The Germans' attention was on the tank. Its great noise meant that Jackson could move closer without being heard. He crept to within ten yards, aimed and began firing. The man at the gun fell immediately, but the ones on either side jerked aside, and Jackson's next bullets missed. In the confusion of battle, the Germans didn't realize they were being fired on from behind. Jackson aimed again, and took down a second man.

The last Kraut rose and turned, realizing at last where the danger lay. But he had been feeding ammo to the machine gunner, and his rifle was not in his hand. Jackson dashed forward—"You fucking Hun cock sucker"—and reached the German just as the man pulled his handgun from its holster. In his rush, Jackson couldn't aim his rifle, so he swung the butt across the man's face. He saw fear and rage in the man's blue eyes, and he saw how very pale the man's skin was. There was a crunch as the butt struck the side of the man's mouth, and the German went down.

Jackson stumbled, struggled to stay on his feet. The Luger was still in the German's hand, and he was trying to point it at Jackson. He fired as Jackson lifted the rifle to smash the man's head, and Jackson felt something singe his upper arm. His descending rifle butt missed and slid off the man's shoulder. It hit the ground with a brutal jolt, and Jackson's arms tingled. He dropped the rifle.

Jackson fell on the German, pushing the pistol hand to the side with one hand, while he clawed the German's face with his other hand. He felt the German's eyeball give way under his fingers, heard the man grunt in anguish. Jackson was splattered with blood and gore, and the German's breath and spittle were in his face. Jackson reared his head back, exposing his throat for a moment, then with all the strength in his great thick neck, Jackson heavily smashed the top of his skull down into the German's nose. The man went limp for a moment and Jackson wrenched the handgun from him, and rolled away on his side. Out of the German's reach for the moment, he stretched both his arms out to steady the gun, pointed the Lugar at the German, heard "*Bitte*—"

The first bullet blew away most of the man's face.

Jackson kept firing until the clip was empty. He didn't hear any of the shots. Then he realized the clicking sound meant there were no more bullets in the gun. The man Jackson had killed did not look much like a man any more.

Jackson was alive. He was trembling, and he smelled blood and shit. Around him were three men he had just killed, and the filth of death. The muck under his legs was that awful mud created when dirt was trampled or ground into pools of fresh blood. Even after Joshua Jackson had seen the horrors he was to see in the coming months, he would sometimes dream of this moment, of lying in this bloody paste. But the shock now was too much for him to take in.

He got up onto his knees in time to see the American tank rumble up nearby. "Kilroy was fucking here!" Jackson tried to shout, but his voice was hoarse, and he didn't know if they could hear him. The man in the front right hatch of the tank looked over, took in the scene, and smiled as he recognized the black man as an American Negro who had cleaned out a German machine gun nest. Giving a thumbs up, he said something to someone else in the tank, and they lurched back toward the Panzers, which were even now firing their cannon.

The tankers of the 761st were blasting away with their big cannon, not getting closer, and the Panzers were doing the same. Suddenly two other tanks Jackson had not seen broke in from the Panzers' flank, firing at their sides. Moments later one, then the other German tank was hit. The first was immediately engulfed in flames. But a German nonetheless popped up from its forward hatch. Grasping his machine gun, even while flames began to envelop him, the German began firing at the American tanks. Another cannon blast from the American tank, and the Kraut and the front of the Panzer disappeared entirely. No one left the second tank, which burned noisily.

Jackson stood up and approached the scene, as the American tankers emerged.

"Nice work, brother," the Negro commander of one of the tanks called down to Jackson. "What you doing way out here?"

"Red Ball Express," Jackson said. "I was with the Red Ball Express until a little while ago," gesturing back toward the smoking remains of his truck. "I the onliest one in sight now, though. Guess I'm gonna need to be reassigned." He paused. "These look like pretty good vehicles," Jackson ventured, nodding toward the tanks.

"Where the Southern cross the Yellow Dog?" the commander asked.

Jackson chuckled. In England, before the invasion began, Negroes from the Mississippi Delta called out this question in a room full of soldiers, to see who else knew this referred to the place in Mississippi where the Southern Railway had intersected the Yazoo Delta line. This was a funny place to be asking the question.

"In Moorhead, a few miles from my home in Greenwood," Jackson responded. "Where you be from?"

"Itta Bena," the tanker said. They were practically neighbors.

There was a rumble of more tanks approaching.

"Now we're shy a machine gunner," the commander said. "I need someone right now. Ever handle one of these?"

"Sure," Jackson said.

"You bull-sheeting, I think, but you get your chance. We work out the reeble-deeble paper shit later if you work out."

Jackson ran toward the tank. The driver, who was in the left front hatch, explained how to feed the machine gun. Jackson was quickly told what to do, and they rumbled forward.

So began Jackson's life as a tanker. He was part of the 761st Tank Battalion when it assaulted and took Morville that afternoon; then later, as part of the spearhead of tanks and infantry driving through Forest De Koecking. Then, in the coming weeks, the battles at Wuisse, Bois De Kerpriche, Dreuze, Bidestroff, Neufvillage.

The 761st Tank Battalion went through 183 days of nearly continuous combat. Jackson and the others fought their way through France, Belgium, Holland, Luxembourg, Germany and Austria. More towns and places than Jackson could remember. He got his Bronze Star for wiping out the machine gun nest that first day. A purple heart, too, for the bullet that creased his upper arm. Another medal for gallantry under fire in the forest of Leisenwold toward the end of the war.

The 761st destroyed hundreds of enemy vehicles, tanks, anti-tank guns, pill-boxes, machine gun nests. They spearheaded drives into the heartland of the enemy, killing or capturing tens of thousands of German soldiers. They were with the army that liberated the Nazi concentration camp at Buchenwald. And Jackson was with them, at the end, when they reached the Enns River in Austria to await the arrival of the Russians and the end of the war.

On 6 May 1945, surrender papers were signed. The 761st performed occupation duties in Bavaria for another year, until June 1946. Then Jackson's unit was deactivated, and Joshua Jackson returned to the United States of America.

* * *

Jackson remembered tank commander Hank White's question about the Southern and the Yellow Dog, the question Hank had asked while he was making his shrewd, swift judgment that Jackson would do. Now Jackson wasn't far from that railroad crossing. He would get off a few miles short of there. In a little while, he would descend from this ratty car at Greenwood, Mississippi, see his wife and child again, and resume his life. But differently.

Joshua Jackson had fought for his country, he had shed his blood for his country, just like the whites. Some of them were much more capable than he was, especially those who'd had schooling. But many were no smarter, no bolder, no shrewder than Joshua Jackson. And damn few of them were as damned determined as he was now. So he was god damned if would go back to scrapin' and shufflin', letting these Mississippi crackers treat him like the "boy" they always called him. He had earned the right to be treated like a man and to move up in the world.

Jackson knew full well that being a decorated war hero would not amount to squat among the whites of Greenwood. In fact, he'd heard tales of Negro soldiers being lynched on their way home for wearing their uniforms. On his own ride home, the quiet and cautious pride of the Negro GIs had come under assault. When the train had stopped at Birmingham for half an hour the evening before, half a dozen Negro soldiers went to look for a place to eat. Jackson decided against joining them.

The only restaurant at the station was for whites only. They were not trying to make a stand against segregation; but the colored soldiers felt they were entitled to a hot meal. Having fought for America, now they were home they meant to be treated at least as well as the German POWs who had been taken to eat at white restaurants when being transported during their captivity.

The colored soldiers walked and sat at a table. A brawl ensued immediately, as the restaurant manager and the short order cook each grabbed a chair and swung at them, and a dozen white soldiers jumped the Negroes to drive them out of the restaurant. Three of the black vets and two of the whites interrupted their trips home for a stay in the local hospitals.

When the remaining Negro soldiers returned to the car, they were bloodied, their faces swollen and badly bruised. They looked reproachfully at Jackson and the other Negroes, saying with a look, "Why weren't you with us when we were fighting?" Jackson was angry. But he had not gone through war and hell to get beaten to death on his way home before he saw his wife and son again.

He looked aside. He meant to stand up for himself. But he had more important things on his list than eating at a crummy railroad restaurant. There had been meetings about the GI Bill of Rights. He could get job training for a better job—building on what he had learned about automotives, taking care of trucks and the tank—and he was told he could get unemployment money to tide him over until they found the right job for him.

The war had torn a chunk out of Joshua Jackson's life, but he'd made it through alive. He meant to get a skilled job. Maybe even go to college. The GI Bill would pay to support him and Fannie Jo and his son Jason while he got more schooling.

The train pulled into Greenwood. Jackson grabbed his duffel bag and hung out the steps as the train slowly ground to a halt. On the side of the station house nearest the rear cars, a mule-drawn wagon stood. An old black man and a large child—Fannie Jo's uncle Benjamin and Joshua's son Jason, not a baby anymore—sat on the board. And there, Fannie Jo was running across the wooden platform toward the slowing train. *"Josh! Josh! Josh!"* He heard her call over the screeching of the braking railroad wheels. His long journey had come to an end.

Joshua Jackson dropped down to the platform, let fall his bag, and took Fannie Jo into his arms. He felt her softness, and her strong arms too, embracing him. He kissed her and took in the look of her, saw her smile wobble as she began crying, crying and laughing at once. Joshua Jackson was home, and his short struggle for a new dawn would soon begin. He laughed, and gently held Fannie Jo in his big hands, and he kissed her.

31

December 1946. The last six weeks had been worse than Joshua Jackson had expected. He had returned from the war with skills and expectations. He did not mean to go back to hoeing cotton. He knew he was good for more than toting crates in a warehouse. He was a fine truck driver. His four months with the Red Ball Express had given him more experience than most truck drivers in the States got in four years! He also knew about engines from his work on the trucks and the tanks.

He was entitled to a skilled job. And if one suitable to his skills was not available, he was entitled to a full year of unemployment while United States Employment Services (USES, it was called) helped him to find the right job or the job training he needed.

The sign on the door read: "Hours: 8:30 a.m. to 4:30 p.m. Closed Noon to 1:15 p.m." Jackson had been there since 0822 hours. (He still wore his uniform and still thought in military time.) By a few minutes before nine, the center had still not opened, but three young white men, also in uniform, had arrived. The white soldiers talked quietly to each other, and did not return Jackson's nod or "Good morning."

At nine a young white woman unlocked the door. The four men entered, and she took her place behind the desk in the reception area. Jackson was at the head of the short line, but the woman said politely to Jackson, "Would you sit down for a moment, on that side?" While Jackson waited, she spoke with the three whites, took their names, and gave them forms on clipboards to fill out. She directed them to a line of chairs on the other side of the small room.

As they sat down to fill out the forms, the young woman called to Jackson, "You can come over now, boy."

"What can we do for you today?" she said.

"I'm a veteran. I was a trucker and then I was an assistant driver on a tank in Europe. I'd like to find work as a truck driver or a mechanic, maybe get some more training as a mechanic."

"Well, we surely do not have very many tanks here in Greenwood, but I think we can find something that suits you. Please fill this out. One of the counselors will be with you as soon as they can."

He sat down and filled out the forms, handed them back to the receptionist, and resumed his seat.

By 9:30, another dozen former soldiers had arrived, and the room was starting to get crowded. Four of the newcomers were Negroes, and Jackson knew one of them, Eli McGee from Itta Bena, who'd spent the war in the Signal Corps. He had also known where the Southern crossed the Yellow Dog. They talked some, but by 10:00 a.m., when still more people had entered, Jackson realized that eight or ten whites had been sent through to meet with the employment counselors, but none of the Negroes. *He thought, I don't want to make no hullabaloo with these people. But I'm not gonna wait forever either.*

"'Scuse me, Eli, I got to talk to the lady." He went up to the desk, and after a moment she looked up at him.

"Miss, I was the very first one here before 8:30 this morning, but quite a few men who came in after me have gone in. Isn't it my turn?"

"Well—" (she looked over at his form) "Joshua. Those men were . . . interested in areas of employment the counselors were handling first. But just you be patient, it won't be but a minute more." As Jackson sat down again, she picked up his card and went through the door to the other room. A few minutes later she came out.

"Now, Joshua, Mrs. Black can see you. Just go through the door. She's in your second cubby on the right."

"Thank you, ma'am."

The room Jackson entered was large, and divided into cubicles with wood and glass dividers around each station to afford a measure of privacy. He looked quickly around. Mrs. Black was white, as were the five other counselors. There was a plastic plaque next to the second cubby with her full name, Gladys Black. Her face looked familiar. He might have seen her around town before the war. She was a few years older than he, mid-thirties he thought, and thickening at the waist. She had washed out straw colored hair.

Jackson put on a big, positive, confident-looking smile, and greeted her first.

"Good morning, Mrs. Black. My name's Joshua Jackson, and I want to work." He was careful not to offer to shake hands.

"Good morning, Joshua. So nice to see you home safe from the war." She looked at his form. "Well, I see that you did truck driving and machine gunning and such like in the Army. Let's see what we can do for you."

"Yes, ma'am. Actually, on the tank, I was an assistant driver as well as a machine gunner. I was a truck driver first, with what they called the Red Ball Express."

"The Rebel Express? Over there? Well, did they teach you any rebel yells, Joshua?"

"Oh, no, ma'am, what I said was"—he articulated more carefully—"the *Red ... Ball ...* Express. That's what they called it, our trucks was running night and day, day and night, to supply the front line."

Mrs. Black did not seem to like to be corrected. "Well, whatever it was, Joshua, we don't have one of those here. Let me look and see what might suit you."

"Anyway, ma'am, I want to be a mechanic or a truck driver—I did repair work on the trucks and the tanks, and I know engines. With some training, or if I can learn on the job, maybe I could get work as a mechanic. And I've got a lot of experience driving trucks."

"First, let me make a card for you." There was a small wooden box for file cards on her desk, with alphabet tab dividers. Jackson noticed that all the cards were white or yellow, mostly white. Mrs. Black neatly wrote Joshua's name in large block letters at the top of a yellow card, put a "C" in a circle next to it, then wrote down some more information in her looping handwriting.

Mrs. Black next looked into a small loose-leaf binder, which evidently had available jobs. There were quite a few pages in the binder, and she would flip rapidly through some, pause, hum to herself, then riffle through some more.

"Well, this will be just the thing for you." She pulled a two-part form out of a drawer, and began filling it out.

"What is it for, ma'am?"

Mrs. Black finished writing without answering, then briskly tore apart the form, handed him the yellow copy from the bottom, and threw the carbon paper into her trash basket. She attached the other part of the form to his file card with a paper clip.

"It's at the Jameson Automotive plant, down on Carrollton Avenue just past the tracks, and you just see if they don't get you back to work right fast." She stood up, but did not offer her hand. "It's been a real pleasure, Joshua. You give it your best try, and you'll be at work in no time, earning an honest living. Right glad we could help you."

Jackson was uneasy. What was the job? Was this what he wanted? But he would be rude if he questioned her now, she was plainly telling him to go.

He walked four blocks down to Carrollton Avenue, and out seven more to Jameson's. It was a new plant that hadn't been there before the war. It looked as though it had turned out parts for jeeps. He walked into the office.

"What can we do for you, boy?" a heavy set white man in a tie asked.

"Mrs. Black from the USES center sent me here. I'm looking for a job." He handed the man the yellow slip. "I'm looking to work as a truck driver or a mechanic."

"We don't have anything like that for colored people. What I need is a boy to stock shelves in the warehouse. The pay's thirty cents an hour."

"No, thanks," said Jackson, and walked out. He walked back down to Main Street, where he sat on a bench near the USES center. Then he walked over to Mabel's, a private house that was a sort of club or bar, on Percy Street, and got a beer. Eli McGee came in after a while.

"Any luck?" said McGee.

"I told them I had experience to be a truck driver or a mechanic. They tried to give me a job stocking shelves," Jackson said.

"Well, I've been going through it with them for months. I worked for the Army Signal Corps for three years, stringing and repairing communication lines. They told me they couldn't find anything for me. I heard later they sent white vets over to the Mississippi Power & Light. They told me if I didn't take a 'suitable' job, I couldn't get no unemployment pay.

"They made me take a job as a porter," McGee went on, "but I keep coming back, trying to get something better. Now they tell me that they are trying to take care of those veterans first who don't have any jobs. The skinny is that for folks with black skins, the USES is useless."

"Well, I'm going back," Jackson said.

Over the coming weeks, Jackson was steered toward a variety of menial jobs which he refused. Dish washing at a cafe. Sweeping at the mill. Wood chopper. "What about job training?" he asked. There was no job training for mechanics anywhere around here. When he pressed, Mrs. Black sent him to Greenwood Cabs, a Negro-owned taxi service that put him to work as a driver, with the promise of on-the-job training as a mechanic. In three weeks, the only time he saw an engine was when he opened the hood of the 1938 Studebaker to put in some oil. He quit again.

Hoping to learn some kind of skill, any skill, he let them put him into a training program at a large bakery. In two weeks, all he did was grease pans, fetch supplies and stack loaves of bread in racks for the delivery drivers.

Eli McGee told him he was thinking of heading for Chicago with his family.

"This state is bad news. We got no future here," McGee said.

"Look," Jackson said, "this is my home. My family is here, and my wife's family is here. We don't want to leave. We shouldn't have to leave."

"Well, hell, that's just the way it is."

"A lot of us are in the same boat," said Jackson. "We fought, and we're entitled to the benefits. Maybe we should get together some of the other guys and start talking about what we can do."

Joshua Jackson's house was a two room shack on a dirt road past the edge of town. Jackson, McGee and three other Negro vets met several times over the next few weeks. They talked about life in Greenwood for colored people. Mississippi's economy had been changed by the war. The farms and plantations had revived from the Depression. War industries had come in, making new kinds of jobs that paid better than cotton. But colored people were going to have to fight for their fair share.

"Either we're gonna leave this state, or we're gonna make changes," Jackson said. "Jobs are just part of the problem. What kind of future can our kids have, in third-rate schools where they never see a new textbook—only old books the white schools stopped using ten years ago? Why do we have to be afraid a deputy's gonna beat up on us just for fun? How come we can't even find a place with a bathroom we're allowed to piss in when we're downtown, spending our money at their stores?"

They discussed registering to vote. "Dammit," Jackson said, "three-quarters of the people in Leflore County are Negroes. We the majority, and we ought to have *some* say in how things go." But only a handful were registered, and few of those were bold (or crazy) enough to actually vote.

McGee had heard of a Negro group called the Mississippi Progressive Voters League, in Clarksdale, but the Voters League didn't seem eager to send someone around to talk to them about starting a chapter in Greenwood. They talked about hooking up with the NAACP. But first, they decided, they would quietly see if they could just register to vote without marking themselves as part of any organization. Then they could consider what next.

On Tuesday at eleven in the morning, five of them met in front of the County Courthouse, walked up the steps together, and went into the Registrar's Office.

"We come to register to vote," Jackson said to the woman behind the counter. She looked at him incredulously, then walked away without saying a word.

Ten minutes later the Sheriff appeared. He was a heavy-set, but powerful man, known for his violent temper. His face was flushed.

"What is this, some kind of god damn darkie parade? What are you boys doing here?"

"We just come to regis' to vote," Jackson said in a soft voice, showing a big smile.

"Well, the Office is closed. Niggers don't vote in this County, and they ain't gonna start now, so you can get the hell out of here."

Jackson opened his mouth to say something, but the Sheriff interrupted him: "Didn't you hear me? Your black ass is gonna land in jail if you don't about face and get out of here. I don't know what kind of shit you niggers got away with in France, but this is Greenwood. You don't talk back when a white man tells you something."

They left. None of them spoke a word to the others as they went their separate ways. That night, Fannie Jo told him that Miss Penny, the white woman she took in washing from, told her she heard that Joshua was making trouble downtown, and what was that about? Maybe the washing would be stopped. When Joshua told Fannie Jo what had happened, she came around the table and hugged him.

"He was telling me I was a dog, Fannie Jo, and I couldn't say a word back. What can we do in a place like this? How can we raise Jason to be a man here?"

The next day, Joshua Jackson went back to the USES center. After a wait, he was at Mrs. Black's desk again.

"Mrs. Black, I'm quitting the bakery. I'm not learning anything there, and it ain't training for nothing. I want a proper job or unemployment until I get one."

"It's not our responsibility, Joshua, to see to it that you learn if you are not able to. You're been given a chance, and you're not getting unemployment to laze around and drink, when we're offered you suitable work."

"I'm a trained truck driver, Mrs. Black, and you send me to a place where I'm greasing pans. Greasing pans isn't training. Greasing pans isn't skilled work. I know there have been truck driver jobs that you keep for whites. They filled one at the bakery two days after I started."

"Well, you already had a position then, Joshua."

"Dammit, *I* should have had the truck driver position, Mrs. Black," Jackson said, raising his voice. "You've known for weeks that I wanted a position as a truck driver, and I got the experience. At least I should have heard about it, so I had a chance."

"Joshua, don't you use that tone of voice with me," Mrs. Black said in a loud but trembling voice. "I'm not here to be scolded by colored boys."

"Don't you call me a boy no more, *Gladys*, because I ain't no boy," Jackson responded. "I'm a man. I fought and bled and killed for this country while you and your hubby were having mint juleps at garden parties, and I'm entitled to be treated fair. And, *Gladys*," he fairly yelled, leaning forward, "if I call you Mrs. Black all the time, I don't see why you can't call me Mr. Jackson."

Mrs. Black grew pale and shrank back away from him. She was trembling and her eyes filled with tears.

"I'm sorry," he began, lowering his voice.

"Don't you touch me," she cried loudly. "Don't touch me you dirty black . . . you filthy nigger." Her voice failed.

Jackson realized that everyone in the room was looking at them, and two red-faced white veterans were advancing on him. The office manager got between them and Jackson, and made an effort to restrain them.

"Nigger," one of them said tightly, "get away from that white woman right now before I kill you. Niggers don't talk to white women that way, ever. If you raise your voice to her again, if you lay a finger on her, you filthy God damn black bastard, you are going to be hanging from the light pole outside this office in five minutes."

"We don't want any trouble in here," the office manager said to the white men crowding behind the soldiers. As he slowed them, Jackson made his escape. *Now I'm in it*, he thought. *This is the end of Joshua Jackson and Greenwood, Mississippi.*

32

July 1964. Susan worked in the Freedom School, teaching children about Negro history from what she had taught herself in the spring. Then teaching basic literacy to adults during the evenings and helping with the voter registration classes. She seldom went out to do freedom registration, only on occasion, when she could be paired with Gideon or another white volunteer.

But Gideon went out. He went door to door, farm to farm, and he learned the introductory patter quickly. How to introduce himself politely, and ask wary black men and women, most of them much older than himself, to sign a freedom registration form and come to a meeting. Over the weeks, he learned how to appear fearless when a police car trailed them. Then he realized that he was actually becoming less afraid.

Many were ready, amazingly ready. He remembered an elderly Negro woman named Cleo Bates, Cleola Bates of Batesville. When Gideon walked up she had smiled, greeted him warmly—"You one of them Freedom Riders"—and told him to come in. While Gideon did his freedom voter registration riff, she set down an out-sized lunch for them: fried chicken, okra, collard greens, coleslaw, corn bread, a great pitcher of lemonade, cobbler. Gideon was at home with this absurdly excessive, food-based hospitality because it was exactly what his Jewish mother would have done. He was pleased with himself when Mrs. Bates signed the freedom registration forms. She promised to come to the next mass meeting and to bring her friends.

It had taken Gideon a while to realize why Mrs. Bates and many other Mississippi Negroes called him a "Freedom Rider." Negroes in Mississippi had long been subjected to crushing oppression. Barred from voting, kept off juries, they had no recourse against lynchings or police violence.

Precisely because open protest was so perilous, and white supremacy so entrenched, the news of the 1961 Freedom Rides had spread like wildfire when it came. The first Freedom Ride—an effort by an integrated group to travel together on a bus from Washington, D.C. to New Orleans—had been terminated by violence. The riders were beaten nearly to death, and the bus was burned by a mob in Anniston, Alabama. The Freedom Rides were taken up by others, but the next trip ended when the riders were all arrested and jailed in Jackson, Mississippi. Yet their courage and defiance inspired the state's isolated Negro populace. So when the Freedom Summer organizers began to arrive three years later, they were all Freedom Riders to Negroes like Mrs. Bates, who had been waiting for the struggle to reach them.

That did not mean they were totally downtrodden. When Gideon returned, later, to spend more time with Mrs. Bates, she told him of the near-slavery conditions she and her parents had endured, sharecropping in the Mississippi Delta when she grew up. But also of the strength they had imparted to her.

"My mother and father taught me not to look down when I talked to

white men, to always look them dead in the eyes and not blink." Gideon
struggled to grasp the courage this took.

Others tried to walk that fine line in Mississippi between conducting
themselves with the simple dignity of men and women, and engaging in
what whites might see as provocation—fatal provocation.

Nonetheless, the climate of fear was palpable. Many Negroes refused
to have anything to do with these dangerous freedom people. A lifetime
of precautionary deference to whites also meant that Gideon's presence
often undermined the message that Negro people could be in charge of
their own destinies. Even when Gideon went with an experienced black
organizer who did the talking, many Negroes would still turn to him, assuming this young white man must be in command.

And Gideon's take-charge attitude aggravated the problem.

Gideon knew they were supposed to keep a phone log to document
the harassment that the volunteers, local people and SNCC organizers
encountered. But it was being done haphazardly.

"Let's make a big chart and write down the details whenever we get a
call about harassment," Gideon told Jimmie Hayes, a young black man he
saw hanging around the office much of the time. Jimmie had been one of
the people in the cars when they went to the church in Batesville that first
night, but Gideon didn't really know what he did. Gideon showed Jimmie
what he had in mind, and drew up the chart. But Jimmie didn't write well,
and his entries were sparse. "Harrased, 1st Baptist," he might write, without indicating who called in or the time or details of the incident.

"Let me get that," Gideon called across to Jimmie, next time the phone
rang. Gideon was eager to show Jimmie how to do it right. Jimmie went
off looking unhappy. Later that day, Brian called Gideon aside.

"Gideon," Brian said, "Jimmie Hayes has been in the Movement around
here for about two years. Whatever you may think, he knows what he is
doing.

"Two years. That's a long time for a local person to be part of the freedom struggle in Mississippi. Did you know he led six people who went
down to the county courthouse in October 1962 to try to register?

"The sheriff shoved them out and arrested Jimmie for disorderly conduct. He spent sixty days in county jail that time. But he just continued, though the word got around that the Klan was after him." Brian paused.

"How long you been here?"

"Um, nearly three weeks," Gideon said.

Brian looked at Gideon for a long time without speaking. Then he went on.

"You're here to help, not take over. There was actually a debate among staff before the summer project about whether bringing a bunch of white college kids down here was going to help or hurt. Some people thought you all would dominate everything, and that it wasn't going to help black people learn how to be their own leaders.

"Jimmie doesn't trust white people too much, and riding over him isn't making you any friends. What matters is not you figuring out the best way to do things. It's local people like Jimmie dealing with everything after you go home when the summer's over. You need to listen and learn from him, not expect him to learn from you."

Gideon reddened. "I'm sorry. I was an idiot."

Most of the time there was no danger of people deferring to Gideon. The Movement's leaders in Mississippi—mostly local people—were a mature and confident group of men and women. In many cases, they drew on earlier experiences as leaders of the Southern Tenant Farmers Union of the 1930s, or with the NAACP in the 1940s and '50s, when the NAACP had to be a clandestine organization in Mississippi.

On the next Saturday, a group was heading for a meeting of the Mississippi Freedom Democratic Party in nearby Holmes County, where blacks were more than 70% of the population. At the last minute, Gideon was put in a truck with Hartman Turnbow, a fifty-nine year old rights leader from the county. No one else was with them, so Gideon took the opportunity to ask questions.

"How did you first get involved?"

"Was last year. We had been hearing about a citizenship class in Greenwood. Some of us invited them to come down to Tchula to speak at our church, and we decided we'd go down to register. About fourteen of us. After about two weeks of classes, we learned how to fill out the forms, and we decided to try it out, see what it was like. We parked at the edge of town, and walked in, two by two, a good distance apart, so they couldn't say we was demonstrating."

"Had there been any demonstrating in Tchula?"

"Nope. When we reached the courthouse, we is met by the sheriff. Everyone stopped. But Samuel Black says, 'March forward.' The sheriff, he puts his right hand on his revolver and his left hand on his blackjack, and he says, 'None of that damn forward stuff here.'

"'We only come here to register,' I says.

"'Go over the North side and wait there,' he says.

"We went over and waited for maybe twenty minutes, then he come over again. He got his hands on his gun and his blackjack again. 'All right now,' he says, 'who'll be first?'

"The fourteen of us just look at each other, and was quiet. When I saw that, I just stepped out and said, 'I will, Hartman Turnbow.'

"And he says, 'All right, Turnbow, go in and do what you have to do.' So I goes inside the building and into the Circuit Clerk's Office. A white lady ask me, 'What do you want?'

"'I come to register to vote.'

"'To register to vote!'

"'Yes, ma'am.'

"'Well, the circuit clerk isn't here.'

"'May I wait until he comes?'

"'Yes, you may.'

"It was about ten o'clock then, and I sit there until twelve o'clock. The circuit clerk didn't come. 'I'll be back after lunch,' I say. We come back around two o'clock, and finally the clerk tells me to come in.

"He has me fill out the registration form, then he say to me, 'Hartman, you always been a good boy. Why you want to go mixing up with these here trouble-makers for?'

"'I just come to register,' I says.

"'Okay, you got to interpret the Mississippi Constitution.' He asked me to tell him what the section means about 'No person shall be elected or appointed to office in this state for life.' We had been preparing for this, so I knew about different sections of the Constitution. I told him, 'It means that government offices are for so many years,' I say, 'and not forever and ever.'

" He asked me to interpret another section, and I got that right too. Section 22. 'No person's life or liberty shall be twice placed in jeopardy for the same offense,' and so on.

"'It mean,' I say, 'that if you accused of a crime, and you have a trial, and the jury say not guilty, the County Attorney can't go for you again to put you in Parchman for the same crime.'

"Me and one other got registered that day. But when they see there's twelve more, they say all the others fail the test. After that day, no one else pass the test. Next day was a write up in the local paper saying Hartman Turnbow was an integrational leader. Two weeks later, our house was fire-bombed in the night. Mrs. Turnbow wakes me up, and she run outside and I hear shooting.

"I pick up my 22 Remington rifle, hit down the safety, and got it in shooting position. No sooner I get out in the open, I sees two white men. One of them shoots at me, and I begin to shoot at them with my Remington right fast. While I am shooting at them, they is shooting at me. After about three minutes of shooting, they left.

"We fought the fire for about an hour before we could get it under control. Then we set on the back porch, waiting for day. After a time, we get in our car, and go to a friend's house, and call the sheriff. The sheriff come out and he says, 'It could have been you, Hartman.'

"'Could I ask you a question?' I say. 'Do you think I would set my own house on fire if nothing was insured?' He got up and went on out.

"Later, he came back and tells me to come out of the house. 'Git 'em up. I got a writ for you for arsony.' He carried me to Lexington and put me in jail. I stayed in for two days. The fire commission come talk to me, while they investigating, and he says to me, 'You a goddamn liar, boy. You a liar. You burned your own damn house.'

"Then a colored man from Greenwood bailed me out. The civil rights lawyers took the case to federal court, and they dropped the arsony charges against me. Judge Cox said he didn't believe I burned my own house, and he didn't believe I had no gun battle with the white men.

"Since then I just been trying to keep up the freedom struggle."

"Were other people afraid to get involved after they burned you out?" Gideon asked.

"Well, sure. Lots of people that tried to register, they cut the credit. All the people that was buying on credit, they cut them off. They done everything they could. And they still burning up stuff, and it ain't cooled off. This Sunday, they threw a couple of sticks of dynamite at the center we're building up here. About a month ago, they rode by and threw a cocktail bomb in a car and burned it out. We all afraid, but we got to keep on keeping on."

33

June 4, 1997. Driving by himself in the growing darkness of eastern Washington, Gideon thought of the Mississippi rules. *I should take the bulb out of the roof light of this vehicle, so I'm not so visible at night when I open the door.* Now he felt a pang of doubt. *Those were the rules to keep night riders from shooting us in the dark. But now I'm more like the night riders. I'm keeping from being seen so I can kill.*

He wasn't sure how he should go about killing Cecil Price when it came right down to it. Price was not owed a fair chance—what kind of chance had his lynch mob given Schwerner, Chaney and Goodman? But Gideon was uneasy with the thought of gunning Price down on his doorstep in the night, silhouetted in an open doorway, the way Byron de la Beckwith had murdered Mississippi civil rights leader Medgar Evers in 1963. When the world learned Cecil Price had finally been brought to justice, he did not want them comparing the retribution long owed Price with the cowardly assassination of Medgar Evers. Or would it be evening the score for Medgar, tit-for-tat?

He also felt, in an inchoate way, the need for some sort of confrontation. He imagined catching Price and taking him somewhere at gunpoint.

"You have no idea what this is about, do you?" he saw himself asking Price.

"No. Why you bothering me for? I ain't got much money."

"I'm here to bring you to justice, Cecil Price." He could see doubt beginning to dawn on Price then.

"I'm here for James Chaney and Andy Goodman and Mickey Schwerner. I'm here for all the others murdered by you and your fellow racists." He imagined seeing the sweat on Price's forehead as Gideon steadily pointed the Beretta at him.

"But that was years and years ago. I done hard time for that already."

"Four years in jail? For a triple lynching? You know that's not enough."

Or perhaps: "That was for violating their civil rights. Tonight you're going to pay for murder." Or: "Don't bother talking to me."

Gideon could not decide whether he preferred the scene better in which Price flopped down, begging for mercy and shitting his pants, and Gideon killed him in disgust, saying something like, "Be a man"—not that Gideon believed in that kind of thing, but he thought Price would.

Or Cecil Price defiant to the end: "The kikes and the darkie deserved it. Kill me if you're going to do it, you nigger-loving Yankee pussy. Don't waste your time. I ain't gonna beg for my life."

Gideon would laugh in his face, then rage:

"So die, racist." And pull the trigger.

Would this be any better than just gunning him down in the street without warning? How much talk was needed?

Gideon tried to tell himself that Price was like a mad dog who had to be put down, not a moral creature who could be made to appreciate the justice of his own death. And the safest, cleanest way to kill Price would be without warning, perhaps at night.

Gideon was convinced that Cecil Price was owed nothing, that he was not entitled to the respect accorded citizens of a civilized society. Price must be the target of one-man justice, rather than the defendant in a community morality play called a trial, not because Gideon Roth had so decreed, but because an immoral white community had itself set Price outside the realm of law. When, for decade after decade, that community held nigger-slaying to be no crime at all, and smiled upon killers like Price, they were also decreeing that the rule of law would not protect such perpetrators.

There was no need, then, for Gideon to think about the matters he himself might ask a jury to consider in the penalty phase of a death penalty case: How had Cecil Price become the kind of person who could commit the crimes he committed? Wasn't he entitled to sympathy, as the innocent victim of an upbringing that had turned him into the heartless killer he had become?

Gideon was sure the answer was No. This was not a matter of understanding an individual who had been twisted and deformed by horrible personal experiences until he had become capable of committing ghastly crimes. Cecil Price wasn't twisted at all. He was a banal man who had acted as the authorized instrument of a deformed social order, the immoral white South of thirty years ago. It was white Mississippi's prurient lust for the suffering of blacks, white Mississippi's unending need to remind the African-American populace of their subordination, which explained the Neshoba County murders, not any personal psychopathology on the part of Cecil Price and his vicious pack of killers.

But what did all that say of Gideon's own moral obligations as Cecil Price's executioner? Didn't he have to conduct the execution in a certain way, so that it fulfilled its purpose? It was not only the echoes of the night riders that caused Gideon to hesitate when he thought of the bullet in the night. It was not only that Gideon wanted this act to be understood by the world at large as a belated execution, as justice long overdue. It was not only that he did not want anyone to compare the righteous execution of a lynch-mob ringleader with Medgar Evers' assassination.

He felt the need to confront Cecil Price, to confirm to Price's face that he was not ashamed of acting as the instrument of retribution. It was for himself that he needed to speak to Price, to utter words of condemnation, for himself and that community which had for so long been rendered silent by murderous violence. It was necessary to speak to Cecil Price in order to affirm—in the name of a community not present—that Cecil Price, like the corrupt society he had represented, deserved death.

But was that all there was to it? Didn't Price also deserve to suffer before he was snuffed out? Didn't he need to understand that an avenger had come? That it had been wrong for him to live out the last thirty years without fear? Gideon felt this longing for cruelty, as well. Although he saw ways of making intellectual distinctions between himself and the South's old regime, he feared that his own hunger for revenge was not entirely different from the delight the old order had taken in inflicting suffering.

Each scenario that Gideon constructed for Price's last moments, to effect his moral purpose—to make Price suffer as he deserved—seemed melodramatic, gratuitous, mean, tawdry. Executing Cecil Price would be a moral act, Gideon was sure, so there must surely be a moral way to do it. But he hadn't yet figured out what that way was.

Gideon wondered what his comrades in the civil rights struggle would think. "Right on, whoever did this," some of them would say, the angrier participants. Perhaps they would use that strange phrase of praise they had back then, "Work out!" But Gideon had misgivings. He was unsure whether those whom he had respected the most, the old Freedom Riders, would be disgusted with the assassination.

But that would not stop him. Had quiet dignity been enough to save Kareem's grandfather from his fate? Had nonviolence saved Kareem? Price and the others were entitled to no reprieve.

34

Toward the end of July 1964, Gideon was in Atlanta for a SNCC staff meeting. The Civil Rights Act of 1964 had recently been passed, finally outlawing segregation of public accommodations like restaurants, motels, public swimming pools and buses, and Gideon was told that lawyers for the NAACP Legal Defense Fund needed a few white people for the first case to arise under the new Act.

Earlier in the month, when some blacks had sought to be served at Lester Maddox's Pickrick Restaurant in Atlanta, Maddox drove them away at gunpoint, aided by white patrons wielding axe handles.

Maddox asserted that the Pickrick was his private property, that he had the right to exclude blacks, and that the federal government had no right to interfere. But under the Constitution, Congress has the power to regulate interstate commerce, and Congress had expressly found segregation was a burden to interstate travelers.

The upcoming legal battle would test whether—one hundred years after the Civil War—the federal government could at last stop the Southern States and their white citizens from imposing badges of inferiority on blacks, from systematically humiliating and demeaning the Negro people in order to maintain white supremacy.

In this great legal drama, Gideon had a small but not entirely trivial role: he was to help prove that even though The Pickrick restaurant was wholly within a single state, the restaurant and enterprises like it were so interlaced with the fabric of interstate commerce that Congress could regulate them.

Gideon and two young white women, also Northerners, had doffed their blue work shirts and dungarees for the occasion, and dressed as nicely as they were able for their outing to The Pickrick. The girls wore light flowered dresses, in one case borrowed from their hosts. Gideon wore light colored chinos and a dress shirt and tie.

They presented themselves at the restaurant and were seated after a few minutes. Service was prompt. Gideon ordered chicken in a basket. It was not as good, Gideon was pleased to find, as the fried chicken at Paschal's, the Negro restaurant near the Atlanta SNCC office that had sustained the SNCC workers during hungry times.

You cannot sell French fries without offering ketchup, and (Gideon observed and later testified) their table at The Pickrick featured a bottle of Heinz ketchup that had begun its life in another state. Likewise, Lea & Perrins Worcestershire Sauce and the Pickapeppa hot sauce from Louisiana, integral to Pickrick cuisine.

The day Gideon testified, Maddox ran an advertisement in the Atlanta Constitution, touting the segregationist cause as well as his chicken:

PICKRICK SAYS:
TO THE WORLD

I will continue to give my all in the fight for survival of my business, the American Free Enterprise System, and for the survival of our civilization and freedom and liberty. In the name of liberty I will resist with my last breath and last drop of blood.

If President Johnson enforces this civil rights bill then he will make a police state out of America. If we are forced to close, forty faithful and loyal Negroes and twenty faithful and loyal White employees will lose their jobs as a result of our closing.

OUR SPECIAL TONIGHT
Order of PICKRICK SKILLET FRIED CHICKEN
Drumstick & Thigh 25¢ Breast & Wing 50¢
Please, no carry out orders at these special prices!

I MAY GO TO JAIL,

My life may be required of me; but I stand ready to give my all in defense of God, America, my family, friends, and freedom and liberty. I promise to resist with all my life such ungodly and unconstitutional civil rights bills.

Should I go to jail, it won't be Lester Maddox going to jail . . . It will be Freedom and Liberty being placed behind bars for LIFE. Behind those dark doors will be States Rights, Constitutional Government, the American Free Enterprise System, and racial pride.

Yours for America
Lester Maddox

AND FOR SUNDAY
Roast young turkey with dressing,
giblet gravy and cranberry sauce 55¢
Baked Spanish Mackerel 50¢   Barbecued Chicken 55¢
Roast Round of Beef 70¢   Pickrick Meat Loaf 50¢

A three-judge panel, headed by legendary Fifth Circuit Chief Judge Tuttle, sat in a gigantic courtroom to hear the case. In due course Gideon Roth was called as a witness, and a black NAACP lawyer quickly elicited the key evidence: Gideon Roth was a New Yorker; Gideon had been freely served at The Pickrick; and sauces of interstate origin had been offered. Gideon was also asked what his race was. Seizing his only opportunity at feistiness, Gideon responded: "The human race." The attorney was allowed to confirm for the record that Gideon was of the white race.

At the end of the trial the three judges ruled that The Pickrick was sufficiently involved in interstate commerce for Congress to regulate it. The court rejected Maddox's claim that the Civil Rights Act was a burden on individual freedom and ordered The Pickrick to admit black patrons. Maddox sold the restaurant rather than comply or go to jail, and later became Governor of Georgia on the strength of his segregationist stand. In due course the United States Supreme Court would confirm that the federal government could require restaurants and motels that offered accommodation to the general public to treat blacks and whites equally.

★ ★ ★

Exercising such rights in Mississippi was another matter.

The Saturday morning after Gideon returned to Hokes Landing, he sat in a small restaurant with two young black people from the town, Charles and Emma Willis. They were brother and sister. Their aunt Ruth owned the place, and Emma and Gideon went freely to the grill to grab the plates, loaded with pieces of chicken as well as grits and eggs. Country folk ate hearty breakfasts around here, Gideon had learned. It was a sunny morning, and the well-used tables and chairs were cheerful in the bright room.

Charles—Gideon had jokingly started calling him Charleston—was the elder of the two, in his early twenties, a short but tough looking man. Emma was tall and thin, just a couple of years younger. They looked a lot like each other, with prominent cheekbones and noses. They were thought to have some Indian blood.

Gideon was explaining where he had been and what his role had been at the trial. They asked him why, now that the Civil Rights Act was law, they shouldn't be served at Humphrey's, the whites-only luncheonette in the five and dime downtown that served Negroes only at a take-out window by the back door.

"Well, Charleston, they told me that COFO was trying to avoid demonstrations this summer. They think things are hot enough already in Mississippi," said Gideon, "and they want to keep the focus on voter registration and the freedom schools."

"But ain't this just like voting?" Charles asked. "They say Negroes don't want to vote, and that you outside agitators are just interfering. We try to register to show they are wrong. Same thing about our right to be served at restaurants. If we don't go, now that we can, won't they say it was just the outside agitators making a fuss over nothing all along?"

Gideon had no ready answer.

"It's the law," Emma finally said. "We won this, and now we need to show we aren't afraid to use our rights."

"Well, then," Gideon said. He took a deep breath. "Okay, if you guys are going, I'll go with you. I came down here to support integration, and for all I know we'll have a nice integrated lunch together. First let me call the Freedom House, so they know what we're doing."

Gideon made the call. Brian told him they would have observers outside, and not to start before they got there.

They drove cross-town to Humphrey's in Charles' car while Gideon explained what Brian had said. Gideon was apprehensive, but tried to hide it. It was important they not back down, and showing fear would encourage the segregationists. He didn't know whether the Willises were unafraid, or just didn't believe in talking about it. But he also did not want them to see his fear. They saw Brian and Brenda across the street, waved, and went into Humphrey's.

A wooden sign on a post stood by the entrance to the luncheonette, "Please Wait to Be Seated." They waited.

"What do you want?" a waitress asked eventually.

"We'd like a booth please, Miss," Charles said politely.

"I mean, what are you doing here? We don't serve coloreds here," she said. "You go to the take-out window and they'll help you there."

"Sorry, Ma'am," replied Charles, "as of July second, under the Civil Rights Act of Nineteen Hundred and Sixty Four, we've got a right to eat here same as white folks."

"And no need to worry about providing us with a white person to integrate our table," Emma added, "we done brung our own."

The waitress walked away without answering. After a few minutes, she returned and seated a group of white people who had come after Charles, Emma and Gideon.

"Let's just sit at the counter while we're waiting," Charles said. They sat, but the waitresses continued to ignore them. Then the manager came out. "We don't serve niggers or communists here," he said. "Get out of my restaurant."

The three acted as though he had said nothing and continued to sit. Soon a group of young white men came up behind them. One of them grabbed a ketchup bottle, and shook ketchup on Emma's head, then Gideon's, then Charles, prompting laughter from his peers. Another added mustard, and soon the muck was dripping over them. The group of young whites grew larger and began jostling them. Then one grabbed Gideon by his collar, pulled him off the stool, and slugged him in the face.

Gideon fell, his lip bleeding. Others threw Charles and Emma to the floor, and the mob began kicking and stomping at them.

Gideon curled himself into the nonviolent protective position he'd been taught, with his arms tight against his head to protect it from the kicks. The blows hurt in a way, but in the agitation of the moment he felt little pain. The anticipation of violence had been worse than the actual thing so far.

"*Fucking nigger-lover.*" One of the assailants grabbed a chair, and raised it over his head, preparing to strike Gideon, but the manager pushed in front of him.

"That's enough, don't you go smashing up my restaurant . . . " He pushed them all back and the whites left, exulting.

The police arrived a few minutes later and arrested Gideon, Charles and Emma for disturbing the peace.

"We'll be back," Gideon said, as they were being hustled out of the restaurant, and then shoved into the back of a police car.

At the police station, ignoring the usual jail practices, Charles and Gideon were put into the same cell in the Negro section of the lockup.

"Well," Gideon said, "we have succeeded in desegregating something, even if it's only the jail."

From the women's cells, they heard Emma singing, her voice rich and compelling:

Jesus on the Mainline, tell him what you want,
Jesus on the Mainline, tell him what you want,
Tell him what you want by and by,

If you're bound in jail,
Tell him what you want . . .

They sang with her, and some of the other prisoners joined them, though others seemed afraid to. After two hours they were bailed out. When they got back to the Freedom House, they washed the blood off and tended their bruises. Gideon called FBI headquarters in Jackson to report that Humphrey's had violated the law. And that they'd been arrested for trying to be served as they were entitled under the Civil Rights Act.

The FBI did not seem terribly interested. Gideon, Charles and Emma would have to come in to file a complaint, the FBI man said. Later, they did. Nothing came of it.

The next morning, ten black high school students tried to hold a demonstration outside the store.

They were carrying hand-written signs that said "End Segregation," "Humphrey's, Obey the Law" and "Freedom Now." No sooner had they unrolled their signs than the police arrested them. Brian and Gideon began calling to see who might go their bail, but were having trouble raising enough money for all ten students. Toward the end of the afternoon, they learned that the police chief had released the students to their parents on condition they not demonstrate again. Many of the parents were frightened and angry, and called the Project to complain.

Gideon argued with Brian about whether more direct action was a good idea.

"We've been down this path before," Brian told him. "They'll just go on with arrest after arrest, and they'll probably charge you with contributing to the delinquency of minors and send you to Parchman for six months or a year. It's happened before. No one's going to stop them from doing it again."

"I just have a hard time accepting that the First Amendment does not apply in Mississippi," said Gideon.

"Let me tell you a story. Two years ago, Charlie Cobb arrived in Ruleville, in Sunflower County near here, with a couple of Mississippi sit-in students, to try to get things going. One day a white man with a pistol forces them into his car and drives off with them, to his hardware store. He rants at them for half an hour. Turns out he's the mayor and the justice of the peace. Also head of the White Citizens' Council.

"When he finally orders them to get out of town, one of them, Charles McLaurin—have you met him?—Mac tells him they were there to help people register to vote, and that they had the right to do this under the United States Constitution. The mayor says: 'That law ain't got here yet.'

"It still hasn't, and the federal government won't protect our rights. Maybe it'll get here some day, but for now we're focusing on voter registration."

"But we're not getting anyone registered either," Gideon said. "Last week, a Negro minister who has two degrees from Columbia University failed the registration test. There are no Negro voters in the entire county."

"That's why we're doing 'freedom registration,'" said Brian, "having Negroes fill out registration forms to show that thousands of black people in the South would vote if we were allowed to." His eyes were intense. "Think of the organizing we're doing like this. It's like snow piling up on the side of a mountain. Someday, there's going to be a thaw, and when that day comes, a mighty river of power will come rushing down."

35

December 1946. Joshua Jackson sat at the table. It was close to midnight, and Fannie Jo and the boy were asleep in the other room. He stared at the dull red glow of the cast iron stove, banked for the night. He stood and looked out the window, then returned to the table. As he and Fannie Jo had decided, he was going to write to a cousin in Chicago about whether they could stay with him while Joshua looked for work there.

He was running away. He knew it. There was nobody here he could fight against and win. It was time to leave Mississippi and make a life elsewhere.

He picked up the pen. Then he heard the sound of cars pulling up. He went to the window again. Three cars had stopped, their head lamps glaring toward the house, and he heard car doors slamming. He went for his rifle. A rock smashed through the window, and as he moved quickly back, he heard glass breaking in the other room. As he turned toward the bedroom, Fannie Jo rushed in with Jason in her arms. He was crying.

"Lay down on the floor, and keep your heads down," Jackson said.

"No, I'm getting the shotgun," said Fannie Jo.

Shots rang out, and they dropped to the floor.

"Jackson," a voice called, "We're all 'round the house. Come out and give up."

Joshua crept toward the front window, swiftly poked the rifle out and shot out one of the headlights, then another. Meanwhile Fannie Jo fired a shotgun blast out the side window. A scream, then angry yells and a fusillade followed.

"Let's burn it down." "You gonna die, niggers," another jeered. "Come on out before it's too late."

"Jackson, you come out by yourself," the first voice said, "or we'll burn the place down with you and your nigger bitch and son in it."

"Don't, Josh," Fannie Jo said. "They'll kill you."

"We'll all burn if I don't. I'll tell them we're moving away. Maybe they'll just whip me. Don't matter."

He put down the gun, and opened the door. He could not see the men

behind the car lights. He stretched his arms out, and tried to talk, "Please
. . ."

"Shut up and come here, nigger."

He advanced, and three white men grabbed him, pulled his arms behind him and tied them. Now a dozen other men came around, and made
a small circle around him. He recognized some of the men from the employment office. Others he had seen around town. Some were strangers.

"This is the kind of nigger who rapes white women," said an old white
man holding a rifle. His thin skin clung to his neck, and his Adam's apple
bulged.

"No, please," Jackson tried to say again, "I never . . . ," then another hit
him on the side of the head with a club, and he fell to his knees, blood
flowing from his scalp.

"You black animal, you."

"Bring his nigger bitch and his bastard out here. Let 'em watch."

Fannie Jo and Jason were being held by two other men, a few feet back
from the ring of men. A man came up and punched Jackson in the face,
and when he fell, another kicked him in the stomach. Through his pain,
as he doubled up, he heard Fannie Jo's cry.

"Stop," said the thin man. "We gonna do this right.

"In my daddy's day, they knew how to deal with uppity niggers like
this. Would have been a notice in the newspapers about the hanging and
the nigger roast for a couple of days. Then people from all 'round the
county would have come to watch and take pictures. Still got the post
cards of the one I went to when I was ten.

"Tie him to the tree."

They piled kindling and branches against the base of the large oak tree
in the yard in front of the house, and pulled Jackson against it.

"No, please sir, we just gonna leave Mississippi," Fannie Jo called out.
"Please don't hurt him, sir, don't hurt him or my boy."

Loop after loop of heavy rope went around Jackson and the tree.
Meanwhile the men had poured gasoline on the floor of the house and
ignited it. There was a great blast of heat, and the flames from the burning
house shone on the scene. Joshua saw Fannie Jo looking on, Jason crushed

against her, trying to hide his face. Blood clouded one of Jackson's eyes, but he and Fannie Jo looked at each other.

"Please, please," Fannie Jo said too softly to be heard.

"They'll both watch, or we'll burn them too," the thin man said. "This'll teach them a lesson." A big man held little Jason's hands behind his back, and turned his head to face the tree his father was tied to.

A man went up to Joshua Jackson, raised his leg high, and kicked Joshua in the chest, breaking his ribs. Someone picked up a burning brand from the house, and thrust it into the wood under Jackson. The wood began slowly to burn. Jackson screamed in pain when the flames reached him, and he writhed, trying desperately to pull his legs away, yelping and calling, "No, no." The man tried to cut off a finger, as a souvenir, but the flames were too close, and he had to give up.

"You'll never rape another white woman again, you damn nigger bastard," said another, as he ripped open Jackson's pants, and cut away at him. Jackson's agonized cries rose above the men's laughter. Another stood over Jackson and pissed on him.

Finally, the soldier from the USES office came over to Jackson, carrying a tin of gasoline. He splashed gasoline over Jackson's chest and the wound in his groin, then sloshed some on the branches beneath Jackson.

With a fierce whoosh, the kindling and the trunk of the tree behind Jackson burst into flame, and Jackson himself began to burn. His vocal cords were scorched and he could make no more sounds, but still, Fannie Jo and Jason saw him bucking and pulling at the ropes. The reek of burning flesh and gasoline filled the air, and the cries of Fannie Jo and Jason were mixed with the whoops of the lynch mob. "Nigger roast! Nigger roast! Nigger roast!"

The ropes burned through, and Joshua Jackson's charred body toppled over. His ordeal was ended. But the fire continued. They poured more gasoline on his carcass, and he burned and burned until nothing was left but a few scorched bones.

When the Klansmen drove off half an hour later, little Jason had stopped crying. He knelt on the ground, gazing at the remains of his father, wide-eyed and catatonic. Three of the men had raped Fannie Jo before they all left, and she lay on the ground nearby, mumbling incoherently and shuddering.

In the morning, Fannie Jo's people came and took them away.

36

Fannie Jo's Mama sat in the back of the wagon next to Fannie Jo, stroking her head, trying to warm her chilled body, as Uncle Benjamin whipped the mules toward the farm. Her other arm was around little Jason. When they reached home, Fannie Jo did not move, and she did not respond to Jason, who tried to lean against her. "Take the boy," Mama told Benjamin, "and jes hold him. Don't you let go of him no matter what. I be there when I kin."

"Climb down from the wagon, Fannie Jo, honey," Mama said. "Climb on down now."

"Come down," Uncle Benjamin said, "so's we can take care you inside." But Fannie Jo lay on the boards, paying no mind.

Mama was old, old at fifty-four from birthing nine children, six of them still alive. Old from years of working hard, and from times of eating too little. But her body was still large and strong. Mama lifted her daughter up into her arms and carried her to her own bedroom, where she put Fannie Jo down on a wooden chair. Fannie Jo didn't topple over, but her eyes did not move. She acted like she wasn't there.

Mama got hot water from the great pot on the back of the big iron stove in the kitchen that never went out. "Lord, guide my hand, while I run this race," she hummed. Mama undressed Fannie Jo and washed her off with the warm water, crooning, "You be safe now, love" and "My poor dear little girl, we gone take care of you." And praying under her breath: Lord Jesus, make me strong so's I kin help this girl live. She washed off the blood from Fannie Jo's face, Lordy, and the blood from her thighs from where the men had hurt her, Lord, hold my hand, she washed the soot from her daughter's face and hair, While I run, the soot, oh Lord, the soot of the burning, While I run, she washed the soot off, While I run this race, and she washed off the dried scum from the men from Fannie Jo's thighs,

For I don't want to run this race in, and she gently bathed the bruises there, Fannie Jo twitched in pain, run this race in vain, the bruises where they threw her down and, Lord, speak for me, throwed theyselves on her, like the animals they was, speak for me, after they'd—

She could not keep herself from seeing the scene: the place where the house had been, the winter garden they'd trampled, the mud where Fannie Jo lay, her nightgown half torn from her, the ruined great tree, the remains. Lord Jesus, Lord Jesus, don't let me think about Joshua no more, not right now, Jesus, or 1 go mad. Lord God, give me the strength. Take him straight into heaven, Lord. Take him by Your side. Take away all his pain, Lord, make him whole again, Lord Jesus.

She held her breath to keep from sobbing. Her eyes filled with tears, but she held them back. She held Fannie Jo in her arms, recollecting the little body she had nourished from her teats, remembering the girl running and playing amidst the rows of cotton, then working satisfiedly in them, remembering the young woman so proud when she married Joshua Jackson, a good man, a strong man.

"My baby," she murmured, "my baby," and Oh Jesus stand by me Jesus she kissed Fannie Jo's cheek. Jesus, make me strong and make her strong to bear this. She wanted to fall into a daze herself, or sleep and never waken. But she couldn't let herself.

Fannie Jo shivered. Mama saw that her eyes were focused on nothing before her. Make her strong so she can take care of her baby again, Jesus. Make her want to live for herself sake. Mama picked up the night dress that reeked of the smoke and worse, and took it outside to throw away, and she brought back more hot water and washed Fannie Jo all over again.

She put a nightgown on Fannie Jo, and put her in the bed and sat by her, holding her hand, and praying for them all. Fannie Jo finally sank into sleep. Little Jason be needing, too, Mama thought, but she could not let go Fannie Jo's hand. After a time, Mama dozed off.

An unending scream wakened her. Fannie Jo's cry.

It went on and on, and Mama's heart pounded and she shivered. Hearing it, Jason cried out from the other side of the house. "It be all right, baby," Mama said to Fannie Jo, patting her, pushing her back down onto the bed, "it be all right now, mama's here," knowing it wasn't all right, Jesus, make it right, nothing would make this right, Please Lord Jesus, "You safe now, honey, you with your mammy now." Keep us safe, Lord, don't let them come again.

Fear from her own girlhood, the fear of the nightriders, rushed into Mama's heart. Fannie Jo ran out of breath from crying out and she gasped and gulped, panted for air. Mama felt the terror around them, terror as heavy as if it were water from a flood tearing through the house.

Mama slipped off her shoes and crawled into the bed, under the covers with Fannie Jo. She wrapped her arms around her. "You safe in Mama's arms, honey, nobody kin hurt you now." I can't be thinking of Joshua now, but who would collect the bones if there were enough left for a funeral? She tightened her arms around Fannie Jo, chanting softly, "I be with you, I be with you." And after a long time Fannie Jo's body loosened and she slept again. You got your reasons, Lord. You must got your reasons.

Fear came back to Mama, the numbing terror from when she was a girl.

Over and over, nearly every month, from when she was old enough to remember to when she married in 1907, she'd hear of the colored folk being tortured and hanged and burned. Sometimes by night riders, but sometimes in broad daylight too. Like they was celebrations.

She was six, seven years old the first time. Her parents had tried to protect her from knowing, but an older cousin told her: "We caint go to town today 'cause the white folk gonna kill a colored man they say raped a white woman."

"What rape, Willie?"

"Never you mind, it be a bad thing, but he didn't do it. No how, they even put in the paper they gonna kill a nigger at noon Saturday in the square, no trial no nothing. If any other coloreds be around, they may get kilt too, so we stayin away."

"Ma," she asked that afternoon, "they gone kill Papa if he go to town?"

"What you talking about girl, ain't nobody gittin kilt round here."

"But Ma —."

"Don't you talk about it no more, you hear, Ellie Lou, and don't let your pa hear you saying nothing bout it too. It be nothing we talk about, and you too young."

A week later they ventured cautiously into town, to the hardware store. She saw a picture there, stuck in the front window of the store, a camera snapshot they'd made up into a postal card. A postal card showing two black bodies hanging from the big tree in the center of the square, heavy ropes round their necks, something smoking underneath.

Standing in front of the burned, hanging bodies were dozens and dozens of white folks, men and women, and children her age too, facing the camera, some of them pointing at the dead colored men, many of them smiling and laughing. When her ma saw her looking at these, she turned her away and took her back to the wagon. Her pa did not return to that store for many months.

She had bad dreams about the picture. She'd prayed to Jesus to make her forget, but the recollection never went away. Like her memory of the lines of scars on grandma's back that she only saw but once, her grandma who had lived in slavery, the scars from the whipping she got when she tried to escape.

Now Mama could not keep her thoughts away from Joshua. From the scene she saw when they had come to get Fannie Jo and Jason, the smell of the burning, the smell of the gasoline and of something else.

So easy for a group of men with hatred in their hearts to destroy. Lord Jesus, turn my mind away from hate, let us live in peace. Hold my hand, Lord, hold my hand, while I run this race, for I don't want to run this race in vain. At last, Mama let herself cry quietly, to ease the heaviness. Then she and Fannie Jo slept.

Mama woke. It was afternoon, and the light was fading.

She slipped out of the bed, and hobbled to the kitchen to find Benjamin and Jason. The kitchen door was open, and Uncle Benjamin was going back and forth between the kitchen and the woodpile outside. He was holding Jason against him with one arm, patting and murmuring to him, while carrying two, three sticks of wood at a time in the other. Little Jason clung silently to Benjamin, his body rigid. He quickly turned his head toward her when Mama entered the room, in a jerky movement, his eyes darting to and fro. His face was a moving mask, as he squeezed his eyes shut tight and then them let go, blinking again and again, his mouth working twitching grimaces.

"How you be, boy?" Mama asked softly.

Jason twisted himself around, and flung out his arms in Mama's direction in a harsh movement that nearly threw Benjamin off balance. She took him, but he did not hold himself against her in a soft way. She sat next to the stove, and held him in her lap. Jason was silent.

"I been holding him," said Uncle Benjamin. "He hurtin inside, course, he hurtin inside. But he don't say nothing. Don't want to eat nothing, neither."

"You got to eat, boy," said Mama. "We got to go on livin, no matter what. You safe here with us. And you momma be better by and by. You safe now. You safe now."

She put him down in the chair. She set corn bread on a plate and sliced a piece of ham and put it on the table in front of Jason. Poured some milk for him. She picked him up, and set him on her lap as she sat at the table before the food.

"You eat now," she said, rubbing his shoulder, and kissing the back of his head. "You kin eat now." After a while he did. But the boy said nothing. His body was stiff and he shook every little while.

Her heart was tore up. After he'd eaten, Jason slipped off her lap, and went into the bedroom, sitting on the floor in a corner where he could see his momma without getting too close.

Mama returned and sat by her daughter.

Fannie Jo slept, but her face was hard and pained. Later she opened her eyes, but she did not seem to be there. She did not respond when Mama spoke. Mama knelt by the side of the bed and tried to pray. Jesus, Lord, forgive my sins. Let her get better.

Fannie Jo took a little water that evening, but said nothing. Mama put Jason in bed next to Uncle Benjamin, and she slept next to Fannie Jo in her own bed. She woke when Fannie Jo talked in her sleep. "Don't go out there, Josh. Don't go," Fannie Jo said softly. Then she yelled, "No, Josh, No!" As her voice rose, Mama gave Fannie Jo a little shake, to wake her from the dream. Again she woke with a shriek of fear and pain, and her cry did not stop for a long time.

Fannie Jo knew who they were the next day, and she ate. But that was all. She did not respond to anything Mama said, to her endearments, her efforts to make her feel safe. Fannie Jo turned away, on her side, to face the wall. Her face was blank, and her eyes unseeing. Still, Mama sat by her, singing hymns, or lay next to her, holding her in her arms, talking softly and rocking her slowly. "Joshua be in heaven with Jesus, now," Mama said into Fannie Jo's ear. She felt Fannie Jo tense at Joshua's name. "He at peace now, and you and Jason be safe here, with mammy."

The next night was worse.

Fannie Jo woke in terror and tore her night clothes off and ran outside, then tried to crawl toward the woods, calling in a hoarse whisper, "Josh, Josh? Where my baby?" Then harshly, hopelessly, "Don't touch me."

Another night, when Mama tried to wake her from her nightmare, Fannie Jo lashed out at her with fists and knees, knocking Mama out of the bed. Through all, Mama spoke softly, "You be safe now, honey." "Mammy gonna take care you now." "The Lord will make us right, honey."

At last, Fannie Jo began talking. "I told him not to go out, ma. But they said they'd burn down the house with all of us in it."

"He save you, then, honey. He give hisself to save you and the baby. He the bravest man on God's earth."

"I shouldn't have let him go out there, Mama." She saw the tears in Fannie Jo's eyes again. "I don't want to live no more."

"He a masterly man, Fannie Jo, Joshua was. He knew what he had to do. You couldn't stop him from saving you and Jason. Now you got to live again, cause that why he did it for. For to save you and for to save your baby. He knowed, and he done it for you and the baby. So they wouldn't kill you and Jason. So you got to live again."

Fannie Jo closed her eyes, and her tears brimmed. She sobbed, then wept loudly and wouldn't let Mama hold her. "You got to live again, girl," Mama said. "We keep you safe and help you."

"I don't want to live no more."

Mama felt helpless.

Fannie Jo seemed to go away again. She turned to the wall and was silent for days. Jason tried to get in bed next to her once or twice, but Fannie Jo's body jerked at his touch, and he drew little sustenance from the contact. So sometimes Mama would be in bed near Fannie Jo, sitting up, not touching her, holding Jason in her lap.

"You be better by and by," Mama said. "Jesus make you git stronger again." Jason watched and listened but said nothing.

A week later, Fannie Jo began talking to Mama again.

"Mama," she said. "Did you do the funeral while I was too sick?"

"Honey, Joshua's people couldn't do no rightful funeral, but they bury Joshua Friday last. There be another service later."

Fannie Jo wept.

"Mama. There's something else I am fearing. What if I am carrying a baby from one of the white men who did it to me?"

"The Lord Jesus won't give you more than you can carry, honey. Is your time of month past?"

"Not for maybe a week more. I'll kill it rather than bear one of their babies, Mama. I'll kill it."

"You mustn't say that, honey."

"I mean it, Ma."

Fannie Jo's period came, and she did not have to decide what to do with a baby from one of the men who had tortured Joshua and raped her. After that, Fannie Jo slowly began to recover.

37

Early in August 1964, a week after the Humphrey's sit-in arrests, Gideon, Charles Willis and Ruby Walker, one of the SNCC organizers, were talking with a group of high school kids from Holly Bluff, a very small town south of Hokes Landing, about schools. The students were attending one of the Freedom Schools the Summer Project had launched. The day before, the church they had been using for classes had been dynamited. A meeting room was demolished, and the County had declared the entire structure unsafe for occupancy until it could be inspected. They said they could not schedule an inspection until September or October.

The Freedom School continued anyway, meeting on the lawn. Now they were collecting information about the public schools for a desegregation lawsuit that the Lawyers' Committee for Civil Rights intended to file.

Segregation had been legally justified between 1896 and 1954 under the theory of "separate but equal." If Negroes saw enforced separation as a badge of inferiority, the U.S. Supreme Court intoned in 1896, this was "solely because the colored race chooses to put that construction upon it."

Separate but equal ceased to be the law of the land in 1954. But ten years later Mississippi schools were every bit as separate—and every bit as unequal—as they had always been. The State of Mississippi spent four times as much on white schools as on black ones, and local school districts were even worse. Holly Bluff spent $191.17 per white student each year, and $1.26 for each black student.

When a student named Paulette told them that she went to school in an old bus, Gideon's first thought was that this wasn't so bad, no matter how old the bus was. After all, in many Mississippi school districts, Negro children weren't bused at all, and families had to make their own arrangements if it was too far to walk.

But after a confusing exchange, it became clear that Paulette was not talking about *taking* a bus to school. Paulette *attended* school in a bus. An old school bus that no longer ran was put up on blocks and used as a classroom! This meant no desks, no blackboard, no classroom library of books, no science equipment, no art materials, no teacher's desk, no place to store supplies (if there were any). No heat in winter.

The bus wasn't the entire school. But the colored school building was so old and out of repair that water poured through when it rained and plaster was flaking from the cracked walls.

"They close one of the classrooms and start using the bus," another student explained, "after my brother twist his ankle falling through a hole in the floor."

"We only get 'new' schoolbooks when they old," a girl reported. "After the white kids have used the books for a bunch of years, they get the new ones. We get their old books. The paper feel all soft and worn out, and there are smudges where they underlined stuff and then erased."

"How many students in each class?" Ruby asked.

"About fifty in mine."

"More than forty in mine."

"Forty-eight on the bus."

"Anything else that's a problem?" Gideon asked.

"We have a science class, but we don't have any science equipment or labs."

"They won't let us talk about voting in the civics class. The teachers are afraid to."

"That's why Negro people need to be able to vote," Gideon said. "So you can change all that. Meanwhile the lawyers need to know about this." Gideon had brought an old Underwood typewriter, and Charles, whom he had been teaching to type, wrote up the statements for the other students to sign.

"Of course," Ruby told the students, "everyone knows things aren't equal. But when the lawyers go into court, they have to have evidence, not what everyone knows. So telling us what you told us and signing these papers is a big part of the freedom struggle.

"We'll give your affidavits to the attorneys from the Lawyers' Committee for Civil Rights, and there will be a lawsuit, and the courts will decide whether Holly Bluff can get away with this."

Hopefully, Gideon thought, the lawyers would be able to find some parents brave (and independent) enough to be the plaintiffs in a lawsuit to force the district to equalize spending or merge the two school systems. But here was proof it wasn't "merely" segregation—it was white supremacy.

Early the next morning, Gideon and Charles Willis drove to a rural area near Holly Bluff, canvassing for Freedom Registration and talking to families about joining the schools lawsuit.

By 7 a.m., there seemed to be no one left at home for them to talk to. Pretty much everyone was out in the fields working. Gideon stopped at what was going to be the last place to visit, an unpainted shack with a rickety porch with no railing. Looked like no one was home. But Gideon knocked a second time, just to make sure, while Charles leaned against the car, at the edge of the road.

Suddenly a truck rumbled down the dirt road toward them and pulled into the yard. The doors flapped open and two white men jumped out. One was holding a tire iron, the other had a heavy chain in his hand, and he was swinging the chain. Gideon saw no way to get to the car before they reached him.

Charles stepped into their path, perhaps fifteen feet in front of the men. He had taken the knife he always carried out of his pocket. Never taking his eyes off the two white men, he slowly unfolded the knife. Everyone heard the snap as the blade locked into place. Its six-inch blade glinted.

Charles held the knife before him, point down, slowly moving it from side to side, while he looked in the eyes of the white men.

The men stopped. Gideon did not run, but walked briskly behind Charles to the car. He got in the driver's seat and started the engine—for once the old car fired up immediately—then he leaned across, unlatched and pushed opened the passenger door. Very slowly, Charles backed toward the car, then quickly turned and jumped in.

Even before Charles closed the door, Gideon let out the clutch, and wheeled around, tires spinning, the car fishtailing onto the dirt road as they raced off. The white men still did not move, and Charles sped a bumpy mile before they turned onto the macadam county road. Then he punched the accelerator.

The rednecks were not following.

Gideon felt the wind whipping through the car windows, drying the sweat on his face and hands. He looked in the rear view mirror again, still seeing no one. He loosened his grip on the steering wheel a little, glanced at Charles Willis.

"Could you have taken them, Charleston?"

"Dunno. Maybe. Depends on whether they knew how to fight together."

Gideon tried to imagine the scene.

"I think you just saved my life, Charles."

"They carries in their minds this scary picture, 'a nigger with a knife.' Sometimes it helps."

"Nothing like a good ole racist stereotype."

Gideon pretended to be calm.

38

When they returned to the Freedom House, Gideon was told there had been a call from home, from his father. His mother had suffered a massive heart attack and it didn't look good.

Brian, Charles and Susan drove him to Memphis, and he caught a night plane to New York. All Gideon could think, on the flight home, was "Don't let her die. Don't let her die." Gideon's mind returned again and again to the phone call when he told them he wanted to go to Mississippi, her fear, her melodramatic threat to jump out the window. It didn't seem so silly now.

He did not reached the hospital until long after midnight. She was gone. She was dead because Gideon had chosen to go to Mississippi.

His father never voiced blame aloud, and the doctors said her heart had been deteriorating for years. But neither did his father utter the words Gideon needed to hear: it's not your fault. And Gideon detected his Dad's unstated condemnation, *Why did she have to spend her last weeks worrying about you?* A lifetime with his father had honed Gideon's sensitivity to the man's anger, whether muted or vocal.

After the funeral, Gideon sat shiva with his father for four days. Aunt Ethel, his mother's sister, brought a lentil casserole with hard boiled eggs and sat with them. They didn't have the little stools that were traditional, but brought the hard chairs from the kitchen into the living room. His father was not a taciturn man, but now he was withdrawn. While they waited for other mourners to join them, Gideon was alone with his thoughts.

His recollections went back and forth between the conversation in which she said she'd jump out the window and the only call he'd made to them from Mississippi. They had never left their Depression-era thinking behind, and a collect long-distance call was a big thing for them, so he'd only called the one time, the day after he had arrived.

"Got here yesterday, no problems, Mom. Oh, hi, Dad." His father had picked up the extension.

"Are you being careful of yourself, Giddy?" he said.

"Yes. Lots of us at this center, and it seems like a safe place. Everyone's being friendly."

He did not mention his frightening adventure in Batesville that first night, when they'd been stopped by the Sheriff and fled the night riders.

They took little comfort in his words as he tried to persuade them all would be okay. The more he told them about the Project's security arrangements, the more it underlined what they were up against.

"Don't try to be a hero," his mother had said in a small defeated voice at the end of the call. Little risk of that, he had thought. But he had not turned out to be such a coward after all.

Before long they read about the disappearance of Andrew Goodman and the others, and Mom's fears grew to terror.

Gideon wished he had written home more than once. He told himself it would have made no difference.

He was trying to think about his mother, about her life, as he knew he ought to be doing now. But his thoughts kept returning to whether he should believe the doctor's assurance that she could have gone at any time in the last few months because of her heart.

His cousins and aunts and uncles began to arrive, most of them congregating in the kitchen, a few sitting by his father and talking to him.

"What a loss, Max. She was a great woman."

Gideon wondered whether his father thought she was a great woman. He doubted it. He suppressed a surge of anger toward his father. That was inappropriate now.

Throughout Gideon's life, his father had subjected his mother to a rain of disparagement, both subtle and overt, regarding everything she did or omitted to do. And his mother had passively borne Dad's never-ending hostility, had forever tried to placate and divert, but never to confront him.

When Gideon was eight or ten years old, he had begun to apprehend that a forever angry man was not part of everyone's life, and he was outraged that his mother never fought back. Mom refused to notice the pattern of antagonism. Instead, she treated each of his father's jabs at face value, as though it were an entirely separate event, embodying a sincere, well-meant if perhaps poorly-expressed, constructive suggestion.

Nor had Gideon's efforts to argue on her behalf made any difference.

Later, Gideon was to realize that the challenge of responding to what seemed lunatic arguments had honed his skill in logical thinking. And still later, he wondered whether this intimate experience of wrongness was the source of his indignation, no, his rage against injustice—the sense that his mother had been the victim of a perpetual and never acknowledged, never remedied unfairness. The long deluge of genteel belittling, from which he never succeeded in protecting her, had eventually drowned her.

His father's brothers talked about his mother while Gideon's attention drifted in and out, until an older cousin asked him, "So what have you been doing this summer, Gideon?"

"I've been working in the Mississippi Freedom Summer project, the civil rights project? I was in Hokes Landing, a small town in northern Mississippi."

Gideon wanted to explain the importance of this work, but felt his father listening with irritation. His father must consider everything Gideon was saying about Mississippi a confirmation of Gideon's indifference to his mother. "I wasn't really there for very long," he said after a few more words, cutting off the discussion. Conversation returned to his uncles' reminiscences about his mother.

Gideon thought back to the trips he and his mother had made when he was small, to visit these relatives in their neighborhoods in far away Flatbush. His mother had been more relaxed, funnier when she traveled without his father, and they took an endless series of trollies and subways to get there.

He remembered being four or five years old, walking with her along slushy cobblestoned streets in the winter cold, and reaching up with his arms, saying "Carry me, Mommy." He recalled her lifting him, the smell of the fur on the collar of her coat, cold at first, the feeling of his legs dangling. He remembered sitting on her lap on crowded streetcars, "Try not to bang your galoshes against my legs, Giddy."

He recalled small kindnesses, childhood conversations. Mom hanging out the second-story apartment window, resting her arms on a pillow, watching Gideon and the other kids playing stickball or stoop ball. Her sympathy as he became a teenager. Their visits to him when he'd started college.

Gideon wished he could articulate a way in which she'd changed his life on some philosophical level, maybe the kind of thing that someone would write up as an appreciation in The Reader's Digest. But it wasn't that. It was just the confidence you get from knowing that you are unreservedly loved. That there's someone who cares for you and your future more than anything else in the world, who will always be interested in you and will always love you.

It was only when he was in college that he met girls whose parents hadn't felt that way. It had seemed so *of course* to him as he'd grown up. But everyone did not have that. And then there was Dad, and his bullying and expectations.

Gideon called Susan each night, and they talked about what was happening with them and with the Project.

When the mourning ceremonies ended, Gideon intended to steel himself to tell his father he wanted to go back to Mississippi. But it was more than he could do. Had there been an argument, Gideon could have said. *I still need to do what I need to do, Dad. I'm sorry, but . . .* But what? *I'm sorry Mom died and I wasn't here. I am sorry that my going to Mississippi killed her a little sooner, but she would have died anyway. I'm going and I'll worry about your feelings later; you've never worried about mine.*

At the end of the last evening, Aunt Ethel had given Gideon's father and then Gideon a final hug and kiss before she left. "Take care," she said to Gideon. "Take care of your father, too."

Gideon's father closed the apartment door and flipped the latch, put the police lock in place. Then he turned to Gideon and said, almost in a whisper, "Giddy, please don't leave me now. I need you." And he kissed Gideon on the lips.

Gideon couldn't remember when his father had last kissed him, it must have been when he was a toddler. Gideon wondered whether Dad had let his guard down for a moment, or had just been manipulating him. He couldn't tell. But it didn't matter. He could only say, "No, of course I'll stay."

* * *

At the end of the summer Susan decided to remain in Mississippi, to go on with the work for at least a year more. And Gideon returned to school for his junior year.

Their calls and Susan's letters grew less frequent and less personal. He received the last one in December.

> Dear Gideon,
>
> Who would have thought, in the Godawful heat of summer, that Mississippi could get cold? It sure has. Now that it's December I'm freezing. Thank God for the pile of quilts Mrs. Dilworth gave me! My folks sent some of my winter clothes, too.
>
> I'm sure you've heard that when the federal court ordered the school district to desegregate, it adopted the 'freedom of choice' plan rather than merging the black and white schools. Only three families from Washington Carver Elementary chose the white school this fall, and two of them have been forced out already.
>
> You remember the Moores. After they filled out the form to put their girls in the white school, they were evicted from the land they had been sharecropping for a decade and had to move. The Leakes withdrew their application after their name was published in the Holly Bluff Reporter and Mr. Leake's boss at the bottling company threatened to fire him.

Amazingly, the Carters are hanging in despite shots being fired at the house a week before school began and the mother losing her job.

I really wish you were still here, Giddy. Now that nearly all the summer people have left, it feels more like what I suppose is the real Mississippi again—I mean, abandoned by the rest of the country. I'm not exactly angry at you for not returning, but it's hard to maintain a relationship when we're in these different worlds. Do the same things matter to both of us? To ask, 'How's school going?' seems completely absurd to me. Or: Have you met any interesting girls in the course of the anti-war work?

I'm spending time with the older women when they are quilting. They got me to join them, so I should say 'when we are quilting.' Though my stitching is poor, and I'm really just slowing them down. They're very patient with me.

On blustery days we sit for hours, quietly working, hearing the wind around the house and under the door, scarcely speaking. It seemed strange at first, but it's very centering. Sometimes one of them will read from the Bible. Sometimes we sing. Mostly, we are just silent or humming. Sometimes I think, what if I stayed here forever? What if I married one of the local people, made a life of this? In between the struggles and the violence, it's such a caring, loving community. A family. It's so calming. So real.

Gideon, I'm not with someone else now, but I may be. I am not seeing a scenario in which we get back together. I am sorry. But you've also come to understand this was how it was turning out, haven't you? I will always care for you.

Love,
Susan

Earlier that fall Lyndon Baines Johnson, the supposed anti-war candidate in the 1964 election, had crushed Barry Goldwater. But then he escalated the U.S. onslaught on Vietnam. Soon U.S. troop involvement rose from a few thousand Special Forces to hundreds of thousands of grunts. And Gideon grew more involved in the emerging struggle against the war.

39

San Quentin. Nine months since Gideon's first visit. He thought about what they'd learned of Kareem's family history, about the horrors that had destroyed Kareem's grandfather Joshua, and their impact on Joshua's young son Jason, Kareem's father. Much of the story still needed to be filled in.

Gideon had visited the prison several times now and thought he knew what to expect. But this time he was told at the sallyport it would be a non-contact visit. He was directed to a new visiting area. There he opened a metal door with a small window in it, and went into a tiny room, a booth really, with padded walls all around. Padding on the door, too.

Set in the wall before him was a plexiglass window, about two feet by a foot and a half, that looked into a similar booth where Kareem waited. The plexiglass plate prevented any contact between prisoner and visitor.

Kareem's face was bruised and his forehead swollen, and he was shackled again. Gideon lifted a hand to wave hello and sat down, putting his coffee on the shelf under the window. They would not be sharing popcorn this visit.

The booth was small and overheated. If he stretched his arms out, he could easily touch both walls. To the left of the window, a telephone handset hung on a hook; its metal-sheathed cord went into the wall. He lifted his phone and Kareem lifted one on the other side.

"Hey, how are you doing, Kareem?"

"I'm fine. How are you?"

The sound was good, but this was weird.

"What's all this about, Kareem? You don't seem in A-1 shape."

"Fight in the yard," Kareem said. "Guards knocked me around too. After, they moved me from East Block to the Adjustment Center. No contact visits til I get out of there."

"That's terrible. How long will it be?"

"Dunno."

"How'd that happen? What's the story?"

"No story. One of the Mexicans was dissing a brother. I jumped him. The guards waded in before everyone got into it and hauled me off. Threw out all my stuff from my cell, I think, and put me down in the Adjustment Center."

"What's that like?"

"It ain't Caesars Palace. Nothing in the cells, and we're locked in twenty-three hours a day. Showers once a week."

"That sounds awful. "

Gideon thought about where this conversation should go.

"Kareem, I didn't have anything all that special to report or anything. Just felt like seeing you." He sipped his coffee, suddenly feeling that even this made him seem privileged. And of course he was. He was free.

"Look, tell me more about what happened, how it got started."

"Naw, don't matter."

"Really, I want to understand how it happened. I care about it."

Kareem was silent. So was Gideon. He waited and looked at Kareem.

Kareem shrugged. Then he spoke.

"Me and my man Jo-Jo was standing there talking, close to the other brothers. The Mexicans always stay in another part of the yard. Whites got their corner, too. One of the Mexs is coming out into the yard, and he walks right along next to us. Gives me a cold look. Then he turns away and makes this loud sniffing noise, through his nose, like he's saying we smell.

"Jo-Jo hears it too and he turn and say, 'What the fuck you sayin, mother?'

"The Mex slowly turns and says, 'You talking to me?' Like he thinks we're shit.

"I can see he ain't backin off, and when he opens his mouth again, I slam him first. He falls down, and Jo Jo stomps his legs.

"The guards are there, real fast, and they pull us off the Mex. The gun rail yells on his loudspeaker, 'Everyone down on the ground or I'll shoot. Don't nobody move.'"

Kareem sniffled his nose a little, and smiled.

"I guess the guards happen to be lookin right our way and saw it all. They pulled their sticks out soon as they dragged us inside. One of them cuffed me and started whacking. On Jo-Jo too. Then they took me down to the Adjustment Center and flung me in a cell."

Gideon thought about how to say what he wanted to say.

"Kareem, you know I'm on your side."

He paused, leaned closer to the window, looking right at Kareem.

"I hear you," said Kareem.

"If I'd a been there . . . Well, actually, if I'd been there I guess I would have been with the white guys, enjoying watching you colored people fuck each other up."

Kareem laughed.

"Let me say something about what I hear you telling me happened. I hear you jumping into something too fast, that maybe could have been avoided. The Mex got hurt. You got hurt. And you got stuck in the Adjustment Center. Is this a good outcome, a good result?"

"You don't understand, Gideon. You got to stand up right off, or they will mess with you. We have got to show these Mexicans they can't fuck with us."

"I get that," said Gideon. "But I'm not so sure there was really something to stand up to . . . Just listen to me," he said, holding up a hand. "Maybe the Mex had a cold . . . I'm serious; you sniffed just now and I didn't think you were dissing me. You were putting a lot into how you thought he was looking, but maybe he didn't mean a thing."

"Gideon, don't take this too hard. But you don't know what the fuck you talkin about. This ain't Harvard law school. Maybe I know more about the world in here than you do?"

Gideon flinched.

"Well, sure. But maybe I know about a more reasonable way to deal with it." As soon as he heard his own words, Gideon knew he sounded lame.

Kareem slowly shook his head, looking at Gideon with pity.

"I been through it, Gideon. You ain't. So you just don't know."

"Well . . ."

Gideon stopped. He looked away from Kareem, then he looked back.

"Okay. Maybe you're right. I don't really know. But it doesn't seem fair, does it? There's gotta be some other way to get through a day without things like this having to happen."

"That's the way it is."

Gideon thought.

"Is it that you want to hurt these guys? Are you looking for a chance to do that? Don't take offense, I just want to know."

"No. I don't give a shit about them. I just want to do my time, best I can, whatever time I got left. But we got no choice."

"Kareem, I'm acknowledging that I'm not the one who knows the answer. But have you thought about alternatives?"

"This is how it is. If I says to the Mex, 'Puleeze don't make that noise with you nose, it hurt my feelings terrible,' he gonna say, 'Fuck you, punk, and fuck you feelings.' They gonna think we're weak, and pile it on."

"I wonder if there isn't another way, something that isn't sounding like a punk and isn't slamming each other. Because the more violence there is, the more you suffer."

"I can take it."

What a narrow set of choices now constrained Kareem Jackson, so different from the hard choices his grandfather Joshua had confronted.

40

Gideon was on a stretch of Interstate 84 in southern Idaho, maybe one hundred miles north of the Great Salt Lake, and he stopped at a rest area for lunch. A small, paved area, surrounded by desert and mountains. Bleak. A few pitiful trees offered a pretense of shade to a pair of metal picnic tables. There was a waterless toilet. An animal-proof trash can. And a pay phone on a short metal pole.

It was hot and windless, and Gideon was the only one there. He had collected a lot of quarters, and used the phone to place another call to Cecil Price. After much less than a minute of silence, Price hung up and Gideon smiled.

He had picked up sandwiches and drinks that morning when he stopped for gas near Twin Falls, but had little appetite. He thought he ought to eat anyway, and read a newspaper he had also grabbed. Mostly local news and sports (of course).

Sports. Like the bread and circuses of the Romans. But inside the paper was a small National section and some syndicated columns on the editorial page. As usual, Gideon could not read the paper without anger, and letters to the editor popped into his head, the kind he had so often dispatched and seldom seen printed.

In the months following Kareem's execution, after Helen's departure, Gideon's lassitude had been interrupted regularly by outrage at national and international events, outrage which swelled with each passing day until he felt every news story and op-ed piece as a personal provocation. He would almost stumble into walls as he wandered from the bathroom in the morning, his face still half covered with shaving cream, distractedly seeking a yellow legal pad and a pencil— *Why the fuck can I never find a fucking pencil in this goddamn house?*—so he could begin jotting down a good phrase or the first line or two of a letter he'd already begun in his head.

On the resistance to the admission of a girl to formerly all-male Virginia Military Institute:

> *To the Editor:*
> *All too much attention has been paid to the pathetic efforts of this third-rate wannabe military high school to defend its brain-dead macho culture against the twentieth century . . .*

On the Clinton Administration's opposition to a treaty banning land mines:

> *Dear Editor:*
> *Each year, the millions of land mines left over from the wars of the last decade—many of them supplied by U.S. arms exporters—cause thousands of innocent children to be maimed or*

killed. How many amputee children, hobbling their lives away on crutches, will it take before . . .

On the Menendez brothers escaping the death penalty for slaying their parents:

Dear Editor:

Your correspondents are too ready to condemn the jury for sparing the lives of Lyle and Erik. Isn't it just possible that twelve jurors who actually heard the evidence might have made their decision in a more informed way than your dim-witted readers, who caught no more than a sound bite on the evening news in between reports of the storm that did not arrive and the outcome of the Podunk High football game?

Gideon had the sense not to send letters to the editor on this trip.

With an effort, he stifled his irritation and put away the newspaper, unwrapped his salami sandwich, popped open his soda. Then he took some maps and papers out of the canvas satchel he'd been using as his "at hand" bag. He stared at the printouts of the photos of Cecil Price he had found online. These included several taken around the time of the murders; one taken when Price emerged from prison after his four year stint, and another from eight years ago.

He looked at the map of the USA he had printed from the Altavista web site, showing with a thick purple line his overall route from the Columbia River Gorge to Philadelphia, Mississippi. He had written dates by his position on the map each night to show his progress. He put the map and the photos on the picnic table, and placed a rock on them as a paperweight. Then he found what he had been looking for, the manual for adjusting the sighting scope on the rifle.

He got the rifle and the scope from the pickup truck, and fixed the scope to the unloaded rifle. Absorbed in the instructions, Gideon only dimly heard another car stop. As he sighted through the scope on a small bird resting on the yellow flowers of a greasewood shrub, he was startled by a voice.

"Howdy."

Gideon looked up and saw an Idaho Highway Patrolman a few feet away, staring at him. He blanched.

"Whatcha got planned?" asked the patrolman.

"Umm, what?" said Gideon, suddenly tremulous. "What say?" his voice shaking.

"I mean, what are you planning with your rifle? Target shooting? Hunting?"

"Oh, uh, hunting," Gideon said, slowly responding out of his daze.

"This is a great state for it. What do you figure to hunt? Elk? Bear?"

Bear? Gideon didn't know whether you could hunt bear. Was this a trick question? He'd never hunted in his life. He hadn't planned for this kind of conversation. Idiot.

His delays in responding were making him look suspicious. But then he realized he did not have to say anything. He was a lawyer, and it came to him that you don't have to answer cops' questions. He just gave a very small nod, and looked down at his stuff.

"Maybe one of those little sage thrashers you were aiming at?" the officer joked. But he did not seem to be enjoying his own joke. He poured some coffee from a thermos bottle at the other picnic table. "Care for a cup?"

Maybe he wasn't a suspect after all. He wasn't sure. He need only calm down, and this chance encounter would end harmlessly.

"No, thanks. Just ate. Actually, I'm just leaving." Gideon pushed his papers together carelessly, not too quickly he hoped, and stuffed them into his bag. He folded the uneaten half of his sandwich back into its paper, and put that in, too. "So long," he said, without looking in the highway patrolman's direction.

Gideon walked at what he hoped was a measured pace to his pickup truck. Placing the bag on the seat, and the gun in the rack behind the bench seat, he started the engine, and slowly drove out of the rest area and back onto the interstate.

I was acting strange, he thought, but it doesn't matter. I did nothing unlawful. Still, maybe it would be a good idea to disappear before the cop can catch up and make a note of my license number.

Just ahead, a state road crossed under the interstate and there was a cloverleaf. Exiting, Gideon turned right and continued on. After a few moments he was out of sight of the freeway. He punched the accelerator, zooming up to ninety miles per hour in a few seconds, racing around the road's broad curves in this desolate landscape for another few minutes. OK, that's enough, he eased off. He came to a halt by the side of the road. His hands were shaking.

If he couldn't even encounter a cop without panicking, how was he going to handle Mississippi and Cecil Price? Maybe he needed more time to think. But he was already thinking too much, almost trying to talk himself out of it.

He looked down at his trembling hands, turned them palm up. He thought of the prison guard shoving a broom into Kareem's chest to force out the remaining cyanide gas after they had turned him into a thing. He thought of Andy Goodman and Mickey Schwerner and James Chaney. Of talking to their parents.

He knew what he needed to do. But he could go more slowly. At this rate, he would be in Mississippi in three days. A little more time would do no harm. What's the hurry? I need to calm down.

He would get off the interstate, take an extra week to get there if necessary. Give himself time to work out how he was going to do it, time to prepare himself for anything that might happen. He couldn't let himself be surprised again.

He looked at a map. Now he was on Idaho Highway 81. A small town, Palma, lay ten miles south. From there, it appeared he could actually go west for a while on another two-lane state road, then north to hook up with the interstate again, and perhaps find another route east. A slower one. He would see where things would lead him. Maybe he'd head into southern Illinois, where Susan had ended up, teaching at the university in Springfield.

The last time Gideon recalled being in touch with her was in 1979, when he became a partner at the firm. He'd scribbled a note on one of the cards the firm sent out, announcing new partners. She wrote back to congratulate him, and then a few months later he received an announcement when her son was born. Otherwise, they had been out of touch for nearly twenty years.

* * *

Officer Phillip Vanderson finished his coffee and looked at the picnic table from whence the bald headed man had disappeared. Fled, really. When you were a cop, you got used to people looking guilty every time you looked at them. Hard to tell, though, if it meant anything in particular. You so seldom dealt with the real criminal element out here, mostly just speeders. Still, the man's reaction had been out of the ordinary. This man must be up to no good, but there was nothing specific he could pin on him.

Vanderson walked over to the other picnic table, and saw that the man had dropped some stuff on the ground. A picture of a middle-aged man, and another of what looked like the same man when he was younger. Computer print-out kind of thing, not real photos.

Maybe he'd see if he could catch up with the man, tell him he'd left these behind. See if he got more of a sense of the guy. The man had been driving a blue Chevy pickup with an Oregon plate. Had a three, four minute head start now, but Vanderson thought maybe he could catch up in fifteen, twenty minutes if he stepped on it. Everyone drove over the speed limit out here, so he'd have a reason to question the man further, even to search the pickup truck if he wanted to arrest him.

After thirty minutes zooming east on I-84 at ninety, then one hundred miles per hour, Vanderson had not caught sight of the blue pickup. He continued for another fifteen minutes, still saw nothing.

The truck's disappearance troubled him. He should have caught up with it by now. Maybe not, if the driver had really been blazing. But people usually slow down for a while after they encounter the highway patrol, and a ten or fifteen mile-per-hour edge should have caught him up with baldy by now.

Of course, the driver could have been headed for somewhere nearby. But that seemed unlikely. Why have lunch in a bleak rest stop if he were close to his destination?

Where did he go, then?

There was no evidence of wrongdoing. No basis for transmitting an alarm to other highway patrolmen to be on the lookout. But the man had something to conceal. Vanderson's instincts told him that baldy had exited the road because of their encounter. He stuck the photos in the glove compartment, then resumed his patrol, going back the other way. He wondered who the man in the photos was.

When Vanderson got back to the station, he checked the All Points Bulletins and the BOLOs (Be On the Look Out). Even the FBI's Most Wanted, on the off chance. Nothing. With nothing but intuition, there was no basis for initiating anything.

No BOLO for baldy.

41

You need to start getting up, for Jason's sake," Mama had told her in January. Fannie Jo did. But when the white men knocked her to the ground and fell upon her, something in her spine had cracked. Now when she walked, her back throbbed, and pains shot down her legs, and Fannie Jo could not lift Jason into her arms.

Winter was a slow season on Mama and Uncle Benjamin's farm, so there was time for Fannie Jo to rest and for Mama to try to take care of her. But Fannie Jo didn't want to be taken care of.

She stood by the kitchen window that faced the shed and the barn, and she thought about her son. He was afraid around other children, and he'd stopped talking. Some nights he wet his bed. It was like he was two, again, not six years old. Sometimes they would be wakened by the boy's nightmares and screams.

"You be missing your daddy, ain't you?" Fannie Jo asked him quietly one afternoon.

"When he comin' back, ma?" Jason asked.

"He ain't comin' back, Jason, baby. You know that." She took him onto her lap, and suppressed a gasp, as pain shot through her back. "He ain't coming back cause he with the Lord Jesus now."

Fannie Jo was frightened by Jason's question, and her eyes filled. "You know he dead, Jason. I be missing him, too, honey."

Jason said nothing, but his eyes were twitching and squinching, and his mouth twisted into a grimace. She tried to press him to her, but he ran away.

That spring, when Jason turned six, Fannie Jo started him at the primary school for colored children. One of the older boys, Willie Marlin, had told the others, "He make funny faces all the time cause he got crazy when the white peoples kilt his daddy."

One day when Jason returned home, Mama and Fannie Jo were shocked to see his clothes stained with blood.

"What happen?" Mama asked quickly. "Who done this?"

"They was saying things about daddy," Jason said. Then, in a puzzled tone, "I done beat up Willie Marlin."

"What you mean, boy?" Mama asked. She began to realize the blood was not all his.

From his halting words, they pieced together the story. During recess, a group of boys made a ring around Jason. Willie had led them as they chanted:

Jason, Jason, crazy mad,
Cause the white men roast his dad.

Jason had hung his head as they surrounded him, but when he heard the chant, and Willie's high-pitched laugh, he flung himself upon the boy.

"Don't you dare hit me," the bigger boy said, shoving Jason down, and then jabbing him on the side of the head. But Jason sprang back up, and a ferocious explosion of butting, scratching and punching burst from Jason, and his unexpected rage overwhelmed the bigger boy. They rolled over each other on the ground. Then Jason was on top, pummeling Willie's bleeding face until a teacher pulled him off. By that time, the boy's nose was bloodied and bent. One of his eyes was badly swollen, and there was blood in the white.

Mama held out her arms to Jason and pulled him toward her, but he struggled free. When Fannie Jo reached painfully for him, Jason ran and hid in the barn.

"Fannie Jo, you got to do something about that boy, you know what I'm saying?"

"I don't know what to do Mama. I got no strength left inside, no strength to deal with Jason." She stopped, then whispered, "I ain't fit to mother him no more."

Mama hugged Fannie Jo to her. "Yes, you is," Mama said. "Jesus give you this cross to carry, and he make you strong enough to bear it. You just keep trying. That all we can do. The Lord will make you get better."

"I can't stop thinking on the night of the burning, Mama."

She looked down in shame. "When I'm trying to do my work, it's like I'm there and seeing the fire while they keep doing it to me, over and over and over."

Mama held Fannie Jo again, holding back her own tears.

She ain't the same girl, Mama thought. *Course she ain't.* Fannie Jo seemed a woman just barely alive. *She act like she jes as old as me.*

* * *

One Saturday morning in late March, they went into Greenwood to shop for staples, cloth and parts for the plow. The adults sat on the board in front and Jason was in the back of the wagon by himself.

Uncle Benjamin and Mama helped Fannie Jo down from the wagon, then she and Mama and Jason went into the general store while Benjamin went on to the farm supply store.

Mama waited as the whites were served. Meanwhile Fannie Jo rested on a small barrel off to the side. Jason stayed near her, trembling as he looked sidelong at the white people. Finally, Mama purchased the large bags of salt, rice and flour they'd come for. She was careful to put the money on the counter, rather than try to put it directly into the hand of the storeowner, because most of the white storekeepers would not want to touch a colored person's hand.

Mama was carrying the flour and dragging a great bag of rice along the floor. Fannie Jo carried nothing but she smiled, looking down on her son struggling to manage the fifteen pound bag of salt he held to his chest.

As they emerged from the store, Fannie Jo looked around, then staggered back. Walking toward them, only a few feet away, was one of the men who had raped her.

The man was speaking to a thin, pale-looking woman in her early thirties, evidently his wife. Three small boys were with them. The man didn't notice Fannie Jo until he and the woman were abreast of them. Then his glance fell on her. For a moment he seemed confused, then contempt seemed to blaze from him as he moved past.

Like a rabbit surprised by a weasel, Fannie Jo could not turn her eyes from the white man's. She froze in terror, collapsed against Mama, and slid to the ground. Mama dropped to her knees by Fannie Jo, patting her checks.

"Fannie Jo! Fannie Jo! What is it?" said Mama. Fannie Jo's limbs began twitching. "Oh Lord, Fannie Jo, wake up."

Mama cradled Fannie Jo's head in her lap and fanned her face with her hat. "What the matter, Fannie Jo? Jason, boy, go run down to the farm store," said Mama, "go get your uncle right quick."

The boy shot down the sidewalk, bumping heedless into people before him, white or black. On the next block, he came up behind the white man. This was the man who had hurt his ma.

Jason dashed into the street, fleeing, dodging cars and horse-drawn wagons. Fear had emptied his mind and he forgot where he was going.

He saw his uncle loading their wagon.

"Uncle Ben, it's ma, it's ma!" he shrieked. "Grandma say come right away. Come right away!"

When they returned, Fannie Jo was lying on a bench inside the store, where the store owner Mr. Meckle had carried her so she could rest easier.

Mama held Fannie Jo to her, her eyes filling with tears.

Fannie Jo couldn't or wouldn't rise, and Mr. Meckle carried her to the wagon with the help of some colored people in the store. Mama and Jason sat in the back with her. Fannie Jo didn't recognize Jason or Uncle Benjamin, and would only look at Mama.

Back at the farm, they put Fannie Jo to bed, and she seemed to sleep.

Mama saw that Jason was terrified. She reached out to him.

"One of . . . One of . . . One of those white men," Jason stammered. "One of them that kilt . . . that . . ."

"Don't talk no more, love," said Mama. "You don't got to say no more, I know." Jason fled.

In the morning Fannie Jo was no better. She hummed little songs to herself, and seemed to think she was eleven years old. On Monday, they brought her to the state hospital.

Fannie Jo spent three months in the hospital. After six rounds of electric shock therapy, she knew who she was again. They gave her pills to take when she got home. But she was lethargic and barely able to care for herself. They said it was probably better if she didn't go into town anymore, and she shouldn't try to do too much.

While Fannie Jo was in hospital, Mama and Uncle Benjamin tried to care for Jason. But they couldn't handle him. He fought at school. He ran into the fields or the woods after eating. He wouldn't mind, no matter how often Benjamin caught him for a whipping, and he scarcely spoke. He shoved Mama to escape her attempts to hug him.

When Fannie Jo returned, thin and empty, she still forgot who she was at times. When her mind cleared, she trembled, distraught, at the sight of Jason.

Mama tried to care for the two of them, but she felt ten years older. For weeks at a time, Fannie Jo mostly stayed in bed. Mama sat by her again, helpless.

Late one night, Mama hobbled into the kitchen, and dropped into a chair at the table. Her brother was banking the fire in the big stove for the night.

"Benjamin," she said, "I caint do nothin' for my baby. Or for the boy. They be hurtin', hurtin', hurtin', and I don't see no way for to make them be right. If only the Lord would help. I been prayin' to Jesus for help, but it ain't come. What we goin' to do, Benjamin?"

Her brother sat by her and put his hand on her shoulder.

"We just got to do what we got to do. The Lord's gonna give us what we need to keep goin', Ellie Lou. We caint make it right no more, no one can."

Mama leaned against her brother and let the tears well up and spill onto her cheeks.

"I could go to Jesus right now if he would take me. What I got ain't enough. It ain't enough to make Fannie Jo and Jason right no more."

She dried her tears on her apron, hung it up and went to bed.

More weeks passed. Mama came to feel it would be better for Fannie Jo to be out of Greenwood, out of Mississippi, for good. She persuaded Fannie Jo's married sister in Memphis to take her in. But, with their own four children, they could not take Jason, too. Taking care of Fannie Jo would be like having two more children around, Grace had said. They couldn't do Jason as well.

After his mother left, Jason became more unruly. Uncle Benjamin, who was sixty-eight, felt his strength draining. Finally, they had to give up. "Maybe he do best if he be away from this place, too," Mama said, "with someone stronger enough."

"Who that be?" Benjamin asked. They had written or spoken with various brothers and sisters and nieces, and to Joshua's family. But none was able to take on another child. None but one of their brothers, Jason's great uncle Seth Barnes, in southwest Mississippi.

"You still think Jason be right with Seth?" Benjamin asked.

"Right with Seth? No. But no one else will take the boy."

"I 'most rather keep him with us than give him to Seth," Benjamin said.

"Me too. But it jes be a matter of time before we got to give him for someone else to raise," Mama said. "We ain't strong enough no more to hold that boy down. So it be now or it be a little while. And we got no better pick to pick."

42

Seth Barnes was sixty years old. Born in 1888, after the violent overthrow of Reconstruction by Ku Klux Klan terrorism, his childhood spanned the early years of segregation, beginning with the times when colored people were first ejected from the spaces that were to be reserved for whites—train cars, coaches, schools, hospitals, eating places, hotels, sidewalks, parks—entire neighborhoods and towns sometimes—through the years of terror around the turn of the new century, when an orgy of near daily lynchings—torture-murders, it would be more accurate to say—swept the South.

Seth had lived through the Great War, when he had been allowed to serve only as a porter in the army in France, and into the Great Depression which had started early in the South, in the 1920s, with the collapse of cotton prices.

Seth lived through a second world war in which farming finally recovered, and through more killings of colored soldiers who returned from the war determined to be treated like men. Mean times and hungry times. Times of humiliation. Times of violence. Times that seemed not far from slavery. And times when colored men fought back.

The land Seth farmed had been in the family since their father, Moses Barnes, bought it in 1874. Moses was born a slave right there in Amite County some time in the 1850s. He did not know what year. After Emancipation, the Freedman's Bureau offered land for sale under the Southern Homestead Act, and Moses struggled for six years to scrape together money to buy forty acres. In later years he added more land, patch by small field, until eventually he owned 125 acres.

Moses' farm lay in a community of former slaves who survived the years after the Civil War, when they had nearly been re-enslaved under the Black Codes. They had known that to be free, they needed their own land. They passed that determination to their children.

Getting the land had been a struggle. Holding the land had been harder. Seth had seen the many ways white men could steal land from Negro owners.

A cousin of Seth's had a small farm in Pike County, and needed a loan for seed. The banks would not lend to him because he was colored. So he got the loan direct from the agricultural supply man, who gave him the seed. But the man made him put up the farm as collateral. Seth's cousin missed one $12 payment, and the supply man foreclosed and took the whole farm.

Another Negro farmer had a loan to buy a team of mules. Come time to make the last payment on the loan, the white man refused to take the money, and foreclosed instead. The farmer was warned going to law would mean the rope. He and his family yielded the land and fled North.

Oftentimes, one family farmed the land, but title was held in common by dozens of descendants because the original owner left no will. No money for lawyers and wills, but the land was farmed, the taxes paid, year in, year out.

A white man with a little money and a lawyer would track down one of the owners, buy his interest, then get a judge to put the entire farm up for a partition sale. The other colored owners had no cash money, so the farm would fall into white hands for next to nothing.

Then there was simply killing.

Seth had known more than one Negro who'd been lynched for looking like he was doing too well. A white man would pick a fight when the Negro came in to sell his cotton, and the Negro was arrested. A mob would take him from the cell, batter and hang him. After the family ran for their lives, the deputy sheriff would hold a sale to a white man in the lynch mob.

*   *   *

Moses and his descendants held onto their land. Seth himself had been well known in his youth among both whites and coloreds in Amite county as a wild nigger who went around armed and whom it was risky to fool with. Few knew it, but Seth Barnes had killed to defend this land. A white man had, in impudent overconfidence, come out by himself one night to threaten Seth. His body had quietly joined the many black bodies that over the years had been put into the West Fork of the Amite River.

When Jason Jackson went to live with his great uncle Seth in 1948, at the age of seven, Seth had already outlived three wives, and begotten fourteen children. Most of the ones who survived were girls, and the sons had either gone north to Ohio or Illinois in the 1930s or not returned to the farm after the Second World War. The war years had been good years for farming, though, and he had put by enough to feel safe. He had lived by himself on the farm for many years.

When Uncle Benjamin delivered Jason to Moses Farm, Jason wore a sullen face.

"'Lo, Seth," said Benjamin. "You got my letter 'bout the boy?"

Seth nodded, looking Jason up and down. He saw a thin boy with a down-turned mouth and bruises under his left eye, looking at the ground.

"He need a firm hand," Benjamin said. "But not too hard."

"I raised nine that lived. Don't need no advice, Ben. I kin raise him too. Have you eaten? Come in and have something."

Seth led them into the kitchen. He put plates down, put out chicken, black-eyed peas, okra, creamed corn. He cut the slices of bread they used instead of forks. No one spoke while they ate.

When they were through, Seth said his first words to Jason.

"Boy, you clear this table and clean up."

Seth and Benjamin put on their jackets, and went onto the porch to sit and smoke, watch the evening begin to darken into night.

"Seth, this boy been through a lot."

"Ain't we all?"

The old anger rose up in Benjamin. In fifty years he'd never been able to talk sense to Seth.

"We all been through what we all been through, Seth. But he been through more. You know what happened with his pa. Them white men made this boy look when they done it. That ain't nothing you or me seen with our own eyes. Made him look when they done what they done to his Momma, too. Now she broken."

"They're dogs, they ain't men," said Seth, with simmering rage. "They worse than dogs, the devil made them. If Joshua'd been my son, there'd be white bodies rottin' in the Yazoo by now. Maybe jes pieces of some of 'em."

The two men sat silently. The first stars came out.

Benjamin seethed. All this talk about what he'd do to the whites. We got no choice but to put up with what they does to us.

Same old fight, agin and agin. But that ain't what we got to talk about now.

"Don't know how to say this right," Benjamin said. "The boy ain't like he used to be no more. Wild. But that ain't all. Don't want no touch, neither, wouldn't let your sister Ellie Lou hug him no more. Don't want to be around people. Whipping don't get him to mind. Just don't know what to do with him." Benjamin paused. "He ain't right with folks. He ain't right in his head, and the rod ain't gonna cure him."

"Why you come here talking this shit to me, Ben? You know what I gonna say. We colored people don't need no damn hugging. We need to be hard, if we gonna hold what we got against the white devils. *He* got to get hard so some day he can come back and find the men who did it. Then kill them."

"Seth, he ain't even seven year old yet. He don't need that now."

"He need it just like we needed it, Ben! How else we made it? What our pa done to us, so's we made it."

"What our pa done?" said Benjamin. "You was one of the little ones, Seth. You don't remember things he done. The times I had to fight him off from beating Ellie Lou and Jamie half way to death. The way he drove us away from him. The way he broke Ma. That ain't the way for raising Jason."

Same old fight. Benjamin had seen the beginning and the end. As the oldest, he'd known the old man's love when he was still proud of his first born son. Later he'd seen how his father had come to love being the one who commanded the lash. Benjamin had had his mother's loving, before Moses' hunger for land and Moses' taunts and Moses' babies wore her to death. Before she became as hard as Moses himself. But Seth had come at the end, had made himself tough enough to take it. Seth had taken pride in being hard.

Seth also knew they were repeating themselves.

"Ben, I know what you be thinking, but I caint raise him your way. You want to take him back with you, you take him back. I won't be angry. We got no soft life living next to these white men, these white dogs. If we be soft, they tear us to pieces and eat us up. May be it be my boys don't care about me no more. May be they hate me. But they hard men now, and they be alive. The white men ain't kilt them. If I raise this boy right, he be tough enough to live, too. "

"Don't know if jes living is enough," Benjamin said. The sky had darkened over the fields while they spoke, and the first few stars glimmered. "Ellie Lou and I can't do no more with Jason. And you the only one left who can do it. You got to take him, Seth. Think on what I done told you."

* * *

Jason had slipped outdoors after he'd cleaned the dinner dishes, and wasn't there to say goodbye when Uncle Benjamin left. He looked about the farm, tried to find places where no one could see him when he went to be by himself. He sat under some bushes by the edge of a field for a long time, losing himself, gazing at the patterns of the field and the stars. It was long dark when he got back to the house.

Seth was waiting with a switch in his hand.

"Boy, did I say you could go way without saying goodbye to your uncle? You ask before you run off, you hear? You do what you're told, and you don't go 'less you told you can. You show respect." Seth paused. "I don't hear you saying, 'Yessir.' You are gonna learn right now to be mannerly."

Seth grabbed the boy by the scruff of the neck, and leaned him over one of the big chairs. He pulled Jason's pants down, picked up the switch, and lashed it across his buttocks.

Jason was stunned by the first blow. He had been spanked by his mother and father, and hard, too. But never lashed with the thin peeled branch that was like a whip, whose every stroke would raise a long, red welt. He shuddered at the blow, and his knees gave. He tried to find the strength to escape as Seth brought it down again, but this angered Seth the more.

"Don't you dare try to git away when I am learning you, boy!"

Seth's arms were strong, and he gave four more strokes. When he stopped, he could hear Jason crying and gasping for breath, and a little smile flitted across Seth's face.

"Now pull up your pants, and I'm gonna show you where you sleep."

Jason did as he was told, but he could barely walk, and Seth carried him upstairs.

The bedroom was large, and Seth's big double bed and a lot of old, heavy furniture filled most of the room. But to one side, there was a small bed with a mattress filled with old collapsed feathers. It smelled funny, but Jason couldn't see anything very clearly through the blur of his tears. He lay down on the bed, and Seth left him.

I'll run away, he thought, *I got to run away.* But the thought of what Uncle Seth would do if he were caught filled Jason with terror. After a while he began to doze through the pain, though it woke him almost immediately. He was afraid to fall asleep in the same room with Uncle Seth. Remembering his mother, and Uncle Benjamin, and Mama, he trembled and silently cried.

Finally he dropped off for the night. After what seemed only a moment, it was morning, and Seth was standing before him, shaking him awake.

"Git up now," said Seth. "You gonna live. You just got to learn to act right. Now git dressed and come down." Seth's voice seemed a shade less mean to Jason this morning.

Uncle Benjamin had brought a sack with Jason's clothing, and Seth had brought it into the room and put Jason's things into an old bureau. Uncle Seth didn't seem angry anymore, but Jason was wary.

Seth had put two plates out, and was loading one of them with eggs fried in a lot of grease, and with sausage and grits. Jason's insides were still quivering, but he was hungry too.

"You sit on the one with the cushion," Seth said, pointing to the chair closer to the big stove, and setting down the plate. Jason sat and looked at the food, but didn't start to eat right away. He looked sideways across at Uncle Seth, to try to figure out what he was supposed to do, how far the kindness of the cushion was supposed to extend. He tried to smile at Uncle Seth.

Seth put his own plate down, poured himself coffee, and put a pitcher of milk on the table. Jason looked up at Seth, and across at the pitcher and hesitated.

"You pour for yourself," said Seth, "I ain't gonna serve you."

Uncle Seth's tone was harsh, but not angry. Jason tried to keep the trembling in his arms from showing. His bottom hurt and he was tired. Uncle Seth did not say grace over the food, like ma used to. He began eating.

"That wasn't nothing," said Seth. "My daddy, now, he would lay into me for ten, twenty minutes at a time. Sticks, too. Didn't know what for most the time. But I learned to obey. You act right, and you won't get beat too often." Jason tried to nod understandingly.

Jason watched Uncle Seth for signs of his mood. As soon as they finished eating, Jason leapt up to put the dishes into the big bucket, found the big kettle with the hot water, and poured some in, just like he'd seem his ma do, and washed them up.

He heard a soft grunt, apparently of approval, from Seth. After breakfast, Seth told Jason what his chores were, and how Seth wanted them done.

Jason couldn't move quickly because of the pain of his bottom and his legs from the thrashing, and it took him a long time to clean the chicken runs. He couldn't figure out where to put the mess, afterward.

"Can't you even sweep chicken shit out of a chicken coop, boy? Didn't your momma and pa learn you nothin'?" Jason's face got hot, but he looked down, choking back anger at the insult to his parents. He wanted to defend them, but he felt shamed, and he was afraid to defy Uncle Seth.

When it came time for dinner, at mid-day, Seth called him into the kitchen.

"Look at the job you did on the dishes," Seth said. "They all greasy. Do them again. You need to use hotter water."

He poured much more from the kettle into the dish tub, and stood over while Jason tried again with the dark soap. Jason flinched when he cautiously put his hands into the hot water, and Seth laughed.

"You got to be tougher than that, boy." He grabbed Jason's hands, and plunged them into the steaming water, and Jason screamed.

"Didn't hurt me any," Seth said, finally letting go of Jason. "How you gonna learn to take care of yourself if you so tender?" Seth taunted. "You ain't no baby no more."

Jason wiped the tears from his eyes, and tried to quiet his whimpering. Seth turned to stir the food on the stove, and Jason gingerly touched the hot water again with the dish rag, grabbing a plate quickly through the heat, and trying to wash it carefully.

After the dinner plates and cups, he reached for the big bowl that had held last night's creamed corn. The bowl was burning hot from sitting in the water, and heavy and slippery. Jason's grasp wasn't firm enough. The bowl slipped from his fingers and crashed, breaking into several pieces and spilling hot water on the floor.

"You fool boy! You damn fool!" Seth cried. "Had that bowl for twenty-five years, from my mother, and now you done broke it."

Seth yanked Jason away from the tub of dishes, "God damn you," delivering a hard, open-handed smack on the side of Jason's head, "Can't do anything right." Jason slipped on the wet floor and slithered into one of the legs of the big kitchen table.

Uncle Seth reached, shaking with rage, pulled Jason up by the arm and smacked him twice, then pushed him back down onto the floor. Jason tried to crawl away, but Seth yelled, "Where you think you goin'? You got to clean up that mess before we have dinner. You think it gonna clean itself up? You think I'm gonna clean up your messes?"

When the water and the crockery shards were cleared, Jason wanted to crawl off by himself. But Uncle Seth told him, "Come back here. We ain't gonna waste all this good food because you made a mess. You gonna finish everything on your plate."

Uncle Seth banged a plate down in front of Jason. Jason's ear hurt where Seth had smacked him, and snot and blood were dripping from his nose. He didn't know whether Seth would hit him for wiping it off on his shirt, so he did it quietly. His stomach was churning, and when he tried to swallow, he thought he was going to throw up. He forced the food down, then asked Uncle Seth if he could be excused.

Jason went to the outhouse and vomited. He stayed on his knees, too exhausted to move.

He pumped cold water from the pump outside by the kitchen and washed off his face, but he couldn't entirely get rid of the taste and smell of puke. It was cold outside, and he was wet, but he did not want to go in. He knew there was no place he could be by himself. After a time, he made himself go inside.

He went up to the room he shared with Uncle Seth. There was a nightshirt on the bed, which Seth had told him to use. Jason changed into it and lay down. He closed his eyes to little slits, to make believe he was sleeping while he watched. He worried that Seth might come in and hit him while he was asleep.

It was to happen other times, when Seth had been drinking.

Jason wanted to stay awake until after Seth had come up and gone to sleep, when it would be safe. He was startled each time he heard the floorboards downstairs creaking, as Uncle Seth moved about. But Seth did not come, and eventually Jason fell asleep in spite of himself.

So ended Jason's first full day at Moses Farm. He would stay with Uncle Seth until he left, alone, at fourteen years of age.

43

State Highway 81 became Main Street as Gideon entered Palma, Pop. 171. Its inhabitants must be scattered thinly, he thought, because it appeared the center of town was only two or three streets and a handful of stores.

There was a luncheonette that looked like the 1950s—big old Coke signs above the windows, with a few rusty patches; booths with puffy red upholstery visible through the big windows.

Gideon thought he ought to be hungry after his interrupted lunch at the rest area, and he parked alongside the store. He stepped out of the pickup's feeble air-conditioning and felt the dry but intense summer heat of southern Idaho. He went into the luncheonette and was assailed by cold air.

Gideon sat on one of the spinning stools at the counter. It had a little frame of a seat back, and Gideon sagged back against it. He arched his back to relieve the stiffness from hours of sitting and driving.

His confidence was returning. True, he had made himself conspicuous by taking out the rifle and the scope in a public place. That was foolish.

But he extricated himself before the cop pressed him further, boldly deciding to leave despite the awkwardness of the situation. Better awkwardness than giving more confused answers or having his ID checked!

It was half past one and Gideon was the only customer. The mirror across from where he sat, on the other side of the aisle behind the counter, reflected Gideon's image. His eyes were piercing and alert, and the efforts he had made to appear nondescript were belied by the intensity of his gaze.

A white apron interrupted Gideon's view of himself, and he looked up to see the waitress. Lisa, as her plastic badge identified her, was a brunette in her mid-thirties with a big chest. She handed Gideon a menu, then leaned across the counter to point out the items that were not being offered today. A generous display of cleavage loomed, and Gideon imagined himself unbuttoning her blouse.

After two or three seconds he gave himself a mental shake. Even as he snapped back to reality he felt his groin quiver. The waitress was looking at him expectantly. What had she said? *You ready to order?* He looked up from her breasts and felt himself blush. It had been some time since he had felt the pull of sexual attraction.

"Do you need another minute or two to decide what you want?" she asked.

"No, I know what I want . . . the tuna on white toast with some fries, and a diet Coke. Tomato no lettuce. Just a little mayo."

"Comin' up," she responded, smiling broadly as she jotted the order on a little green pad. She tore out the page and pushed it into the wheel in front of the kitchen, returned a moment later with Gideon's soda. As she moved away, there was now a slight, self-conscious saunter to her movements. She seemed to have recognized that he was looking hungrily in her direction, and not for want of fries.

His attraction to the waitress confused him—he didn't need to make new friends on this trip—but he'd be gone in fifteen minutes, and it didn't matter. It was just how close she had put herself to him. It had been a while.

"Don't get many visitors this time of year," she said, returning. She was leaning against the cooler, resting her weight back on her arms behind her in a way that emphasized her bust. "Here on business?"

"Just passing through," Gideon said. Maybe he had to say something more. "Thought I'd get off the Interstate for a while, slow down." Gideon didn't want to draw attention to himself, but he also did not want to seem mysterious.

"This is a good place to pass through," she said. "Maybe I'm passing through myself and I didn't know it 'til now. Might have more in common than what you were thinking," she said, raising her eyebrows.

Gideon said nothing about what he was thinking, and tried to tamp down his sexual calculations.

"My name's Lisa," she said, touching her name tag in a way that moved her breast a little. "What's yours?"

What is it again? "Jim," he said. "Jim Cargill." *Dammit, why didn't I just give another name?*

Ding! went a bell. Gideon's sandwich appeared on the shelf between the kitchen and the counter area.

Lisa turned and got Gideon's plate, and put it down before him. She got ketchup for his fries. Put it down with deliberation. Gideon ate, while they looked at each other, without speaking. When Gideon had finished nearly half the sandwich he spoke without having planned to.

"Listen, can I take you some place for a beer? Seems slow here."

"Sure. Time for my lunch break."

Gideon had another bite of his sandwich, looked at the check next to the plate, and put down some money. She picked it up, carried it to the register at the end of the row, rang him up, and brought his change, not looking at him. She cleared his place, and Gideon left the change for the tip. She came back and picked it up. Went round to the door to the kitchen, pushed it open a crack.

"Lee, I'm taking my break now. Back around two forty five." She walked straight out the door without looking in Gideon's direction. He followed. She was standing at the sidewalk, looking outward, guarded, Gideon thought. She turned to him, and he could see wariness in her eyes next to the boldness.

"There's a seven-eleven down this way," she said, leading them. "People sometimes sit at the picnic table outside and drink their beer."

They walked that way until the sidewalk gave out a half block away.

"Actually," Gideon said, "I might stay overnight. Is there a hotel or something you'd recommend?"

"Palma look like the kind of place that has hotels?" she asked.

"Look," he said, touching her arm lightly, "Actually, I just want to sleep with you."

"That was fast, but that's okay," she said, then laughed. "I want you too, case you didn't notice. I got a room in what used to be a hotel long time ago. You come and have a beer with me there."

He walked next to her around the corner and down the next street, past a dry goods store and the seven-eleven, past a bar on the corner. They were both getting sweaty from the heat and Gideon thought he could detect her scent.

Across the next street stood a two story building from early in the century. You could see where it used to say "Palma City Hotel" in paint on the side on the building, in a big old-time font, but the letters had faded nearly entirely. Next door was a snowmobile dealership.

They crossed over, still silent, went through the glass doors, past what had been the desk and up the stairs to the second floor. He rested his hand on the small of her back as she unlocked the door to her room, felt her press backward to confirm the touch.

He sat down on the edge of the bed, and pushed his shoes off as she turned on the air conditioner in the window and then went to the bathroom. When she came out, she took two beers out of a small fridge next to the bathroom door and opened them. Gideon caught a glimpse of himself in a mirror on the wall. He looked strange to himself, not just the baldness. He realized he had devised no made-up identity to go with his alias.

He had not anticipated a meeting in which he would present himself, and was not sure what to say, what persona to adopt or reveal. He felt, for some reason he could not say, that he wanted to be himself in this encounter, however brief it was. But he was no longer sure who that was: The recently-unmarried husband, ready to score a little nookie? The man at sea, seeking the comfort of imaginary intimacy with a stranger? Or the prospective killer, asserting his reawakened manhood with a tramp? Gideon didn't like any of these.

"Come over here," he said. "I want to hold you for a little while, and we can get used to each other and see how we feel. See what we want."

She put the beers on the end table and turned to Gideon.

"I know what I want," she said. "I just want you to screw me. You don't need to take care of me special like. It's okay. I can take care of myself. I've been doing that for a long time, and I ain't so delicate I need some guy who likes my ketchup delivery style or my tits treating me like I'm breakable."

She sat next to Gideon. He leaned back on the bed and pulled her toward him. She lay on him, her head on his shoulder, her hair in his face. Her legs opened a little so Gideon's thigh was between them. He felt her heat and his own.

Gideon stroked her back lightly, touched the skin of her arms and under the short sleeves. Put his arms inside hers, and held the sides of her chest, then stopped. He let his breath all the way out. Inhaled a little, feeling his chest raise her body a little, then let it down again. Let his breath stay down, and felt her breathe in and out. She turned and put her tongue into his ear, and Gideon felt an electric surge through his body to his cock. He rocked his pelvis to push against her, and touched her breast. She kissed, licked him under his chin, then stopped.

"What do you do, Jim Cargill? What's your trip about anyway?"

Now what did she want from him? She said she just wanted to get laid.

Though extramarital liaisons had not been a regular event for Gideon, this was not the first time. Gideon had told himself before that each encounter deserves its own honesty, and sometimes convinced himself he was forging a meaningful connection with a woman he'd only known a little while. But this time tension and fear—and the violence of his plans—had added a charge to the impersonal chemistry of his response to this woman.

He didn't know what it was on her side—was she just a horny chick, interested in a quick fuck, or did she recognize something in him that she needed? His head was too busy. The hell with all that. *I am going to fuck her brains out.*

"Doesn't matter about me and my trip." But he said it gently. He took her head in his hands, lifted and turned it so he could look into her eyes, felt her lips resting softly against his as she closed her eyes. His mouth was soft, and he opened his lips a little and put the tip of his tongue between her lips. The touch sent a throb through him, she shuddered and pressed against his thigh.

She put her hand behind his head, and kept their lips together as she rolled on her side, sucking his tongue in her mouth. She rested her other hand on his chest, and started unbuttoning his shirt. Gideon put his hand inside her blouse, felt her softness, her nipples through her bra. He was moving slowly, and as his hand slid around to her back, he could feel her softening, her edge of wariness leaving. The tension was now in himself.

"Well," he said, "maybe I'm the one who's a bit nervous."

She paused in what she was doing along his back, took his head in her two hands and kissed his forehead.

"Don't you worry too much," she said. "Just take off some more clothes," she said, "and all that will be fine."

She sat up, quickly undid her white blouse and removed it, unzipped and moved out of her skirt, put the blouse and skirt neatly on the back of a chair. She kept on her satiny slip and underpants and bra, peach colored with a shiny pattern. She unbuckled, unbuttoned and unzipped his trousers, and slid them down off his legs while he was twisting to get out of his shirt and undershirt. She was slow and attentive in removing his socks, held one of his feet in both hands for a moment, then sidled her length against him again.

Gideon felt a cat-like familiarity in her flesh as it melded around him. Then his mind drifted, and he wasn't working at it, just touching around her ears, under her chin, the small of her back, behind her knees, then places of very soft skin, toward the top of her thighs inside, kissing her navel. She caressed his back, pressed against him, let her hands lightly brush over his stomach, his underpants, let her tongue alight here and there.

In his mind, . . . *But it ain't me, babe*—then an embarrassed recollection of his encounter with the highway patrolman. Unhooking her bra, a memory came of Kareem chuckling at an anecdote he'd told Gideon about sex in the visitors' rest room. His thoughts darkened, that faded too—

"I can drift off and still be here," he murmured, "I mean in my mind, mostly here."

– Lisa held his cock more firmly, and he gasped—heard her intake of breath as he finally put his fingers between her thighs, felt how moist she'd become. She took him into her mouth for a long moment, his heart pounded as he pushed into her, *I need to fuck you.*

Now their underwear was gone, she held back briefly as they started to enwrap arms and legs together, his erection against her. "God, I want you," Lisa said. Then she sat up again, pulled open the bedside drawer, and took out a condom, tore open the wrapper and put it on him.

Gideon pushed her down and rolled on top of her as she opened her legs. Gideon slid into her, felt himself enveloped, pressed all the way in, then held himself still at the bottom, deep within. Then began moving.

She gave a little high pitched cry. "Fuck me hard," she said hoarsely. But Gideon, silent, moved slowly, then at last a little faster.

"Fuck me, fuck me," she chanted in a whisper, "fuck me, fuck me, fuck me, fuck me."

Then her voice broke and she thrust herself against him, crying out, then gasping, "Oh, oh, oooh," and came to rest. Gideon sucked and bit her neck as he shoved himself in, *I need to ram it into you . . .* his pace quickening. Helen came to mind for a moment, his anger, and then Susan. Then, no one, and he suddenly knew that starting-to-lose-it throbbing, and it wasn't shoving anymore, and then he burst into her, again and again, then continuing to pump in and out even after there was nothing left to spurt. Then finally slowing down and at last stopping.

They lay together, taking in the friendly stickiness, the odor of bodily fluids, the slipperiness of their barely moving bodies. She ran her fingers lazily along his back, and around the curve of his ass. After a few minutes, he began giving little kisses on her eyes, her nose, her neck near her ear, tickling her. He was conscious of acting a part, spontaneous affection, to avoid speaking.

"You moved so sweetly," Lisa said, finally. "It was different. Talk to me."

"You are a sweet thing, you really are," he replied. He could not think what else to say.

She was quiet. He knew she was disappointed with his withholding response.

"Oh, Lordy, what time is it? I've got to get back to the restaurant."

"I'll walk you back. Is it okay if I stay here tonight with you?"

"God, yes."

She gave him a key, and he drove the pickup and parked in front of the former hotel. There was no special reason to worry, but he didn't want to leave his cash and papers and all in the truck. So he moved the money from the tool kit into one of the compartments of his duffel bag, grabbed his satchel too (leaving the Mississippi maps under the seat). He put all this in her room, by her closet. The guns stayed locked inside the Delta Pro box.

Gideon sat on the edge of the rumpled bed, thinking. It was crazy for him to spend more time with Lisa, and he wasn't sure what he would say to her. But after the "Wham, bam," he hadn't felt able to say, "Thank you Ma'am" and drive off. Now he regretted he hadn't. He would not be doing her any favor, though he couldn't believe she actually expected any more from him.

Maybe it was his belief, not hers, that it would be wrong for him to just walk out. He could still do it. He could leave her a note, saying he had to move on, and adding something sweet. Why didn't he?

He wanted her again. And something else. To have someone else know him.

It had been a long while. And he wanted to believe that sex meant he was making the kind of human contact he had so long spurned. Even though Lisa the waitress was a stranger, and this was just a good fuck, he wanted the intimacy he had been rejecting. And he reveled in his restored virility, his sense of power. The power of a man who would hold life and death in his hands.

But staying meant having to resist opening up to her. How could he connect with someone through lies?

He heard again the question he hadn't answered, "What's your trip about?" *It's about running away after you let someone die who has de-*

pended on you. He thought of Kareem smiling at some temporary legal triumph Gideon had reported, and he thought of the fear in Kareem's face at the end, when they walked him into the gas chamber. And finally, Kareem slumping in death.

A surge of emotion filled Gideon's chest and his eyes blurred with tears. He thought of his mother's death. And of Schwerner and Goodman and Chaney. He wiped his eyes on a sleeve, took a deep breath. He had no choice. There was no way out other than through Mississippi, and the men he was appointed to bring to justice.

Gideon walked around what there was of Palma. He bought a couple of real cowboy shirts at the dry goods store. He got a bunch of change at a gas station, and used the telephone booth to place another call to Cecil Price to make sure he was still in town. Price answered, and Gideon heard Price swear at him, "Stop bothering me, you stupid pussy." Gideon was still, holding the phone even after Price hung up, feeling the familiar surge of anger.

He went back to Lisa's room and read until he dropped off to sleep. Around four thirty, there was a knock at the door, then it opened. It was Lisa. She gave him a kiss, "You still look sleepy," she said, and went into the bathroom. He followed. She turned on the shower, stripped off her clothing, and stepped in. Gideon took off his clothes and got in with her. He washed her back, then turned her around and soaped her breasts and the front of her body. They kissed again as the hot water cascaded over them, and Lisa ran her hands over him, and they rubbed their soapy bodies against each other. She turned, pressing her ass against his slippery hardon, and turned off the water. They toweled themselves nearly dry, returned to the bed and made love again.

"That was lovely, Mr. James Cargill."

"Thank you ma'am. You have a sweet body and you are a sweet woman."

Her fingers traced circles on his chest, then she looked at him.

"So just who are you, actually, and what are you doing out here?"

"I'm a man passing through. Let's leave it at that."

Gideon looked at the dusty window sill, the stained lacy curtains, the browning window shade.

"And you?" he asked. "You from here? You seem to have an eastern accent. How did you come to be in Palma?"

Lisa's gaze turned away, to the window. Then back.

"I'm from Philly, originally. Worked as a waitress for a while, then in an office as a secretary. Didn't like the feel of office work. Two years ago, I hook up with this guy who dealt drugs sometimes. After we'd been together a couple months he goes, 'I'm drivin' to the coast. You can come along, or this is good-bye.' Asshole, I think. But what the hell, I go, I'm tired of this shit, I'll try somewhere else.

"We leave at night, and he's secret-like. Stop in odd places, where he makes a lot of calls he don't want me to listen in on. Finally, in Salt Lake City, I overhear him on a call to someone. After we leave town, I try to talk to him about it. 'Sounds like we're carrying some heavy shit for a delivery.' I go, 'If I'm along on this, don't you think you could tell me about what I'm letting myself in for?'

"None of your fucking business,' he goes. 'You don't like it, you can get out right here.'

"'OK,' I say, 'just put me down somewhere. I'm not gonna do time for some shit I don't know a god damn thing about, for a dickhead who's keeping secrets.'

"An exit comes up, and he pulls right off the freeway and pulls out a map. Figures out where we are. Drives south to here. Stops at the edge of town, reaches across the front seat, and opens the door on my side. Sticks his foot across and pushes it open. 'So long, baby.' He pops open the trunk. I step out and slam the door, walk around the back and pull out my suitcase, slam the trunk lid down with all my might. He takes off, leaving me in a bunch of dust.

"I thought about taking a bus back to Salt Lake City. But I think, 'What the fuck, what difference does it make where I am?' I walk up to the luncheonette, ask whether they need a waitress. They do. Winters, things are busier round here with hunters and winter sports people. It's a place.

"How 'bout you? What's your story?"

Gideon was silent. "No story. Worked in high tech in California. Got tired of it. Now I'm going East to see some people. End of story."

They were silent for a while. Lisa held him. Gideon imagined she was thinking she'd come on to another loser.

"Let's get some dinner," she suggested brightly. "Let's have a good time." They drove to a restaurant that was part of a winter resort twelve miles away. They had cocktails, and talked on and off, but not about themselves. After dinner, they went to the bar and drank gin for a while. Gideon paid cash for everything, and around nine they returned to the former Palma City Hotel. They had sex again, but now it was more desperate.

"Take me with you," Lisa said. "I need to get out of Palma. We can go to wherever you're going in the East, and give this a try. I don't care what you're doing. Maybe we'd be good for each other."

Gideon looked away. "No. I can't do that. I've got something I've got to do, and I've got to do it on my own."

Lisa looked wounded. She turned her back to Gideon, and pulled the covers over herself. After a time she seemed to be sleeping, and Gideon drifted off too. Later he heard her crying softly.

When Gideon woke in the morning, she was sitting on the floor with his bags next to her. The zip compartment with the money was open, and his manuals and photos of Cecil Price were on the floor next to her. His wallet, too.

"Who the hell are you?" she asked. "How come the only thing in your wallet that's got your name on it is a temporary drivers license from California? What's all the money for? Who's the guy in the pictures?"

"You know all you need to know. This isn't another drug thing, and I'm not a criminal. Now I've got to go." He pulled his clothes on, and shoved his stuff back into the bags. He didn't count the money, but he didn't think she'd taken anything.

"Look," she said, "just take me to Salt Lake. I'll take a bus from there. To somewhere. Anywhere. I'm through here."

Gideon pushed down a surge of anger. She wasn't going to entangle him. He had a job to do. Price was going to pay. He didn't need her. He didn't want her.

"No. I can't do that either. I'm on my own. That's it."

She went to the window, looking out, her back to him, her back very straight.

"Goodbye, Lisa. I'm sorry."

"Fuck you," she said.

He closed the door quietly, went down, and drove away. When he was half way to the freeway, he pulled over and checked the money. Of course, she hadn't taken any. He reddened. He put it back into the tool chest under the front seat.

44

Seth Barnes, harsh in his dealings with men, and brutal toward Jason, was gentle and even affectionate with the farm's animals. So when, a few months after Jason's arrival, Uncle Seth found him tormenting the mules, deliberately startling them with sudden noises until they were frantic, Seth's rage was out of control. Yet the savage whipping did not render Jason as abject as it once had.

Jason was terrified of the beatings. But each time he nonetheless returned to the condemned activity, as though he had forgotten the response it was to provoke. So the mules suffered until Jason grew bored of the mean game.

Jason avenged himself in new ways, usually by breaking things he thought Seth cared about, only some of the time in ways that Seth could not ascribe to Jason. It was worth the thrashings.

At the school for Negro children, Seth was called in so the teacher could berate Jason, and by implication Seth, over Jason's defiance and fighting. Seth had tanned Jason when he was told the teacher needed to meet with him, so Jason was surprised to hear his uncle standing up for him. "Ain't the boy supposed to show some spirit, defend hisself?" Seth challenged. "Boys got to take care of theyselves, and they gonna fight. Why don't you let them settle their own damn wrangles without butting in?"

Despite any punishments, Jason understood that Seth was not displeased that the other boys had come to fear Jason.

But Seth's secret pride was not shared by Jason's teachers, and after being held back several times, Jason was expelled from school for good when he was eleven.

Over the years, Jason learned to monitor Seth's moods so that he could avoid, or try to placate, Seth when a bad time was coming, or at least not be surprised at the onset of Seth's rage. He always knew where, along the scale of Seth's anger, from simmering indignation to rampaging fury, the needle would point.

But as the years went by, Seth's drinking increased and his pleasure in having someone to batter also increased. Jason never grew entirely inured to his uncle's harsh and unpredictable discipline.

At fourteen, Jason was big for his age, and often thought to be sixteen. He was as tall as Seth, though he had not attained his full growth. Years of work on the farm and plenty of food had made him strong.

Early Sunday afternoon, Seth had begun drinking. Jason sat on the porch, mending a halter, and he felt an uneasiness build in his stomach as he heard Seth muttering bitterly to himself.

"Come in here, nigger," Seth called loudly. "Worthless little nigger," Seth grumbled in a low voice. Jason had heard the phrase a thousand times.

As Jason approached, Seth rose unsteadily to his feet, and Jason felt his heart pounding. He knew Seth was about to ask questions to which there was no right answer.

"Why ain't you fixin' supper yet?" Seth demanded.

"I'm working on the weak spot in Jen's halter," Jason said carefully, "and there's lots of time before supper." Jason felt time begin to slow down. Each moment contained a horrible fullness as he began to make himself remote from what he knew was about to happen.

"Don't you talk back to me that way, boy," Seth said.

"I was not trying to talk back, sir," Jason said, looking down respectfully. "I was jes tryin' to answer your question."

"*Jes tryin' to answer your question,*" Seth mocked. "Don't you talk that way to me, you insolent bastard. Do I need to teach you how to be respectful again?"

Seth advanced toward Jason, and Jason felt his stomach seething, the muscles in his chest twitching and cramping. He took a step back.

"You trying to run away again?" Seth's arms hung loosely by his sides in the ready way Jason knew. "Come here and take your punishment like a man."

Jason hesitated. He wouldn't get away with escaping. But he could not get himself to walk toward Uncle Seth for another beating.

He opened his mouth. His heart was thumping and only the croak came out, "Uncle . . ." He cleared his throat.

"Please don't hit me, Uncle Seth, sir. I didn't mean to show no disrespect. Please, Uncle Seth, I'll do whatever you tell me to."

"I'm telling you to come here."

"No."

The word had rushed out of him without thought, with finality. Then he realized it was true: he was not going to come when called, he was not going to let Seth beat him again.

"What you say to me?"

"I said no. You're not going to hit me no more."

Seth rushed at Jason, bringing his right fist around and swinging at Jason's face, but liquor and age had made him slower, and Jason dodged and gave Seth a shove. The old man tottered, regained his balance. Jason held his hands out, palms toward Seth, pleadingly.

"Now, Uncle," he said. "Please . . ."

"You little—," Seth said, not finishing as he rushed in, his blows connecting this time. Jason was knocked back, but he responded with a punch to Seth's head. Then another to his chest. Hurting Seth came naturally once he embraced the notion he could strike his uncle. It felt good.

Seth didn't expect to be hit, and he fell, tripping over the couch and stumbling to the floor.

"You sneaky bastard," he said, rising a little then suddenly trying to throw himself at Jason's legs. Jason dodged and kicked Seth in the ribs. Jason still feared Seth. But he was even more afraid he might not hurt Seth enough to stop him. Seth cried out, and Jason kicked him again, viciously in the stomach. The wind went out of Seth and he stayed down.

"You not going to whip me no more," said Jason, releasing the rage he had so long contained. "It ain't right. I didn't do nothing to you, and you got no cause to hurt me, and you not gonna whip me no more. Not ever."

"Get out, you worthless little shit," Seth said. "After all I've done for you. After all I done to make a man of you. Get out of my house and don't never come back."

Jason stood over the old man. His fists were tight. *After all I put up with, I got to leave? This farm was gonna be mine one day, wasn't it?* He looked down, ready to strike again. But only words came from Seth Barnes.

"It's no use," Seth said tearfully. "I always knowed you come to nothin'. Get out, you nothin'."

Only words.

"You're just no good. I'm through trying to help you. After all I tried to do."

Jason felt guilt, but he wasn't going to back down. Even if he had to leave.

He went upstairs and into the attic. He pulled out a small cardboard valise, took it to his room, and stuffed his clothing into it. In his drawer was the photo of his parents that Uncle Benjamin had left with him when Ben gave him to Seth. It was all that he had of them. He looked at the picture, wrapped it in a shirt and put it in the valise.

Jason put a folding knife and a small change purse into his pockets. A pack of cards and some dice.

Jason went into Seth's room and to the drawer where Seth kept his money. He took fifty dollars in small bills. He'd earned it, and he couldn't start out with nothing. He took Seth's pocket flask of corn liquor, too. He'd been sneaking it since he was ten years old, and Seth could get hisself another flask.

Jason put on the ragged jacket that was his only outer coat, picked up the valise, and went downstairs. Seth was sitting on the couch, rubbing his ribs.

"I tried to make a man of you, this be my thanks."

Jason went to the door without a word.

"Go to hell," Seth called. "Don't never come back here. I don't never want to hear from you agin. You gonna end up in Parchman State Farm."

Jason began walking the nine miles to the town of Liberty.

He was free! Free of Seth Barnes. Never again would he worry about Seth hurting him. He would take care of himself and no one would ever beat him again.

45

Jason had not spent much time among white people when he lived with Uncle Seth, so he had to catch on fast. He got and lost a number of jobs before he learned to observe the whites more carefully and to display the mood they wanted to see. Soon he found work, sweeping and cleaning and helping the colored customers, in a dry goods store owned by Mr. Robert Jenkins, a white man in his late thirties.

After trying living with a much older cousin's family, he got a room in town in a boarding house where they gave him meals. He felt like a grown-up, even if he had next to no money left from his small wages.

The county was mostly Negro, and so were most of the shoppers at Mr. Jenkins' store. Jenkins did not trouble to conceal his contempt for them, often cursing and even slapping his colored customers.

One day a thin, very small Negro women in her sixties came into the store and asked Jason to help her reach a bolt of cloth that was stored higher up. Jason put the bolt onto a counter, and the woman unrolled it to feel the cloth.

Jenkins flew at them. "Boy, don't you let that old nigger paw my goods with her dirty black hands," he yelled. He snatched the fabric away, rolling it back up and jostling the old woman. Her face became stony. She looked to one side.

Jason stared with astonishment. "Sorry, ma'am," he said in a low voice, embarrassed.

Jenkins glared at Jason. Jason looked down and stopped talking.

"How much you want me to cut for you, girl? You behave yourself in my store. Don't you go handling my merchandise—it ain't yours till you buy it. I cut it and you pay. Then you get it."

"Three and half yard, suh."

Jenkins carelessly measured what looked to Jason like only a little more than the three and a half yards. "Well," he said, "we'll round it down and call it four yards. That'll be five twenty."

Jason opened his mouth as though to start to say something.

Jenkins looked at him hard, and Jason shut his mouth. He was afraid, and tried hard not to show his feelings.

The woman paid, putting the money down on the counter. She folded the piece of cloth, and put it into her shopping bag, bowed a little to Mr. Jenkins, and shambled out.

"I never let these niggers handle nothin' before they buy," the owner told Jason, even before she had gone out the door. "Our white customers wouldn't want their goods handled by niggers before they buy them."

He could see something in Jason's face. "You got a problem?"

"No," said Jason promptly, "no sir." *I could smash your pointy nose flat and knock out your teeth,* Jason thought, *and you'd have no idea how to fight back.*

"You don't look happy, boy."

"Oh, I'm fine, Mr. Jenkins, suh." Jason tried to put on what he thought was a big niggery-looking grin. He tried not to think, even as he simmered with rage. "You de boss, boss, suh. I happy. You knows best."

"There are lots of niggers who'd love to have your job, boy."

"I know, suh. Thank you, suh. I proud to work here." Jason looked down some more, and tried to make himself look even happier and more simple-minded. He struggled to keep his face soft.

"Next time one of these old niggers ask you to get something, you tell her, 'Girl, the boss don't let you touch nothing before you buy.' You got that, Jason?"

"Yassuh, Mr. Jenkins. Yassuh, that jes what I say to them old gals."

"Let me hear what you're going to say."

"I say, 'Girl, boss man don't want you touch *nothin'.* Keep yo hands off.'" His voice broke as he spoke.

"That's right, boy," Jenkins said, patting Jason on the head in a friendly way. "You're a good boy, and you keep clean. I just don't like these dirty, smelly old niggers around my merchandise."

Liberty was a small town, with high wooden sidewalks in front of the stores in the shopping district. After work, Jason walked quietly down the sidewalk, his eyes downcast. He was afraid he would have to look into the eyes of another Negro. He was afraid he'd have another explosion once he was with people he wasn't afraid of.

Suddenly, a large, young white man came up to Jason. "What the hell you doin' up here?" he asked loudly. He grabbed Jason by his shirt front and shoved Jason off the sidewalk and onto the dirt street. Jason fell to the ground, but swiftly rolled back onto his feet and made fists of this hands. The white man jumped down to the ground, followed by two young whites who had been with him..

"You think you a white man, boy?" the man asked.

"No, sir," Jason said meekly. He opened his hands

One of the white men came right alongside Jason, and the other stood behind him, while the one who had shoved Jason did the talking.

"Didn't you see that white lady walking on the sidewalk, nigger boy? Sidewalks in Liberty are for white people, not niggers."

"No sir," Jason said. "I mean, yes sir! I'm new to town, sir, I just didn't know."

The man crowded Jason, and he tottered back, bumping into the white man behind him.

"Don't knock into me, you black bastard. Show respect, nigger," he said. He smacked the back of Jason's head sharply. Jason stumbled and the third white man knocked Jason down.

The three men stomped on Jason's legs and he tried to curl himself up on the ground to protect himself. They kicked his back and head, grunting with the exertion, while some white people stopped and looked silently on. Three middle-aged Negro men turned and hurried away, taking care not to look.

"That's enough," the first white said equably. "This nigger boy just needed a little reminding." He squatted down next to Jason, and patted his head. "Ain't that right, boy?"

"Yes, suh," said Jason, trying to catch his breath.

"You as good as a white man, boy."

"No, I ain't as good," Jason said in a low voice.

"Can't hear you. Not as good, what?"

"I ain't as good as no white man, sir."

"You want to go to school with white girls, nigger, like Earl Warren say you should?"

"I don't know no Earl, and I don't go to no school. Sir."

"Well then, get up and get your damned black ass the hell out of here."

The white men moved on, laughing to each other. Jason limped off, trying to get away from this street, trying to turn the corner to another part of town not filled with people who had seen him humiliated. But his face burned and his shame came with him.

Only a month earlier, Jason knew, a fourteen-year-old black boy from Chicago, visiting his relatives in Mississippi for the summer, had been taken from his bed in the night, brutalized, murdered and mutilated by two white men who were later to sell their story to a magazine. Young Emmett Till's crime: he whistled at a white woman coming out of a grocery store in Money, Mississippi.

The photos of Emmett's ruined face were published nation-wide, and they spread rage as well as fear among black people in Mississippi. When the men in Liberty attacked Jason for his supposed disrespect to a white woman, Jason thought: *They gonna kill me just like they done Emmett Till. They gonna put my eye out, then beat me to death and shoot me.*

Jason was almost exactly as old as Emmet Till when he was murdered. *Or maybe they'll burn me up like my father.* Jason longed to strike back, but he knew he couldn't.

In this world of white people, Jason realized, you always had to be paying attention to them, figuring out what they were thinking, what might offend them, what they might do next. You always had to watch what you said and try not to attract their attention, and you had to put on the expression they wanted to see. Jason had run away from Uncle Seth. But being around white people was like being in a world full of Seths.

Jason had nothing. He was nothing. White people killed Emmett Till, just like they killed his papa, and they could kill him any time they wanted-ed. Nothin' he could do about that.

Jason retreated to a colored street. When he reached the place near his room where he went to drink, he saw one of the Negroes who turned away when the white men started to beat him. The man came over and tried to be friendly.

"You made a little mistake out there, boy. But you got out of it okay," the man said.

"I ain't no boy," Jason said. "That was getting out of it okay?"

"You still alive. You done right to play the fool after those crackers beat on you."

Jason knew it. But he didn't want to be around people who said it out loud. "Mind your own god damn business," he said leaning toward the man, "or I'll show you who the fool, you old bastard." The man went away in a huff.

A month later, Mr. Jenkins fired Jason. He held back most of Jason's last week's wages, claiming that Jason had been stealing. It was true.

Jason got another job, mopping and cleaning at the bank. From time to time he got odd jobs in the homes of the white folks who worked there, mowing and hauling. Some of them seemed as though they were trying to be nice to this respectful black boy. But he wasn't always careful enough around them. He needed to stay in his place or they would grow sharp and mean. He had to hold in his anger until it was safe to let it go, when he was with other black folks.

46

After leaving Palma, Gideon stayed off the Interstates, meandering eastward on mostly empty state highways. He thought about all the murders that had been done in Mississippi, and he thought about Cecil Price.

He thought of three young men, boys, cut down because of the vicious idiocy of white supremacy. He thought of the anguish of their parents when he called with the news of their sons' disappearance the night of the murders. The memory of their voices and their terrible fear was still alive in his memory. He thought of his failure to get the FBI to act in time.

For once, he would not feel helpless in the face of injustice. For once, his need for revenge would be satisfied.

Gideon recalled sitting in a joint in Jackson, Mississippi, about a week before he went back to the Bronx, drinking beer with another summer volunteer, Ron Carver, a white guy from Massachusetts Gideon had met at orientation.

Back in New York, he wouldn't have hesitated to call such a place a dive. But here it was just agreeably run down. And the barbeque was something.

Gideon had come with Brian and a few others from Hokes Landing for a meeting, and this place was next door to the office.

The owner had shown his support for the Movement by feeding SNCC workers during the winter, when they had had no money. And every now and then, he'd slip a summer volunteer a free beer.

There was a double line of wooden booths running down the middle of the place, and Gideon and Ron were sitting in one. A dark wooden panel, nearly shoulder high when you were sitting in the booth, separated theirs from the booth joined to it.

Brian and SNCC head Jim Forman had been sitting with them at first, but they'd moved to another booth to talk to some local people, and they hadn't invited Gideon and Ron to join them. They were okay.

The people who frequented this place were getting used to having these strange white people around, and one of the black girls in the booth adjoining theirs looked at Gideon every now and then, perhaps invitingly.

The white volunteers were objects of curiosity and often, too, of desire.

They embodied many kinds of strangeness, sometimes as the first Jews that the young blacks had ever met. Gideon remembered suppressing a smile when a teenager asked him whether all Jews were atheists—all the Jewish volunteers she had met were.

It was around eleven at night. The heat and humidity were still cloying.

Ron got up to feed the jukebox some nickels. He stayed there for a few minutes, jiving with a black girl—he insisted she pick her songs first. "No, if you're waiting behind me, it's a line, and you've got to get to the front of the line," he was telling her. "Like the freedom song," Ron sang, "'*If you don't see me at the back of the jukebox line, I'll be picking songs up front . . .*' Besides, this way I get to look at you in front of me."

It would be a while before the music that Ron had selected started playing, and they were in no hurry. They were in a safe place, and Gideon was feeling comfortable on his second beer, waiting for their barbeque to emerge from the kitchen in the fullness of time. It was plenty noisy, so they could talk privately despite all the people around them.

He and Ron had had the same reactions to this new thing they were experiencing, the Movement, and to this quintessentially un-American place, Mississippi. Which was at the same time also so entirely American.

Ron grew quiet as Gideon shared his experiences of fear and embarrassment about his first night in the state, about his efforts to fit himself into this big thing that was happening in this remote place, into the growing struggle of ordinary local people.

Ron told him about having spent a week in the Atlanta SNCC office before the summer project started. There were volunteers there, too, working to support the Mississippi project from outside.

"They weren't well organized in Atlanta," Ron said, "and they didn't know what to do with us at first. I thought, well, it's a privilege to be here at all. I don't care, I'll do anything that helps.

"For the first few days, I just picked up a broom and went around the whole place sweeping. One evening I mopped—the office really gets dirty with all these people running in and out all the time.

"A white kid mopping the floor in an office run by black people. They were plenty amused.

"And I took some ribbing—'Hey, boy, you missed over here, don't you know how to handle no mop?' That was okay.

"I also helped proof-read and get out their publication, The Student Voice, while I was there. Finally the summer project got under way here, and I was assigned to Greenwood."

Ron talked to Gideon about what he was learning about the strength of ordinary black people, about the balance they maintained between submission and resistance, a balance that was shifting now.

Ron got up to get two more beers. Gideon was sweating heavily, and his shirt stuck to his back. The girl in the next booth chanced a swift look at him, and he gave her a broad smile and raised his bushy eyebrows a couple of times. She turned away, but she was smiling.

When Ron returned, Gideon told him of his experiences on the night of the three murders, when he had been on the WATS line and had tried so desperately to persuade John Doar and the FBI to do something. How he had been the one to call Mickey's and Andy's parents in New York City to tell them their sons were missing. The folks in Meridian had called James Chaney's people.

"Those were horrible calls. They were frantic. You can imagine. I told them about all of our efforts to get the FBI to act. . . gave them some numbers to call." Gideon looked grim, remembering. "I hope I never have to make another call like that."

"Those fuckers," Gideon went on after a pause. "Now that the three are obviously dead, two hundred FBI agents are crawling all over the state looking for bodies. But they refused to do anything when it might have made a difference."

Later, after Gideon had returned North, the story came out how the killings actually took place. The three young men had in fact been alive when he had been going back and forth between the FBI in Meridian and John Doar in Washington. They were in jail in Philadelphia when the local FBI men were saying they could do nothing. The jailor's wife lied when she told him they weren't there.

If the FBI men had called or just gone out to the jail—maybe if Gideon had been more persuasive, more forceful dealing with them—the three men would be alive today.

It didn't have to have happened.

As Gideon drove toward Wyoming, twenty-three years later, on his crooked path to Mississippi, he still couldn't figure out who was most to blame.

His memories were wearing him out. He was exhausted from his conversations with himself. He needed to talk to someone else. Someone who understood what he had gone through. Yes, he would stop and see Susan Channing.

47

"He's on the move, Mr. Jeffers, and he don't mean no good," said Timmie Ray Phelps as he walked into the D.A.'s office in Meridian, Mississippi.

"What's up, Sheriff?" said the District Attorney.

"For three weeks, no calls to any of the perps from our anonymous friend. Then, like I told you, Mr. Quiet Caller calls from southern Idaho. Twice. From phone booths. To Cecil Price. That was day before yesterday. Now, just five minutes ago, he's called again from Jackson, Wyoming, just below the Grand Tetons. Another public phone booth, Wyoming Bell tells me. He's on the move, Mr. Jeffers. He is on his way. And I know it means trouble."

"Wait a minute, Timmie. Has he finally said something?"

"Nope. That's just my point."

"So how do you know it's the same person—okay, the same man?"

"I recognize the sound of his silence. And I have a feeling."

The DA snorted.

"Mr. Jeffers, don't make fun. You think there's a whole bunch of different men in Idaho, Wyoming, all calling Cecil Price and the others, and not saying a word to them? Different people checking up on them for no reason?"

"But Timmie Ray, your theory isn't making any sense. If we posit that it's all one quiet man, and he's on the move, he is not headed here. You don't get to Mississippi from southern Idaho by going Northeast to Wyoming. Whatever he's doing, he's not coming here."

"Something's happening, Mr. Jeffers. Mr. Quiet Caller is no longer just being quiet. He's traveling. I don't know why he's goin' round about, but he is in motion. And why is he in motion, Mr. Jeffers, if not to get to Mississippi?"

"Timmie Ray, that is speculation pure and simple. Nothing but wild speculation. Coincidences do happen in the real world. He could be heading somewhere else, and just making his usual calls along the way."

Now it was Timmie Ray's turn to snort.

"But even if they are not coincidences, it could mean anything or nothing. And it certainly does not look like someone heading for Mississippi. Whatever they might do when they get here. I mean if they get here.

"And what do you propose we do about it, anyway, Timmie? Even if we knew that someone from the other side of the country intended to commit some unspecified illegal act in Mississippi, we don't know when and we don't know who and we don't know where. We don't know who he is. We don't know what he looks like. We don't know what kind of car he's driving, if he's driving. We don't know a blessed thing, including whether he's done anything more unlawful than disturb Cecil Price's sleep a few times and waste his money for the honor of hearing the voices of some aging citizens of Philadelphia, Mississippi."

Timmie Ray snorted again.

"What are we supposed to do, Timmie Ray? Ask the Highway Patrol in all the states between Wyoming and Mississippi to be on the lookout for men making calls from public telephone booths? Put up a cordon around the state? Arrest anyone who crosses into Mississippi with a suspicious number of quarters in his pocket? What good's your suspicion when there's nothing we can do?"

"What good is it?" Timmie Ray retorted. "It's better than waitin' until it's too late. I don't know what we can do. But making a closing argument to me as though you were in court, speechifying the jury senseless the way you do, don't speak to the issue, and you know it.

"For months someone's been calling a bunch of men we know were murderers, calling Cecil Price over and over, and not saying a word. I say he's checking whether they're still alive and well and in Philadelphia. And now we finally started tracing the calls, we see he's heading East toward us. Don't know exactly why he's goin' the way he's goin'. But when he turns up at Cecil Price's door in Philadelphia, Mississippi, I don't think he's gonna ask Price to buy Girl Scout cookies or offer him a subscription to the Jackson Clarion-Ledger. Neither do you."

Jeffers was silent. His expression acknowledged the justice of Timmie Ray's complaint.

"Well, Timmie, I was only saying what any reasonable person would say. There's no hard evidence of any wrongdoing, actual or planned. But the truth is I'm worried too. I was just seeing if I could convince myself there was nothing to it.

"Someone else is interested in our quarry. Too interested. I just don't know what we can do on the state of the case. Take Cecil Price and Billy Wayne Posey and Jimmie Snowden into protective custody? Give them police escorts from now on? Tell them we've been tapping their phones, and they should shoot first if a stranger looks at them funny?

"What do you really think we should do, other than wait for further developments?"

"Mr. Jeffers, we have identified two public telephones from which long distance calls have been made, and we know the exact time of the calls. It's probably a long shot. But let's see if the phone companies can tell us if a credit card was used for the calls, and whose it is."

"Worth a try," Jeffers agreed. "And if that don't work?"

"I can only think of one more thing, really," Timmie said. "Another long shot. Next time there's a phone call to Price, let's call on the local police and ask them to head right over to the phone booth. See if he's still around. See if there are any witnesses who saw someone in the booth lately."

"What are we supposed to tell them we're investigating, Timmie? I don't think we can do that, based on what we have. What else?"

"Well, we could ask them to check the phones for prints. If we find the same prints on public telephones in two different towns that have been used to call Cecil Price, well, we'll have our man," said Timmie Ray.

"Assuming, that is, that I see my way clear to troubling two sets of police and two phone companies in two states over idle suspicions, and assuming he's not wearing gloves and assuming there are enough readable prints on both phones and assuming that our man's prints are on file somewhere.

"I am afraid, Timmie, that what we've got to go on is too thin for that."

Timmie Ray checked the credit card angle. But no credit card had been used for the calls.

48

Over the next three years, young Jason Jackson drifted from job to job, moving from Liberty to Magnolia to McComb. Eventually, he got work at the mill. The pay was good, but wrestling the logs and the cants for the saws was dangerous. Working the machinery was white men's work, so they didn't let Jason touch any equipment, and he had to listen to a lot of "nigger" and "coon" talk. He did the dirtiest work and swallowed the insults.

After work, he hung around the private clubs that were in people's houses, where black folks went to drink. He joked around with other young men, but he drank more and often started fights, in which he seemed to spin out of control.

One night, a man he knew slightly began one of the familiar games of young black men, playing the dozens.

"Jason, can you help me find my dick? I can't remember whether I left it in your sister or your mother."

"Leon, don't you talk about my mother."

"Why, I got nothin bad to say 'bout your momma, Jason. I loves your momma. She so nice to me, she shine my shoes while she already down there on her knees."

Jason's move was so fast he surprised the man despite the warnings, knocking Leon off balance, then slamming his fist into Leon's stomach. Leon crumpled, and as he started to fall, Jason yanked him up by his shirt and smacked him twice. Leon banged into a chair, and fell to the floor. He decided against getting up, and the fight was over.

An admiring group crowded around Jason, and he also noticed a group of young women looking interestedly in his direction.

Tessa Griggs was one of them. Her eyes were bright with excitement and she smiled at Jason. She drifted toward him, then let him buy her a rum and soda. She flirted boldly, but when she left, it was in the company of her girl friends.

Tessa was sixteen—just a year younger than Jason, though he still looked older than his age—and she was on her own. Her father had gone to Chicago some years earlier, and after a while the money he sent home stopped coming. Now her mother was too busy struggling to keep food on the table for Tessa's three younger brothers to pay much attention to Tessa.

She worked in white folks' houses, cleaning and ironing, and lived on her own. She and her roommate often went to clubs or roadhouses where there was dancing and where people drank out back. Tessa had good hair, so she could straighten it without using much lye, and her skin was not dark, so she didn't need to use skin lighteners. Her breasts and hips were large, and she wore tight dresses that showed them off, now her mother couldn't tell her what to do.

Tessa didn't let the men she met at the club go too far. Nonetheless she got a reputation for being fast. Jason was strong and good looking, even if he was very black. His power, and the rage below the surface, drew her. Eventually, it became more than flirting. Tessa's roommate moved out and Jason moved in.

After they started living together, Jason began to change.

"You were making eyes at Dorsey last night," he said. "Why you want to hurt me that way?"

"No, I wasn't," she said. "I was just—"

He slapped her. "Don't you talk back to me, girl," he said. "Show me respect. Ain't I entitled to no respect nowhere?" He turned from her and left the room.

Tessa was shocked, but confused, too. No man had smacked her face before. But he looked so hurt, she must have been in the wrong. She knew what he had to put up with at the mill. Maybe it was her fault.

"Honey," she said softly, later. "I'm sorry if I upset you. I was just having fun like I always do."

"I shouldn't a hit you, baby. I dunno know what came over me. I'll never do it again."

A few nights later, Tessa got to the club before Jason. He was working late, and promised to meet her around 8 o'clock. But it was nearly nine and he still wasn't there. She began joking with her old friends, then when the music began, she danced with Dorsey. She could feel him press his thing against her through her thin dress, and feel his hand near her bottom.

Jason arrived, and she saw his face darken.

"What the fuck you doing with my woman?" Jason asked Dorsey.

"We just dancing, Jackson, man," said Dorsey. "Just dancing while Tessa waited for you. Your gal's a great dancer."

"The fuck you were. You touch my Tessa like that again and I'll kill you."

"Hey, man," said Dorsey.

Jason took a knife from his pocket. He started to unfold it, his eyes never leaving Dorsey's.

"Put that away, man," said the owner of the club. "Here, have a drink on me." Dorsey left and Jason quieted.

Tessa cautiously moved a little closer toward him, but Jason ignored her. When they returned to Tessa's room, she tried to talk to him.

"Don't go treating everything so seriously," she started.

He wheeled on her, smacking her full in the face, then he flung her against the bureau. She tried to push him away.

"Let me be, damn you," she kicked his shins, and Jason yelped. He punched her twice in the stomach. She went down, gasping, and didn't get up this time.

"You trying to make me look the fool, ain't you? 'Jason's woman is layin' everyone in the club,' they be sayin'. 'Jason don't seem to know nothing bout what Tessa do, do he?' I ain't that big a fool."

"Who say that to you? That be a lie."

"Thas what they all be thinking. Jason can't control that woman of his."

"That ain't the way it is, baby. You the onliest man for me."

Tessa thought that if she were more careful, she could avoid provoking him. Jason's apologies and promises moved her, and it was her fault she didn't try harder to support him, so he wasn't always so upset.

Jason and Tessa got married a few months later, in June 1958. Jason's wages went up, and there were good times in between the beatings.

Early one afternoon in August, a white man came by in a truck. Jason had an accident at the sawmill, and they'd taken him to General Hospital.

He drove her to the hospital, where the doctor told her Jason's right leg had almost been cut off by a saw. They'd managed to save the leg, but Jason would never be able to walk without a cane.

Tessa took in laundry, as well as working at white people's houses. Jason drank more, and Tessa did, too. When both of them had been drinking or smoking Maryjane, they fought. When Jason learned Tessa was pregnant, he asked, "How I know whose baby that be?"

"There ain't never, not once, been anyone but you."

In November, they laid Jason off at the mill, and they decided to go North, to Chicago. They moved into a small apartment on the south side, near to where a friend of Jason's lived.

49

The cold was a shock to Tessa, and she was frightened of the rats and roaches that were everywhere. But it was a powerful relief that white people did not openly abuse them. They faced discrimination, sure. But Jason need not fear injury or death for saying the wrong thing to any white man. Jason got jobs and quickly lost them when he lost his temper. He challenged a white supervisor who criticized his work.

"Mr. Hillary, sir, Mr. White Man, Massah. here's what I got to say to that—take your god damn job and shove it up your pretty white ass!"

Walking out the door, he felt a dizzying power. He could say anything and no one would hurt him.

But it didn't pay the rent. They were evicted from their apartment for nonpayment. A dealer called Sickle helped them find another place, more run down than the first.

One morning in February, Jason returned to the apartment after an all-night outing with Sickle and his friends. Tessa was in her seventh month and she was tired. She turned on Jason.

"You and Sickle and them been with a woman, ain't you? Sharing her like dogs with a bitch in heat. Sickle gets to go first, don't he? I can smell her from here."

Jason was bright and intense, and he seemed high.

"Who you think you talking to, you fat hog?"

"I'm talking to a dog who smells like he just lick up his own vomit."

Jason grabbed Tessa and kneed her between the legs. She grunted in pain, then scratched his face. Jason punched her on the side of the head, and Tessa fell. She kicked at him. He pulled her up, pushed her in a corner between the bureau and the wall, then he punched her in the stomach several times.

He stepped back and she slumped to the floor, her eyes still open, but dazed.

"No more, Jason, you gonna hurt the baby."

"Fuck the baby," Jason said. "That baby ain't mine."

"Yes it is . . ."

He kicked, but she twisted away and caught it in her ribs. He stood above her and swung his foot again, into her swollen abdomen. She screamed in fear, then gasped as his shoe thudded into her.

"Don't . . ."

"Stinking bastard," Jason said, stomping her. "I'm gettin rid of it."

After he stopped, Jason went to the bathroom to wash off his scratches, then walked out the door. Tessa lay half curled up on the floor, moaning. She was bleeding between her legs and throbbing with pain.

She couldn't get to her feet. She crawled to a neighbor's apartment, knocked at the bottom of the door and called hoarsely for help.

"My baby's coming, help me."

They brought her to the emergency room, where she told them she'd fallen down the stairs. The doctor looked skeptical, observing Tessa's swollen face and the pattern of bruises on her body, old and new.

"We'll do what we can, but you're nearly two months early, and it looks like you've been hurt badly."

Forty-five minutes later, the baby was delivered by Caesarian section, four pounds ten ounces. They had to work on him for a while to get him breathing, but the doctors said there did not seem to be anything profoundly wrong with him; he mostly needed time to grow. It was six weeks before they discharged him.

After the baby came home, people told Jason that the boy looked like him, and he was proud to have a son. Tessa had named him Charles Joshua Jackson, after his two grandfathers. It was not until he became a teenager that he would become known as Kareem Jackson.

"You don't even know where your daddy is, or whether he still alive." Jason complained. "So how come his name come first? If I the father it ain't right."

"You even remember why you wasn't at the hospital to help name the baby? Why he came early?"

Because of Tessa's condition when she'd come into the hospital, the child welfare assigned a social worker to come out to the apartment and check on how Tessa and the baby were doing. But after the social worker visited three times in the first month, they moved to another apartment without telling the welfare and they did not see her again.

50

Jason and Tessa were drinking more. Tessa got money and food stamps from the welfare for the baby, and they hustled to get by without real jobs.

Charlie cried and cried, even after six weeks. Tessa didn't know what to do. Her mother was far away in Mississippi, and Tessa didn't remember her brothers going on this way when they were babies. Her few girl friends had no babies, and no one could advise Tessa whether her baby was acting normal.

She would walk around half the night carrying Charlie, but his shrill cry was unending. The apartment was small, and Tessa and the baby could never get far enough from the bedroom where Jason was trying to sleep.

"Make that damned baby shut up!" Jason said one night. It was two in the morning, and Jason stumbled out of bed into the kitchen. He got himself a drink. Tessa sat wearily rocking her body back and forth in a hard kitchen chair, hoping to lull Charlie to sleep with her movement, or at least to quiet him down a little, so she could get some sleep herself. Jason stood in front of her, glowering.

"How come you don't know nothing about taking care of my son?" he asked.

"He's just a fussy baby. I don't know."

"You don't know cause you worthless. He drivin' me crazy," Jason said.

Tessa shook her head, opened her mouth to respond, then closed it. Jason slapped her anyway, then turned and got back in bed by himself. Charlie finally quieted, and Tessa put him down and went to sleep.

In the morning, Jason and Tessa lay in bed drinking, half-dozing on the bed, feeling good. Charlie was crying softly enough that they didn't have to pay attention.

After a while, Tessa got up to change him. He had a bad diaper rash that didn't seem to go away, and now it started oozing blood, so Tessa got dressed and took him to the emergency room.

"You're not changing him often enough," a nurse told Tessa sternly. "He's gotten like this because you're leaving him sitting in his mess for hours." She gave Tessa a hard look, and Tessa turned her eyes away.

They gave her salves to apply to the sores, and the nurse talked to her about how to do it. She was to bring Charlie in for testing in a week. But Tessa was afraid they'd take him away so she didn't go back.

Often she could forget about Charlie entirely while she and Jason were drinking together. But he whimpered when Jason beat her, and flinched when Jason came near. At eleven months, Tessa thought Charlie was a little behind other babies. She sat him up in a high chair, but he didn't hold himself up real good.

One day, Charlie was sitting in his chair, eating from a bowl of soggy Corn Flakes with his fingers. He dangled his fingers over the edge, dropping cereal mush onto the floor.

"Don't you be doing that, honey," Tessa said. Charlie looked appealingly at her, then he pushed his baby cup off the edge of the highchair tray. It clattered to the floor. Tessa picked it up and Charlie pushed it off again.

Suddenly Jason was there.

"He shouldn't ought to make messes like this," Jason said. "You're spoiling him."

"He's just a baby, Jason."

"Don't you do that," Jason scolded. Charlie was pouring juice from his cup onto the tray.

"Stop that," Jason yelled. "Didn't you hear me?"

Charlie grabbed the cup by its handle and banged it up and down on the tray, splashing the juice, and gurgling.

"Don't make fun of me, you little bastard," Jason said. He struck Charlie on the side of the head, hard enough to knock the high chair over with Charlie in it.

"Leave him alone!" Tessa cried, going to the baby on the floor. Charlie was wailing and choking, and blood was coming out of one of his ears. Jason stormed out. Charlie's body began shaking funny.

She brought him to the emergency room. The shaking had stopped, but now he seemed too quiet and she was afraid. Soon they took her and Charlie into an examining room. While the doctor examined Charlie she told her story about the high chair accidentally falling over when she bumped into it. The doctor glanced sharply at her for a moment, then resumed his examination. He was shining a light into Charlie's eyes, then into his ears, then pulled on both of his legs.

The doctor took Charlie off for X-rays, and the nurse got out a form, wrote something down, and asked Tessa to say again how the accident happened. She wrote some more and left Tessa alone in the examining room. After a half hour, a woman with a hospital name tag came in. She sat down and looked sympathetically at Tessa for a moment. She seemed calm. But Tessa was fearful.

"Mrs. Jackson, my name is Joan Berger. I'm a social worker. The doctor's going to tell you more about this," the woman said, speaking slowly, "but your baby's had a concussion. They want to keep him here for a couple of days to see how he's doing."

"What does it mean, what he had?"

"A concussion. It's like a bruise or a hurt to the brain, from a hit or a bang to the head. The doctor's the one who will explain this to you—you need to make sure you ask him any questions you have. Sometimes the injury is worse than other times. They have to see how bad this is by observing him for a while."

"Okay," said Tessa.

"The doctor will also talk to you about what you have to look out for after you take him home. So you know if he's getting worse, and if you have to bring him back in." Mrs. Berger paused for a moment, seeing if Tessa wanted to ask her anything about that. "You look like it's been pretty rough for you, too, hasn't it?"

Tessa was conscious of the still-swollen bruises on her own face. She wanted to make up some story, but could not think of another story. Her eyes filled with tears.

"I can see that you love your baby," Mrs. Berger said, nodding slowly as she spoke. "You know it's really important to keep him safe, no matter what else you do."

Tessa looked down and nodded too.

"It looks like there are a lot of things happening in your life right now. Whatever else is happening, though, you know you have to protect him, right, because he can't protect himself?"

Tessa nodded again.

"When a baby has injuries like this, we report it to a county agency called Child Protective Services. They are going to send someone out and make sure that you have a safe place for Charlie to be, and they can help you to keep him safe."

Mrs. Berger stopped talking. She was still looking at Tessa understandingly. But she was waiting. After a time, Tessa spoke.

"I need to keep him safe."

"Sometimes it's not easy," Mrs. Berger said. She paused again. "What do you think you need to do to keep him safe?"

"I . . . I'm not sure . . ."

"Is your husband still with you in the house, or is there another man?"

"There's just my husband, and he don't live with us now," Tessa said quickly. She was thinking about the welfare, and the fact that they'd cut off the AFDC if they knew there was a man in the house. "I don't know where he is."

"When someone really loves you, Tessa, he doesn't hurt you. You're here for your baby today. But it's not good for your baby to be in a place where someone's hurting his mom." She waited again, but Tessa didn't take the opening.

"Would you like to be able to come back and talk to me about this? Perhaps we can help you figure out how to deal with being with a man who hurts you."

"There's no dealing with it," Tessa said. "If you with a man, sometimes he's gonna get angry, and he gonna beat up on you when that happen."

"All men don't do that, Tessa. And a woman doesn't have to stay where it's happening to her or her child." Mrs. Berger wrote something on a card, and gave it to Tessa. "You call me here if you decide you need help."

When Tessa returned home, she stayed by Charlie, to make sure he didn't fall asleep for too long. After a while, Jason returned.

"Hey, baby. How's it going?"

"You gave Charlie a concussion when you hit him and knocked him down."

"Look like he's fine now."

"He's not so okay. And the child protective and the welfare people are going to be coming to check things, so you better not be here."

The child protective people came out a couple of times and talked to her about making the apartment safer for a baby. Tessa didn't go back to the hospital.

For three weeks, she didn't hear a word from Jason, and she was getting anxious. Then she got a letter. He had gone to Los Angeles with some people he knew, and had a place there, and had found work. He was going to send her money so they could come out and be with him.

51

"I knew something stupid was happening when he had me playing with those little blocks." Kareem said. "That's supposed to show that I'm a retard, right? What a load of shit."

Gideon had just told Kareem about the psychologist's report. It was a year and a half after Gideon had started on Kareem's case, and the investigation of Kareem's functioning had included a neuropsychological work-up. The psychologist concluded that Kareem Jackson suffered from brain damage.

Gideon planned to use these findings in a report he would submit to the California Supreme Court with his appeal brief and habeas corpus petition. Gideon wanted to show that Kareem's first attorney had been incompetent, and that his omissions had left the jury without critical information about Jackson—that his brain had been damaged by childhood abuse. But first Gideon was discussing the findings with Kareem.

"That's not what it says, Kareem. This isn't, like, you're retarded. I have spent a lot of time getting to know you and talking to you, and you're obviously not dumb. Do you feel dumb?"

That was a bad question, Gideon suddenly realized.

Kareem sat in silence, scowling, his muscular arms folded across his chest, looking at the wall.

"This is something else, Kareem. The brain's more complicated than just smart or dumb. And the shrink's not saying you're a dummy, he's saying that there's a problem with the way you've gotten on in the world. And that part of it has got to do with how your brain processes information, and how you are able to control violent impulses."

Kareem remained silent, but he looked back at Gideon. Gideon chose to be silent too, as he stared into Kareem's eyes. After a few minutes, Kareem spoke.

"You're supposed to be able to tell about that kind of shit from the way I played little games with the blocks and all that?"

"That and the other tests he gave you. These are scientific tests, Kareem, and I'm not equipped to judge them. But I can tell you real doctors use these in the real world to decide how to treat patients. This is not some scam they invented for court.

"It's one of the things that should have been done the first time around, before your trial. If your first lawyer had been on the ball. Maybe the jury might have thought the results were part of a reason not to execute you, to be merciful, if they had a question about whether you were a person with brain damage."

"After I fucked and knifed the mom and fucked up her kid's mind, you think this white jury would have given me life because this doctor says I don't know how to move these little blocks around just right?"

"I don't know what they might have decided. What the doctor would have told the jury is that your brain works differently from the brains of people who haven't had your problems. So you're not entirely in control of yourself because of the condition of your brain."

"Someone in the yard say that bout me—*you brain damaged, Kareem*—I'd whack them. I don't want to hear no one saying that about me."

"I'm out of patience with you, Kareem. Aren't you listening? You think I shouldn't give the judges information that helps your case because it might be embarrassing? Would you rather be embarrassed or dead? I don't find that a hard choice."

Kareem said nothing.

Gideon stood at the door, looking out through the bars, resting his hands on them. He knocked to signal the guards to let him out.

After many minutes, a guard moved slowly down the corridor toward them. Gideon looked down for a moment, and saw himself as he must appear to Kareem—a white man in his nicely-polished, black wingtip shoes, sleek in his pin-striped suit, wearing a tie that cost more than two weeks wages when Kareem had been growing up. The one with all the advantages and all the power.

He looked over and saw Kareem, neatly dressed in blue denim prison garb, the shirt pale blue, the pants darker. The pants had a sharp, hard crease that Kareem had pressed into them by putting them under his mattress overnight.

Gideon sat down. He waved the guard away.

Kareem was still smoldering over the report. And angry at Gideon for getting ready to walk out.

Would you rather be embarrassed or dead? What a stupid remark, Gideon realized. When everyone despises you, when you have nothing and self-respect is the only thing you can try to hold onto, the answer's not so obvious.

"I'm sorry," Gideon said. "I shouldn't have said that. I wasn't thinking. And I shouldn't have started to walk away."

Kareem's eyes were boring a hole in Gideon.

"I'm sorry," Gideon said again. He looked at Kareem, then he looked away, at the little wooden table that stood between them, at the last pieces of popcorn on the brown paper towels that served as napkins, at the empty soda cans Kareem had crushed while they were talking. He looked out the window at the Bay, saw cars in the distance on a bridge Kareem would likely never see up close. His eyes returned to Kareem's.

"Okay," Kareem said at last.

"Maybe it is a hard choice. These are tough things to hear about yourself. Hard to take in. Hard to take. I'm sorry."

Kareem was holding himself stiffly, still silent. But his face softened a little. Gideon wanted to give him a hug, but Kareem wouldn't want that. He reached across and took one of Kareem's hands in his, squeezed it gently.

"I'm not saying the report isn't true," said Gideon. "I think it is. I think it helps explain why you've done some of the things you've done. But I know it makes you feel bad."

Kareem did not respond. But neither did he move his hand away.

"We can talk about this again when I'm back next month."

52

CALIFORNIA SUPREME COURT

CHARLES JOSHUA JACKSON, PETITIONER, VS. WARDEN OF SAN QUENTIN STATE PRISON, RESPONDENT.	NO. 82-0558 JLH DEATH PENALTY CASE PROCEEDING ON PETITION FOR WRIT OF HABEAS CORPUS

REPORTER'S TRANSCRIPT

OF EVIDENTIARY HEARING PROCEEDINGS

BEFORE JAMES L. HANNIGAN, JUDGE, SPECIAL MASTER BY

APPOINTMENT OF THE CALIFORNIA SUPREME COURT

TERESA MORENO, CSR

OFFICIAL COURT REPORTER

****

Franklyn Jones, M.D., having been called as a witness
and duly sworn, testified as follows

DIRECT EXAMINATION BY MR. ROTH

Q   You work as a psychiatrist in a clinic in South
Central Los Angeles and you teach at USC Medical Center,
correct?

A   Yes.

Q   You have performed a psychiatric examination of Mr.
Jackson, and have reviewed the records of his life and
that of his family, is that correct?

A   Yes, that's correct.

Q   And you ordered neuropsychological testing for
Kareem Jackson?

A   Yes.

Q   Was there something in Mr. Jackson's background
that suggested the need for such testing?

A   Yes, a number of factors, beginning with the
circumstances of his birth.

Q   Please tell the Court about that, Dr. Jones.

A   When Kareem Jackson's mother was in the seventh
month of her pregnancy, his father literally tried to
kill Kareem in utero by punching and stomping on his
mother's abdomen. The assault precipitated Kareem's
premature birth.
Neuropsychological testing confirms he has brain damage,
and the pre-natal battery is a likely cause. But there
were other documented insults to his brain, so we cannot
isolate this one as sole cause.

Q   What were some of the other injuries that Kareem's

brain suffered when he was in the care of his father and
mother?

A   As a baby, a toddler and a small child, Kareem
received serious blows to the head from the father,
repeatedly, including at least one assault that resulted
in concussion and a seizure.

Q   How old was Kareem at the time of that assault?

A   Eleven months old. The seizure strongly supports
the conclusion that the assault caused brain damage.

Q   Have you formed a neurological diagnosis?

A   Yes. Mr. Jackson suffers significant, diffuse brain
dysfunction, suggesting the likelihood of frontal
and temporal lobe brain lesions and anterior brain
disruption.

Q   What does brain damage of this kind mean for the
subject's behavior?

A   The impairments that Kareem Jackson suffers from are
associated with impulsivity, inability to exercise self-
control, inability to plan, impaired decision-making,
and violent outbursts.

Q   What does that mean in ordinary terms?

A   Let me put it simply. There are parts of the brain
that allow normal people to exercise judgment and to
control their anger and their violent impulses. These
parts of Kareem Jackson's brain have been damaged and
they don't work very well. So because of these injuries
to his brain, he is much more likely to engage in
violent acts than ordinary people, much less able to
control himself . . . .

CROSS-EXAMINATION BY MR. CONTI

Q   Would you agree, then, Dr. Jones, that Kareem
Jackson was programmed for violence?

A   Well, "programmed" is too strong. Someone with
Kareem's hardware is much more vulnerable to becoming
violent than the average person. But, if he had had the
right kind of support and treatment at the outset, he
could have been guided toward an education and a future
suitable for his abilities, and his problems might not
have led to drugs and violence.

Q   Are you aware that Jackson has been disciplined for
attacking other inmates at San Quentin?

A   Yes, I am.

Q   It's your testimony that his difficulty in
controlling violent impulses is now built into his
brain, correct?

A   Yes.

Q.   Isn't it true, then, that Jackson is more likely
than people with ordinary brains to injure or kill
guards and other inmates?

A   Not necessarily. People change on death row. It
can actually be a more stable environment than the one
that people like Jackson had previously been living in.
It's usually drug free, and things can happen that are
healing. They meet some people who genuinely care about
them.

It's not too late for him to change, to improve.

Q   So even though his brain was supposedly damaged
when he was a baby, he could be capable of controlling
his impulses and his propensity for violence if he
wanted to?

A   It's not that simple, Mr. Conti. There are a range
of psychological factors in play, as well as the effect
of drugs when they are available and when they are
abused.

53

Jason had rented a small flat in South Central LA. He was proud of having made the move and of finding work right off. A friend from Mississippi had pointed him to a job in a body shop, where he did spray-painting after the dents had been fixed.

He got headaches from the fumes, but the pay was good. He saved enough to bring Tessa and Charlie from Chicago on the Greyhound bus. It was early March when they joined him. For a while they had money for booze and for food and rent, too, and Jason felt good about holding it all together.

At work, an occasional drink made his head better when the paint fumes got to him. It became routine during his morning break and at the end of lunch. Then more often.

Jason was in the paint locker, getting a five-gallon can of primer for the sprayer. He had put a fifth of vodka in a paper sack behind a stack of cans that morning. He took it out, twisted the cap open, and was taking a long pull when the owner walked in.

"Told you when you started, Jason, no drinking on the job. Take that with you when you go."

"Sorry, boss, won't do that again."

"I don't do second chances. You were told. Now you're fired. Go to the office, and collect your pay."

Jason had met some dealers in the neighborhood, and they gave him a small supply of drugs which he sold to friends and acquaintances. He also did occasional deliveries and other small jobs for the men who dealt in a bigger way.

Tessa kept Charlie out of his path as much as possible, but that was harder after they had to move to a smaller place. Now Jason was around more, there were more times when the child irritated him.

"That boy is going to learn to behave," Jason said when the boy had an accident in his pants. Jason took off his heavy belt to whip the child. Suddenly, he thought of Uncle Seth's belt. But this is different, Jason thought. Seth did it for no reason.

When Charlie was four, Tessa found out about Jason having sex with a girl on the next street.

"Seems everyone know you been screwing Carmen. And she got a big belly now."

"I don't need to answer to you."

"You gonna support that bitch and her bastard and us too? You think you the big man because you got two women? You ain't' nothing but dirt."

"Mind your fucking mouth. Least I know this one's mine," said Jason.

Tessa laughed. "Ever' body but you know that slut lays for anyone who got a belt that unbuckles."

Jason punched her in the mouth, and lashed her with his belt. He turned on Charlie when the boy began to scream.

"I don't want to see your ugly black face no more, you little piece of shit." He yanked Charlie up into the air by his arm, then he swung Charlie against the dresser. He opened the closet, threw the boy in, and slammed the door shut. "You just stay in there."

Tessa escaped out the front door while Jason was shoving the dresser in front of the closet so Charlie couldn't get out. Jason poured himself a drink. Then he left.

54

Saturday morning. Helen and Gideon had just made love. "That seemed mechanical," Helen said. "You were thinking about Jackson's case, weren't you?"

"Sorry. I guess I was. I thought you'd be upset if we stopped."

"Stopped and talked about what's going on in your head? Instead of performing your duty? Yes, that certainly would have been terrible."

Helen found her underwear and started dressing, then sat on the edge of the bed.

"Gideon, there's something I'm concerned about. When you tell me about your visits with Jackson, you talk about him as though he were a friend."

"I'm not sure what to say. I'm starting to understand a lot about what makes him tick. And we need to develop a relationship he can trust in. He's going to need support to survive the years in San Quentin."

"Is becoming his friend part of your job description? Or is it your duty to appear to be his friend?"

"I wouldn't put it like that."

"Because it seems a phony kind of friendship if that's what you're thinking it involves. You need to be clear that you're his lawyer, not his friend."

"Well, I'll admit I've started to genuinely like him," Gideon said. "Does that change things? Is something wrong with that? I don't think it conflicts with my responsibilities."

"I'm not talking about your responsibilities. I'm talking about the fact that your new friend, if that's how you see it, is a man who butchered a young mother in front of her child."

"And shot the store clerk, too, Helen. Don't forget the clerk, while you're talking like the prosecutor. What is your problem, Helen? We're just beginning to understand the forces that made Kareem into what he is. I thought you recognized that. We need to comprehend how he came to be what he is, not condemn him. I expected more of you, Helen."

"Gideon, you are treating him as though he bears no responsibility for what he did, as though he's less than human. Is that what you really think?"

"No, he's human. He's a very damaged human being, who still needs to be treated as a person. How responsible he can be is limited by the damage he's suffered."

"But you don't expect anything of him. What kind of friend are you then?"

"Maybe the only kind he can deal with right now."

"That's a cop-out, Gideon. Has he ever told you he's sorry for what he did?"

"I . . . I'm not sure he has. I don't think it's my role to judge him."

"Gideon, maybe you are the one who is contemptuous of Kareem Jackson. I'm not saying it's your job to lecture him. But he did something really, really horrible. Sometimes I think you lose sight of that."

"The crime is in my mind all the time, Helen."

"Yes, but only as a problem you have to solve. As something you want to make people 'understand' and forgive."

"Not forgive."

"All right, not forgive. But almost forget. Forget from the perspective of the victims. It's like the joke about the two therapists who come upon a mugging victim, lying battered in the gutter. 'This is awful,' one says. 'Yes,' the other replies, 'the person who did this really needs our help.'

"Sometimes, Gideon, it seems that the crime and the suffering of the victims is only significant to you because it reveals how much Jackson must have suffered in order to allow him to do things like this."

"Fuck you, Helen. That's a terrible thing to say about me."

He got up and started dressing, angrily pulling on his clothes. She watched.

"All right. That's an exaggeration," Helen said. "An unfair exaggeration."

She stood behind him and put her arms around him.

"Helen, at first I went back and forth between the horror of it and just blanking it out. Now it's stopped being vivid. I can't function if I really feel the awfulness of these crimes all the time."

"I'm sorry. I can accept that you need to deal with it that way. But it disturbs me to hear you talk about the case with so much detachment. And there's still the question of how you think about Jackson."

Gideon could feel her breathing deeply against him, but he refused to relax the tension in his body.

"All right," she said. "This is what I mean. Jackson committed a terrible crime. And you are going to try to save him from death by showing that he was so damaged by things in his background that he could not appreciate what an evil thing he was doing."

"Right."

"But what about now? Are you saying that this damage is permanent? That Kareem can never come to understand that he did wrong? That he can never feel genuine remorse or repentance?"

Gideon unclasped her arms from around him and went to the wooden chair beside the dresser. He turned it around and sat with the back of the chair between him and Helen. He rested his arms on the chair back, and put his head on them. She sat down on the bed and waited. Finally he lifted his head.

"I don't know. I hadn't thought about that. It's not part of the job I've got to do. Maybe his moral sense is permanently impaired."

"If that is what you think, then you are the one who believes Kareem will never be fully human. Because being human means being able to empathize with others, and accepting responsibility for the pains we cause. If you think he can never do that, then you certainly can't be his friend. How could you be a friend of someone who can feel no sorrow for what he did to Marisol Flores and Luisa Flores? Can Marisol ever be an intact person after what she witnessed? Your confusion about befriending him is twisting your judgment. And he's not a friend, no matter how long you know him. He's a client. There's a boundary between the two, and I'm afraid of what will happen to you if you lose sight of it."

She got up and finished dressing.

"Gideon, I don't know what made Kareem Jackson what he is. And I don't know just what you should do or say, or when. But you can't avoid this forever."

55

In his drive through Yellowstone National Park, Gideon did not stop to see the sights. But he had stopped for dinner at the Lake Yellowstone Hotel. Afterward, he found a phone booth outside and called Wayne Roberts. Dropping the quarters in, Gideon noticed that someone was standing nearby, waiting to use the phone. Gideon smiled. No worries over anyone overhearing, because Gideon didn't plan to say anything. He pressed the handset tightly against his ear, so only he could hear Roberts' voice.

"Hullo," Wayne Roberts said. "Hullo." After a few moments, Roberts hung up noisily, and Gideon also hung up.

He picked up the phone again. Perhaps he should call Susan and let her know he was coming. He got her number from Springfield directory assistance. After four rings her answering machine came on. "Hi, Susan here. Please leave a message and I'll get back to you." *Beep.* Her voice was familiar, but different. Gideon opened his mouth, then thought, a recording is evidence. Was there danger in leaving his voice and a message? Did he really need to talk to her now? He hung up.

A few minutes after the Wayne Roberts call, a special phone company operative in Mississippi called Timmie Ray Phelps and gave him the number from which the call to Roberts had been placed.

Area code 307, Timmie Ray said to himself. Still in Wyoming. This time we'll see!

Timmie called the Wyoming state police. He identified himself as a Mississippi police officer, working on a special matter for a District Attorney deputized by the Mississippi State Attorney General, and explained his interest. He was somewhat vague, trying to make the matter appear more definite and ominous than he had a right to, without uttering any outright lies.

In a few minutes, a Wyoming state police investigator called back. The number was a public phone booth at the big hotel in the park, the Lake Yellowstone Hotel. It was after hours, but they would ask the hotel to close off the phone booth, and in the morning they'd have a latent print man go to the hotel and see what they could lift from the phone or the booth. They would not do anything with the impressions they lifted but would send them directly to Mississippi.

Timmie was nervous. Southern Idaho. Grand Tetons. Now, Lake Yellowstone Hotel, on the road to the eastern exit from Yellowstone park. It would not take Mr. Quiet Caller long to get here once he stopped dawdling. But as Jeffers had predicted, this wasn't the kind of matter the Wyoming police were inclined to consider urgent.

The phone box was a busy one, it turned out, and someone else was using it—a young woman with two small children in the booth with her—when the police arrived next morning. They didn't bother trying to lift prints from the handset.

They dusted the rest of the booth, found about a dozen good prints, sprayed and lifted them, and sent them on to Mississippi.

When Timmie learned the circumstances, he was pessimistic. He dropped the prints into a file.

56

Charlie huddled in the corner of the closet, gasping and trying to stay quiet. Clothes had fallen on him, and his shoulder throbbed with pain where Papa yanked him by his arm. His nose was bleeding. His chest hurt where he'd hit the edge of the dresser. It hurt bad when he took a deep breath. His heart was thumping, and he hoped Papa wasn't going to come back for him.

After a long time, the light under the door began to fade, and he called cautiously. "Momma?" There was no answer. He had been in the closet for hours. He was hungry and he had to pee. He reached up for the handle and turned it slowly, so it wouldn't make a noise. But the door wouldn't open when he pushed.

"Momma, let me out! Let me out! I got to go."

He called again, louder. No one answered. He didn't hear anyone moving.

Charlie was scared. No one was there. Even outside the closet it wasn't light. He flailed at the door with his fists, crying and screaming.

He was all alone. No one was there. He shrieked and shrieked, until his throat hurt.

He heard little scampering noises on the floor outside. Rats or mice.

He had to go.

"Momma, Momma, let me out. I got to pee. I'm gonna pee my pants." Finally he let go and wet himself. He was ashamed and afraid of what Momma or Papa would do when they found out. Stinky.

After a while the pee got cold. He was tired and he was hungry, and his shoulder hurt. He pulled down a coat that was hanging above him and fell asleep.

It was morning. Still no one was there. He cried softly. The pee had dried out but his pants felt funny. Now he had to go shit. He held it in. Then he knew he couldn't anymore. Charlie didn't know what to do. He didn't want to mess in his pants and he didn't want to mess the floor. Would they be madder if it was his pants or the floor?

"Momma, Momma, where are you?" He banged on the door some more, but still it didn't open.

While he was trying to decide, it came out. Charlie pressed his nose against the crack along the bottom of the door so he didn't have to smell it so much. He was hungry. He felt weaker and he slept.

When Charlie woke, he started banging against the door with a shoe that was in the closet. After a while he heard noises in the apartment.

"Tessa honey? You here?" It was one of the neighbors.

"Auntie Myrlie! I'm in the closet. Lemme out."

"Hold on, what you doin' in there, boy?" He heard the dresser scraping along the floor.

"Papa hit me and put me in here. I was bad. I had to go, and I couldn't hold it in."

The door opened and he saw Auntie Myrlie. She was lots older than Momma, and she was nice.

"I saw the door flopping open, and I thought your momma was here. They leave you alone?"

He nodded.

"Whew, what a smell." She carried him down the hall to the bathroom and took off his clothes. She put his pants and underpants into the toilet to soak, then stood him in the tub and turned the faucets on. She ran water over him with the shower attachment, and rubbed the mess off him with her hands, until it all ran down the drain. She turned toward the door.

"Don't leave me alone, Auntie Myrlie," Charlie said softly.

"I'm just going to my place to get some soap, honey."

She returned and soaped him all up, then rinsed him off again.

He was clean now, it felt good. Auntie Myrlie's hands were strong but gentle, and the water was nice and hot. She put the stopper in the drain this time and filled the tub and washed him all over again. He cried when she touched his hurt shoulder, then she was careful. He was tired and her hands felt good. "You was pretty dirty even where there wasn't any dookey," she said.

Charlie began to feel sleepy, and his head lolled against the back of the tub. The hot water softened him. Auntie Myrlie was holding his pants and flushing the toilet so the water ran through them. After a few times, she squeezed them out.

"I be right back, don't you worry." She went out and came back with a big towel. She pulled the chain that held the plug, and he heard the gurgle-whoosh sound. She held the towel open and he stood up. She wrapped it around him and lifted him out. Charlie was surprised, the towel was warm from the radiator. It felt good. She patted him dry, wound the towel around and carried him to her apartment.

"There weren't no clean clothing for you in your place, so I'm gonna put my John's old things on you for now." They were too big, but she dressed him in them anyway. She sat him in the kitchen and gave him breakfast.

Charlie spent the day watching TV in Auntie Myrlie's living room, and eating and sleeping. When John came home from school, he wouldn't play with him because Charlie was a baby.

That night Momma returned and carried him back to their apartment. He was happy to see Momma, but he didn't want to go back. He'd felt soft inside when he'd been with Auntie Myrlie. Now he was tightening up again.

His eyes darted around, to see whether Papa was there. Momma didn't have that look, so Papa was probably out. He peeped at Momma. Was she cross? Anyway, it didn't hurt so much when she was the one who smacked him.

⋆ ⋆ ⋆

Six years old. They moved again. Momma and Papa screamed at each other all the time, and sometimes Papa hit Momma and Momma hit Papa and Papa hit him. Charlie was good at dodging. Momma and Papa didn't notice him much, and lots of times they acted sleepy and funny.

"Why you jump away, honey?" Momma asked one day, when she had reached out to stroke his head. He felt ashamed, but he'd been afraid she was going to give him a smack.

Charlie tried the stuff Momma and Papa drank. It burned, but make him feel funny, and he decided he liked it. He drank whenever he could. Sometimes Momma laughed when she saw he was drunk. Sometimes she slapped him for stealing her liquor.

A lot of people were in and out of the apartment. There was a big mattress on the floor for Momma and Papa, and a smaller one in the corner for him. He listened to what they were saying, in case he had to dodge, but he didn't always understand. Sometimes they thought he was asleep, but he was listening.

"When you gonna score us some more shit, honey?" Momma asked. Something in her voice made Charlie nervous.

"Tessa, baby," Papa was saying, "my man Hunter want to do it with you. He say he give us a hundred dollars if you do him."

Papa left. Then a big man came in. Momma talk sweet to him but she didn't sound sweet. Momma hugged the big man, and the man started taking his pants off.

Charlie closed his eyes tight, but he could hear them. They were doing the pussy, and the man was hurting Momma.

* * *

Seven. Charlie had rolled a piece of newspaper tightly, and held it over the burner til it caught. He swung it back and forth in the air, gazing intently as the flames got bigger when he waved the rolled paper, then a little smaller when he held it still. When the fire got close to his fingers, he dropped it into the sink, where it burned down. He watched closely as it turned into black crinkling paper. Then he turned the faucet on and washed it down the drain. It left a scorch.

Charlie started again.

All of a sudden Momma was there, and she smacked Charlie on the side of the head.

"How many times I got to say don't play with fire? You going to burn the house down one of these days, and Lenny's gonna whup your ass."

After the big fires that had burned across Watts last year, Papa went away to the Penitentiary, and Momma and Charlie were on their own. Except now they lived in an apartment with Momma's new friend Lenny.

Charlie grabbed the box of matches he'd used to light the burner and he ran. Downstairs, there were vacant lots from where the fires had burned. Charlie and a friend built a little house of sticks, then carefully tucked bits of dried weeds and wrappers inside.

They lit it and watched. "Burn, baby, burn," Charlie's friend said.

Charlie liked to smell the smoke and the burning. When it was done they collected rocks and went to look for cats. Once they'd killed one with rocks. Charlie had wanted to tie sticks and paper to a cat's tail and light it. But the only time they'd actually caught one, she had scratched them so bad they had to let her go before they could tie anything to her.

Charlie was afraid of Lenny. One afternoon after school, Momma wasn't home when he got there. Lenny was there. Charlie's heart was pounding, and he felt a churning in the center of his stomach. Lenny was reading something from the school, and scowling.

"You've been ditching school again. They're going to leave you behind. Come over here."

Lenny took his belt off his pants, and doubled it.

"Pull down your pants and lean over."

Lenny made it worse if he tried to run away. He bent over the edge of the couch. Lenny put his left hand on Charlie's back and held him. He pulled down Charlie's underpants and lashed his bottom with the belt, making red welts until Charlie cried.

"I'm just doing this for your own good, you know that," Lenny said in a soft voice when he had stopped. He patted the hurt places on Charlie's bottom, then rested his hand on Charlie's buttocks, and probed him with a finger. Charlie tried to hold his breath. He heard the man unzip and drop his pants, and heard him spit. A small cry escaped Charlie as Lenny's finger wet his anus, and tears ran down his face.

Five months later, Charlie was removed from his mother and sent to the first of many foster homes. After Charles Joshua Jackson turned ten, he was never to see his mother or his father again.

57

"Well, if it isn't Officer Vanderson," said Lisa. "We haven't had the pleasure of your distinguished company hereabouts for some time." She put down a cup of coffee and a glazed donut immediately.

"No, I've been taking my valuable business elsewhere, Lisa, where I don't get sassed by waitresses."

"Not sure how much valuable business there is in the same cuppa-coffee-and-one-donut three times a week," said Lisa. "And a handsome man like you must meet sassy waitresses everywhere."

"So, how you been, Lisa?"

"Actually," she dropped her voice and her regulation smile faltered. It had never been much use flirting with Phil Vanderson. "I've been glum lately. Thinking about moving on."

"Sorry to hear that, hon. How come?"

"Just, well, maybe I've stayed in Palma too long. Any chance you could give me a ride to Twin Falls on Friday some time, so's I can catch a bus to Frisco?"

"Well, sure. Guess so. When you figure to leave?"

"After lunch time be okay with you?"

He picked her up in front of her hotel a little after one. Lisa's worldly goods occupied one suitcase and an overflowing shopping bag. They picked up some coffee at the cafe, where Lisa gave the other waitress a hug and they exchanged the traditional empty promises to keep in touch.

Lisa and Vanderson drove in silence for a time.

"Well, I'm going to miss you," he said. But I can't say I'm surprised. What made you decide now was the time to go?"

Lisa didn't answer. Phillip Vanderson was used to people who didn't say much, and he didn't necessarily expect an answer right away. Or at all.

Lisa watched the desert unroll past them. Empty and flat, and in the distance on all sides, low mountains. Looked from afar like pretty scenery. Nothing but ugly brush and dry dirt up close. After a while of driving, without exactly noticing it, you passed on into another place where there was another set of low mountains all around, different, but the same. They were like big rooms, and after a while you passed from one room to another. One empty room after another.

"I was headed for Frisco when I happened to stop here. So I'm just finishing the journey, Phil."

Officer Vanderson said nothing and neither did Lisa for a time.

"I met some guy last week. He was just passing through, but we spent a little time together. You know. Different from your big dumb Mormon type—don't take offense, Phil," she added quickly. He just nodded.

"Different from the tourists, too. I liked him, but he wouldn't take me with him. Wouldn't even give me a ride to Salt Lake. Bald-headed asshole. I'm not sure why I cared the tiniest bit, anyway."

She was quiet again until they passed into another room of the desert.

"Anyway, I got no more to wait for here, and maybe I can get my life goin' again in California."

She looked out at the mountains on her side of the car for a while. Trying to see something interesting in them. Nothing but the hawks or vultures or whatever they were floating overhead.

"Phil, there was something else. Don't know whether I ought to be telling on him or not. Feels funny, but oh well. I don't owe him nothing. This guy was up to something, Phil."

"What kind of something?"

"I peeked at his stuff while he was sleeping in the morning, and he didn't have any real identification, and he was carrying lots of cash. Like thousands and thousands of dollars. But he wasn't part of no drug thing. I know those kinds of people, and there weren't any drugs there anyway."

"Guns?"

"Well . . . I didn't see any, but he had a manual for one of those little telescopes they have on rifles. But he didn't seem like the militia type, either—not at all. Who the hell knows?"

"This guy have a name?"

"Jim Cargill, or that's what he said. He had a temporary California drivers license with James Cargill on it. But it didn't have his picture. That was the only thing in his wallet except for money. No credit cards, no ATM card, no work papers, no Blue Cross, no other crap. I mean nothing. Weird, huh? Who has a wallet like that?"

"Yeah, but that doesn't make him a criminal. James Cargill. You happen to notice the license plate on his car? What state it was from?"

"No, but it was an old blue pickup truck, camper kind of thing."

Vanderson suddenly grew alert. "You said he was bald. But did he have dark hair on the sides and in back? And thick-rimmed glasses?"

"Yeah. You know this guy?"

"No, but I think I ran into him at a rest stop on I-84 last week. He acted strange. Real startled when he saw I was a highway patrolman, practically ran away."

He thought for a moment. "Would this have been on Wednesday?"

"Yeah."

"Take a look in the glove compartment. There's a photo he dropped when he jammed everything he'd been looking at into this leather satchel he was carrying."

Lisa took out the photo. "This isn't him."

"No, but it's a picture he was carrying with him."

"Jim's stuff was in a leather bag," she said softly. "Kind of rawhide like?" she asked sadly. "He's into something bad, isn't he?"

"Well, I don't rightly know. But before I drop you in Twin Falls, I want to stop at headquarters and take down everything you remember about Cargill and his vehicle."

58

Charlie lasted four months in the first foster home. He was seven. The woman had two boys of her own, ten and thirteen, and they hated Charlie for invading their home and getting any of their mother's attention.

"Your Momma was a junkie," the younger boy mocked. "That's why she didn't want to keep you."

"You don't have no mother," the older one said. "You got to do what we say or they put you on the street."

Charlie didn't know whether to believe them and was afraid to find out. He said nothing when they made fun of him. He was afraid to defy them when they told him to do things.

The foster mother made Charlie clean the bathroom and the kitchen with a spray bottle of stuff, and wipe all the walls every day. She prayed a lot and made the children pray with her. She carried something like a short leather leash for her keys in her pocket all the time, and would hit Charlie with it unexpectedly, to drive out the devil he had in him. Charlie was on the lookout all the time.

It was summer, and the boys spent most of the day outside on their own, playing. Charlie was glad school was out, because he couldn't read very well, and everyone made fun of him.

While Charlie was doing what the foster mother had told him to do, he looked about for some of the drink that Momma and Papa had told him was only for grownups. He'd gotten used to the bad taste, and it took away the tight feeling in his chest. He yearned for more, but the foster mother was against "devil rum" and he couldn't find anything like it in the house.

He went outside. But the older boys wanted nothing to do with Charlie. Once some other kids let him join while they were sniffing glue. That made him feel better. But mostly Charlie was by himself.

He caught a small abandoned dog in a vacant lot, and squeezed its stomach until the dog squealed. Charlie liked to hear the squealing noise. It was funny, and it made him laugh. He tied a rope around the dog, and dragged it around with him, squeezing it every now and then to hear the sound. He pet and hugged the dog too.

"I got a dog, I got a dog, I got a funny dog, I got a dog," he chanted. He knew he couldn't take it back to the foster home. He let it go after a while.

The younger boy had asthma, and early one morning the foster mother told the older boy to look after Charlie while she took the younger to the clinic. The boys all shared a bedroom, and after the mother left, the older boy came in. Charlie was in bed looking at a comic book, but something in the large boy's manner made Charlie uneasy. When Charlie looked up, he saw the boy had nothing on but his underpants, and the front was bulging.

"Time to get out of your pajamas," the boy said.

Charlie got up to get dressed, but the boy pushed him back onto the bed.

"Take 'em off and lie on your belly."

"I don't want to . . . leave me alone," Charlie said. But he heard his voice break, and knew he sounded scared.

"I'll tell my mom you tried to grab my dick while I was peeing and she'll throw you out."

Charlie's heart was pounding and he could hardly breath. He knelt on the bed, passive, as the boy took off his pajama top, then pushed him down and pulled down the bottom, then separated his legs.

The boy laid himself on Charlie, and Charlie felt a wave of revulsion at the boy's sweaty skin against his. The boy stuck his hard thing into Charlie, and Charlie lay still, trying not to move at all. He kept quiet, the way Lenny had made him be, even though it hurt.

"If you tell anyone about this," the boy said after he finished, "I'll wait 'til you're sleeping, then I'll stick a fork in your eye and you'll be blind."

Charlie was afraid to tell. And it happened more times. Now he worried about when the foster mother might leave them alone together. He tried to stay outside as much as he could, and to do his jobs in the house as quickly as possible.

One day when they were all out, Charlie started a little fire in the bathroom after he finished cleaning it. He put an ashtray on the floor next to the toilet bowl, made a little pile of crumpled toilet paper, and lit it. When it burned down, he dumped it into the toilet and started again. He loved the sound of the match scratching the side of the box, and the smell as the match burst into flame, and the way the fire slowly grew along the edges of the paper. He loved the shapes in the fire, and how you could look through it. As he gazed at the flames, his eyes grew wide and unfocused, and his breathing slowed. Everything left his mind.

I could keep it going by feeding toilet paper from the roll on the wall, Charlie thought.

The ashtray wasn't big enough, so he got a small bowl from the kitchen and put it on the floor beneath the toilet paper dispenser. He loosely crumpled some paper into a ball without tearing it off the roll, and put it in the bowl and he lit it in three places. As it burned, he pulled slowly and steadily on the roll and pushed the paper into the bowl.

The fire kept going and going. He had nearly used up the roll, and he stopped unfurling as he wondered if he would be punished for using it all up. Suddenly, the fire leapt the length of the paper to the dispenser, and it was all burning at once. He tried to hit at the flame to knock it down, but it didn't go out.

Charlie was scared. He ran to the kitchen to get a glass of water to pour on the fire. But he rammed his toe into a chair on the way. Blinded by pain, Charlie staggered. He made himself go on and get the water, and went back to the bathroom as fast as he could without spilling.

The towel next to the toilet paper had caught, and the flames were starting in the curtains. Charlie threw the water at the fire and tried to splash water from the sink but it wouldn't go out. He ran out of the apartment crying "Fire, fire!"

A neighbor ran in and pulled down the burning curtains and beat down the flames. By the time the foster mother returned, the fire department was there. The walls were charred and the entire apartment smelled of smoke. The firemen had pulled open part of the wall next to the window to make sure the fire was entirely out, and they broke the windows to let the smoke escape, and they wet down everything.

"That was a close call, ma'am," the fireman told the foster mother. "Whole house would have gone up in another five minutes."

She made them take Charlie back immediately.

At the next foster placement, the foster mother was very old, and her own children were grown and gone. Mrs. Clay took in several foster children, and they came and went. There were two others when Charlie arrived. Charlie felt safer because both were girls. Phyllis was eleven and Josie was five.

Mrs. Clay put Charlie in the tub with Josie, told them to wash themselves, and went to watch the TV. Charlie soaped her up, though she told him she could do it herself. When he put his hand between her legs, Josie tried to pull away, but Charlie told her, "Be quiet or I'll stick your eye with a fork when you're asleep." She became still. Her skin was slippery, and Charlie pressed his prick against her backside and rubbed it back and forth against her. It felt good.

Mrs. Clay put Charlie and Josie to bed earlier than the older girl, who watched television with her. When the TV got loud in the other room, Charlie went to the bed the girls shared and made Josie turn over. He pulled up her nightie and lay down on top of her, pressing himself on her, then he put his prick into her butt. She whimpered but was quiet.

Charlie found the "medicine" that Mrs. Clay drank to make her feel better, and he had drank some too. But the bottles were little, and he was afraid she'd catch him if he took too much. There were cleaning fluids in a pantry, and he sniffed that. It made his head hurt, but he liked the way it made him woozy.

Charlie had been in school for two months when they'd moved him to the new foster home, and he had to start at a new school again.

A boy teased him in the school yard the first day during morning recess. Charlie tried to ignore him, but he knew the boy was looking for a fight. Always the same. Stupid questions and jeers. Then a shove, then the fighting.

The boy was bigger than Charlie, and Charlie was afraid. But if they were going to fight, he was going to hit first. As soon as the boy said, "You fosters ain't got no fathers, do you?"—Charlie wheeled and punched him in the face with all his might. The boy went down, and Charlie kicked him and fell on him, punching until the yard duty pulled him off. It felt good to hurt someone.

Mrs. Carson didn't like having to come to school for the principal to tell her about how bad Charlie was. And when Josie finally told on him, he was taken away and put into a youth shelter.

59

Gideon was trying to make him talk about what happened when he'd been on his own, as a kid. *I am not going to go there.*

"Maybe you're shy about things that were done to you," he heard Gideon say, "because they're not the kinds of things you'd talk to your friends about? But this is more like the kind of confidences you might share with your family doctor . . . "

What the fuck was Gideon talking about? "Family doctor"? That's what people have on TV shows.

"We've already learned a lot about what happened to you when you were a child. Private things about how your parents acted, things a child shouldn't see, things they did to you." Gideon spoke softly. "Things other people did to you. But even though it's hard to talk about, we need the whole picture. How it was for you. So we can help you."

Kareem stiffened; his face grew warm. Why the hell did Gideon think they could . . .

Gideon was looking at him, to see how he was reacting. Gideon wasn't embarrassed. And Gideon wasn't making fun of him.

"I know," Gideon said softly. "It hurts to think about it. We're only going through all this to help you, right? You know that. Because we care."

Kareem saw he was working himself up. He stood, turned away from Gideon. He looked out the window. He took a breath, then another. Then he swallowed, sat back down. *Okay, I don't need to blow up.*

"There's nothing to talk about," Kareem said quietly. "Forget it."

"We don't have to talk about it right now, no more than you want to. When you're ready."

"Gideon. Stop acting so fucking patient with me. I'm not a god damn mental case. Let's talk about something else."

60

Charlie was fourteen. He was through with the youth shelters and through with school.

Junior high had been a war zone. Charlie tried to steer clear of the two gangs that fought over control of the school. But one of them regarded him as from enemy territory because he lived in a neighborhood the other gang dominated. He had to be careful which bathroom he went to, and he couldn't go to certain classes because they were in the part of the building controlled by the first gang.

Kids were knifed in the yard, and once he had been at a basketball game when gunfire had broken out. After the initial burst of shots, he joined the mob running for the exits. One of the players, someone they'd said was going to make it to the NBA, was on the floor under the home team basket, blood spreading under him.

Charlie had been on his own for three months now. When he'd run off, he thought a slightly older friend would give him a place to stay. But that fell through.

Charlie had spent the next day wandering around on his own, trying to look as though he knew what he was doing. That night he tried to sleep curled up against his backpack in the foyer of a decaying apartment building, but one of the tenants ran him out.

It was nearly midnight. Charlie thought of breaking into an abandoned building and sleeping there, but he was afraid of who might find him. He kept walking so he looked like he was someone who had some place he was going to, stopping after a while to rest by leaning against a telephone pole. He hadn't eaten since morning, and now it was getting drizzly.

An older white guy in a car slowed, ducked his head down as he went by so he could get a look at Charlie. He parked his car next to an all night diner up the street, and walked toward Charlie.

"You look like you're down on your luck. Can I buy you a meal?"

"Sure."

The man joked with Charlie while he was eating, and made small talk. He had a beer while Charlie put away a burger and fries, and then some pie. When Charlie was through, the man asked, "Need a place to stay tonight?"

"Yeah."

They went to his apartment. It was warm and clean inside, and the man got out a couple of beers. Charlie sat on the sofa, and the guy sat next to him. He rolled a joint, and they smoked it together and drank. The man got up to put on some jazz, which Charlie didn't like, then the man sat by him. Charlie felt how close the man was, was aware of his leg touching Charlie's leg as he nodded with the music. While Charlie was toking their third joint, the man rested his hand inside Charlie's thigh. The man was gentle.

After the sex, they went to sleep. The next morning the man did it again, then gave him some money and sent him off.

Charlie realized he was young and pretty, and could get by this way. Some of the men who paid for him were kind. Others liked to be rough. But being knocked about was nothing new, and at least he could run away afterward. Sometimes he would get even by breaking or stealing something that seemed precious to the men who bought him. Once he poured lighter fluid on the bed near the sleeping john, lit it and left. He was disappointed he never found out what happened.

Every now and then he wished there were something else he could do with his life, become a doctor or a fireman or something, but he had no idea how to get from here to there.

The cops picked him up every now and then, but when he told them how old he was, they let him go. "They'd just send you up to CYA," California Youth Authority, a tolerant cop once told Charles, "and that ain't calculated to give your ass-hole a rest."

It was Friday night and he was sitting by himself on a curb in Inglewood, waiting for his friend Jamaal. Jamaal was sixteen and had been living with his parents until he had run away a year ago. Charlie had been suspicious when Jamaal first befriended him, but Jamaal preferred girls and just wanted a sidekick. Jamaal used to be called Michael, but he told Charlie this was a slave name, and that he had given himself an African name.

Jamaal persuaded Charlie he should have an African name too, and helped him pick "Kareem" as his new name. He liked the way it sounded. Kareem Jackson.

Jamaal had shown Kareem how they could get by, shoplifting and selling small radios and other stuff they lifted from stores to a guy in the neighborhood.

They expected to crash tonight with some older girls Jamaal knew, but first they would score some weed. Jamaal always found something for them to try. Rum coolers, weed, cocaine when they were with someone flush, or glue or just gasoline to sniff. The dope and the fumes made the tightness in his chest go away, the tightness he always seemed to feel.

"Hey, Kareem," Jamaal said. "Come quick, easy pickings." Jamaal was better than he was at planning.

Jamaal had seen a guy tottering out of a liquor store, putting a fat wallet into his back pocket. Now the guy was sitting by himself, with the car door open, drinking from a small bottle of gin in a paper bag.

"You tell him you'll blow him for five bucks, and when he gets up to reach for his wallet, you pull him out of the car, and I'll rush him. We'll hit him and take the wallet and run."

They separated, and Kareem sidled up to the man, and crouched down a couple of feet from him.

"Hey mister," he said softly. "I'll suck your dick in the back of your car for five bucks."

"Come here, baby."

"First give me the money," Kareem said.

The man stood and reached for his back pocket, but when he saw Jamaal approaching, he kicked out at Kareem, knocking him down. Jamaal had a length of rebar in his hand and he struck the man, hitting his shoulder. The man grunted, but threw himself at Jamaal, butting Jamaal's face with his head and punching. He was tougher than he looked.

Kareem tried to pull the man off Jamaal, but he wasn't so drunk after all. As they struggled, a patrol car came by. The cops jumped out and grabbed them.

Kareem went to Juvie Hall for the first time.

Just like in school, if you didn't want to be the next victim, you had to show right off you could kick ass. Kareem always let himself go when he fought and became ferocious. He also knew that if you didn't want to get fucked, you had to join the stronger kids who did the grabbing and the fucking. When they did a train on a new boy, he was part of it. It was fuck or get fucked.

The grownups tested him while he was there, to see where he should be in school. Kareem couldn't read much and did poorly on tests. One of the teachers thought it had to do with stuff Kareem had been sniffing. "You ought to lay off the glue and the gasoline," he told Kareem. "It can really screw up your brain." Kareem said he didn't care, but he worried about being thought stupid.

Kareem was tired of having to watch out for himself all the time, and he felt down. The other guys got pills from their visitors, and some of them shared with Kareem. These made him high, but then there was the crash.

Late one night, Kareem decided to off himself. He took the sheet off his bed and tore it into strips, which he twisted and tied together to make a sort of rope. He tied one end around his neck. The light in the ceiling had a heavy metal frame around it to protect it from being smashed. Kareem stood on a chair and tied the other end of his makeshift rope to one of the bars of the fixture. Then he jumped.

But the frame bent, and his rope tightened without strangling him. Partially suspended, and sagging against the chair, Kareem became woozy as the sheet squeezed his windpipe. One of the guards found him before he became completely unconscious.

They sent him to a psych unit for a few days and gave him some pills. He told them he didn't know why he did it, but he was feeling better now. The pills made him feel dull, and he stopped using them. A few days after he got back to the regular dorm, someone offered Kareem meth for the first time.

Nothing in his life had been like this. Doing meth was as good as sex. Better. It was like coming again and again and again, all at once. But the downer when you stopped was awful.

After two months, they sent him to a CYA special school. A month later he escaped.

Kareem spent the next few years on the street, and in and out of the camps and jails of the California Youth Authority, to which he was committed for prostitution, selling drugs, petty thefts and assaults. For a while he was with a girl from Mexico called Chantico, who was a year younger than Kareem. Sometimes he pimped her.

Together, they tried every kind of drug there was. One night he decided, again, he would end everything. He took a big handful of downers and washed them down with vodka.

When Chantico got up in the night to pee, she noticed Kareem was too still. When she couldn't shake him awake, she called 911. An ambulance brought him to County General, where they pumped his stomach. After he had recovered for a day, they had him talk to a shrink for fifteen minutes. The shrink prescribed an anti-depressant and made a follow-up appointment. Kareem sold the pills and didn't keep the appointment.

They went back to hustling and getting high. Chantico was careful of Kareem when they were short of meth, because he was so touchy then.

At seventeen, Kareem was tried as an adult for auto theft, and sent up to Folsom State Prison for two years. Chantico was sent to CYA's Ventura facility, as an accessory. He never saw her again. In Kareem's two years at Folsom, he had not a single visitor.

Kareem was good at taking a plan someone else came up with and doing it right. At Folsom, he met Dave Hollister. They'd become buddies and protected each other. When they got out, another friend from Folsom, Jimmie Henderson, taught them how to do armed robberies: Brandish or fire a big gun as soon as you entered a small store. Whatever you do, don't shoot anyone. Grab whatever there was to grab and go.

Jimmie went down one night when the owner of a convenience store pulled out a handgun and shot him three times pointblank in the chest. Dave exchanged fire with the man, then he and Kareem ran off.

Afterward, they tried the robbery number on their own. Kareem liked being the leader. He had no thoughts on how to do anything different from how Jimmie had taught them. But they were able to work the robberies, as well as other hustles with no big problems. They'd never hurt anyone.

Not until the Sunday afternoon at Kentucky Fried Chicken and the Dark Nines Motor Lodge.

61

"So grandpappy was a war hero," Kareem said to Gideon. "I never knew that."

"Yes. He was someone to be proud of. He was even braver when he came home to Mississippi. He was really a civil rights hero. An unrecognized civil rights hero. He died a terrible death for demanding equality."

"At the hands of those white fuckers," said Kareem, his fists clenching. "No offense, Gideon."

"I'm not offended. They did what they did for white supremacy."

"And you were in the fight against that when you were a Freedom Rider back in the day."

"Just for a summer."

Kareem smiled, reached across and softly punched Gideon's shoulder. He stood and went to the window, looked out at the Bay. At the ships out there, at the bridge and the cars that looked tiny from here, running across it. This was the only time he could actually see the world outside San Quentin. The world Gideon could return to any time.

He sat down.

"Kareem," Gideon said cautiously, "we knew about how badly your father treated you when you were small. Tried to kill you, actually, when you were still inside your mother. Now we see what he went through himself, the terrible things that formed him. How they made him watch the lynching. How he was battered throughout his childhood. The racism he faced, and his substance abuse. Why he became the kind of man he was. We had to find out about all that, to understand him."

"He was one bad nigger," Kareem said. "Not in a good way. But . . ." His voice trailed off.

"I'd been afraid to talk to you about the things he did to you, Kareem. The way he abused you and your mother. The way they never took proper care of you. I was afraid you were going to think I was bad-mouthing them."

"Shit, Gideon. I remember what he done to me when I was little, before he disappeared. I hated that man. When I grew up, I wanted to go back and find him and kill him. I just didn't want nobody throwing it up to me. Dissing me, that I had a dad like that. But what you told me about him and seeing the lynching . . ." Kareem shook his head.

"About grandma losing her mind, and Uncle Seth, and the rest . . . about what it was like being a black dude in Mississippi back then. I can sort of feel for the man, now . . . I don't know what to think."

"What he did to you wasn't right, Kareem. But he was a damaged man. No one could go through what he did and come out intact. And maybe that applies to you too? You went through your own hell. We need to dig into what happened to Kareem as well as what happened to Jason. Uncovering what was done to you."

Kareem was silent.

I don't need to hear this shit about being like my dad, Kareem thought.

My father should have got what he gave me. But he's long dead. I'm almost as old as he was when he died. If only gramps had been my father.

But then it would've been me seeing him burned alive.

"Kareem, there were people, innocent people, who were your victims. But earlier in your life you were the innocent victim. You need to think about both of those things and you need to talk about both of those things. Just like you're thinking about your father, who was a victim of awful cruelty . . . and who made you his victim. He made you his victim without understanding what he was doing."

Dad isn't around to get back at. Or Lenny. None of the people I want to hurt is there anymore.

He felt shame . . . shame and anger when he thought about what they'd done to him. Did Gideon also want him to feel bad about the woman he'd offed and the kid?

Nothing I can do about any of it now. Why go into it?

"Start with whatever you can talk about," said Gideon. He reached across and squeezed Kareem's shoulder.

Kareem did not shrink from Gideon's touch. But he looked away, through the barred plexiglass door, at the condemned men in the other visiting cells, talking to their lawyers.

He was tired. All of us in here, waiting for death. Meanwhile fighting with each other. What's the use? Why not get it over? They'd kill him in the end anyway. He should tell Gideon to give up the appeals.

But Gideon would be disappointed. Gideon wanted to go on fighting for him, no matter what.

Kareem smiled a little. What kind of reason is that? For letting it go on, for letting himself hope? But maybe that was enough. Because Gideon cared.

He felt dirty when he thought about what they'd done to him when he was a kid. And now he felt dirty about what he'd done to the woman and her girl. But Gideon and the others didn't think he was dirty.

"Gideon, what was it you told me once about the strong and the weak."

" 'The strong do what they can and the weak suffer what they must.' An ancient Greek said that a couple of thousand years ago. I also said suffering from the power of someone stronger than you is not a mark of shame—even though American culture glories in the illusion that everyone can be powerful, that bad things are your own fault. That's not so. Enduring is also a virtue."

Did I endure? Or just do the hurting?

What does Gideon want from me? I don't have to talk about the worst parts right off. I can start with other things.

"I remember a neighbor letting me out of a closet . . ."

62

RE-DIRECT EXAMINATION BY MR. ROTH

Q   Doctor Jones, yesterday afternoon Mr. Conti questioned you about the sexual assaults Mr. Jackson inflicted on others when he was in foster care and then as a teenager in Juvie. Can you illuminate this conduct?

A   Human behavior is complex, and it is hard to explain it fully. But one key factor in Kareem Jackson's case was certainly that Kareem himself had been a childhood victim of anal rape.

Q   Please tell us what happened, Doctor.

A   Kareem's father was incarcerated following the Watts riots, and afterward, mom took up with a new boyfriend. This man, who was thirty years old, began raping Kareem after school. Kareem was seven at the time. These sexual assaults went on for more than five months.

We know how deeply traumatizing a single episode of rape can be for an adult. But adults have emotional tools to try to cope with it, to rebuild their ability to connect with people and the world after the violation.

A seven-year-old just doesn't have those tools.

Q   Kareem was taken from his mother after the authorities learned of the sexual assaults. What kind of

therapeutic intervention was provided to him after these
traumatizing experiences?

A   None. He was removed from the home. Which also
means he was removed from the only person, his mother,
who had shown him any love, problematic though it may
have been. But there was no therapy, no treatment.
Instead he was shuffled off to a series of foster homes.
Most of these were cold and unloving, and in some he was
sexually victimized again. And Kareem started to do unto
to others what was being done to him.

Q   Before we get to what Kareem did, can you say
some more about why sexual assault is so damaging to
children?

A   Several reasons. To begin, when an adult is
sexually assaulted, he or she is usually clear that they
are being victimized. But children who are raped tend to
blame themselves, in part because the assailant — often a
caretaker — tells them they are bad. They are ashamed, and
they accept that they somehow deserved what was done to
them.

At the same time, particularly when there have
been sexual assaults by a caretaker, the child lives in
fear of recurrences. Because they are ashamed and blame
themselves, they don't tell anyone. Usually, there are
threats, too.

They cut themselves off from others, and in their
anxiety, they regress to earlier behavior like bed-
wetting or thumb-sucking. They are self-destructive.

And though they blame themselves, they also have a
lot of anger. They have to suppress their anger since
they are powerless against the rapist. But eventually
it comes out. They start fires. They abuse animals. They
self-medicate with alcohol or anything else they can
lay their hands on. They understand sex as aggression,

and when they grow up, they become adults more prone to engage in sexual violence.

Q   Would you say these are the natural consequences of child abuse?

A   In many cases, yes.

Q   Can you relate this now to the rape and murder of Luis Flores and the interrupted assault on the child, Marisol Flores?

A   All of the overwhelming experiences of Kareem Jackson's childhood — the nearly-lethal abuse, the damage to the parts of the brain that govern our ability to exercise self-control, the beatings and rapes he suffered and could not escape, the violence and sex he witnessed as a child — made him a person ill-equipped to withstand an impulse to act violently.

These things also made him more vulnerable to drug abuse. And the methamphetamines and other drugs he took to help him cope with depression and anxiety — recall that he made multiple suicide attempts — these only exacerbated his problems. Some drugs are calming, but meth in particular increased his volatility and made him still more likely to engage in impulsive acts of violence. Obviously, nothing excuses the rape of Luis Flores or the attempted assault on her daughter. But as Luis understandably fought back to try to defend her daughter — and I want to note that she did succeed in the end — Kareem Jackson was incapable of a measured response. So a man who had been twisted by extreme abuse resorted to extreme violence.

Q   And regarding the assault of the child Marisol Flores?

A   For adults who have had normal lives, the thought of raping a child is deeply repugnant. But Kareem Jackson did not have a normal life. He had experienced

this outrage himself and had been left with confused
feelings about it. At some level, he had been forced
to accept the rapes as something he, as a child, had
deserved.

Marisol's screams at the horror she was witnessing
triggered Kareem Jackson's memories of his own
victimization, at what he himself had endured as a
helpless child. So he lashed out at her in his misplaced
rage and anger—misplaced, because Kareem's brain damage
and his other impairments made him unable to come to
terms with what had been done to him, to understand who
was to blame for what he had suffered.

Q   But he didn't actually sexually assault her, did he?

A   Not in the end.

I don't think raping a child was in his mind when
he and his accomplice decided to take the mother. But as
the violence spiraled out of control and Marisol's cries
broke through, he turned to her with a kind of "take
that" in mind. But in the end, he hesitated and seems to
have been holding himself back from raping or stabbing
Marisol.

We're in the zone of comparative horrors here,
so I'm not saying this marks Jackson as a person of
compassion.

The bottom line is this. A chain of cruelty led
from the lynching of Kareem's grandfather through
the suffering of Kareem's father Jason—who had been
traumatized and brutalized as an innocent child—through
Kareem—who Jason in turn brutalized and profoundly
impaired when Kareem was an innocent child—to the brutal
crimes against Luisa and Marisol Flores. The tragedy is
that no one tried to intervene in a way that might have
broken that chain of cruelty and brutality.

RE-CROSS EXAMINATION BY MR. CONTI

Q   Doctor Jones, most children who have been subjected to sexual assaults do not respond by committing such crimes themselves, correct?

A   Not most. But many do. It often takes a set of further extreme stresses before that happens.

Q   By the time Jackson was a teenager, he was deciding that he would engage in sexual assaults against younger, weaker victims at Juvie, isn't that true?

A   As I think I've already testified, it is misleading to think of Jackson's actions as though they were free choices, not deeply influenced by the brain damage he suffered or by his psychological disabilities.

Q   Your Honor, would you direct the witness to answer the question?

THE COURT: Doctor, please provide a yes or no answer to the question.

BY MR. CONTI: Please read the question back.

(COURT REPORTER READS THE QUESTION.)

THE WITNESS: Yes, he quote decided unquote he would join the sexual assaults on other young people at Juvie for the reasons I have discussed.

Q   Was Jackson innocent, when he committed the terrifying kidnappings, the rape and murder and assaults of Luisa Flores and nine-year-old Marisol?

A   That's not what I said—I never said he was innocent of the crimes he was convicted of committing.

Q   He was no longer an innocent child—that's what you called him, right?—when he tore the clothes off little Marisol and threatened her, was he?

A   No, but what happened to him earlier in his life helps explain how he got there.

Q   Your Honor, can we have the witness answer

my questions without adding speeches that are not
responsive? These are simple yes or no questions.

THE COURT: Doctor, please just answer Mr. Conti's
questions. Mr. Roth can ask you to elaborate when it is
his turn if he considers that necessary.

BY MR. CONTI: Thank you, your Honor.

Q   Twenty-two year old Kareem Jackson was no longer an
innocent child when he viciously raped and then attacked Luis
Flores and stabbed her in the throat and stomach, was he?

A   No.

Q   But in your view, every criminal starts out as an
innocent child, isn't that correct?

A   Yes.

Q   Yet at some point in their lives, they choose to
engage in conduct that is not so innocent, right?

A   I'm not sure what you mean by "choose" in this
context.

Q   No one forced Kareem Jackson to go on a crime
spree on the afternoon of June 14, 1981, when he robbed
three stores, terrorized dozens of innocent people, and
personally shot a shopkeeper, correct?

A   That is true.

Q   No one forced him to kidnap Luisa Flores and her
nine-year-old daughter, right?

A   True, no one person made him engage in these
specific acts.

Q   No one forced him to use the money he stole in the
course of these crimes in order to indulge his desire
for alcohol and methamphetamines, correct?

A   I don't agree with that statement — that way of
putting it is misleading and is certainly not the whole
truth, which I was sworn to tell.

Q   Who forced Kareem Jackson to consume tequila and
meth on the afternoon of June 14th?

A   The circumstances of his life forced him to do so.
When his father damaged Kareem's brain before he was
born and assaulted him when he was a baby . . .

Q   Let me re-phrase my question, Doctor.

MR. ROTH: Objection, Your Honor. Mr. Conti needs to
let the witness finish answering his question, not cut
him off because he doesn't like the answer.

THE COURT: You can finish your answer, Doctor.

THE WITNESS: Thank you, Your Honor.

A   When his own father inflicted injuries that caused
brain damage and made Kareem more vulnerable to becoming
a drug addict, when his mother failed to protect him,
and exposed him to terrors from which alcohol was his
only escape, when the State left him in the custody of
caretakers who did not protect him from rape, the child
and young adult Kareem Jackson was forced to medicate
himself with alcohol and drugs. And his use of these
drugs continued to represent self-medication.

I don't say Kareem Jackson has no responsibility for
the crimes he committed. But if you want to understand
why he became a drug addict and why these crimes took
place, you cannot ignore what was done to Kareem Jackson
when he was a small baby and a young child.

63

Under California law, judgments of death go straight to the California
Supreme Court for appellate review. When he began the case, Gideon had
been cautiously hopeful because the court's liberal majority had scrutinized the imposition of the death penalty closely, and overturned dozens
of death sentences under the state's ill-drafted death penalty laws.

In 1986, conservatives (bankrolled by oil companies and big agricul-
ture) began a campaign—exploiting popular resentment of the court's
death penalty decisions—that ended in the electorate's removal of Chief

Justice Rose Bird and two other liberal justices. The conservative judges who replaced them affirmed nearly every conviction and death sentence that came before them, no matter what.

In one case Gideon read, the court upheld a murder conviction even though the trial attorney failed to investigate the defendant's alibi defense—so the jury never heard there were seventeen witnesses who would have testified he was in Mexico at the time of the murder. In another, the court held that the lawyer in a death penalty case must be presumed competent even though he was drunk throughout trial—he drank each morning before trial began, during recesses, and each evening, and was arrested for driving to the courthouse with a blood-alcohol level triple that for drunk driving.

Five years after Gideon had been appointed to represent Kareem Jackson, and one year after the liberal justices had been replaced, Kareem's case came before the California Supreme Court.

"May it please the Court," Gideon began in the traditional manner, "my name is Gideon Roth, and I represent petitioner Kareem Jackson.

"The issue in this case is whether the attorney the State provided to Mr. Jackson was deficient in performing his duties—so deficient that Mr. Jackson was denied the effective assistance of counsel that the California Constitution and the Sixth Amendment to the United States Constitution guarantee to someone charged with capital murder. As we have argued ..."

Gideon was interrupted almost immediately.

"We've read your papers, counselor," said Justice Bradley, "and even if we considered trial counsel's performance to be imperfect, it is not so clear that any deficiencies rise to the level of a constitutional violation. You are complaining he did not engage in the exhaustive investigation going back four generations that you did. Your model investigation was commendable. But the Constitution does not require every defense attorney to do everything you did, with years to work on the case.

"Defense counsel did interview the defendant about his background and he investigated. He obtained the records of Child Protective Services and the California Youth Authority. He presented the jury with evidence that Mr. Jackson had been abandoned by his parents as a small child, that he had been poor, that he had been on his own as a teenager, and he argued that Jackson's sad youth caused him to drift into drugs and delinquency and crime.

"The fact that defense counsel failed to persuade the jury that the defendant deserved life doesn't mean he was incompetent. Some cases can't be won, no matter how great the advocate, wouldn't you agree?"

"Your Honor, with respect, we agree that the issue is not perfection— it is whether the defense attorney's performance was reasonable for a death penalty case. His performance was not. First, although ostensibly he made the points you mentioned, he did so in such a hollow manner that it had no impact. He offered not a single witnesses, and presented only the cold records from Child Protective Services and CYA. The length of the jury's deliberations—only fifteen minutes—shows the jurors could not even have read the evidence he introduced."

"Mr. Roth, you know very well that it is improper for us to pry into the jury's deliberation process, and we won't start now. Though the fact that they deliberated so briefly really shows this was not a close case, doesn't it?"

"I'm speaking of the nature of the mitigation showing and of the objective facts, your Honor, not the jury's mental processes. And they might have considered the case a closer one had trial counsel given them more information.

"My second point is that because counsel's investigation was too limited, he never presented the evidence of extreme abuse that explained *why* the defendant came to be the kind of person who could commit the crimes . . ."

"But Mr. Roth," Justice Conklin interrupted, "couldn't trial counsel have reasonably decided that this kind of evidence might have caused the jury to see your client as, quote, damaged goods, unquote, and therefore deserving to be put down, like a mad dog? Wasn't it a close decision for him, how to present the case?"

"No, Your Honor. For a lawyer's decisions on such matters to be reasonable, first he has to engage in a thorough investigation so he knows what the facts are. Defense counsel never discovered the brain damage, never learned Mr. Jackson's own father gave him a concussion when he was less than a year old, never learned that he'd been raped as a seven-year old and in foster care, his lawyer never learned of the emotional damage Mr. Jackson had suffered as a result of that kind of abuse or when he witnessed his mother being pimped by his father . . . so he never actually made the decision you have hypothesized."

"But what difference would that have made, Mr. Roth, when Mr. Jackson had ordered his attorney not to offer that kind of evidence? Doesn't a defendant have the right to say, 'I'd rather take a greater chance of a death verdict rather than have my mother's life and the intimate circumstances of my life exposed to public view'? Shouldn't we respect Mr. Jackson's dignity, his right to decide how he is defended?"

"Judge Conklin, if I may respectfully correct you, the record indicates that Mr. Jackson only said he did not want them, quote, bad-mouthing my mother, unquote. He did not tell his attorney not to investigate. His defense counsel still could have told the story of Kareem's terrible abuse at the hands of his father, his brain damage, the rapes and neglect he suffered as a child. An expert like Dr. Jones could have explained how these events shaped him into the person he became. The jury might have concluded that a brain-damaged person who had been traumatized by these childhood experiences was not fully responsible for his acts."

"But what if we understand your client's words differently, Mr. Roth? What if we conclude that Mr. Jackson meant that he didn't want *any* of the intimate circumstances of his life held up to public view? Wouldn't the defendant be entitled to make that decision? And aren't we obliged to assume that, since we begin with the presumption that defense counsel provided competent representation?"

"Not in the face of the record, your Honor. With all due respect, the presumption of competent representation is not an excuse for conjuring facts that contradict the actual record. The record makes it quite clear that Mr. Jackson made a specific, limited statement, your honor, about his mother. This court may not . . ."

Gideon saw the judges were echoing the arguments the State's lawyer had made in her written submissions.

"In any event," said Justice Tan, "can you show it is likely that the marginal information that was not presented would have made any difference? We see many death penalty cases up here. The facts of this case—kidnapping and raping a mother in front of her nine-year-old, attempted rape of the small child herself, then butchering the mother with knives—all on top of a lethal crime spree—this is one of the most barbaric cases we have ever seen."

"Before I answer you directly, your Honor, I have to say that this case also presents some of the most powerful mitigating circumstances ever presented—that the abuse Kareem Jackson suffered as a child was far more horrible than the typical case.

"The evidence the jury did not hear was not 'marginal.' It was critical evidence of the kind that courts have always recognized to be strongly mitigating—brain damage and child battering and rape, mistreatment beyond his control that deformed Kareem into the person he became.

"Of course, as the Court understands, these considerations do not excuse Jackson's behavior, but a jury might well have concluded that Jackson did not bear the same kind of responsibility for his actions as a person did who had an entirely intact brain, who'd had a normal childhood. This court cannot be confident the jury would have voted for death no matter what they had heard."

"Isn't this case on all fours with *People versus Helms,* where we upheld a death verdict against similar arguments?" asked Justice Bethany.

Yes, it was much like *Helms,* Gideon knew, an earlier case in which you turned justice on its head.

"*Helms* can be distinguished, your Honor . . ."

"You discussed that in your brief, counselor," said Justice Conklin. "Why don't you move on to another issue?"

Afterwards, the argument seemed to Gideon a blur of hostile questions embodying skewed assumptions about the law and the facts.

Six weeks later, Gideon received the California Supreme Court decision: Affirmed. The conviction and the death sentence were upheld by a six-one vote.

64

Phil Vanderson methodically interviewed Lisa. Then he took her to the bus station for San Francisco, knowing he would never again see the only other witness to the strange behavior of "Jim Cargill." Now he was typing up his notes.

Obviously, there was nothing to warrant holding her as a material witness—a witness to what?

He had not the least doubt the man who had falsely called himself Cargill was going to commit a crime. But he didn't know what to do about it.

He went to his supervisor, sighing on the way. Lieutenant Thatcher was not a man of great imagination. In fact, Thatcher reserved the word "imaginative" as a term of contempt for officers whose thinking strayed from the reliable.

"Lieutenant, can I talk to you about an unusual case? Not a clear violation or crime yet, but I'm troubled."

"I'm doing the monthly statistics now, Phil. Are you sure you wouldn't be less troubled if you racked up a few more tickets for twelve over the limit?"

"I'll just need a few minutes of your time, Lieutenant." As Thatcher lightly drummed his fingers on his desk, Vanderson outlined his encounter with the bald-headed nervous man and Lisa's report of the same man, who was strangely lacking in identification and strangely flush with cash.

"That's all?" Thatcher asked.

"Well, pretty much," said Vanderson. He thought it would be better not to say anything about the photo the man had left behind; that would seem even more speculative to Thatcher.

"And you think the Idaho Highway Patrol's resources would be well spent on this so-called mystery?"

"My instincts tell me this man's up to no good. Might just be a drug deal. But I feel strongly an act of violence is being planned. Maybe if we set something in motion, for once we can stop a crime before it happens. We should at least put out an all points for the state police in each of the states east of here, and we should see what we can pull up for the name and vehicle. Then see where we're at."

"You want to open up an investigation," Thatcher said in a flat voice, "based on nothing. Then at the end of the year we will have one more open matter that will be listed on our books as unresolved."

Vanderson opened his mouth, then closed it as Thatcher held up his palm.

"Look, even if your suspicion is right and the man is going to commit a crime, so what? Thousands of people intend to commit crimes every day. Nothing we do can stop them in advance ninety-nine point nine percent of the time. And ninety-nine point nine nine percent, thank God, they don't happen in our jurisdiction. You don't have anything to go on, so you'd just be spinning your wheels anyway. You need to forget about this and get back to work."

Thatcher's chair rotated, and he turned back to a chart he was filling in.

Vanderson's face felt warm as he went back to his desk.

Damn fool, he muttered to himself. I'm a damn fool for having said anything to him. Now what can I do? Whatever it is, I better keep it real low profile.

Even if Thatcher had approved, though, on what basis could I ask the police in another state to start an investigation?

He sipped a cup of lukewarm tea and he thought.

Hoping Thatcher wouldn't be venturing out of his office for a cup of coffee, Vanderson went over to the computer in the operations room and checked an online database. He was discouraged to see there were dozens of James Cargills out there.

Lisa said the man had a California driver's license, and he narrowed his search to six in California. He nervously printed the result. What's someone with a California temporary drivers license doing with a truck with Oregon plates? Now he wished Lisa were still here so he could show her the list of addresses from the print out and see if she recognized any from the drivers license she'd seen. He did another James Cargill search for the State of Oregon, then printed that too. Then he scrambled back to his desk before Thatcher emerged.

He pinned the photos Cargill had left behind onto his bulletin board and went home.

65

Gideon was moseying along, slower than ever, often getting a late start. He drove only a few hours each day before stopping at a park or campground. A couple of times he missed the turn for the freeway exit he'd meant to take.

It didn't matter. He had his job to do. But he needed to be sure he would be steady enough to do it when the time came.

He wanted to visit Susan in southern Illinois before he went on to Mississippi, and he hoped she would be around, maybe teaching a summer session course. Another day or two getting there would make no difference.

Now he paused at the famous Wall Drug store in Wall, South Dakota.

Wall and its drug store were as close to nothing as you could get, as an attraction. But its minimal somethingness and its promise of "FREE ICE WATER" (as a series of signs had, since the 1930s, beckoned for a hundred miles on each side of Wall) had been enough to give it what passed for celebrity in the greater nothingness of the Dakotas. In fact, tens of thousands of cars decided each day that Wall would be the place to take a break from driving Interstate 90.

Gideon was one of them. He wandered through the endless chain of stores and departments, all part of Wall Drug in some way or other, with their various useless things. An "art gallery" featuring western paintings and small bronze sculptures of bucking broncos. An American Indian mural. Fur-trimmed tchotchkes of various kinds. Restaurants.

And ice water.

Gideon resumed his drive, but on the outskirts of town stopped for gas. After going to the men's room, he noticed a pay phone. He dropped in some quarters and called Cecil Price.

It was not Timmie Ray, but another cop who was on the phones in the basement of the police station in Meridian, Mississippi that afternoon.

Most of the calls were pointless, and the automated tape recorders would have captured anything of value to the investigation of the 1964 murders. The only reason to have a live human being listening at all was to try to catch the location information if and when there was another call from Mr. Quiet Caller.

"Hullo," said Price, picking up.

Silence.

Sergeant Bernice Williams was working on a puzzle, and almost didn't notice it was one of those calls.

But as the silence went into the third second, Williams realized this was what she was there for, sat up, and triggered the tracing equipment.

"Hullo," Price said again. This time he did not hang up immediately. The Sergeant heard Price cough, then sigh heavily as he waited. She thought she heard another person breathing.

"What you want, Mister?" said Price after a while. "Why you bothering me? Leave me be."

Quiet Caller was not drawn into responding. Price waited another a few seconds, then added, "I'm getting real tired of this, mister. Maybe I'll just have this phone taken out." Then he hung up.

There had been ample time for the trace. Sergeant Williams copied the numerals from the registers on the device and called Timmie Ray. By the time Timmie Ray arrived, the Sergeant had determined that the number was that of a public telephone booth in Wall.

It took little time to find someone at South Dakota Bell who could give them the address of the call box. Then another difficult call to the local police.

"You want us to go out and find someone you're looking for who made a call from a gas station? Tell me his name, what he looks like, and what he's wanted for. This someone dangerous?"

"Well, we know he's stalking someone in Mississippi, but we don't know his name yet and I don't know what he looks like. Not sure if he's armed and dangerous. Probably armed."

The cop in South Dakota laughed. "How in hell can someone in South Dakota be stalking someone in Mississippi? And how in hell are we supposed to help you find someone when you've got no who he is or what he looks like? Is this a crank call?"

"Shee-it, I'll give you my damned number and you can call me back here in Mississippi, or look it up through directory information. Police Department, Meridian, Mississippi. Timmie Ray Phelps. I'll be here."

"Okay, relax, I believe you. But you got nothing to go on . . . What do you want us to do?"

"It's a long story. But we have reason to believe there's a plot to commit a crime of violence in Mississippi, and there have been a series of calls from places on the way here. If you can send someone right away, maybe someone at this gas station remembers who used the phone at a quarter past twelve. But mostly, if you could get them to rope off the phone, lift whatever prints there might be and send them to us."

"People use these phones all the time, and our fingerprint guys are busy. We're not gonna get a latent fingerprint guy out there for something like this, not without an order from higher up. At least tell me what your guy sounds like on the phone. Young, old? Regular American or colored? Foreign accent? Give me something to go on."

"I'm not in a position to help too much on that kind of thing." Timmie Ray paused. He really didn't want to say all they had was someone who didn't speak—'A crank caller?!' he could hear the South Dakota officer saying. He decided it was better to be inventive. Most weird murderers were young, so if that's what this was about, he would probably be right.

"It's a white guy in his late thirties, average height and weight, dark hair . . . cut short. Don't know about any accent. Look, just do the best you can. We've done this before, if you can lift any prints, we'll take care of analysis on our end. Please, just do what you can."

Two days later, Timmie Ray received several sets of fingerprints from the booth.

66

After the California Supreme Court affirmed Jackson's death sentence, the State got an execution date. Kareem was to be put to death in six weeks.

Gideon asked the state trial court to stay the execution pending federal review, but the trial court refused to issue a stay.

"The people of California have voted to have a death penalty," proclaimed LA Superior Court Judge Ono, "and after a fair trial, Mr. Jackson's jury sentenced him to death. The California Supreme Court has at last—after five years—upheld the jury's verdict, and the State is entitled to have the verdict carried out. There's been enough delay, delay, delay of justice. The process is over as far as the State of California and the courts of California are concerned."

Nice rhetoric that made perfect political sense. State court judges are elected. Why seem weak on the death penalty, when you can sound tough and pass the buck to a federal court?

A federal district judge issued a stay of execution, on condition Gideon file a petition for writ of habeas corpus within ninety days.

U.S. District Judge Jacqueline Cole was assigned to the case, and she would be their judge for the duration. She was a Reagan appointee and, Gideon noted, in reviewing her bio, that she had been born the same year as Gideon. She had been a college Republican. In 1964, while he was in Mississippi fighting for civil rights, Jackie Cole had been campaigning for Barry Goldwater.

Judge Cole, who sat in Orange County, was said to be highly conservative, smart and fair. Only the first proved to be true.

As in any federal case, a range of preliminary matters came before the judge before she had to decide, finally, whether to uphold or overturn the death sentence. She ruled against them on issue after issue. Kareem's claims were destined to be denied by this judge. All he could do was to lay the groundwork for the possibility of prevailing on appeal to the Ninth Circuit some day.

67

The fingerprints from Wall arrived in Mississippi two days after Gideon left South Dakota. Timmie Ray forwarded them to the crime lab in Jackson, along with the Lake Yellowstone Hotel set.

Timmie Ray's puzzle did not intrigue the head of the crime lab enough to bump other matters. Two days passed before there was a call from Bob Hogan, the head of the fingerprint section.

"Hi, Timmie Ray. Got your two envelopes here in front of me. What's this about?" Hogan liked talking to people instead of reading their usually confused memos.

"A person of interest has been placing suspicious calls to certain perps we are surveilling in Neshoba County," said Timmie Ray. "We want to identify him."

"And the prints came from where?"

"The set marked 'Yellowstone' are from the inside of a phone booth at the Lake Yellowstone Hotel in Wyoming. The set marked 'Wall' are from a pay phone at a gas station outside Wall, South Dakota. Our man placed calls to certain parties in Mississippi from these phones. If anyone's prints were in both phone booths, it's going to be our man. "

"I'll see what I can do."

Timmie was anxious. It was four days since the South Dakota call. By now Mr. Silent Caller could be in Mississippi. Timmie feared something would happen before they got results.

"Do what you can to hurry it. I'm trying to stop a crime before it happens."

A day later Hogan called.

"Out of the thirteen prints from Yellowstone, seven of them were pretty good, and there was one clean set of three that appears to be the middle fingers from the left hand of one person. The Wall set wasn't so good, but there were four partial prints I could work from. I compared each of them to the seven good Yellowstone prints."

"Was there a match?"

Hogan was silent for a long time.

"It's like this, Timmie. You know fingerprints aren't as much of a science as people think. Judgment goes into deciding whether you have a positive identification.

"Most fingerprint experts in the U.S. say you got a make if there are twelve points of comparison between the latent and an inked original. But opinions differ. In England, they want 16 points of comparison. The FBI is often satisfied with eight."

"And you got . . .?"

"Here, I'm doing latent to latent, so it's even harder. I saw one possible match. For that one, I have seven points of similarity. Am I sure enough to put someone in the electric chair? No. But between you and me, and I think the same guy left these prints on the two phones."

"So now can you figure out who he is?"

Hogan smiled.

"I took the next step and ran the print through the database. Working from the best Hotel Yellowstone print, we get eleven points of similarity with a print on file in California for a man named Gideon Roth.

"I've done some investigating for you, Timmie. Roth is a California lawyer, and they take a full set of finger and palm prints when they do bar admissions. I pulled down a digitized set of all of his prints, went back and compared them to all the other prints we've got. Another of the Yellowstone prints was also his, no doubt about it."

"So he's our man," said Timmie Ray.

"Well, maybe," said Hogan. "Just to make sure you understand what we've got here. I'm confident Roth left his finger prints at the Hotel Yellowstone phone booth. I'd say he probably also left a matching print at the Wall, South Dakota phone, but I wouldn't absolutely swear to that."

"Good enough for me."

"Okay. I'll fax you my results."

Timmie Ray called the State Bar of California and asked what information they could provide on attorney Gideon Roth. The person who answered the phone referred him to the State Bar's web site, where he learned that Roth had been admitted to law practice in 1972 and was a partner at the law firm of Harkin & Lessman in Menlo Park. And that there had been a disciplinary proceeding against Roth earlier that year that ended in a reprimand.

What was that about? He picked up the phone again.

"Harkin & Lessman, how may I help you?"

"I'd like to speak with Gideon Roth or his secretary if he isn't in."

"I'm sorry, sir. Mr. Roth is no longer associated with Harkin & Lessman."

"Is there a number where I can reach him?"

"I'm sorry. We have no other phone number for Mr. Roth at this time."

"My name is Timmie Ray Phelps. I'm a law enforcement officer from Meridian, Mississippi, and I'm trying to locate Mr. Roth. It's urgent. Is there anyone in authority at the firm who can assist me?"

"Hold on for a moment please, and I'll see."

Timmie Ray wondered what Roth might have been disciplined for. Stalking? Threatening phone calls?

"Good morning, Mr. Phelps. My name is Laura Fuji, and I am the Chief Administrative Officer of the firm. How may I assist you?"

"I'm the Sheriff of Lauderdale County in Mississippi, and I am trying to locate Gideon Roth in connection with an investigation."

"An investigation of what? I'm not aware of Mr. Roth having had any connection with Mississippi."

"The subject of the investigation is confidential. I would just like to talk to Mr. Roth or learn more about what he has been doing from someone who works with him."

"He no longer works at the firm, and he has provided us with no phone number for forwarding inquiries to him. We have a home phone number, but I'm not at liberty to provide that. I am afraid we don't provide further information on attorneys formerly with the firm except through formal legal process."

"I don't have time for that. Did he leave the firm recently? How did that happen?"

"I really can't tell you much more. He left this February, but the details of his departure are confidential."

"Even to law enforcement?"

"You can talk to the firm's counsel, but I can't do any more informally. Look, I can't really talk to you about this, but the story was all over the newspapers, with the Jackson execution and the fight and all, that night, and you can read between the lines . . ."

A few minutes on the Internet gave Timmie Ray most of the information he needed, including news photos of Gideon Roth on the night his client was executed. Now he knew what Mr. Silent Caller looked like. All he lacked was information on where this Gideon Roth was and what he planned to do.

68

Kareem looked up from what he'd been reading. The transcript of the testimony of the psychiatrist Franklyn Jones rested in Kareem's lap. Gideon sat close by.

Kareem thought about the woman he had raped and killed. He felt a heaviness in his chest, and the heat of shame in his face. He'd nearly raped the girl too. They were just coming home from a nice day at the beach. Why did they have to run into him? And why didn't he just take their car and leave them there at the Kentucky Fried Chicken?

He knew why. Because, then, he didn't see anyone else as really people.

He touched Gideon's arm lightly, then slowly returned his hand to his lap. He glanced again at Jones' testimony.

"Not sure I get all this," he said. "But maybe it's only what you guys been saying all along."

They were in one of the inside visiting cells. From here, Kareem could see the general visiting area, where prisoners who had not been condemned to death met with their wives or girlfriends and their kids.

Small children were playing with blocks and well-used plastic toys in a space surrounded by low shelves. Kareem never had any visitors other than members of his legal team. Except for such occasional glimpses, Kareem had not seen a child in nine years.

"When I look at them, I think about Marisol Flores," he said.

He turned back toward Gideon.

"Like Doc Jones says, the things my folks and the others did to me— what happened when I was a kid—that's got to do with who I am. Who I was. But I'm the one who done it. It was me, not dad, not Lenny, not the others, who murdered a little girl's ma, and shot the kid at Kentucky Fried Chicken. People who done me no harm.

"They didn't deserve what I did to them. I wish I could go back and not do it. But there's no way I can make it right, except maybe I accept my punishment."

"You are responsible for what you did," said Gideon. "It's right that you've accepted that. But having to spend the rest of your life in jail, decade after decade, no possibility of parole, would be a harsh enough punishment."

"If they say that's not enough, Gideon, maybe they right."

"Killing is just as wrong when the state does it."

"I hear you, Gideon. I ain't saying you got to stop what you're trying to do for me. I agree with you. 'Course, I got personal reasons for that. But I also got personal reasons for agreeing with them." He took a slow breath. "What will be, will be."

69

Habeas corpus provides an opportunity for a condemned inmate to challenge his trial or sentence as unconstitutional—on the ground that it failed to meet the standards that those who wrote our Constitution considered necessary for a criminal trial to be fair and reliable.

But constitutional rights were dismissed by conservative politicians as "technicalities." And over the years, an increasingly right-wing Supreme Court had devised procedural roadblocks and traps for the unwary, to thwart efforts to remedy constitutional violations.

After the enactment of the Antiterrorism and Effective Death Penalty Act, the AEDPA, federal courts became still less concerned with whether a defendant's rights had actually been violated. The AEDPA required federal judges to defer to state court decisions whether they were right or wrong— so long as they were "reasonable." Reasonably wrong was good enough.

Consistent with the principle of deference, Gideon had to jump through a set of procedural hoops in state and federal court. Litigating whether he had properly observed these formalities had itself caused years of delay. Instead of weighing whether something fundamentally unfair had taken place at trial, the judge dismissed many of Jackson's claims based on supposed procedural flaws.

Eventually, Judge Cole held a mini-trial on the remaining claims. This focused on whether the trial attorney had been incompetent for failing to present expert testimony on the childhood abuse Kareem had suffered, his brain damage and his psychological impairments.

After taking the matter under advisement for eleven months, Judge Cole rejected all of Jackson's claims and affirmed the death penalty. Eight years after the case arrived in federal court, Gideon turned to the U.S. Court of Appeals for the Ninth Circuit. Here, he thought, they finally had a chance at justice.

70

After another nine months, the two sides had filed all of their lengthy appeal briefs, and the case was set for oral argument.

The Ninth Circuit was widely considered a liberal court. But the reality was that Presidents Reagan and Bush had, by 1995, appointed more than a third of the judges of the Ninth Circuit. It wasn't so liberal anymore.

Jackson drew a bad panel. Two of the judges were conservatives who had never set aside a death verdict, and the third, a quirky moderate, hard to predict.

If fairly considered, Gideon thought, this case ought to be about two things: the awful nature of the crime, on the one hand, and what we now know about Kareem Jackson, on the other. The judges should be considering in a balanced way whether—even with a crime so terrible—a jury might have been influenced by evidence of Kareem's own victimization and how he had, through no fault of his own, been shaped into the damaged man he had become.

But it won't be like that.

The case was argued in one of the Ninth Circuit's elegant courtrooms in Pasadena, California. The room, with its glass French doors connecting to the hallway and the large windows looking out onto a garden and grass lawn, was an airy and welcoming space, an elegant and charming venue.

Everyone rose as three black-robed jurists, two men and one woman, swept into the courtroom promptly at 10:00 a.m.

"May it please the Court," Gideon began a few moments later, "my name is Gideon Roth and I represent petitioner Kareem Jackson.

"Your Honors, I would like to focus on two of Mr. Jackson's claims for relief, his claim that trial counsel was ineffective in the penalty phase and his claim that the prosecutor violated due process in using his peremptory challenges to exclude African Americans from Mr. Jackson's jury.

"The issue before this Court, regarding the first claim, is whether the evidence Mr. Jackson's trial attorney neglected to discover and present—including evidence of brain damage resulting from severe child abuse—undermines confidence in the death verdict."

"Counsel," said Judge MacVey, "in assessing whether this evidence might have made any difference to the jury, shouldn't our starting point be the highly aggravated circumstances of this case?"

"All the more reason, Judge, for trial counsel to put forward the greatest possible effort. Instead, trial counsel . . ."

"When you say, 'the greatest possible effort,'" Judge Dallan interrupted, "you are going far past the constitutional standard. The Constitution doesn't require the greatest possible effort, and we do not overturn death verdicts just because trial lawyers do not do everything that is conceivable."

"We do not say perfection is required, your Honor. The standard a defense attorney must meet is simply the one this court stated in *Caro,* that 'all relevant mitigating information be unearthed for consideration.' Trial counsel never even lifted the shovel."

"But we recently held in *Hendricks* that counsel's duty to investigate is not limitless," said Judge Bead. "Jackson's lawyer did interview Jackson and he did obtain the key records that contained the essence of the mitigation you say he should have presented with live witnesses."

"The issue, Judge, is not whether the duty is limitless; it is whether stopping after reading two sets of files, without interviewing any witnesses himself, without consulting with experts, without learning of his client's brain damage and history of severe abuse, is reasonable . . ."

"Mr. Roth," said Judge Bead, "you have a more fundamental problem, don't you? You are asking us to determine that the California Supreme Court made an incorrect decision. But since this case is governed by the Anti-terrorism and Effective Death Penalty Act, the issue—to be blunt—is not whether their decision was right or wrong. Under the statute, we have to defer to the state court's decision unless you show that the state court was unreasonable. In the *Drinkard* case, the Fifth Circuit recently held this standard requires—a state court judgment can only be set aside—only if the decision was so clearly incorrect that it would not even be debatable among reasonable judges. Can you meet that standard?"

Gideon had entered jurisprudential never-never land. Yes, under *Drinkard*, even if the state court was wrong, a death penalty will stand so long as a 'reasonable' judge could have *debated* the issue. Meaning that a man can be executed even though his trial did not actually meet constitutional requirements.

"Your Honor, we understand that requirement. But in light of the heightened obligation to uncover all evidence that would support a life sentence in a death penalty case, we say no reasonable judge would have denied Mr. Jackson's claim."

"Yet the California Supreme Court did."

"Well, it's an objective standard, Judge Bead."

Judge MacVey interjected, "Even if I were to tend to agree with you that trial counsel was incompetent, I am hard pressed to say that every one of the justices of the California Supreme Court was unreasonable in coming to the contrary conclusion."

Gideon's argument went downhill from there.

When the deputy attorney general took the podium, he kept the discussion on the deference issue: "Your Honors, petitioner's claims can be disposed of on one simple point. Kareem Jackson perpetrated a heinous, vicious, merciless crime, including—after they courageously endured hours of terror—the rape and murder of a mother and the battery and attempted rape of her nine-year-old daughter. And why? So Jackson and his confederate could escape from the scene of a murderous robbery they perpetrated to get money for drugs. Those are the undisputed facts that were before the jury.

"Petitioner's defense attorney gave the jury 86 pages of evidence, documents on Jackson's sad life history—86 full pages of evidence—but the jury concluded this did not outweigh Jackson's ghastly crimes. The California Supreme Court held that more detail on Jackson's background and testimony from dubious 'experts of the night,' as Judge MacVey has referred to such witnesses in an insightful article, that more of such evidence would have not have changed the outcome.

"Petitioner cannot assert with a straight face that all reasonable jurists would disagree with the California Supreme Court's decision to reject petitioner Jackson's feeble argument."

Two months later, the panel issued an opinion unanimously affirming the decision of the district court to deny the writ of habeas corpus. Gideon had lost the best hope for saving Kareem's life.

71

Officer Vanderson was in his cubicle, talking to a visitor. A delegation from the Criminal Justice program at Idaho State University had come by. They had been studying whether race played a role in traffic and highway stops, and were giving presentations to highway patrolmen on the subject. A lively discussion ensued, with most of Vanderson's colleagues denying there was any problem. Vanderson had allowed as he wasn't entirely sure, prompting a big frown from Lieutenant Thatcher.

Afterward, one of the older professors came by to talk with Officer Vanderson. He wanted to know how hard it would be to keep statistics on reasons for stops and race.

As he was leaving, the professor noticed Vanderson's bulletin board, and asked why Vanderson had put up pictures of Cecil Price.

"It's a long story. Actually, I came across these but I didn't know who the guy was," said Vanderson. "Who did you say?"

"He's Cecil Price. He was a sheriff in Mississippi, part of a lynch mob that murdered three civil rights workers in 1964. It was a big case, don't you remember it?"

"Umm. 1964. I was ten years old at the time. Doesn't ring a bell. Tell me about what happened."

"Sure. I had just started as a teacher at the time, in Fayetteville, Arkansas, but I am originally from western Alabama, not far from where it all happened. Mississippi was a real die-hard segregationist place back then—so was Alabama—and the civil rights organizations had brought a lot of students down from the North to protest and try to register African-Americans to vote."

The professor explained what he recalled about the killings and the case. "The first photo you've got there was a famous one. There's Price, along with the others, smirking at the camera in court. They were facing some court charge—I forget exactly what, but I don't think it was murder."

"So what happened to Price?" Vanderson asked.

"Best I recall, he did a little jail time for a minor charge. I don't know what became of him after that. So what are you doing with his picture?"

Vanderson gave a not-overly-informative response, and the professor went on his way. Vanderson sat and thought for ten minutes. Then he picked up the phone, got a phone number from information and placed a call.

"Police Department? This is the Idaho Highway Patrol—I'd like to speak someone in charge of investigations. That would be . . .? Timmie Phelps. Thanks . . .

"Hello, Sheriff Phelps. This is Phil Vanderson. I'm a highway patrol-man in Idaho, and I've got sort of an unusual concern I'd like to talk to you about. This may be completely off the wall. But first let me ask you a question. Do you know whether a guy named Cecil Price still lives in Philadelphia, Mississippi?"

72

The final ten months of the *Jackson* case was a flurry of skirmishes that failed to deflect the approaching defeat. The last weeks were no more than desperate, brief charges in a futile battle to stave off the inevitable.

The legal team asked for reconsideration by a larger group of Ninth Circuit judges. Such "en banc" review was rarely granted. But Gideon thought the claims were strong enough to sway the moderates to at least hear the case. He was shaken to learn a narrow majority voted against another hearing.

He met with Kareem to discuss what had happened.

"Not good," said Gideon. He explained that the denial left them few places to go and none especially promising.

"How come they wouldn't listen?" Kareem asked.

"We don't really know. Judge Reinhardt, the grand old liberal of the court, wrote an eloquent dissent from the denial of rehearing. Four other judges joined what he said."

"What about the rest of them?" Kareem asked.

"That's all they tell us, other than that a majority of the judges did not vote for reconsideration en banc. I understand from someone inside that it was close."

"Close don't pay the rent," said Kareem.

"No. As I told you before, this court now has a lot of conservative judges who are rabid about not setting aside death sentences. And maybe—I don't really know—the so-called moderates felt this was not a good case for using up political capital. With a crime this bad, maybe they thought they'd be giving too much ammunition to critics of the Circuit."

"Better to throw me to the dogs," said Kareem.

"That's what it comes to."

Gideon looked at Kareem without flinching.

"Well, I never hoped for a lot," said Kareem. He hunched over, his hands hanging loosely between his knees, staring downward. Then he sat up straighter and looked at Gideon.

"You done a lot for me, Gideon. It's gone on a long time. I don't understand all of it, but I know you've gone the last mile. I want to thank you. You and Jennie and the others."

"It's not over yet."

"Some of them sayings, like 'Never say die,' they feel a little different in here. I know you won't stop. Thank you. Thank you. But you just told me where it's gonna end, right? And I done bad things, and a price is gotta be paid. Luisa Flores and Marisol . . . If it weren't for me, Luisa might a been watching Marisol graduate from college last year. Marisol might have had a brother who could have been there too. Luisa might a been a grandma by now. I stopped their lives, so maybe . . .

"It don't matter what now, I want to thank you."

Gideon stood up, and they embraced. "I wish I could have done more," he said.

"Gideon," Kareem said, looking him in the eye and firmly holding his shoulders, giving him a little shake. "Gideon, Gideon. You done so much. It's okay now to cut yourself some slack."

Gideon and his team waited the full ninety days they were allowed in which to file a petition for writ of certiorari, asking the U.S. Supreme Court to take up the case.

Denied.

Gideon could no longer see a path but he soldiered on. They petitioned the governor for clemency, but Gideon had little hope. His pessimism was warranted.

The Governor's prime-time refusal: "Forty-three state and federal judges have considered Kareem Jackson's claims many times, and they have all rejected them. I decline to stand in the way of the just reward that all of these judges and a jury of his peers decided was the appropriate punishment for Jackson's despicable crimes."

To be accurate, all 43 judges had not decided that death was appropriate in this case. Most of them had either simply declined to hear the case or had deferred to what the state court had decided.

73

The live coverage of the clemency hearing had one useful result. Jennie reported to Gideon that one of the Jackson trial jurors, a Joan Stanton, had contacted them. She wanted to talk to Gideon.

"You remember her from the transcripts of the jury selection, Gideon? Housewife in her forties, then, from Torrance. Husband worked for the city.

"She's read some of the stories about the case and watched the clemency hearing on CNN, and she is having second thoughts about the verdict."

Gideon flew to Los Angeles to speak with her. It was late afternoon when he arrived at Stanton's house in Palos Verdes Estates, a rich suburb of LA. Joan Stanton was now in her early sixties, a neatly dressed, slightly heavy-set woman with cropped graying hair. She invited him in and gave him a cup of tea after he had refused a drink. She sipped a small glass of Scotch.

"All I know about you," Gideon said, "is from a transcript of what you were asked and what you answered during jury selection at Jackson's trial fourteen years ago. I appreciate your willingness to re-think what happened. Most people never want to do that."

"Well, it was a horrible crime, and we were still stunned by the evidence when we got to the penalty trial. The things the newspapers reported on, we got to see even closer. The bloody clothes and all and the color photos."

Gideon nodded. "I've seen them too."

Stanton went on. "I was one of the jurors who felt we should at least read some of the reports that Jackson's lawyer put in. But there was such a rush to get it over with, I was embarrassed to insist.

"We didn't hear any of the things about Jackson that you were talking about on television last week. Maybe they would have mattered. Maybe not. I'm not so sure about the death penalty as I've gotten older, but then it seemed right."

"Again," said Gideon, "not many people want to reconsider their views. Thank you."

"There were a couple of things that happened at the trial that were wrong, just plain wrong. That's what I want to tell you about.

"One of the other jurors, an older guy named Harold Axelrod, was a terrible racist. During the first part of the trial, we all used to have lunch together and I sat at a table with him a couple of times. Most of us talked about other things, our families or jobs, what kind of ties the lawyers were wearing, whatever. Because every time there was a break in the trial, the judge told us that we were not to discuss the case—not until it was time to deliberate—and not to form any opinions on the case.

"Well, Mr. Axelrod says to me at a lunch break, 'This is an open and shut case.' Quote unquote. He says he knows there was even worse evidence they were keeping from us, and he can't wait to get to the penalty phase, because—these were his words—'This nigger needs gassing, and I'm going to see to it that he gets it.'

"I'll never forget that. I told him I didn't approve of that kind of language, and we should wait to hear all of the evidence.

"I avoided him after that. But during the penalty phase deliberations, he was the same. When we start deliberating about life or death, Axelrod is the first one to open his mouth, and he says, 'This is the kind of thing they do all the time.'

"Everyone knew what he meant, but someone goes, 'I beg your pardon?' 'The . . . Negroes,' he goes, hesitating before 'Negroes,' just to sort of tell everyone he had another word in mind. 'They are animals,' he says, 'and no loss if we did away with all of them.' His words.

"Everyone was shocked. The foreman says, 'We're not going to talk that way here. There isn't much to say for Jackson, but we'll discuss the penalty in a civilized way, without blaming a whole race for what one bad man did.' 'Nothing to talk about,' Axelrod comes right back. Not the least bit ashamed. He says he didn't listen to anything either lawyer said because there's nothing to talk about. 'If anyone's thinking about voting for life,' he says, 'they don't need to talk to me about it because I've known he deserves death since before they picked me,' he says."

"Since before?" said Gideon. "He'd decided Jackson was guilty and deserved death before the trial even started?"

If only they'd had this information earlier. But none of the jurors, including Stanton, had been willing to talk to them when Gideon got the case fourteen years ago.

"One more thing," Stanton went on. "Maybe I should have told the judge about this at the time. But it's so embarrassing to feel you're tattling on someone you've been talking to. And I was trying to be tolerant, because we were all going to be there together for a while.

"During one of our lunches, before he said the 'N'-word, Axelrod mentioned something he hadn't talked about during the jury selection. The judge had asked everyone whether they, or any member of their family, had been the victim of any crimes. Axelrod said no. But he told me he wanted to be on this jury to see that it was 'done right' this time. He said he had a niece who had been sexually assaulted by a colored man a long time ago, and the jury let the man off. He'd read all about this case in the papers, and he didn't want it to end the same way."

"So he was biased," said Gideon, "even before the trial started. Biased because he disliked African-Americans. And biased because he wanted a death sentence before he'd heard any evidence."

Stanton thought for a moment.

"Yes. That would be a fair statement," she said. "One of the twelve of us who voted for death was biased."

"Would you be willing to sign a sworn statement about this, about all of the things you heard Axelrod say? I don't know what the judges will do with the information at this point in the case, but they should hear the facts, don't you agree? Would you do that?"

"Yes." She sighed. "I don't want to be in the newspapers and all. But yes. It's only fair."

Gideon had a laptop computer and a small printer with him. He wrote out a declaration under penalty of perjury for Joan Stanton, and she read it over and signed it then and there.

Gideon knew it would be tough going, making anything of this. Even apart from how late this was in the process, once there is a verdict, the courts are loath to look at how the jury got there.

Gideon discussed the juror misconduct with the two associates who were now working on the case with him and with the paralegal Jennie.

"I've looked into this before," said JoAnn Peterson. "To be brutally frank, it won't matter to most judges that the verdict was tainted by racism, that a juror said he wouldn't listen to the evidence, that he made up his mind before the trial. But the juror's lies during voir dire are something else. That's the kind of misconduct judges should recognize."

"The bigger problem," said Gideon, "is that we didn't allege anything like this in the petition for habeas corpus we filed earlier. So this will be what's called a 'successor petition.' And successor petitions have to clear an even higher hurdle, even though there's no way we could have learned of this violation of Jackson's rights before now.

"Under the legal standard for successor petitions, we have to show by clear and convincing evidence that except for the misconduct, no reasonable juror would have found Kareem guilty of the underlying offense."

"You mean the murder?" asked Jennie.

"Right."

"But that's not fair. That gets it backward. The most important thing is whether Kareem is executed. No matter what happened, even if we couldn't have known of the claim earlier, you're saying it doesn't matter if it's 'only' the penalty? It doesn't matter he got the death penalty because a biased juror lied and was ready to impose death before he even heard any evidence?"

"That's right. Unless we can prove Jackson was actually innocent of the murder, the death sentence stands."

So outrageous, Gideon thought. So much for a fair trial. But it's no use becoming enraged. He closed his eyes for a moment and choked it all back.

The successor petition was swiftly denied, first by the California Supreme Court and then by Judge Cole. Exercising another power granted by the 'effective death penalty act,' Judge Cole refused to authorize a further appeal. The state's new execution date loomed.

The refusal of a "certificate of appealability" was itself appealed by Gideon. But the same three appeal judges who had denied relief the first time around agreed with Judge Cole and refused to hear another appeal.

Any judge could grant a stay of execution, so Gideon asked Judge Reinhardt to put the execution on hold for ten days, pending an emergency application to the entire Ninth Circuit for a rehearing en banc on whether Jackson was allowed to appeal.

Reinhardt granted the stay. But within hours, the Ninth Circuit set it aside. The only thing left, an emergency appeal to the U.S. Supreme Court, was manifestly an exercise in futility. Kareem asked Gideon to be with him at the end, while his associates engaged in the final, pointless maneuvers.

74

There was no one to visit with Kareem at the end—no relatives or friends—other than Gideon Roth. They sat and talked about their long history together, even smiled at some memories. Then they were silent. Kareem looked down.

"Gideon, I'm scared. I don't want to die. I don't want them to kill me."

Gideon took his hands. "I'm sorry . . . I'm so sorry. I wish I could stop them."

Kareem's face became more resolute.

"Gideon, you a man who is hard on hisself. But you got to accept that some things can't be stopped, and it ain't your fault."

A guard walked over and clanged his keys against the bars.

"Two more minutes."

"You know, Gideon, before, I didn't want you lookin' into all that stuff about my family and what had happened when I was a kid. But now I understand. When I see all the things that happened to me, I understand what made me and what I was about.

"I dunno how to say this exactly. They're going to kill me in a little while. But you gave me back my life. Tell everyone on the team . . . Tell them thank you. Tell them I'm so sorry for the things I done."

They embraced. Then Gideon left. They led him to the observation room that looked into the gas chamber.

75

Gideon did not call Susan before he arrived in Springfield.

He made his way to the university and found the Sociology Department.

A chart on a bulletin board gave the room number for Susan's office, and the schedule on her door indicated she was teaching just then.

Class had already started, and Gideon slipped into a seat in back. There was Susan, speaking from the podium to a class of seventy or eighty students. She was older but familiar.

He had forgotten how tall she was, almost as tall as he. She had put on some weight and looked solid. Her hair, falling to just above her shoulders, was tinted a silvery tan color that looked good without attempting to conceal her age. Her eyes flicked in Gideon's direction for a moment, without recognition. The class was on Culture and Social Movements, and she was discussing how the music of the civil rights movement had emerged out of gospel.

This is a life I could have led, Gideon thought. Instead of becoming a business lawyer who salved his conscience with a little pro bono work on the side.

The class ended. A few students came up to talk to Susan, then left. She began pulling together her notes and papers. Gideon saw her look up toward him, this stranger at the back of her classroom. He rose and walked down to her.

"Hello, Susan."

"Hello," she said uncertainly. "Do I know you?"

"We've been much closer than this, but it's been some time," he said, a smile spreading across his face.

"Omigod . . . Gideon? Gideon Roth!"

She hugged him.

"What a surprise. What are you doing here? It's been so long. You look so different, not turned out like the lawyer I thought you'd become."

Gideon flushed. Direct as ever. While he was happy with his appearance as disguise, he had not shed all vanity and he was uneasy about looking poorly to an old friend.

"It's a long story."

"Such a surprise, just turning up this way. Do you have business at the university? Why didn't you call?" She grasped him by his upper arm and shook him a little, in her friendly, confident way. But she seemed perturbed. Perhaps his appearance was disturbing, not just unflattering.

"Oh, I don't know. I've been on a slow cross-country drive, sort of, and I decided at the last minute . . . I remembered you lived around here, and I just thought I'd stop by."

"Are you in town for long?"

"Could be a few days. It would be great if we could spend a little time together before I move on."

"Gideon, and not quite the Gideon I recall," she mused, almost to herself, as she looked at him, her hand still on his arm. "How mysterious. Well, I can't talk now; I've a committee meeting in five minutes and then conferences with my students for most of the afternoon. Come for supper. We can catch up then."

76

The streets of Susan's neighborhood were sheltered by thick, high trees that came together overhead, making it dark in the late afternoon. The old houses were well maintained and not overly large. They had been individually constructed, and so were unselfconsciously marked by satisfying architectural details that the builders of entire neighborhoods from scratch, in California, did not bother with—carved finials on fence posts, triangular brackets in the eaves, well proportioned shutters, front doors with their own distinctive moldings or transoms.

Here was the very image of small town America. They needed only a few flags and a Fourth of July picnic with the neighbors to complete the picture.

Gideon walked to the front door of a small craftsman-style house. The door opened, and there was Susan. She had changed from her professorial slacks into a relaxed, knee-length, brick-colored skirt and a soft top.

She stepped out, opened her arms and gave him a long hug. Her softness enveloped him.

"I'm so glad to see you, Gideon."

She drew him into the house.

"I don't think I would have recognized you if you had walked past me in the street. Your shiny head . . . but it's a little fuzzy on top. Did you have chemo or something?"

Gideon looked down self-consciously and shook his head.

"No, you look too healthy for that. I see you shaved it. . . Well, whatever."

"My appearance," said Gideon, stumbling, "it's part of a long story. But . . . I'll tell you later. But first, what's been going on with you all these years?"

She led him into the kitchen. It was a big room with prints and small bright paintings on the walls. French doors opened onto the back yard. Susan was preparing a pasta sauce, and she poured him a big glass of red wine. He leaned against a counter and listened while, from time to time, he passed ingredients as directed.

Susan was a sociology professor, well-known in her field. "I study the intersection of race and communications, race and education." Her articles had influenced thinking in the field.

She talked about her work, then had Gideon open another bottle of wine. A timer dinged, and Susan drained the pasta.

They sat at a small table in the kitchen. Gideon asked a question every now and then, to draw her out, but volunteered nothing about himself.

Susan was involved in a local group struggling against de facto segregation in the public schools of Springfield and its suburbs, and she led a religious coalition that had opposed U.S. support for the murderous military dictatorships in Central America. She described the successes and frustrations of this work.

She paused for Gideon to respond, looking uneasy with his silence. But he shook his head. "No, you go on."

Susan had had a marriage that ended about a decade ago. A son, Jeffrey, was in college in Ohio. She was with no one in particular right now.

"It's been a good life. Our country's a maddening place, and southern Illinois is not an undiluted haven of progressivism. But I have to say I've been happy. I have friends and I work with kindred spirits, even if it's not what we had in the Movement."

Gideon felt the want of similar friends and compatriots in the life he'd chosen. He would never have called his partners—his former partners— kindred spirits. He had called Kareem a friend, but he hadn't really been one. And in the end, his choice of career had been for nothing, had accomplished nothing. It was too late to go back and create a life of camaraderie. So now he was on another path.

She hadn't finished eating, but her talk wound down into silence. She pushed the food around on her plate. She looked at Gideon expectantly.

"You're taciturn, Gideon. What's going on with you? What's your cross-country trip about?"

"Not sure where to begin."

She gave him a small smile to encourage him, but looked guarded. Now that he had someone to talk to about Mississippi and his plans, he wondered whether he could explain.

"Hasn't all that has happened since the sixties made you feel defeated?" he asked. "The white backlash victorious. Both parties working together to destroy the welfare safety net. Indifference toward the poor. The same old Southern reactionaries back in control of Congress."

"Things have their ups and downs. It's not all fun, but that's what struggle is about. We just have to keep on keeping on, like we used to say in Mississippi."

"What's the point? They've won. We've lost."

"Is that what you think, Gideon?"

"They destroyed everything we accomplished."

"Well, no. There's much to be done, but we brought about some big things that haven't been reversed. We ended American apartheid. We triggered the women's movement. We inspired the anti-Vietnam-war struggle." She paused. "It's not too much to say we re-kindled American democracy."

"But public schools are now more segregated than they were under Jim Crow laws, and our rulers are as militaristic as ever."

"You don't have to tell me. We just have to fight harder."

Who had fought harder and longer than he? Much good it had done.

"Fight harder?" he said. "Every time we make progress, they take it away and then some. You've got to be a fool to still think we can get anywhere."

"You're being offensive, Gideon. And defeatist. I don't understand where you're coming from."

"Is it offensive to see the truth? To say it out loud?"

"You've been weird all evening, Gideon. Remote and strange. And now belligerent." She looked at him searchingly, but still he did not speak. She pushed the food around on her plate and waited, looked up again, but he remained silent. "Once I wouldn't have had to explain what I meant. Now I think there's no point. I don't know you anymore. Perhaps our reunion's gone as far as it can, Gideon. I think it's time for you to go."

He was taken aback. He didn't want it to end like this.

"You can't . . ." he whispered, suddenly tearing up. "I need to talk to you." He slumped.

"Gideon, what's on earth's going on? 'Talk to me'? You show up unannounced and all mysterious after twenty years, want to hear all about my life, but you don't share a thing about yourself. It's like you are a stranger disguised as Gideon. Who are you? What are you doing here?"

He tried to pull himself together.

"My life's taken a bad turn in the last six months, Susan. Everything has come apart."

He took a deep breath and let it out.

"You know that I became a lawyer for a big technology firm. I thought I could balance that with fighting for social justice, with pro bono projects. But nothing I did worked." He told her of his fourteen-year struggle to save Kareem Jackson, about its price, and his failure. The last months of the case, and the collapse of his legal career. And about Helen leaving him.

"Nothing I've done my entire life has done any good. It's all been meaningless."

"No," said Susan fiercely. "No, it hasn't. Everything we did, everything you did was important." She reached across and grasped his hand. She looked at his fingers, saw the skin he'd bitten and scratched away at the nails. She leaned back, not letting go of the hand.

"Fourteen years," she went on. "That's hard to take in, devoting so much of your life to one case. To trying to save one human being. You gave Kareem Jackson fourteen years of life."

Gideon began to make a gesture with his hands, dropped them in futility, shook his head a little, and was still.

"I was there at the end, when they killed him," he said finally. He felt his throat tighten, his voice become a whisper.

"I saw them strap him in and seal the chamber. Now I hear that sound, the screech of the door, over and over. I looked into his eyes. He was afraid, and then he was in pain. Then I saw him die.

"I sat in a room of observers, the audience. As though it were a play. I couldn't stop it. All I could do was be another observer."

"My God," Susan said softly, coming around the table to hold him. She squeezed him against herself.

"No, not just an observer," she said. "You fought for him. Then in the end you were with him, and you bore witness. You bore witness in the place where the evil was done."

Gideon's eyes blurred with tears. "Why . . ." he tried to begin, shaking his head. He began crying.

She held him for a long time, stroking him, wiping his tears with the edge of her top, sharing his grief. After a while she took him upstairs. She paused at the head of the stairs for a moment, then brought him to her son's room.

He was empty, drained of tension and of will. She sat him on the bed and took off his shoes, and laid him down. She put a light cover over him and lay next to him. She held him until his tears stopped, her left arm across his side. She felt his chest rise and fall with each breath as he dropped off, his face finally relaxed. Then she got up and went downstairs to clean the kitchen.

Gideon's plate was nearly full; he had hardly eaten a thing. When she finished, she went to sleep in her own room.

77

Gideon woke in the night. It was too early to get up. He lay in bed, listening to an owl in the distance, *Ur-rrr, hoo-hoo-hoo, Ur-rrr, hoo-hoo-hoo.* He heard the sounds of the house creaking. Though he was sleeping by himself, he felt comforted knowing someone else was nearby. He had been alone for so many months.

He thought of what Susan said about bearing witness. He knew he had had to be there, for Kareem to have someone who was with him at the end. But he'd felt sullied. As though he had joined in the rite of death. Now he saw his presence had deprived the immoral ceremony of its unanimity.

But Susan did not understand that he had failed Kareem, as he'd failed the others, and that he must now place something into the balance, against Kareem's death. He wasn't sure whether it was atonement or vengeance, but things could not lie as they were. He drifted off again.

It was light. He heard Susan moving about. He rose and quickly dressed. His pants seemed loose.

He went downstairs. Past the French doors there was a small deck under the big oak in the back yard. Susan sat at a table under the tree, a pot of coffee and a rack of toast before her.

"Thank you," he said, joining her, "for listening last night. I didn't mean to say the things you have been working on were pointless."

"I wasn't offended for me, Gideon, but for you. You've gone through a horrible time. You've witnessed terrible things. And then all the news media, and your law firm coming down on you. Helen leaving. So many problems.

"But it doesn't mean all you did was meaningless. You've got to regroup now. Maybe it's time for you to take up some new project."

I have.

"Maybe you have something in mind already?" she asked. "Is that what your trip's about?"

"Hard to explain," he said, then he was silent.

She seemed disturbed again, unhappy about his reticence. Was she going to ask him to leave? She got up, took the pruning shears from a small wicker basket that was next to her chair, and dead-headed some roses.

"I'm trying to get used to the way you look, Gideon," she said, not glancing his way. "If it had been real baldness, I would have adjusted. But it's part of the costume, isn't it? Like the eyeglasses and the Sears Roebuck shirt and pants . . . the bushy moustache, too?"

She sat down. "No self-respecting Silicon Valley lawyer would look the way you do. This isn't your usual appearance, is it?"

Gideon shook his head.

"Not so much a costume . . . a disguise. It's a disguise, isn't it?"

Gideon did not contest it, and Susan looked alarmed. "What's going on, Gideon? What are you going to do?"

He stiffened. "I'm going to Mississippi. To render justice."

"What is that supposed to mean?"

"Justice for Chaney, Goodman and Schwerner. I'm going to make their killers pay for what they did."

"What?" she asked, shaking her head.

"It started with you in a way. After Helen left, after I was by myself I started thinking about my life. About making the wrong turn when I became a corporate lawyer. I thought about you and Mississippi, and about the murders . . ."

Now he could not stop talking.

"It was the middle of the night and I couldn't sleep. I've slept poorly since the execution."

He told her about the first call, hearing Cecil Price's voice. And the others. About buying the guns, and how his preparations had unfolded as though on their own.

"I needed to talk to someone who would understand, that's why I came here. Price and the others deserve death. It's wrong they're just living out their lives unpunished. I know where Price lives, and I can take him out. It won't be hard."

"Gideon. This is crazy, you can't be serious . . ."

But she knew he was. He could almost hear her thinking: the disguise, the guns, the driver's license, the truck.

"It wouldn't have to be death if there were another way. If the state really punished them. But no one will, so it's got to be me."

She spoke in a rush.

"Gideon, no. You're really thinking of killing someone? Are you part of some group? Has some Weatherman-type collective talked you into this, done a number on your head? Oh, God, Gideon, what's become of you?"

Her eyes were wide and frightened.

"No group, there's just me," Gideon said. "It's okay, Susan, really. I haven't gone nuts. It's okay."

"Gideon," she moved closer, taking his hands in hers, speaking louder. "It's not okay, and you're not okay. You're not okay at all. Can't you see right away this is crazy? Completely crazy?"

"Don't tell me I'm crazy. It's just that I'm the only one who is ready to do what needs to be done, what everyone should know needs to be done." He shook his hands free of hers.

"This is crazy in so many ways I don't know where to begin," she said. "You really think you can hang around small-town Neshoba County, picking off these old guys one by one without anyone noticing you? Or do you want to get caught so there can be a big show trial about you bringing them to justice."

"No, I'm not going to get caught," he snapped. "I'm going to disappear after I kill Price, then wait and see how things look before deciding whether to go on."

"And so you have come here, to talk to me about your new mid-career plan to become an assassin? And this is not crazy?"

"You don't have to talk about a damn thing with me—I'll leave right now."

"No, Gideon! Please, don't—I didn't mean to insult you. Don't run off and do anything before we can . . . before we straighten this out. Before we talk it through."

She reached toward his hands again, then thought better of it.

"I'm sorry. It's just a shock. That you, Gideon Roth, the gentle and funny and smart Gideon I once knew and loved, mean to kill someone."

"It's too late for gentleness. That's what they count on, that our side will always be gentle, while they kill. Now it's time to strike back."

"Strike back? Against whom? The people who killed Kareem Jackson aren't in Mississippi."

"That doesn't matter."

She shook her head.

"I'm feeling cold. Let's go back inside."

They sat in a big sofa in the living room, and Susan moved to put an arm around him. He pushed her away.

"Don't treat me this way," he said. "I'm not deranged and I'm not going to be patronized."

"Then let's talk sense. Tell me why you think you are entitled to kill someone."

"Because it needs doing. Because they got away with murder for thirty years. Because no one else is going to do anything about it. Because I'm through being a Sunday liberal who's afraid to act."

"What kind of answer is that? The fact that someone deserves punishment doesn't mean you've got the right to kill them. That's why we have law. And even if we didn't, you're not the Lone Ranger."

Gideon had rehearsed this part many times.

"The murders of Schwerner, Chaney and Goodman were key events in the battle to preserve white supremacy. Everyone else may be content to forget and forgive, but I'm not. And execution is the only way I can do anything about it."

"But the crime wasn't forgiven. The entire nation condemned it. It was part of the reason the Civil Rights Act and the Voting Rights Act were passed, why segregation was dismantled. How can you think it's been forgotten?"

"All too late for Kareem's father or his grandfather who was lynched."

"Gideon, Gideon . . . What happened to Kareem's grandfather doesn't happen any more precisely because of what we were part of. Things aren't perfect, but there have been huge changes. We achieved something big. You achieved something big. You were part of it."

She looked at him for acknowledgement, but he refused to provide any. She withdrew, shifting away from him on the sofa.

Gideon felt the truth in what she said. But there was another truth. Kareem deserved to have his death avenged. Kareem and the others he had failed.

"The world has moved on," Susan said. "Cecil Price's fight has been over for decades, and they couldn't stand in the way of history. We won. They lost. But now you're going to make Price a martyr to the lost cause."

"Not a martyr, no more than any killer who gets what he deserves."

"Gideon, listen to yourself. You're glorifying executions. You spent half your life fighting that kind of thinking. Now you're for it?"

"Yes," he said. "I spent half my life fighting it and I lost. Every week someone's executed. Well, let them be on the receiving end for once. If it was okay to kill Kareem, it's okay to kill Price."

"You're not making sense, Gideon. Neither is okay."

She moved closer again.

"Do you even know anything about what kind of person Cecil Price is now? Whether he's repented? What he thinks about his crime, thirty years later. Do you know? You don't care, do you?"

"No, I don't. Kareem repented and it didn't save him. Why should Cecil Price get a free pass?"

"You're standing everything on its head. What happened to Kareem doesn't make it okay to inflict injustice on others."

"That's only what you claim I'm doing."

She was at a loss for words.

"And what about the consequences? Haven't we learned over the years that assassinations beget a cycle of killing?"

"Maybe they do and maybe they don't. You don't really know."

"*Maybe?*" Susan said angrily. "*Maybe?* Maybe other people are going to be swept up into this and die, and you think *maybe* that's okay? Okay for people to be killed so you can work through an emotional problem you're having?"

He was silent. Then he responded.

"Executing Price may have consequences. So what? There's always someone to say justice is inconvenient right now. Didn't the Movement turn white people to the Republican Party and give conservatives the presidency for a generation? Would it have been better for segregation to go on?"

"That's not the same," she said. "If that was the price, it was to end the entire evil regime of segregation. All you want is revenge. Or to become a martyr."

Sometimes you just have to bite the bullet, he thought. Or take one.

"And what about the legacy of our Movement?" she asked more softly. "We were part of something noble and good, something that achieved great things for America without violence. You're going to re-write our history. You're going to turn us into the first act of a nasty, degrading, trivial vendetta."

"I just don't see anyone who's going to launch a blood feud over Cecil Price."

She pushed him away.

"You don't see because you're the fool. What about the white supremacist militias? They'll kill a random black person to even the score."

She was my oldest friend, Gideon thought. Why can't she support me?

"If Price is killed by persons unknown," she said, "they'll look to his past for the motive, right? Right?"

"Sure, but . . ."

"The State of Mississippi will punish someone. If they don't catch you, they'll frame a black person. Someone connected with the Movement. Chaney's brother still lives in Mississippi. What if he doesn't have an alibi on your day of reckoning? I'm not going to let you get him killed."

Gideon took a deep breath. "That's not bound to happen. But if it does, worst case, I'll turn myself in."

"And end up in the electric chair. As though both of you might not be killed for your acts. Do you expect me to be the one in the observer room this time, watching them strap you into the chair? Watching them kill you?"

He was silent. His fantasies hadn't gone that far. So what? Maybe that would be for the best. Maybe that's why he wasn't bothered by the supposed risks.

"Isn't this loony, Gideon? Why aren't all these things bothering you? Why won't you stop?" She grabbed his shoulders and shook him. He did not try to resist.

"I don't want you to die, Gideon. Or to kill."

Gideon felt the tension in his jaw. He was gritting his teeth. They're just arguments, I don't have to agree with her. He hated her for trying to beat him down. It made no difference. Kareem was dead. His life was empty, evil-doers had prevailed, and he was going to have the final say.

"Killing is just wrong, Gideon, as wrong as anything can be. Can't you see that? Wrong when they do it. Wrong if you do it. And you can't just kill someone and go back to being yourself afterward. You'll change, change in ways you can never undo."

Her fingernails were scratching him, and her eyes bore into his. "You're going to become a killer, a hardened, heartless person."

"Don't say that about me! I don't care what you think, you're wrong."

"How can you not care about what you're going to do to yourself, about destroying yourself?"

She was undermining his resolve. But it didn't change anything. To agree was to surrender. His whole life has been compromise and surrender. *I'm not going back to that.*

"There's nothing else for me to do," he said. "Nothing else for me to be."

"No," she said. "No, no, no." She pulled him down on top of her and wrapped her arms tightly around him. "Don't do it, Gideon. Stay here. Stay as you are. I'm not letting go."

She took his face in her hands and kissed his cheek.

"Stay who you are."

But who am I? A failure. His skin shivered and he grasped her with sudden desire. He wanted to be tender, but he also wanted to dominate, to shut her up, to brutalize her. He pressed his pelvis against her and he was erect.

She wrapped a leg around him, pressing back and feeling him, she was panting. Then she pulled his hand away from her breast.

"No, Gideon," she whispered hoarsely. "No, this isn't the way. Not now. I still love you, but this isn't the way."

He stopped, and they held each other. She stroked his head, then he laid it on her shoulder. Her breathing slowed, and he saw she was exhausted, dazed. They were still. But Gideon could not stop thinking.

What did it all mean? He was confused. Tired and resigned. But he didn't know what he was resigned to.

Susan seemed to be dozing. Twenty minutes later she stirred and was alert again, looking up at him with concern. They disentangled and sat up. She touched his cheek, and Gideon squeezed her side. She got up and went into the kitchen to make more coffee.

He joined her and they sat at the table.

"Why do you want to throw away your life?" she asked.

"That's not . . ."

"It all seems so theoretical, Gideon. The things you've said don't seem like enough to explain why you want this. What does all this have to do with you?"

He hunched over, not looking at her. He didn't have good answers. He didn't want to be asked anything more. He wanted to smash something.

"I've failed so many people," he said. "My whole life I've failed people and they've died. Schwerner and Chaney and Goodman. My mother. Kareem."

"Gideon, all of these things aren't the same. This isn't one big pattern with you at the center of it. That's egotism.

"Chaney, Goodman and Schwerner were murdered by the Klan. Not because of anything you did or didn't do . . ."

"But it was my job to get the FBI to act—if I'd done it right that night, I would have made them do something."

"Gideon, that's crazy. John Doar couldn't get the FBI to lift a finger. You really think there was something a nineteen-year-old Jewish kid from the Bronx could have said to a bunch of good ole Mississippi boys who only happen to be FBI agents, to make them challenge the local racist establishment?"

"I had the last clear chance to prevent it."

"No. Once Price had them, there *was* no clear chance to stop the murders. The federal government had turned a blind eye to everything the South did to black people and their supporters since the end of Reconstruction. For nearly a century. If John Doar could not turn that train around in 1964, you sure as hell couldn't.

"As for your mom . . . She had the heart condition you told me about that summer. That's what the doctors told you. She was dying before you went to Mississippi, right?"

"Yes, but . . ."

"But nothing. This is your father's voice inside you, still finding fault, cultivating guilt. You were entitled to your own life, even if she was afraid for you."

Susan became quiet, and appeared lost in thought. Then she spoke more softly.

"At some point you've got to let yourself off the hook."

Do I?

"When I think of what you did for Kareem . . . When you have the courage to struggle for someone's life, you run the risk of losing. That doesn't make you responsible for their death."

"Susan, I made bad mistakes in how I handled the case. Some of it is technical legal stuff, but it might have made a difference."

"So you weren't the perfect lawyer. You really think you lost because of technicalities? Aren't technicalities the excuses judges use to get where they want to go? Given Kareem's crime, how could you have hoped to save him? How could it have ended otherwise, in a state that executes people? When you took one of the most awful cases?"

"He trusted me, Susan."

"He expected you to get him off death row?"

"Kareem didn't expect much of anything."

"Did you promise to save him?"

"No, of course not."

"Then why do you act as though you betrayed him?"

"Not betrayed, just that I failed."

"Yes," she laughed grimly, "you failed to perform a miracle. How much did Kareem regret having fourteen years of life after the jury condemned him?"

But Gideon thought of the gas chamber. Kareem helpless and Gideon helpless.

"Your besetting vice is grandiosity, Gideon. You picked Kareem's case because everyone else thought it would be hopeless, right?" Gideon hadn't told her that. "But still you expected to win. And when you didn't deliver the miracle, you felt there was nothing left of your life—except martyrdom in Mississippi."

78

Susan had run out of things to say, and Gideon had run out of answers.

She took him for a walk through the shaded streets of Springfield and showed him the house Lincoln lived in when he'd been a state legislator in Illinois. They walked to the three story office building where Lincoln and his partner William Herndon had practiced law before he became President. Then they returned to Susan's house.

"What are you thinking, now, about what you're going to do?"

"I don't know."

He felt stubbornly resentful. "I can see that what you've said sort of makes sense. But I'm tired of sensible. I guess I wanted to talk to you as a reality check. But I'm tired of reality. I just want to do what I came to do."

"But you weren't sure. That's why you had to stop and talk to me before you went to Mississippi. Did you really expect me to say, 'Gideon, I'm thrilled, this is the most wonderful idea I've heard in years, why didn't I think of it myself? All our old SNCC comrades will be so proud, they'll give you a medal.'

"You came here to hear me say no, you can't do this. But you want to go on anyway. Because you aren't making sense anymore. Or because you're suicidal. Literally.

"People who kill get hurt inside, hurt and damaged—we've seen this in so many of the men who saw combat in Vietnam. Their ability to connect with other human beings is marred, they lose the ability to live full, happy, productive lives. And witnessing killings can mar people in just the same way.

"You know that already, don't you Gideon? That's what's happened to you, right? You had to sit there while they killed someone before your eyes. Someone you'd known intimately for fourteen years. And they strapped him down, and they killed him in cold blood and you had to watch." She stroked his hand softly, and he looked at her hands.

"It was barbaric, Gideon. It was traumatizing. And now you're readying yourself to end your own life, by first committing murder."

He thought, that doesn't sound wrong. But . . .

She spoke patiently and moved her hand to his cheek, then to his back. "That's what this is all about, Gideon. You've been traumatized. You've gone through some very, very bad times, that ended with a devastating experience. And these traumas have bent you entirely out of shape. And they could lead you to something that would be even more ruinous, more ravaging if you don't succeed in getting yourself dead along the way.

"You know that, Gideon, don't you? Haven't you known this all along? Wake up, Gideon."

She stood next to him, rubbing his back. "I'm going to call a friend who's a therapist, Gideon. I want you to see her today, right now."

Gideon looked down, embarrassed. She does think I'm crazy. I guess I am.

Susan looked at him, then went to the kitchen to make the call.

Gideon heard her voice, murmuring on the phone. He got up, walked to the front door, opened it quietly. He stood at the threshold, hesitated, uncertain.

The afternoon light was beautiful in the trees on Susan's street, the way it came through the trees. It looked idyllic, like a green tunnel. Why didn't I live here? I might have, in another life.

He stepped outside and slowly closed the door, releasing the knob carefully to prevent the latch from making a sound. I have to decide this myself, he thought. He walked to his truck and quietly drove away.

79

Gideon was driving south.

Part of him wanted to believe Susan, to believe he'd done his part, and that it had meant something. That the path of his life was not strewn with a trail of his dead. But Gideon knew the ghosts were around him, the ghosts of those he'd failed. Susan had an excuse for each of them, but there was a pattern. She'd just said what an old friend would have to say. Who would be so brutal as to acknowledge that too many had died on Gideon's watch?

Gideon drove south on Interstate 55, the great conduit connecting the South to the Midwest. From New Orleans up through Jackson, Mississippi, skirting the Delta on its way north to Memphis, then on to St. Louis, Springfield and finally Chicago.

The Interstate followed the route of the old highways and railways over which had passed the Great Migration of nearly two million black people early in the twentieth century, fleeing from hunger and degradation and lynching to Chicago and the North. Not the promised land, but not that land of terror which was the South.

This was the route Kareem's parents had taken North in mid-century, Gideon thought. He was pointed the other way, south, toward Mississippi.

South toward the source. America's heart of darkness, the darkness of hatred and loathing cherished in the hearts of the white people who lived there. For a century, African American people—first enslaved Africans, then their oppressed descendants—had been the majority of Mississippi's population. They had literally built the state out of swamp, scrub and forest. This was their land in the most fundamental sense. But Emancipation had not included the forty acres and a mule General Sherman had promised. So they remained the dispossessed. And still they were despised by the white majority who ruled the state.

South toward the source. Gideon was pointed toward the place where Kareem's grandfather Joshua had been tortured and burned to death, the place where Jason had been broken and tormented, where he had been mutilated and had become the shattered man who had in turn twisted and crippled his own son Kareem.

South toward the source. Where the slowly unfolding tragedy had been launched so long ago, the tragedy that had enveloped and destroyed Luisa and Marisol Flores as inexorably as it had destroyed Joshua and Jason and Kareem. And perhaps, in a way, Gideon Roth.

Gideon wanted to confront those responsible. But the tragedy was too catastrophic, it had too many roots to pull out individuals and say they were responsible. Killing Price might only be a gesture. But the evil was too big to accomplish anything more.

It was Gideon's only remaining choice.

PART THREE

80

Gideon approached the big I-70 freeway interchange at St. Louis. He sailed through, south on I-55. Four hours later he approached Memphis.

Perhaps, he suddenly thought, *perhaps it would be better not to take this vehicle into Mississippi.* Suppose Helen, suppose someone contacted Susan and she tried to help them find him. Or suppose he'd made a mistake along the way. Suppose someone, somehow, was going to try to intercept him.

Gideon exited the Interstate in Memphis and drove through town until he found a large hardware store. He bought a small tool bag and selected tools and electrical items. Then he found a pharmacy, where he purchased a package of latex gloves.

Memphis International Airport had a three-story garage for long-term parking. Gideon pulled into a spot in a largely-empty section and waited. Other cars began to fill in the section. Eventually it became quieter.

Finally, a middle-aged couple emerged from a big green-and-silver Ford pickup. The man hauled out two large suitcases. Good. They were going on a long trip.

It was a four-door, crew cab style behemoth, a vehicle built to carry five or six people to a job and haul a ton of materials too. Mississippi plates. The side said "Yalobusha Contractors."

Gideon made himself wait twenty full minutes, in case they came back for something. Then he slipped on the latex gloves and grabbed the bag with the small pry bar he'd bought. The bag also contained a long wire on which he had bent a small hook at the end, an electrical connector and other tools.

No one was around. Gideon boldly approached the truck. Piece of cake. He peeked into the window. Good. They had left the parking receipt in the cup holder.

Swiftly, Gideon pried the window wide enough to slip the wire down to the door lock button. Deftly, he angled the wire toward the button and pulled.

The wire slipped past the button.

He tried again. And again.

Just be calm, he told himself. But getting the hook in place, with the right pressure, wasn't as easy as Gideon imagined. After four tense minutes—a long time for manifestly criminal behavior in a public space—Gideon stopped and walked back to his own vehicle.

His heart was pounding. He looked down and saw that his hands were shaking. Breaking into cars apparently involves real skills, Gideon realized, and he did not have them. No time to take a community college course on this, either. Maybe he should give up?

No. Fuck that shit. Just means a bolder step is needed. Gideon put a roll of duct tape into the bag and strolled back to the Ford. The place was still empty, and it was still okay.

Swiftly, Gideon applied the tape to the wing window on the passenger side, and smacked it briskly with the pry bar.

It broke neatly and made little noise. Gideon reached in, opened the door, and got in. He slid across to the driver's side and sat still. No one was about. No one had noticed him. He carefully put the shards of glass from the wing window under the seat.

Gideon opened the glove compartment and looked at the registration. Yes, a 1995 F350 pickup.

Thanks for the truck, Mr. Lester Washington and Yalobusha Contractors.

Gideon opened his bag and took out a chisel and a hammer. He looked around again and saw no one. He gave the ignition a great whack with the hammer. Again. His success with the window had encouraged him not to worry about noise.

Three more, harder smashes knocked the ignition loose. Gideon crawled under the steering wheel and yanked the unit down. He used his new wire cutters to sever the ignition wires from the lock, and drew them out. He sat back up and put the pickup into neutral. He touched two wires together and gave the accelerator a light push.

Ignition. First try.

Gideon smiled. He looked in the mirrors. Still no one about.

Gideon pulled the wires apart, and the engine stopped. He attached alligator clips to the wires that went to the starter engine so he could start and stop the engine more easily.

Gideon returned to his own pickup and decided what to bring along. Some clothes, his satchel and the handguns. And the rifle, the most obtrusive item. No one was about. He carried his things to the Ford pickup.

The pickup had a double gun rack behind the second bench seat. Gideon thought that putting his rifle in it would make him seem more a native. But his nerves weren't up to it. He put all of his things on the floor in back and covered them with a blanket.

Gideon started the pickup and pushed the wires out of sight below the steering wheel. He drove to the exit, paid for the parking, and returned to I-55.

Minutes later he crossed the state line. Gideon Roth was in Mississippi.

81

Gideon Roth was in Mississippi. Timmie Ray was sure of it. And he was afraid.

He summarized what they'd learned for District Attorney Jeffers.

"So what's this California lawyer want with Cecil Price and Mississippi?" Jeffers asked.

"I ran the name through our databases. One of the civil rights workers who invaded the state in 1964 was named Gideon Roth. He was in Hokes Landing. Maybe the same man. Must be the same man."

"I feel real bad about this," Jeffers said. "Especially if he and Cargill are the same. Or are working together."

"Helluva coincidence if they got nothing to do with each other," Timmie Ray said. "Well, it ain't enough for an arrest. But I've put out an all-points bulletin for him and his blue pickup truck anyway. He'll be stopped and held for investigation if his truck's sighted."

"I do not like the part about the telescopic rifle sight and the photographs of Price," Jeffers said. "Not at all."

He was fooling with his giant bolt while he looked at the large trees outside his window. This won't be my view much longer if we fuck this up.

"I surely do wish I knew if they were the same man," Jeffers said. "The other way it's two of them working together against Price and Roberts. Maybe . . ." He had a new thought.

"Timmie Ray, if this is a conspiracy, Mr. Silent Caller might have been calling other people we'd like to know about. Can you find out who else was called from the Yellowstone phone and the Wall phone just before and after Roth called Wayne Roberts and Cecil Price?"

⋆   ⋆   ⋆

Later that afternoon, Timmie Ray reported back to the District Attorney.

"First thing, Cargill and Roth. I went back and checked where the earlier calls were from. The first call to Price after I talked to you was from a public phone at a rest area on I-84 in southern Idaho. Appears to be the rest area where the Idaho Highway Patrolman saw a nervous man with a rifle and photos of Cecil Price. The next call was from Palma, the town where the same man spent a night with the woman the Idaho cop told us about—a man who called himself 'Cargill' but probably isn't.

"Then there's the man who also called Price twice from further east, from Yellowstone and Wall. The fingerprints show him to be Gideon Roth. Gideon Roth, who was a civil rights worker in Mississippi the summer Price helped murder three civil rights workers in Mississippi.

"No way two people are making these calls to Price, so Roth and Cargill are the same man—a man with a rifle, a telescopic sight, and a photograph of Cecil Price.

"You wanted to know if Roth called anyone else. Drew a blank on the phone in Wall. No other calls from that phone for hours. But two calls were made from the Lake Yellowstone Hotel phone a few minutes after Roth's call to Wayne Roberts. First was to a number in Springfield, Illinois. Lasted fourteen seconds. The second was to a number in Custer, South Dakota. Lasted four minutes, twenty-seven seconds.

"The Custer number goes to the reservations desk of a hotel near Mount Rushmore. They were able to tell us someone had placed a reservation on that date and time. It was a family of five who asked for a room with a double double and a rollaway bed. Don't sound like our man."

"And the Springfield call?"

"The home number of a woman named Susan Channing. A college professor. I ran her through the database. She was also a civil rights worker in Hokes Landing in 1964."

82

Flipping on the car radio, Gideon was awash in country western. Men and women sang of misguided love and impulsive foolishness, of pigheaded mistakes and lost chances—

The night I spent with my best friend's baby sister . . .
I let a woman I love slip through my fingers . . .
Took a swing at my old man at Christmas . . .
Wrap me up beside the jukebox if I die . . .

These songs must resonate with the lives of people who lived here. Was it because the songs were authentic or because they embodied stereotypes of themselves they preferred to reality?

The colorless character of the land undermined the feeling Gideon had anticipated, of re-entering a place of menace. It did not feel so different from the monotonous farmland of southern Illinois or the forested places between cities in Tennessee. The countryside's bland physical character seemed to belie what it had stood for three decades earlier: the searing, defiant heart of racism in America.

Over the years, characterless dealerships and franchise food chains had largely replaced the local stores. Mississippi had been exotic and ominous in Gideon's personal history. But now it looked like any another state, one that happened to be located in the southern part of the country.

Then there was Christian radio. More densely packed on the dial than in Kansas or Illinois, these stations played music with worshipful lyrics of Resurrection Day and born-again Christian love, strangely set to rock-and-roll or country western tunes.

We need to thank God for all that we have,
And the blood of the lamb,
And the Heavenly Father . . .

I need a hand, in a fallen world,
I just want to stand,
What would Jesus do walkin' in my shoes
Workin' at my job and goin' to my school?

Fifty miles south of Memphis, Gideon started seeing signs for the Batesville exit off the Interstate at US 278. His eyes were tired, and he had trouble focusing on his driving. Was Cleola Bates still alive? Probably not, or surely in a nursing home.

Driving in the right lane just a little over the speed limit, Gideon saw a highway patrol car in his rear mirror. As it came up rapidly, he recalled a SNCC poster depicting an ominous Mississippi cop, with the heading, "IS HE PROTECTING YOU?" Gideon glanced across as the car passed and was startled to see that the Mississippi patrolman was African-American.

It was early evening and Gideon had spent a long day on the road. At the bottom of the exit ramp, he pulled over to look at the Mississippi map he'd found in the glove compartment. Philadelphia was maybe 120 miles southeast of here.

Time for dinner. Gideon went into a restaurant next to the freeway exit. He sat in a booth, and while he was eating, he looked out the window at the motel next door. He saw what would have been unimaginable in

1964: little white kids and little black kids playing next to each other in the motel's swimming pool.

Gideon knew that dirt poverty and discrimination were still the lot of too many black people in Mississippi. Nonetheless, he was stirred by the liberating results of the struggle he had been part of. They had broken the vicious, soul-crushing system of American apartheid, the system that had imposed badges of servitude on black people for a century after the end of slavery.

White and black children could play next to each other in a swimming pool, unnoticed, simply an everyday event.

Gideon returned to the truck. He checked the back seat to see whether the owners had left anything for him to work with. A couple of construction helmets and orange highway safety vests, a clipboard with a punch list. On the floor behind the front seat, a stack of nested orange traffic cones.

Back on the road, Gideon found a black gospel station that was playing spirituals.

Can't no one know at sunrise
How this day is going to end.
Can't no one know at sunset
If the next day will begin.

Gideon turned off US 278 onto State Highway 315. There was road construction, but it was dusk and no one was at the work site. And there was little traffic on either side.

Traffic barricades lined the road for a quarter mile on each side. These were the saw-horse type folding barricade, with orange and white diagonal stripes and mounted at the top, a yellow plastic box with a flashing light.

A good risk.

Gideon pulled over, onto the rough muddy shoulder of the road, and backed up to the last barricade. He took a helmet and an orange vest from the rear seat and put them on. And a pair of work gloves, a size too large but usable. He stepped down out of the high truck, slammed the door, walked around and dropped the tailgate with a clang.

Gideon turned off the light on the nearest barricade, folded it, and slipped it into the bed of the pickup truck. Then three more.

There was no traffic on the road this time of the evening. And if there had been, they would only have seen a highway worker at work. Gideon worked unafraid. Then he got in the truck and drove off.

He returned to US 278 and continued east in the gloaming, through Oxford. Oxford, where segregationists had actually mounted an armed rebellion against U.S. authority in 1962 to resist James Meredith's lonely effort to desegregate Ole Miss.

Driving still more slowly, he continued toward the small town of Pontotoc, thirty miles further east. From there he would begin the hundred mile drive south to Philadelphia on small local roads.

Tired, Gideon slowed down and tuned the radio into more black gospel.

I was standing by the bedside of a neighbor
Who was bound to cross Jordan's swelling tide
And I asked him if he would do me a favor
Kindly take this message to the other side . . .

The sky grew darker, and Gideon's headlights, illuminating by turns this side then that of the twisting roadside, picked out abandoned houses and barns covered with a layer of kudzu. It was so familiar from long ago. He recalled the feeling of danger, driving at night, danger, but also the anonymous darkness.

If you see the Savior tell Him that you saw me
When you saw me I was on my way
When you reach that golden city think about me
Don't forget to tell the Savior what I say . . .

He was moved by the singer's confidence she would arrive into the arms of a comforting god. This kind of religion didn't seem so benighted. Part of him wished he had that kind of belief.

Though you have to make this journey on without me
That's a debt that sooner or later must be paid
You may see some old friends who may ask about me
Tell them I'm coming home some sweet day.

Gideon stopped at an old Sinclair gas station, with the green dinosaur on the sign. The station looked unchanged since the 1950s. He bought gas, chips and beer, a couple of sandwiches wrapped in cellophane and a soda.

At Pontotoc, Gideon turned south on Highway 15 in the direction of Philadelphia. At Davis Lake, a few miles along, he stopped at the campground. No one was at the entrance. Gideon found an empty campsite then went back and put four dollars into a little envelope and dropped it into the slot of a metal post.

Gideon ate his snack and had a beer at a picnic table, then a second beer. It had been a long day. He found a grassy place not far from the truck, put his sleeping bag out and lay on it. A warm night. Still in the 70s and it didn't seem it would get much cooler.

A few birds sang in the darkness. Different from those in the west. Gideon heard laughter from another campsite. The campground had an RV section from which he could hear the dim sound of a television, and canned laughter.

After a time, the talking and other noises quieted, and the last lights went off. There were many stars overhead. He drifted off to sleep.

83

Gideon and Kareem were having their last conversation. This time they were in the gas chamber, with Kareem strapped in. When Kareem told him not to be so hard on himself, all Gideon was thinking about was that he was running out of time to leave.

He saw the observers examining him through the windows and he rose without speaking. When he tried to move, he could only inch forward.

Then he heard the screeching of the door and then there was silence. He heard a clank and the soft splash . . .

He woke shaking, and chilled. It was still dark. He rubbed his arms until he warmed up, and the dream faded. He wanted to sleep more but he was afraid. Soon, he thought, I'll stop having these dreams.

He got up. He unwrapped the sandwich he had saved for breakfast. Then he threw it away.

Gideon walked along the lake, still in the morning mist. On the other side, there were lush trees right down to the water.

Gideon did not know what Price's street actually looked like, but he had an image of Center Avenue as part of a small downtown, a street lined on both sides with two or three story buildings. Perhaps 444 Center was an apartment or flat.

Gideon thought about walking up to Price's flat and knocking.

The door swung open wide, surprising Gideon as he raised his hand to knock again. The small Glock was still in his pocket.

Cecil Price was older than in the last photo Gideon had seen. His right arm was hanging at his side and he held a large revolver.

Cecil Price's eyes held Gideon's, then his gaze dropped and he recognized the lump in Gideon's pocket as a handgun. He swiftly raised the revolver. It was too late to go for his own pistol, and Gideon reached to hold the arm down. But Price was the stronger, or the momentum carried the gun far enough that when it went off, the bullet tore through Gideon's thigh.

A major artery was severed. He would bleed out before help got there.

His confrontation with Price could play out that way. Maybe all those phone calls hadn't been such a good idea.

Two hours later, Gideon saw a highway sign, PHILADELPHIA 5 MILES. He stopped to study the street maps he had printed before he left the West Coast. A couple of miles from town, the state highway swung toward the west, and Gideon could pick up County Road 561 into town. Road 561 became Pecan Avenue, a block from Cecil Price's home.

Philadelphia was a smaller city than he had imagined. One mile north of the center of town there were still fields. After that it started to look suburban, with big houses, grassy lawns and white fences. It continued that way until a block or two from Main Street; then finally there were businesses in brick buildings one or two stories high on Main and Beacon Streets. No apartment houses.

Gideon turned west onto Beacon and saw the courthouse. It was an undistinguished red brick building with four exaggeratedly large, ill-proportioned white columns. Gideon drove around the square, parking near a big black clock on a tall black stand just back from the sidewalk. Far above the courthouse steps, in letters a foot or two high, was carved ""NESHOBA COUNTY."

In Gideon's mind, this was a badge of infamy. But, obviously, everyone didn't see it that way. He checked his map and saw he was just three short blocks from Price's house.

Gideon walked around the square. It was late afternoon and there were many parked cars, but few people about. Stores faced the courthouse on each side, but business did not seem to be thriving. Like most small towns, Philadelphia was dying.

Gideon didn't talk to anyone. Why expose his Yankee accent to curiosity? He wondered for a moment what Kareem would have made of this place, a town not so different from the one where white men had abused his father as a young man for daring to walk on a sidewalk. Now black people passed without fear.

A mix of establishments graced downtown Philadelphia: River of Life Christian Bookstore. M&S Furniture. Philadelphia Printing & Office Supply. Chuxter's Guitar Shop. There was a pharmacy with a soda fountain like the ones there'd been in the Bronx when he'd grown up, but this one had big glass cases displaying memorabilia of earlier times. Most of the buildings looked as though they had been there for decades, and featured old-timey metal or cloth awnings that shaded the sidewalks.

The door of *The Philadelphian* newspaper warned, in lettering neatly painted on the glass: "NO Solicitation of Any Kind." "Management Will Prosecute!" And: "Door Locked."

Gideon wondered what solicitations could be so threatening.

About a half block south stood the Ellis movie theatre. The flaking marquee indicated the Ellis's last show had been The Wizard of Oz on "NOV 30 DEC 1 &" of some year, apparently long ago.

On the Beacon Street side of the square, the statue of a young confederate soldier stood beside the courthouse. It looked like the soldier was made of plaster of Paris. He carried a small backpack, and he held his hand by the brim of his hat to shade his eyes as he gazed into the distance. His right hand balanced a rifle whose stock rested on the ground.

The young soldier stood on a tall column on a high plinth, elevated up to second story level.

The Daughters of the Confederacy, he saw, had put up the memorial. It had been dedicated in 1912, during the orgy of lynching that had swept Mississippi and the rest of the South early in the century. On its base the Daughters had caused to be carved:

LOVE'S TRIBUTE TO THE NOBLE MEN WHO MARCHED
'NEATH THE FLAG OF THE STARS AND BARS AND
WERE FAITHFUL TO THE END
C. S. A.
OUR HEROES

The soldiers of slavery, heroes, still celebrated. Gideon returned to his Yalobusha Contractors pickup truck and started up. The east side of the courthouse square was Center Avenue, the street Cecil Price lived on. Gideon turned left onto Center. A block ahead, Gideon drove past the jail where Price had held Schwerner, Chaney and Goodman on the afternoon and night of June 21, 1964.

About a hundred yards further he found 444 Center, Cecil Price's address. Gideon did not know what Price now thought about what he had done, but apparently it did not trouble him to live near the jail he had used to perpetrate his crime.

Price's house was on a block of small, not-overly-prosperous looking homes, with here and there a few scraggly bushes. Each was surrounded by low weeds that had survived the cars, trucks or boat trailers that rested on them.

Cecil Price's house looked to be two or three bedrooms, one story with tan shingle siding. The houses on that side of the street were on a hill, so the back of the houses overlooked those on the street behind. A small portico shaded Price's front door. A lawn mower sat there, and a couple of folded chairs leaned against the wall. There were no houses across the street, and the lot next to Price's was vacant.

Gideon saw he could not hang around this street for five minutes without being conspicuous. Even though it was close to the courthouse square, there were no apartment buildings here and nothing that would pass for a downtown neighborhood with pedestrian foot traffic.

Gideon observed this in a moment as he drove slowly past. He wondered if Cecil Price, the man he had come all this way to kill, was at home.

Center Avenue ended half a block further, butting into another street where there was an empty church parking lot. Gideon was shocked to see a Philadelphia police car in the parking lot, facing Center Avenue. But the cop took no action as Gideon slowly drove by.

Gideon turned right, and right again, to leave the area. He stopped to wait for the light to change at Main Street, which was State Highway 16. Why was the cop there? Was he hiding from work until his shift ended? Or was he on the lookout for someone? For Gideon?

He turned and drove east out of town.

84

After twice driving past it, Gideon located County Road 747, eight miles away. His windows were down, and the midday heat was oppressive though it was only June.

The narrow macadam way was much patched and only a little better than a dirt or gravel road. For most of its length, the road passed scrub and weeds and small trees, with muddy patches to the side of the road. A few houses.

After a mile and a half, Gideon saw the roadside plaque that had been erected by the Mississippi Department of Archives and History:

"FREEDOM SUMMER MURDERS."

The plaque stood on the shoulder of the road beside the church. It declared that on June 21, 1964 Chaney, Goodman and Schwerner had been murdered after coming here to investigate the burning of Mount Zion Church.

"Victims of a Klan conspiracy, their deaths provoked national outrage and led to the first successful federal prosecution of a civil rights case in Mississippi."

Gideon would have been more impressed had the murders been memorialized in downtown Philadelphia, by the jail where the young men had been held captive, or along the State Highway where Price and his fellow killers had seized them for the second and last time. It was impossible to imagine a place where it was less likely to be noticed.

Putting an historic highway marker in a location destined to see no passers-by amounted to mockery. Neshoba County, true to its heritage, had succeeded in relegating the memory of their struggle to a secluded, segregated place.

Mount Zion Church, rebuilt of brick, had been there for many years now. Nearby, on a white pipe framework, was mounted the bell from the old church whose burning had brought the three to their Gethsemane. A few feet away was a carved, marble stone topped with fresh flowers.

THIS MEMORIAL IS PRAYERFULLY AND PROUDLY
DEDICATED TO THE MEMORY OF

JAMES CHANEY
ANDREW GOODMAN
MICHAEL SCHWERNER
WHO GAVE THEIR LIVES IN THE STRUGGLE TO OBTAIN
HUMAN RIGHTS FOR ALL PEOPLE

Gideon gazed at the stone for a long time. They, too, had also been faithful to the end. But Mississippi treated them as dead history, embalmed and forgotten.

Soon he would give them cause to remember.

Gideon pulled lightly on the chain that hung down from the bell, and heard the bell ring softly. An elderly black man stepped out of the church and came up to Gideon. He was short, perhaps five foot six, very dark, with wiry gray hair. His features were sharp and alert, and he seemed much older than Gideon, though he did not move like an old man.

"That bell was all that was left in the ruins when the Klan burned our church to the ground in 1964," the black man said. "But with God's blessing, we rose up from the ashes."

Both men were quiet.

"Pull it hard, friend, and hear that bell ring out for freedom, ring out for God," the black man said in a larger voice.

Smiling, Gideon set the bell vigorously pealing, again and again, for a full minute. Then he stopped, and as they heard the vibrations fade, he and the black man stared at each other.

"They can never long silence the ring of the truth," the man said.

"I was a volunteer in Hokes Landing during Mississippi Freedom Summer in 1964," said Gideon. "I knew about the burning churches. The many burned churches. And about Chaney, Schwerner and Goodman."

"Then I thank you for coming to pay your respects, sir. Bless you for what you done then. My name is Ezekiel Samson, and I was a deacon in those days, when we decide to let the church be used for the freedom school. Now I come round from time to time to fix things, to keep an eye out."

"My name's Jim Cargill," Gideon said. He felt shamed by the lie.

"Come inside and lets us visit together a while," Ezekiel Samson said.

Next to the main church building was a smaller one with offices and work areas. There were boxes of books and stacks of donated clothing to be sorted.

"Would you like a cup of coffee or a coke?" Ezekiel Samson asked.

"Whatever you are having, sir," said Gideon.

Mr. Samson pulled two cokes from a refrigerator, and he and Gideon sat together. He set out an open package of sandwich cookies.

"What you do now, Mr. Cargill, and what bring you to Philadelphia?" the black man asked politely.

"I'm an attorney, and business brought me to this area. So I borrowed a vehicle from an old friend, and came to pay my respects, as you say. But I'd like to hear about Neshoba County, if I can trouble you. Tell me about how things are around here now for African American people, could you?"

"Well, of course, what used to be is no more. It has passed away, thank the Lord. With the Lord God's help, we swept the worst of those bad times away. The Ku Kluxers and the dynamiting. The beatings and the killings. The danger and the fear to stand up like a man. We swept all that away."

Listening, Gideon had the feeling that the old man was telling a tale he had told before.

"The price was paid in the blood of the three young men and others, many others. But with God's help we done swept away the evil.

"We don't got to cower no more, and we can surely vote. There are schools with white childrens and black childrens all together in the class-room. And librarians at the Public Library are African American, and we are not kept out of that library as we had been. We even got black deputy sheriffs, and they are allowed to arrest white people.

"But I can't say we got equality. We still the poorest of the poor. We don't get what few good jobs there be in Neshoba County. We vote, but no black person been elected to a county or city office. There are white teach-ers now, teaching colored and white children together. But there were few colored teachers left after they put the schools together.

"Our young people see no future for themselves here, so they leave for Memphis or St. Louis or Chicago. And we have a big drug problem here, a very big drug problem afflicting our youth. Perhaps the white people planned it this way, to keep us down and them up.

"Maybe white folks don't spit in our faces no more. But they still walk on us, trampling us without even noticing some times what they doing.

"Forgive me, Lord, for seeming ungrateful and bitter. But our cup doth not overflow with justice yet. Neshoba County is not yet a place of righteousness."

"Which President was it," Gideon asked, "who said the black people and their problems needed 'benign neglect'? Whoever said it, that was one promise that they kept, and those who followed them too. They have succeeded in neglecting equality for a long time, neglecting equality and justice."

"That be the truth," Samson said. "The struggle has got to continue, though I am getting too old to do much more struggling myself. You a younger man, you must still be part of it."

Gideon sat quietly for a few minutes. *Is that what I am going to be part of?*

"And whatever happened," Gideon asked, "to the men who killed the three young men? I mean after the trials—I know some of them were convicted on the civil rights charges, not for murder."

"Most of them still live in Neshoba County. But no one respects them no more after they got out of the prison. At first, in the first years after the murders, there was an element here, an element of white people that considered those who done it their heroes. But after it brought the federal government down on the county, and then the Voting Rights Act and all, and after the killers were actually sent to prison, that started to change. You wouldn't have known it right away. But the white leaders finally accepted that segregation had got to go.

"And the respectable people in the county, the people with the power, they realized it had been a mistake what Price and the others had done. They quietly stopped fighting integration, and they stepped in and they have kept their power."

Mr. Samson laughed softly.

"By the time Price and Barnette and Posey and the others got out of jail, they had gone back to being white trash. They don't matter no more."

"But is that enough?" Gideon asked. "Enough for justice?"

"I don't know if it be enough—I am a just God, saith the Lord—and God may have other plans for them. But we got today's fight to fight, don't we?"

85

Timmie Ray was tired from his flight and anxious about whether this trip would accomplish anything. He knocked sharply on the door. The middle-aged woman who opened it looked like her photograph on the university's faculty web page.

He took out his identification.

"Susan Channing?"

"Yes."

"My name is Timmie Ray Phelps. I'm a sheriff from Mississippi."

She blanched.

"Might I come in and visit with you for a few minutes?"

"Is Gideon all right?"

"Well, that's what I come to talk to you about."

Channing showed him into the living room. By the time they sat, she looked wary. Timmie Ray waited for her to return to her question, but she was silent.

"When was the last time you were in touch with Gideon Roth, Ma'am?"

She took a long time considering the question.

"Gideon and I have scarcely seen each other for many, many years."

"You didn't answer my question, Ma'am. When were you last in touch with him?"

"Not in years."

He leaned forward toward her.

"You know very well that isn't so, Ms. Channing. Gideon called you eleven days ago from the Hotel Yellowstone. The third of June, at 6:42 p.m. We've got a record of the call."

"I don't know anything about any such call," she said. "If you've been tapping my phone, that's what you really know."

He looked at her hard, and she looked away. She wasn't much of a liar. Now she was telling the truth. But not the whole truth.

"Tell me about the last time you and Gideon spoke," he asked in a softer tone. "What did he tell you about what he intends to do in Mississippi?"

"I don't have to answer any of your questions. Has Gideon had an accident or something?"

"What kind of accident or something are you imagining, Ma'am?"

"I'm not imagining anything," she said, looking at him stone-faced.

Timmie Ray knew he had taken a chance, coming to talk to Channing. Now he had to decide whether this seemingly respectable, middle-aged lady professor who was fencing with him was part of a conspiracy to commit murder in Mississippi. If a middle-aged lawyer from California, why not a college teacher from Illinois?

Timmie Ray sighed. He just didn't know enough. But if she was in it with Roth, it was already too late. She would warn him when Timmie Ray left, anyway, if she could.

"It's been a long time since you were a freedom school teacher in Hokes Landing, Susan. Mississippi's come a long way since then."

"Not far enough," she said briskly.

"Not as far as she needs to go, but a long way. Who knows that better than you?"

He knew from the description of her writings, on her faculty web page, that she still cared about the education of minorities and the disadvantaged. What could that have to do with shooting Cecil Price?

"What do you think it'll take to get us the rest of the way home, Susan?"

"That's a big question. A good question."

She looked right at him, deciding to take him seriously.

"A real commitment to confronting poverty would go a long way. A major investment in education for all races, with truly integrated schooling. A mass movement of the kind we had back then, to force you to do what's right."

"Anything else?" He ventured a small smile.

"Maybe we need our own Truth and Reconciliation Commission, like they've got in South Africa. So we can come together by recognizing the history of pain. By acknowledging all the evils."

"What was involved in that?"

"In South Africa, after apartheid ended, they had hearings in a court-like setting. To let the silent victims speak the truth, to tell of what was done to them, and have the wrongs recognized. And for the perpetrators to testify as well. Not for punishment—just because there had been so many who had been part of the enormous, immoral system. But to help the guilty to accept their responsibility."

Timmie Ray wondered how such an enterprise might fare in Mississippi, and whether it might do some good. But his thoughts quickly returned to Gideon Roth. He did not think Susan Channing was the kind of person who would help someone who was a terrorist.

"Susan, you asked me whether Gideon was all right before I said a word to you. So you know he's involved in something wrong. Gideon's heading into trouble, right serious trouble, and I want to stop it before it becomes so serious that Gideon never comes out the other side. Don't you want to help me stop him?"

"I . . . I tried to myself. I don't know where he is now or what he's going to do."

"He's armed and dangerous, and he is fixin' to kill someone. Maybe more than one. Is that clear enough for you? Is murder truth and reconciliation?"

"I don't think Gideon will, but I don't know. I've done everything I can."

"He visited with you here. Tell me what he told you about what he's going to do. Tell me everything you know."

Her glance fell to her feet. She was quiet for a full minute, then she looked him in the eyes.

"I can't say any more."

"Can't or won't? Where is he? Just what is he planning? How can we stop him?"

"I don't know where Gideon is and I don't know how to reach him. That's the truth. He was here two days ago. But he left suddenly. That's all I'm going to tell you. Now, if you please, you can leave my house."

86

It was mid-afternoon. Gideon drove back from Mount Zion Church toward Price's neighborhood.

Neshoba County's banishment of the memories of the three victims angered him. And he was disturbed by the old man's lack of interest in the fate of the killers in the here and now. Was he the only one still to feel indignation that Price received only a slap on the wrist for triple murder? To feel that justice must be done?

As he drove along, in his head a phrase repeated: *Price deserves death. Price deserves death. Price deserves death . . .*

He knew this wasn't logic.

They had other fights to fight, the old man had said. The struggle had to continue. But Gideon was tired of struggle and failure. Let others take up the struggle. He had another agenda.

Many evils *had* been swept away, swept away by what they'd done. By what he had been part of. But not enough.

No, we'll never turn back
Until we've all been freed
And we have equality.

Let others take up the struggle. The old man hadn't accused Gideon of shirking, because he'd assumed Gideon was still part of the struggle for equality, for justice.

Price deserves death.

The police car was probably still there. It would be foolish to drive past it a second time. Gideon turned back onto Highway 19 and continued north out of town.

Maybe it would be a good idea to get out of sight for a while, if the Philadelphia police were hanging around Price's house. Perhaps he should give them a few days to lose interest.

After a while he pulled over to the side of the road. There were no houses here, not even fields, just dead land no one was using for anything.

He would get out of town. But where should he stay? He didn't want to be by himself in a campground or in the pickup. He needed someone to talk to.

Charles Willis. His comrade in 1964, who'd saved his life. He'd see

Charles. But there was no way he could explain what he was doing with Yalobusha Contractors' truck.

It took Gideon an hour and a half to drive to Winona. Outside of town, he saw a half-collapsed, tilted barn, on an abandoned farm with a weathered 'For Sale' sign. He parked the pickup truck behind the barn, out of sight. It took him an hour to walk into town.

There was a bus to Batesville around dinner time. He found a phone booth at the station.

"Hey, Charleston, can you guess?"

A brief pause, then, "A white boy with a Northern accent. And nobody call me Charleston in thirty years. It be you, Gideon, right?"

"Yes, first try, my man."

"How you doin'?"

"Doing well, Charleston, doin' real well for a man who's thirty years older. Listen, I am here in Mississippi and I need a place to stay. Can I crash with you tonight? Maybe longer than one night."

"Surely," said Charles. "Where are you? You need directions?"

"I'll be arriving in Batesville on the Greyhound at six forty this evening."

"I'll pick you up."

In front of the bus station, a middle aged man waited in an aged purple Pontiac. He had very black skin, flat features, a narrow moustache, and a few last puffs of white hair on his scalp. He was carrying a fair amount of weight but looked fit.

He had changed, but Gideon recognized Charles Willis. Gideon opened the car door and sat next to him. "Shall we have another shot at desegregating Humphrey's, Charleston?"

"Gideon. As I live and breathe. I'd never have recognized you. Both of us have gone bald, too!"

"Speak for yourself, baby . . . well, this is a long story, but part of it is that I need to be somewhere for a few days where no one's going to notice me too much."

"You in some trouble, sounds like. You don't need to tell me more'n you want. Thirty years or ninety years, I'm here for you."

Gideon hugged Charles.

"I inherited the farm after daddy passed on, and I been nearly on my own since Essie died of cancer two years ago. If we go there, won't be no problem for anyone who's visiting with me. No one else live there but my old Auntie Lillie. And she be fine with you. And Hettie Williams, you 'member her? She's a cousin, she come by to cook for us."

"Sorry to hear about Essie, Charles. Must be tough without her, all these years."

"She gone to the Lord. Be a while before I join her, but I gotten used to being by myself."

"What's become of your sister Emma?"

"Emma went to Wayne State in Detroit, then to night school in Memphis to get a teaching credential. Took her three years, but she become a history teacher. Now she's an assistant principal in a high school in Memphis. Married, three kids and all. Doin' well. Though one of her boys had a drug problem."

Gideon wasn't going to involve Charles Willis in his plan. But he told Charles about losing his job and his wife. And about his client being executed.

"You been havin' tough times, Gideon. Maybe this can be a sort of rest for you, staying with us for a while."

An hour later they got to Charles' farm outside of Hokes Landing. Gideon hadn't brought much clothing along, and Charles gave him something to change into. They sat on the porch in the mid-afternoon heat, drinking very cold beers.

Gideon told Charles more about what had happened to him at his law firm in the time after the execution.

"Looks like that whole part of your life come down, Gideon. Can you get work with another company, build it up again?"

"Not sure. Wouldn't be easy. Not sure I want to anymore."

"Maybe the Lord got something else, something different in mind for you, for the next part of your life."

"May be."

87

Gideon watched the news for clues something was happening with the police and Cecil Price's neighborhood. But there was nothing.

Gideon read, and he went for walks, though not too far afield. His inactivity at the farm started to disturb him. *I ought to be doing something to help with the work around here.* But knowing nothing of farming or laboring on a farm, Gideon thought there was nothing he could do that would actually be helpful.

Charles Willis had become more religious in the years since Freedom Summer. Trust and companionability still connected them, along with their history of past danger and struggle. But as adults whose lives had run along different courses, they now found little to talk about. Charles told Gideon about his life over the last thirty years, and caught him up about various people he'd known back then. And Gideon recounted his life since 1964.

Gideon found it hard to express the depth of his disquiet with his life. When he tried, Charles suggested they pray together—something too alien for Gideon to embrace—and urged Gideon to put his problems into God's hands.

"I see something is disturbing you, Gideon, though you don't want to talk about it yet. Jesus can give you the peace you're looking for. He's done it for me."

Gideon respected Charles. He did not feel disdain for Charles' religious beliefs. But this was not the way Gideon could come to grips with his problems.

Aunt Lillie was the only other permanent member of the household. Gideon's conversations with her had so far been limited to respectful politeness.

Lillian Lincoln was evidently old, but Gideon had been surprised to learn just how old. Born in May 1902, she recently turned ninety-five. She had lived through nearly the entire twentieth century.

She stood only four foot eight inches. She was a creamy medium brown color, like coffee with more than a little milk, and she had many age spots on her skin, which was thinly stretched on her bones. Her short white hair had also thinned, and she covered her near baldness with a skull cap of African colors that accentuated her sharp features.

Alert though frail, she had a strong voice. But at first Gideon found her heavy southern black accent so thick that he literally could not understand much of what she said. He recalled being similarly confused in encounters with many African Americans in the summer of 1964.

Gideon sat quietly with her and they talked about this and that. And he listened as she spoke with Charles and with other old women who came to visit, including some of her daughters who were themselves very old. After a while he grew accustomed to the accent and found himself automatically translating the southern black syntax and usage.

One hot afternoon, after Gideon and Auntie sat together on the porch, and Gideon had brought her the cup of scalding tea she had requested, he asked, "Aunt Lillie, how did you come to have Lincoln as your last name? I'd never met or heard of any Lincolns in the South before I met you."

"You ask a good question, young man.

"My daddy Adam was eleven years old when Emancipation come, and he had the name of the old master, Greene. Adam Greene my daddy was called.

"He grew up during the time after the war with the North, when we voted and we even ran the government in Mississippi. Colored people was three out of four of them who lived in the Delta then. Black Reconstruction they call it. My daddy was old enough to vote just one time, in 1875, before the white folks stopped us voting. That was the last time anyone in my family was allowed to vote for ninety years. Daddy held his anger over that his whole life.

"My daddy decide when he was a young man he didn't want the name of no enslaver. So he take the Great Emancipator's name. Later, when the white people crush us down again, and there was the segregating and the insults and the lynching, he got in trouble over that name. They near killed him in Coahoma County for being called Lincoln. Whipped him, like he had not been whipped as a boy in slavery, and made him say he was Adam Greene again. I saw the scars many years later, the raised welts that criss-cross his whole back.

"So he carried himself to this county and give himself a new name, Jameson. After a time, he was able to buy some land, and that was this farm. He held it in the name of Jameson, but he kept his true name, Lincoln, a secret.

"My mama born after slavery, and she marry my daddy in 1889. He sixteen years older than herself, and she was his second wife. His first wife died in childbirth with her third baby. Mama raised all them nine childrens that lived, his and hers.

"Daddy learnt us childrens that our real name was Lincoln, but to keep it secret. I decided to take my name back in the 1920s. But when I married and had children I give it up, I took my husband Amos's name.

"Amos died twelve year ago. After a time, I reflected there was no more Lincolns in the family. 'Course, my children all had Amos's name, Clay.

"My daddy's children was mostly girls and we all had took our husbands' names. My two older brothers stayed Jameson and never went back to Lincoln.

"I decided I would go back to my father's name. So there would be one with that name, to respect him, at least as long as I am spared. So I been Lillian Lincoln again since 1987. I been planning for my gravestone to say Lincoln."

Aunt Lillie sipped her tea, sitting very erect. Examining him, Gideon felt.

I've got another name, too, Gideon thought. But mine doesn't honor my father. Nor the Emancipator.

Aunt Lillie put her tea cup down on a little table next to her and slowly stood.

"You come along and keep me company while I quilt. I've been thinking on one I'm working on, and I need to piece it for a while now."

The wood floors of the Willis house were rough and somewhat irregular, tilting here and there, and Gideon watched anxiously as Aunt Lillie hobbled to her room. But she did not fall. Once, he reached out to assist her. She glared at him, and Gideon quickly put down his hand.

Awaiting her on a big table were eight or nine rough piles of scraps, strips of cloth of different patterns and colors. Aunt Lillie sat at the table, and out of a big basket that rested on the floor, she drew the edge of the large part of the quilt that she had so far completed, pulling it into her lap.

Gideon sat in a rocking chair right by, and he watched her reach unhesitating for a particular piece from one of the piles. She began sewing and Gideon was quiet.

"You don't work from a pattern?" he asked after a while.

"You got to talk a little louder when you on that side. That ear ain't so good. Didn't I tell you that already?"

"Sorry," he said in a bigger voice. "You don't use a pattern, Auntie?"

"No. It's in my mind. While I been sitting quiet on the porch before you got there, I was thinking on the quilt and what needs to go where. After this piece it's time for that itty biddy red piece I'm holding on the side there. Then some of the narrow strips over there."

Since only a small part of the emerging quilt was in Aunt Lillie's lap, Gideon had no sense of the pattern, but he understood that she was holding it in her head. She stitched briskly, her hands moving with steady purpose, her bright eyes surveying him from time to time.

"You seem troubled," Aunt Lillie said after a while.

"I am," Gideon said slowly. "But I'm not sure where to begin. Or maybe I mean, how to begin it." He did not want to talk much about Kareem and his death. Nor about Cecil Price.

"Every story starts in the middle," Aunt Lillie said. "There always be something else been before you begin telling. Just start yours anywhere, and you can go back another time if you need more beginning."

"Well, as you know, I was a civil rights volunteer here for a little while in 1964. Later I became a lawyer. Doing things I came to feel weren't what I should have done with my life."

"You made a good beginning, back then. You done some important good when you was a young man."

"It's never seemed to me that what I did mattered all that much."

She looked up sharply from her stitching, resting the hand with the needle in her lap. She opened her lips. Then she shook her head, closed her mouth tightly and went back to the quilt. Her face became hard, and she resumed her work, muttering inaudibly.

Gideon felt her scorn. He was being treated like a child not worth scolding, and he didn't understand why.

She finished with the dark brown piece, took a long blue strip, and began slowly sewing it into place. After five minutes, Gideon thought of quietly leaving, but he was afraid to move.

"Aunt Lillie, I'm not sure what just happened. I feel sorry for something, I guess I said something wrong, but I'm mostly confused."

She looked him in the eyes. Then her face softened.

"When you say what you did didn't matter all that much, that was like saying we colored people didn't matter all that much."

Gideon's face reddened. He shook his head, but said nothing. Aunt Lillie held his gaze.

"From when I was growing up, a little girl 'round 1905, 1910, to when I was sixty year old, I was afraid of the white people every time I went to town. Afraid, because any one of them could do anything they wanted to us. Nothing to stop them. Maybe humbling us. Maybe a push or even a smack. Maybe worse.

"We ain't afraid no more. I can walk down a street now and not worry a white man might humiliate me. Can you see what that means? That's because of what the Freedom Riders done, and you was part of it."

He felt embarrassed, and looked down. "I'm sorry. . . Thank you, Auntie."

He remembered, as she spoke, the humiliation and worse that Joshua and Jason had suffered on the streets of the South. He recalled the parents he'd encountered in Mississippi who feared what might happen to their children if they got involved in the movement. And the men who hadn't wanted to speak of what they had been forced to endure.

The unpredictable, but always present, background of dread and violence was what Susan had been talking about when she said they'd ended American apartheid. That sounded abstract, rhetorical. This was what it had meant.

"Thank you," Gideon said again. "I think I'd lost sight of what we'd done."

Aunt Lillie nodded, and reached across to touch his hand. She went back to stitching, and Gideon tried to go back to his story, even as he reflected on what she'd just told him.

Where does it really start?

"At the beginning of this year my wife left me. It was after a long bad time that ended when a man I represented, I was his lawyer for many years, he was executed for a crime, a terrible crime he had committed.

"I couldn't think of anything else, anything good for a long time. Lost my job. Then Helen left me. Not her fault. She tried, she tried hard. I've failed at a lot of things, and I don't know what's next with my life."

"So much opportunity you've had," Aunt Lillie said. "But even having opportunities don't protect against tribulations. Maybe more'n your share."

Aunt Lillie hadn't stopped working, and now she reached for the small red piece. Gideon could see a little of what it was doing for the pattern where she fit it in.

"Do you want to tell me more about the man who was executed?"

Gideon shook his head. "Too much on my mind as it is."

He continued to gaze in the direction of her quilt but he stopped seeing it.

"I think about what happened when I was here in 1964, Aunt Lillie. Doesn't it bother you about the racists of Mississippi, who committed all those murders back then? Who got away with all that killing? Do you ever think about whether something's needed for the victims' sake—to restore the balance?" He halted, hoping he hadn't said too much. "Maybe to give peace to their souls?"

"All those who been kilt by racists in Mississippi," said Aunt Lillie. "All those who murdered them. Could be a lot of people, if a body could figure out who they all was. Been a lot of killin' in Mississippi over the years. 'Course, most of the killers probably passed on theyselves by now."

"I was thinking especially about the men who killed the civil rights workers in 1964. Cecil Price and the others."

Gideon heard himself, and suddenly he felt embarrassed about what he'd just said. The way he put it revealed a kind of self-centeredness, maybe even racism. As though he, too, focused only on the crime whose victims were mostly white and like himself, not the many anonymous blacks who'd been killed and forgotten by the world. Though how could anyone even know who they all were, and who their killers were?

"It's not that they are forgiven," Aunt Lillie said. "But to think on it too hard, all these long years after, may be to give new life to the hate they birthed."

She looked on Gideon with worry.

"You best stay with us some while longer," she said. "Maybe you can find the comfort you looking for with old friends, on this farm that God's blessed so."

She turned back to her stitching, not needing an answer from him.

Gideon stood up. For the first time he noticed a quilt of vibrant design on Aunt Lillie's bed. He turned to consider it more closely.

He was stunned. Comprised mostly of what appeared strips of old clothing, here was a work of art—for that it surely was—a work of startling expressive power and originality; confident, witty, challenging.

A series of thin strips of fabric, irregularly shaped, made up most of the quilt. Faded purples and blues, varying subtly in darkness, teased each other, and were juxtaposed with three larger rectangular elements, unexpected variations in hue on a nearly peachy orange theme. A group of smaller strips and small squares were set roughly at an angle from the main group, adding an unexpected response that in turn was anticipated by a few very small pieces of bright fabric that had been fitted elsewhere in the work.

There was no question of anything accidental here. This was the work of a mature artist.

The large quilt reminded Gideon of paintings by modern artists like Richard Diebenkorn or Hans Hoffman. But it made its own wholly original statement.

Gideon turned to Aunt Lillie.

"This is incredible," said Gideon. "This is yours?"

"Yes," said Aunt Lillie. "Thank you."

"I don't know what to say. I'm astounded. Are there others I can look at?"

"You can peel that one back," Aunt Lillie said. "There be one more under it. And in the chest over there are some more. Most has been give away or worn out over the years. And I have sold many through the cooperative, too. I made the one on top around 1975."

"How did you learn to do this?"

"I been making quilts since I was eleven year old, Gideon Roth. My mama and grandma and my aunts learnt me when I was a girl."

She stopped talking; her silence seemed abrupt. *Have I made her wonder again whether I'm worth talking to?*

"I didn't ask that question right," said Gideon. "What you are doing is obviously more than what you have 'learned' from others."

Aunt Lillie saw he understood.

"Yes," she said, "I learned how to do things from them when I was a girl, how to stitch and tack down and such. But by and by I learned how to be myself, how to show myself in the quilts. As I got older, I saw they each had a way, and their ways wasn't the same. And we tried out each other's ways for whiles. Or some of it. What we learned from each other wasn't just how to stitch cloth together.

"And now I mostly have gone my own way. But there be many other women round here who do this too, in their own ways. You should see their work too."

Aunt Lillie took Gideon around the house to show him where the other quilts were stored—not many were in use in the summer. Gideon tried to take it in. Some of them were mainly geometric creations, like the first one; others were more patterned; others he could not categorize. All shared an air of improvisation, an eccentricity and humor within a discipline.

The first, Aunt Lillie told Gideon, included cloth from her daddy and mama's pants and dresses, clothes they had literally worn to pieces. When she slept under that one, she told Gideon, she felt their presence.

88

Gerard Jeffers and Timmie Ray Phelps sat in the luncheonette across from the courthouse. The waitress had refilled their coffee cups, and Jeffers was eating a second donut in spite of his diet. Phelps was finishing his breakfast.

"It's been a week," Jeffers said. "I'm hopeful nothing's going to happen. There's reason for cautious optimism."

He's repeating himself, Timmie Ray thought, for no good reason.

"Right," he said. "No more calls. Price and the others still alive and well. No sign of Roth or his truck."

"And nothing on the all points on the truck."

"A few blue pickups stopped, but none of them was Roth."

He picked at the remains of a biscuit.

"We couldn't guard Price and them the whole time," Timmie Ray said. "I can't keep someone out there, keeping an eye on Price's house forever."

"What do you think it means?"

"Maybe Channing talked him out of it. Maybe I imagined the whole thing. Maybe he just was never the kind of person who would shoot Cecil Price."

Maybe he's going to do it next week.

"You think we should warn Price?" Jeffers asked. "Tell him to go fishing for a few days? Or to a whorehouse in Memphis?"

"I don't think we need do that. We'll keep an ear out for more calls."

"I'm really worried," the DA said, "to tell you the truth."

89

Gideon visited with other very old women who quilted. Some were in their 70s and 80s, some in their 50s and 60s; only a few of the quilters were in their thirties. Gideon wondered how long this medium would survive.

He spent many mornings sitting by Aunt Lillie, watching quietly as she worked. Sometimes she talked to him about how it had been, and sometimes she worked quietly and he sat quietly.

She let him hold the larger part of the work that she had started, stretched across his lap so he could see what was emerging. Though she did not need to look at it to know how the whole quilt would develop, Gideon was allowed to see the work of her mind slowly unfold before him, as she stitched in place one piece after another. Other times he went into another room and looked at a quilt and sat by himself with the work for a long time.

He had spent days doing nothing but contemplating the creation of these works of art, and it had opened up something in Gideon. It was like being in a museum for weeks, a very personal museum. Some days he sank into a kind of daze, gazing at the quilt and Aunt Lillie's hands, thinking nothing or drifting into reveries of times gone by.

One of those days, he felt her wrinkled hand touch his cheek, and he realized his face was damp with tears. Some feeling evoked by the quilts had released them. Aunt Lillie stood by Gideon and pulled his head to her, resting it against her chest.

"Who these for, Gideon?"

"My wife . . . or Kareem . . . myself maybe. Or maybe this whole terrible country and what it's done to us all."

There was a knot in his throat, and he tried to breathe deeply and slowly to make it go away. He wiped his eyes on her sleeve, and thought what to say.

"Everything's twisted together . . . My life has come apart, my marriage, my profession. It was because of my work for Kareem, the man I couldn't keep the State of California from killing. I put everything into trying to save Kareem, nothing else really mattered."

Aunt Lillie sat and held both his hands.

"Tell me," she said. "Now you got to go back and this time find the earlier beginning."

Gideon told of his decision to take Kareem's case, of the crime, and of the long fight to turn around the death sentence. He told of Kareem's grandfather Joshua, and of what had happened to him. He told of Kareem's father, and of Great Uncle Seth. He told of Jason and Tessa, of Kareem's childhood of terror.

Gideon told of the long breakdown of his marriage. He told of all of the courts of justice of America where he had sought justice without success. He told her of his failure.

"I seen plenty men like Seth in my time," Aunt Lillie said. "I heard tell of men who done suffered like Joshua, but thank the Lord, I never saw such a thing. I know it happen many times when I was a girl."

She stroked Gideon's hand with both of hers, and he saw, against his own fingers, with his skin torn at the cuticles, Aunt Lillie's creamy-colored, strong, brown hands, her smooth skin spotted and tracked with many thin blue veins.

"Were you responsible for Joshua's and Jason's fate?" she asked. "Or for what happen to Kareem when he was a baby?"

"No."

"That's right. What happen to them was because of hundreds of years of slavery and discriminating and hate. And when they made Kareem what he was and wanted to kill him for it, you tried to stand in front of the locomotive and stop it. You held it back for . . . how long you say it was?"

"Fourteen years, Auntie."

"And you think stopping that thing for fourteen years was nothing?"

"No. But I didn't stop it. I couldn't save him. I just slowed it."

"That locomotive been maiming and running down us black folk for four hundred years. They been throwin' us onto the rails since they took us from Africa, and they ain't stopped. How could you stop it?"

Gideon felt it was more complicated than that. Then he thought about what she'd said. Maybe it was not so much more complicated. Maybe that's what it all came down to.

"Because you white, you thought you could control it. And that was good, good that you had that faith, because it help you fight so strong for so long. But you couldn't change the system, and you ain't responsible for it. Why would you think you was?"

He had no answer.

"You give that boy fourteen years of life, Gideon Roth. Tell me how he use them."

Gideon remembered that Kareem himself had told him. "He used them to come to understand who he was. To understand, and to regret what he had done, with understanding."

"Then you gave him more than fourteen years. You did a great, great thing for him. You let him become a human being."

They were both silent.

"Gideon, in my time I seen colored men turned into animals by what white folks' hatred done to them, seen them hurt their wives and childrens. I've seen my own children hurt, hurt so deep when they understood how they had to live, what they could not be, my heart near burst. And I hated and I done wrong myself. Do you think my art was a waste, my life was a waste, 'cause I couldn't stop those things?"

"No, of course not."

"What's the difference? We do what we can do. We bear what we got to bear. We use the one life God's given us best we can. You done that, and no one can do no more. We only here one time before God takes us back to Him, and we got to try to do good as best we can. And to understand. If you had been the onliest man on earth who understood what happened to Kareem, what happened to his daddy and mama, what happened to his grand daddy and grandma, the onliest man on earth to know why that poor woman died and left behind her poor baby, your life would not be a waste."

She squeezed his hands, more strongly than he thought she could.

"We can't understand God's ways, Gideon, but that woman—and Kareem and the others—are all with Jesus now, at his feet. Comforted forever for what happened. I see that ain't your way of seeing it, but it's mine. I don't know why God made it happen this way, and you can't know why it happened, or what you might ought to have done that would have made it end any different. Afterward, we always think we can see what we should of done different. But we don't know and we never know. You can't throw away your life too. You been a good man. Now you got to forgive yourself."

As she looked at him, the arguments drained out of Gideon. He began to feel he did not have to be ashamed of wanting to live.

"Now you go for a walk, Gideon Roth, while I work on my quilt until dinner."

90

Time for me to move on, Gideon thought, late the next morning. To move forward. Maybe that bastard Price just isn't my business. But I don't know that I can move forward.

But still. How could he just forget about it all, walk away? Maybe to confront Price in some other way. Or just to see what it would be like.

Would have been like. What more was there for him to do with his life? If there isn't going to be a final act?

Gideon told them he was going off for a few days to attend to something. He said his good-bye to Aunt Lillie, and Charles drove him to the bus station. A few hours later, he was back at the barn outside Winona.

The Yalobusha Contractors truck sat undisturbed. He got in and rolled down the windows, pushed the doors open to let in a breath of air. The heat was cloying, even though he'd parked the truck in the shade of a tree.

He sat on the edge of the driver's seat, his feet dangling out the door. He stared at the sagging barn and wondering how long it would be before it fell over and if anyone would see it collapse. A jumble of morning glories were growing wild along a fence beside the barn.

He walked around the truck, looking at the traffic barriers he'd placed in the cargo bed. He returned to the cab and sat quietly. Forty minutes went by. The gospel song he heard yesterday was playing in his head.

Can't no one know at sunrise
How this day is going to end.

He started the engine with the alligator clips and drove to Philadelphia. It was late afternoon when he got there.

The police car was no longer parked down the block from Price's house. Even if at worst they somehow suspected something, in some vague way, Philadelphia was a small town. They could not keep a police car occupied indefinitely, staking out Price's home.

A large vacant area stood between Price's house and the next one. Gideon parked the Yalobusha Contractors truck across from there, on the side of Center Avenue without houses. There was a clear line of sight from the truck's windows to Price's front door. Yes, this was how it could be done.

He picked up the clipboard and, on a blank form it held, quickly wrote up a work order for 402—490 Center Avenue for the following three days. He put on the orange reflector vest and a pair of heavy work gloves, stepped out of the truck with the clipboard, and took the traffic cones from the back seat. Ostentatiously consulting the clipboard and the street addresses of houses along the street, Gideon placed lines of cones ahead of and behind the truck, spaced to occupy much of the length of the street across from Price's side.

Gideon taped paper sheets to the four traffic barricades he had appropriated, and with a heavy marker pen wrote:

NO PARKING
WED—FRI

He carried two barricades toward the south end of the block. He unfolded them about ten feet from each other and turned on their flashers. Then did the same at the north end of the street, close to where the police car had been. It looked official.

No one was around. Gideon put the orange vest and the gloves in the pickup truck. On the floor of the back seat, under his sleeping bag, were his satchel of cash and things, and his rifle and guns. Without a key, he couldn't lock the truck. He would have to rely on how law-abiding Philadelphia folks likely were.

Gideon walked toward downtown. At the end of the block, he looked back. The truck and the barricades and cones were persuasive. Some sort of construction work was to begin the next day.

Gideon walked past the courthouse square and found a local restaurant. *The Magnolia of Philadelphia* was etched on a small glass window, *Southern Cuisine*. He had dinner.

Gideon lingered, nursing a glass of bourbon. Though his mind returned again and again to Cecil Price and the alternative ways this day could end, Gideon tried to make himself think of other things.

He thought about the partnership meeting when they'd forced him out. And the brawl he had embraced the night of the execution, the brawl that had step-by-step led to the end of his life at the law firm. That he had let end his life at the firm. Tearing loose, as well, the last fraying threads binding him to Helen.

He thought of their early days together. He recalled going to the movies with her in Boston after they'd first met, the casual, uncomplicated plea-sure of those evenings. Once, when they'd gone to New York to meet his dad, he had taken her to one of the gigantic old movie palaces in the Bronx where he used to go as a kid. Sometimes Mom had kept him home from school, just to give him a day off, and they had gone to the movies together.

Gideon thought how long it had taken him to understand Kareem and his life, of the years over which they had become—well, not friends, but to form their special bond. He thought of decisions he had made, and mistakes. But he did not feel so much pain, so much guilt over them.

He thought about the years that had stretched between taking on Kareem's case and the rainy afternoon when Helen had driven out of his life. He tried to think past it, to the times they had enjoyed together, been something for each other.

Gideon's sadness was accompanied by lethargy, by the wish not to have to continue struggling. It wasn't so much that his depression was too much to bear. It was that he was exhausted with the need to construct reasons for being. He didn't want to try any more.

He recalled a quotation from St. Exupery: "Each man must look to himself to teach him the meaning of life. It is not something discovered; it is something molded." Once Gideon had seen this as inspiration. Now he felt it as a challenge, a burden that daunted him. Here, in the darkness that was Neshoba County, Gideon felt it might be easier simply to act. And then end himself.

Dusk was approaching. Gideon left the restaurant. He stopped at a phone booth near the courthouse square on Center. From the booth, He could see the confederate soldier on the column, and also the jail. It was a two minutes walk to the truck and to Price's house.

He dropped in two quarters and dialed the number by now so familiar to him.

"Hullo?"

Gideon hesitated, smiled.

"Hullo? Damn it . . ."

"Hello, Cecil."

"Oh, sorry. Thought you was someone else. Who is this?"

"No need to apologize, Cecil. You were right. This is the man who's been calling you. But this time I am doing the talking.

"Don't interrupt me and listen closely. If you want these calls to end—if you don't want to worry about what I intend to do for as long as you may have left of your life—you need to do precisely what I'm about to tell you to do.

"There's a place out Highway 19, a place where black folks go to drink called LaVerne's. You know it?"

"Yeah, sure."

"Leave for LaVerne's exactly ten minutes from now. No sooner. No later. You'll arrive a little before I do. Get yourself a beer and sit by yourself and I'll join you and we'll talk."

"Why the hell should I . . ."

Gideon hung up.

✶ ✶ ✶

The cop on the wiretap duty in Meridian had taken a break, stepping outside to smoke. When he returned 15 minutes later, a red light was blinking, indicating that the tape had run to record a call. He listened to it, then immediately called the dispatcher.

"How fast can you get a car out to Cecil Price's house at 444 Center? And another to LaVerne's, on Highway 19?

"Do it faster. Price is probably heading there and maybe also someone who's fixing to kill him."

Then he called Sheriff Timmie Ray Phelps.

91

Gideon walked briskly down Center Avenue. The street was empty. He got into the pickup truck, started up briefly so he could lower the left-hand front window, on the side facing Price's house. He turned the engine off.

The night was somewhat lighted by a rising quarter moon. The dim light it cast on the street and on the outside of the pickup truck made the inside seem blacker and even less visible from outside. Gideon moved to the rear seat and removed the head rest from the driver's seat.

He picked up the rifle, rested it on the back of the driver's seat. He hesitated, then snapped a magazine of four cartridges into the rifle. He had a clear view of Price's door and of the path Price would take to walk to his car in the driveway.

Gideon let his eyes get used to the darkness.

The position was uncomfortable. Gideon put the gun down. He folded his light jacket to make a cushion and sat on it to raise himself a couple of inches. Now he could hold the weapon without strain or tension. He could swing the barrel freely to track Price's position between the door and the driveway.

Gideon lifted the rifle a small amount and aimed at the front door. At this distance, there would have been little need to compensate for wind even had there been a moderate breeze. But the night was still. Gideon flipped off the safety.

Katydids made their usual commotion. Gideon breathed evenly and held the stillness in himself as he waited, at ease. He pressed lightly on the trigger. There was a kind of blankness in his mind, perhaps a numbness. What did he want? Was there anything to go back to?

He knew the point of pressure that would cause the rifle to fire, and squeezed almost to that point. One minute went by and he relaxed his finger to avoid cramping or stiffness. Then he squeezed again. In less than two seconds I could put a pattern of three bullets into Price's chest, he thought. Gideon loosened, then tightened his finger for another minute. He relaxed his finger.

The door opened and over the sights he saw a woman in the lighted doorway. Price's wife? He sensed a murmur but could not hear what she was saying. She moved aside, and Price stepped into the back light of the doorway. Gideon saw the silhouette and lined up the sights with Price's chest. Just like Medgar Evers, but this time it's one of them. Gideon thought of the trigger and the blast, and the kick of the gun. Price falling. The blankness in him grew louder.

Price stopped in the doorway as his wife gently rested her hand on his upper arm for a moment.

Price moved toward his car. Gideon followed him, shifting his aim to Price's head. Gideon thought of the small force of his finger squeezing, the infinite force passing through the barrel in a line that leapt between Gideon Roth and Cecil Price to shatter Cecil Price's skull and brain. He thought of the body slamming onto the ground next to the car. He thought of Cecil Price ceasing to exist as a person, remaining only as memory in the minds of those who recalled him. Price, dead, the victim of a violent act, like Mickey Schwerner, James Chaney, Andy Goodman.

Cecil Price paused to open the door of his car as Gideon squeezed the trigger, and . . .

He sat inside himself, remote, unmoved, watching a man in a pickup truck who was himself, sitting suspended. In his hands an instrument of death, aimed at another human being, poised to kill. Gideon saw himself watching Cecil Price hesitate, then get into his car, start the engine, and— still in the rifle's cross-hairs—back onto the street. Unmoving, Gideon saw Price drive away.

The rifle pointed at the now empty driveway. Gideon heard the katy- dids again. He loosened his finger and leaned back against the rear seat. His self rushed back into his benumbed mind.

It was over.

He slipped on the rifle's safety, pulled out the magazine, and, hands shaking violently, threw the magazine to the floor of the truck. He ejected the bullet in the chamber. He put the rifle down more slowly, covering it with his sleeping bag. He felt his heart thudding, and he closed his eyes, seeking to calm himself.

He opened the door and stepped down out of the back seat, onto the running board, and then to the ground. He stood in the night, looking at the lights in the home of Cecil Price.

Gideon heard a siren in the distance, coming from the west. He wait- ed for a moment, waited for them to arrive. Then he got into the front seat and started the engine. Without turning on the headlights, he came around and slowly drove the three small blocks to the edge of the courthouse square. At the stop sign, Gideon turned on the headlights and headed toward Highway 19.

92

Past the city limit, on Highway 19, Price was speeding south ahead of him. Just as—thirty-three years ago this very night—Schwerner, Chaney and Goodman had tried to flee from Cecil Price, vainly seeking the safety of Meridian. But Gideon was no longer considering an act of homicide.

Even a three or four minute head start can be hard to make up, Gideon thought. But the big pickup was powerful, and as the road straightened Gideon cranked it up to ninety miles an hour. Going into mild curves, he felt the vehicle swaying to one side then the other, and he slowed a little, then regained his speed. Before ten minutes had gone by, Gideon saw tail lights in the distance.

Gideon let up on the accelerator and closed more slowly. It appeared to be Price's car. He could just follow it to LaVerne's. But Gideon was not going to have a drink with Cecil Price.

Gideon eased closer to Price's vehicle, then swung into the left lane as though to pass. As Gideon came abreast of Price, Price slowed to let him go by, but Gideon also slowed, and began pushing to the right with the big vehicle. Price moved right too and braked, but Gideon also braked and continued to press toward Price's car, forcing Price off the road.

As he was about to get out, Gideon thought, There's danger here. Should I pocket the handgun?

But when you carry a gun into a situation, he reflected, it becomes more dangerous. I'll take my chances.

Price had backed up to give his headlights full play on the big pickup truck, but he was not trying to get away. Gideon slowly stepped down into the headlights' glare, his hands in front of him a little below waist level, palms outward, to show he was unarmed, almost a gesture of offering. He heard Price's car door open, and as Price stepped to the side, Gideon could see that he held a gun, pointed in Gideon's direction.

"Who the fuck are you, and what do you want?"

Gideon smiled. "Don't worry Cecil, I'm not carrying a pistol. A little different from the way you organized it around here in 1964, isn't it?"

Price was silent, and Gideon slowly let his hands down. They looked at each other for long moments.

"That was many years ago," Price said more softly. "What do you want?"

"I want to talk to you."

"You called enough times without talking," Price said.

Gideon did not respond.

"All right," Price said. "Come with me. No, wait. First pull your pockets inside out. Do it slowly." Gideon complied.

"Now turn around and do the same with your back pockets."

Gideon slowly turned. I can't see any reason for Price to shoot me in the back. Gideon took his wallet out and put it on the ground next to himself, slowly rose and pulled out both back pockets. Price came up to him and felt around Gideon's waist for a gun, then checked Gideon's ankles. Strange to feel Cecil Price's hands on him, the intimacy of Price's touch, to have placed himself within Price's power. It balanced, in a small way, the violation of Cecil Price that Gideon committed when he aimed a rifle at him.

Price stepped backed, looked through Gideon's wallet.

"Not much in here but your temporary license, Cargill."

"No, there isn't," said Gideon, turning around toward Price and pushing his pockets back in.

"That means you're not really Cargill, right? And this is the truck that was parked across from my house earlier this evening, isn't it?" Price tucked the gun into his waistband.

"Where shall we go to talk?" said Gideon.

Price thought for a moment. He handed Gideon his wallet.

"Why don't we just go to LaVerne's?" said Price.

"No," said Gideon. "We must be close to where it happened. Where you seized them. We'll take your car. That's where you're going to drive me."

Price paused. "I've never gone back since 1964."

"Well, you are now."

They got into Price's truck. He drove south three miles, to County Road 492, and turned onto it. About a mile down the road he pulled over.

"I stopped them right around here. Do you also want to see where the others shot them? You want a tour of the whole thing?" He had sounded thoughtful before, but now he seemed surly.

"This is enough," said Gideon. He said nothing, and Price was also silent. He did not know what to make of Price. He could no longer summon the rage he had felt.

"It's hard for you to understand what it was like back then," said Price.

"I was there that summer," said Gideon angrily. "It could have happened to me. I understand perfectly well."

"I mean what it was like on our side. It was a bad period. Integration was being thrust on us all of a sudden, and we acted hastily, probably."

"Acted hastily?" said Gideon. "Probably? You murdered three young men in cold blood."

"Look, I paid my debt to society. I did something wrong. And I was punished. Though I didn't shoot any of them myself."

Gideon said nothing. This is just a hollow man. Like so many people who kill. Like my friend Kareem, too, whom life had first crushed and flattened. Is Cecil Price more hollow than Kareem Jackson was? Is it too late for Price to understand?

Price had turned the headlights down. Gideon saw his sagging face, old and tired, and a little stupid, in the dim moonlight and the green light from the instrument panel.

"I was on the phones that night," Gideon said. "I was the one who tried to get the FBI to go down your jailhouse, to stop you. But they wouldn't listen. Then I had to make the calls to their parents. Can you imagine what that was like? What they went through?"

"I paid my debt to society," Price repeated. He sounded as though he had said this many times before.

"Fuck your debt to society," Gideon said. "It will never be paid." He looked at Price, then at the quiet, empty road where it had happened.

"Andy's mother hoped it was just a mistake," Gideon said. "She hoped he hadn't actually reached Mississippi yet and he was still safe. I had to take that hope away from her. She was trying as hard as she could to be calm and brave, so they could do something to try to save their boy's life.

Can you imagine what the fear in her voice sounded like, Cecil? But it was already too late. By the time I was talking to her and Andy's father, and to Mickey's folks, by the time someone else had broken the news to Chaney's people, you and your friends had already murdered the three boys."

Price was quiet again. "Back then," he finally said, "people just couldn't grasp the way things would be afterward. But finally we had to accept this was the way things were going to be, and that's it.

"Look, I wound up sending my own kid to integrated schools in Philadelphia, though I could have sent him to an academy where there weren't any coloreds. I thought, society's going to be integrated, so it's better for my boy to be brought up in it."

Price was saying the right kind of thing, but he did not appear pained by the memory of what he had done. Neither repentant nor burdened. A hollow man. Maybe too hollow, Gideon thought, to stand for all the things I wanted to kill with you.

Gideon had nothing more to say. Both men were quiet for a while. The only sounds were the engine idling, and every now and then, the faint drone of a car going down Highway 19, a mile off.

"I thought you wanted to talk to me," said Price. "Is this all? What do you want with me? What were you doing outside my house?"

"I was thinking I'd kill you," said Gideon. "But then I stopped thinking that was right. And now I'm not going to do anything."

Price laughed nervously, then was silent.

Gideon supposed he could challenge Price's feelings about the victims, tell Price what he thought of him. But in the end, the conversation would only confirm that all of this did not matter much to Cecil Price anymore. Price was an empty man and Gideon realized that what Price might have to say for himself did not matter to Gideon. He had tried to give Cecil Price the opportunity which fourteen years had given Kareem Jackson, but he couldn't tell whether Price had grasped it.

Gideon Roth opened the car door and he stepped out, into the oppressively humid Mississippi night. Right here, on this spot, Mickey Schwerner, James Chaney and Andy Goodman had been seized, to be taken to a place where minutes later their lives were ended. He felt the sadness of it, the loss, though it was thirty-three years ago. Nothing he might have done could have changed that. And nothing he could do to Cecil Price now could further enhance their glory. Tears came to his eyes, and he wiped them away.

He stepped away from the car.

"Hey, mister, don't you want a ride back to your car?"

Gideon began walking to Highway 19.

93

It took Gideon an hour and a half to get back to his pickup truck. I am not sure why I am feeling liberated, he thought, as he walked by the roadside. I came within the tremble of a finger of committing murder.

The frame of mind in which this had seemed a reasonable thing to consider was retreating rapidly.

As he approached the truck, he recalled there was still the small matter of grand theft auto.

* * *

At LaVerne's, Sheriff Timmie Ray Phelps questioned the bar man again. Was he sure a strange white man with a northern accent had not been there this evening? Or any other time recently? Or placed a phone call from there?

"Sheriff, there ain't been no white man in here in weeks 'cept you right now and 'cept the man who deliver the beer. And there ain't been no one, no color, no how, here tonight who ain't a regular. That's it, Sheriff. You think I ain't gonna notice a strange white man in a place like this?"

A few minutes ago Timmie Ray had been on the radio with the car that was outside Cecil Price's house. Officer Harmony reported that Price had returned home an hour ago, hale and healthy as far as could be told, and by himself.

Time to talk to Cecil Price.

"If any white man shows up here," he told the bartender, "or any other stranger with a northern accent, you call me immediately, you hear? Might be someone about six feet tall, bald on top. But anyone, any stranger or white man shows up, you call me or the station right away."

"Sure, Sheriff. Don't know no white man who looks like you say, but I'll call if he walks in here."

Timmie Ray grew increasingly irate in the fifteen mile drive to Philadelphia.

Worrying about this caller for weeks, then there's the break with the fingerprints. Then the call from the Idaho Highway Patrolman, then I talk to his old girlfriend. We identify Roth. We know what he looks like. We know what his pickup truck looks like, too. He slips through anyway and calls Price, and we actually hear him. And we still can't catch the fucker.

God damn it.

A police car sat outside Price's house. Timmie Ray went up to the officer.

"He see you? Say anything?"

"Sure he saw me. How could he miss? He eyeballed me good then he just went inside."

"Okay. Come with me. What's with the construction barriers and the cones?"

"Beats me."

Price was sitting at the kitchen table with his wife. He let Timmie Ray and Harmony in, and they all sat there.

"You've been out for a ride, Cecil."

"Well, yeah."

"Tell me all about it."

"Not much to tell. Some crank's been calling me for months, ringing my phone all hours. Never says a word. No idea who it was. Tonight he finally says something. Tells me he wants to meet me at LaVerne's. I head over and on the way he runs me off the road.

"He's driving this big crew pickup that was parked across the street with the road work or something they're about to do. He comes up behind me on Highway 19 and forces me off the road. Shit, begging your pardon, Conner, I could have been hurt. We stop around there and talk.

"Says he wants to talk about 1964. Except he didn't say all that much." Price stopped, he looked down. His face became looser, then his jaw tightened.

"What else?" Timmie Ray asked.

"He said he'd been thinking of shooting me, but he changed his mind. He didn't have no gun on him. I checked.

"We was riding together then and we stopped at Road 492. We talked some. Then all of a sudden, he gets out and walks away. Just like that. Didn't want a ride back.

"I drove home. That's it. Last I seen him."

"What did he look like?"

"A little shorter than me. Bald on top, messy dark hair on the sides and in back. Bushy moustache. Heavy black glasses. Yankee accent."

"Did he threaten you?"

"No, not a threat. Don't know what to call it. He said he wasn't going to bother me no more. I guess I believe it."

"What's going on with the work on the street? He had something to do with it, you said?"

"Well, he had a big pickup truck that I think said something construction on the side. It had been parked out here. I wasn't noticing much about it until I see it looks like the truck that's driving me off the road on Highway 19."

"License plate?"

"Mississippi. I didn't notice the number."

"Color?"

"Green and something. Maybe white. It was dark and I was thinking about him, not the truck."

"What make?"

"A Ford, one of the big F-350s I think."

"Harmony, see what you can learn about the construction company. But first, put out an all points for the truck and the driver."

All points, Harmony said to himself. Lot of damn good that's gonna do this time of night, and no license plate!

Harmony left for his car radio, to do the Sheriff's bidding. Timmie Ray turned back to Price. "Mrs. Price, you can be excused for now, Ma'am."

When she left, Timmie Ray asked, "Now, Cecil, you tell me the whole story, top to bottom again. Exactly what happened, exactly what you said and what he said. Don't leave out anything this time."

94

No police car was waiting for Gideon when he reached the pickup truck, so Gideon inferred that Cecil Price had not called the cops on returning home. But he could not count on that going on. Getting out of Neshoba County right now would be a good idea, and back roads were the best way to go. If he could get a half hour lead, the chances were slim anyone would find him or figure out who he was.

Gideon drove south to County Road 492 again, then west until 492 connected to 487. In forty minutes, he passed through a number of tiny towns. Union, Sebastopol, Salem and Madden. He scarcely saw a moving vehicle. When he reached State Highway 35, he turned north toward Carthage.

A small bridge crossed the Pearl River. It was past 11 p.m. and Gideon had seen no traffic for a long while. He pulled over and put on the latex gloves he had purchased in Memphis. He took the rifle and the two handguns from the floor of the back seat, and with an undershirt he wiped them clean of prints.

Gideon stepped out of the truck and casually looked both ways. Still no one in sight. He carried the weapons to the middle of the bridge and dropped them into the Pearl River. Gideon looked down into the darkness for a time.

At Carthage, he turned southwest in the direction of Jackson. After twenty minutes he stopped at a campground. He parked out of sight of the highway. He slept in the back seat of the crew cab.

Gideon rose around 8 o'clock and considered what to do about the truck. He would have liked to return it to long term parking at the Memphis airport. He liked the idea of it being found where it ought to have been, a little the worse for wear, perhaps with money from his cash store to compensate Mr. Washington.

But it might have been reported missing by now. And Cecil Price had had two good opportunities to see the truck, on Highway 19, and earlier, across the street from his house. Gideon had to assume Price would soon tell his story to the cops, if he had not done so already. And at least one of his neighbors might have noticed the name on the side of the truck while Gideon was having dinner at The Magnolia last night. So the sooner that Gideon and the vehicle parted company, the better. Then there would only be Price's ability to describe him that posed any danger to Gideon.

He thought about the scope of his exposure to criminal charges. He knew that his plan had gone far enough, technically speaking, as a matter of law, for it to be considered attempted murder. Though it might be difficult for the state to prove that. But the simple matter of grand and petty larceny—stealing a pickup truck and the highway barricades—were doubtless good for many years in Parchman Farm.

Sitting at a picnic table in the campsite, Gideon desperately wished for a cup of coffee. That would have to wait. He focused on the problem at hand.

No one was in the bathroom when Gideon clipped his moustache and then shaved it off. He also cut the shaggy hair on the sides of his head and in back as short as he could with a pair of scissors. It looked decidedly home done, but that would not matter for long.

The campground was mostly empty when Gideon returned to the pickup truck, and there was no one to notice him wiping clean all the surfaces that might have taken prints. When he finished, Gideon put on the latex gloves and drove into Jackson.

He parked in what seemed to be a large, high end shopping mall. He jotted down Yalobusha Contractors' address as shown on the registration and noted where he was leaving the pickup truck. Gideon tucked twenty $100 bills from his cash store in the glove compartment, next to the registration. That should pay to fix the ignition and for any parking fines, as well as make up for hurt feelings.

Goodbye, old Paint, I'm a leavin' Cheyenne.

Gideon pushed down the buttons to lock the doors of the pickup truck, closed the door, peeled off the gloves, and walked away with his satchel. This was a busy place; no one seemed to notice him.

In the mall, Gideon found a barber shop and had his head shaved entirely clean. Gave his face a shave too. He ignored the barber's attempts at small talk.

Gideon took a bus from the mall to downtown Jackson. He found a taxicab and asked the driver to take him to the best men's clothing store in town. He bought an expensive cream-colored summer suit, a white shirt and a tie, and a pair of dark, aviation-style designer sunglasses. He paid cash and wore his new clothes. Nearby, he bought a pair of expensive boots.

The clothing and shoes he had been wearing since yesterday were in the shopping bag from the clothing store. Gideon walked a few blocks then tossed the bag into a dumpster. He dug in his satchel and confirmed that he still had his regular narrow, tortoise-shell eyeglasses. He discarded the thick, black-framed glasses, and put on his own.

At a pharmacy Gideon bought a comb and a pair of small scissors. After lunch, in the restroom of a small restaurant, he used these to thin his usually bushy eyebrows. He had also bought tanning oil, the kind that darkened your skin to make it look like you had a tan from the sun. He rubbed this into his scalp so his head looked darker where the hair had been.

Can't no one know at sunrise
How this day is going to end.

The man in the mirror looked considerably different from the man who had driven Cecil Price off the road last night.

Gideon walked eight blocks to the bus station. Along the way he pitched his maps of Philadelphia into one trash can, and his printouts about Cecil Price into a another a couple of blocks away. For now, he still had his James Cargill driver's license. But nothing else remained to tie Gideon to his quest in Philadelphia.

He bought a bus ticket to Memphis and a few picture postcards that said "Greetings from Mississippi!" Being careful not to touch the shiny side, Gideon addressed a card to Yalobusha Contractors. In small block letters he wrote:

FORD PICKUP FORMERLY AT MEMPHIS INTL NOW AT McALISTER'S DELI, NORTHPARK MALL, JACKSON. SORRY AND THANKS. SEE GLOVE COMPARTMENT FOR FULL APOLOGY.

He dropped the postcard into a letter box shortly before the bus left.

When the Memphis bus stopped at Batesville, he went to the rest room and stayed there until the bus left without him. Then he called Charles to get a ride back to the farm.

"You look differenter every time," Charles said. "I'm worrying about you."

"Well, it's over now," Gideon said, "and no harm done to anyone."

On the drive back to the farm, Gideon recounted all he had done in Philadelphia the previous day.

"Not sure I get what you thought you were doing, Gideon. But I guess it turned out okay. You telling me it could've gone the other way?"

"Maybe. I'm not sure. I don't think I ever exactly intended it, but maybe."

"You had a close call, Gideon. The Lord saved you from an awful mistake. I hope you ain't never gonna do nothing like that again."

"No, never again, Charles."

"Well, whatever you have done or thought of doing, however long you need, you got a refuge here."

"I think it might be a good idea for me to stay out of sight until my hair grows in," Gideon said. "And . . . and anyway, I'm not sure where to go next."

95

There was nothing in the news to suggest the police were on the trail of Gideon Roth or James Cargill, and after a week of apparent silence Gideon began to relax.

Although Sheriff Timmie Ray Phelps had connected James Cargill with Gideon Roth, in searching for him they had little more to go on than Price's and Officer Vanderson's somewhat vague descriptions of a partly bald man with disheveled reddish brown hair on the sides and a big moustache, a man who wore thick, black-rimmed glasses. In the days following Gideon's confrontation with Price, no such man was sighted by the Mississippi Highway Patrol or by any local police department. Timmie Ray concluded that Roth had left the state.

Since the possible crime for which they sought Gideon, as they understood it, seemed vague, and they had no real evidence, they soon lost interest. Price was alive and unharmed. The phone calls stopped. And they did not believe they would see Gideon Roth again.

Eventually, Memphis Airport Parking towed away the blue pickup truck and sold it at auction when no one claimed the vehicle. As for the Ford pickup truck Gideon had "borrowed" from the airport, after getting Gideon's postcard, Lester Washington's partner at Yalobusha Contractors retrieved the vehicle from the Jackson mall. When they discovered $2,000 in the glove compartment, they concluded the money more than compensated for any inconvenience. They also agreed that if they reported the crime, the police were likely to seize the cash as evidence. So they decided to leave the law out of it and ignore the temporary theft.

✳ ✳ ✳

After two weeks, Gideon's mostly white hair had begun to grow back, though it had the severe crew cut look of someone in the service. His apparent similarities to the James Cargill who had stalked Cecil Price were steadily declining, along with his fears of apprehension so long as he stayed out of Neshoba County.

Early in July, he sent one of the picture postcards to Helen:

Been through a thing or two, but I'm okay now. No need for any worries. Will be here for a while longer. I hope you are well and happy.

Love, Gideon

And another to Susan:

Finding myself (so to speak) in Mississippi. But no harm done to anyone. We'll meet again, in time.

Love, Gideon

96

In mid-July, the Clarion-Ledger reported Cecil Price's death.

Price had fallen off a lift at an equipment rental store in Philadelphia and fractured his skull. He had been taken to the University of Mississippi Medical Center in Jackson, where he died three days later. As the article noted, this was the same medical center to which, three decades earlier, Cecil Price had himself helped to transport the bodies of Mickey Schwerner, James Chaney and Andy Goodman for autopsies.

Gideon felt a sort of bewilderment over Price's death.

Price's long life of undeserved freedom had ended, and his passing was a matter of public note only because of his infamous criminal acts. Yet in the end Price had escaped any substantial punishment for three murders. Gideon still considered this regrettable. But he no longer regarded it as a matter that he personally bore responsibility for.

Gideon felt as though he had been composing a work of performance art, whose resolution was to have been an act of dramatic violence. Gideon had cancelled the piece, but Price himself had nonetheless performed a coda.

97

Over the next week, Gideon sat with Aunt Lillie again and again. He remembered and recounted happy times with Helen, and told stories about them without so much pain.

"Sounds like there were a lot of good things that happened in your life with Helen, Gideon."

"Yes. But we were not much connected for the last fifteen years. I don't think it can be put back together if that's what you're asking."

"I'm not asking nothing. You got to do your own asking and your own answering."

Aunt Lillie was sitting in a hard chair on the porch, arranging strips of cloth for a new quilt, and Gideon sat beside her in a rocking chair. Her calm had flowed into him, and he felt no impulse to speak.

Gideon mused over the places where their histories were indirectly connected. He thought of what Aunt Lillian had meant to him, and realized he needed to tell her the truth.

"Auntie . . ."

He recounted his phone calls to Cecil Price and the others, and told her of the planning that had started in California. His trip across the country, and his meeting with Susan, and his first visit to Philadelphia. And what he had done and come close to doing in Philadelphia that final day.

Toward the end Aunt Lillie had stopped her stitching, and sat looking at Gideon.

"How terrible it would have been," she finally said, holding Gideon's eyes with hers, "if this Cecil Price's sinful deed had reach across thirty years to cause one last, most evilest wrong: turning a good man into a murderer. You had a close call, Gideon. The Lord stayed your hand and He denied Cecil Price that final victory."

Gideon listened to the creak of the chair as he slowly rocked back and forth.

"After you and I talked last week, I felt I no longer wanted to kill him. But something in me still wanted to see what it would have been like. If I had pulled the trigger, it would almost have been an accident. Maybe an accident on purpose. I don't know if killing him would have been the accident or if not killing him was the accident. Or maybe it was meeting you that was the accident, meeting you and coming to understand some things I had been blind to."

"In quilting, we got something we calls 'accidentals,'" said Aunt Lillie. "Into the design, something unplanned happen because of the materials. Irregular as life. Bringing in something you did not plan. But then you improvise on it, you build with it. Maybe you play with it. And you find it lead you to something new and beautiful."

Gideon thought about talking with Aunt Lillie. And about the odd bends in her quilts.

"This Susan who tried to talk you out of coming to Mississippi," Aunt Lillie said slyly, "she may be a big bright patch you found by accident that's too big to fit in easy, but too good to leave out now that you done seen it.

"But then maybe you got more than one good patch to work with."

Gideon laughed. "Maybe it takes a better quilter than me."

"You get to be as good a quilter as you need to be, as good a quilter as you care enough to be," said Aunt Lillie.

98

Gideon went to visit a southern poverty law center and explored the possibility of working with them in some way. He knew he could not do another capital case. But there were other possibilities, and Gideon lined up meetings with a few public interest law firms.

He wrote a long letter to Susan, and she wrote back.

His time in Mississippi was coming to a close, at least as a temporary resident at Jameson Farm. But his departure was delayed by Aunt Lillie's illness. The August heat had sapped her strength, and she somehow caught a summer cold.

While she lay in bed, Gideon read to her from her Bible. And sometimes he just sat by her, holding her hand.

"Gideon, could you start at Joshua?"

He read:

"'Only be thou strong and very courageous, that thou mayest observe to do according to all the law . . . This book of the law shall not depart out of thy mouth; but thou shalt meditate therein day and night . . . Have not I commanded thee? Be not afraid, neither be thou dismayed . . .'

"Auntie, is this for you or for me?"

She smiled, and he read on.

"Read me the part in Judges about Gideon's trumpets," she asked finally.

" '. . . And he divided the three hundred men into three companies, and he put a trumpet in every man's hand, with empty pitchers, and lamps within the pitchers.

"'And the three companies blew the trumpets, and brake the pitchers, and held the lamps in their left hands, and the trumpets in their right hands to blow withal: and they cried, *The sword of the LORD, and of Gideon.*

"'And the three hundred blew the trumpets, and the LORD set every man's sword against his fellow throughout all the host: and the host fled . . . .' "

"Gideon," said Aunt Lillie, "you must be like that Gideon, who was not afraid to test the Lord himself. He has set you, too, to fight for the good against great odds. And like the first Gideon, you must use trumpets and lights and guile, and you will overcome. . ."

Her speech softened and slurred. She seemed to drift off.

"But Gideon," she murmured after a while. "Don't go having threescore and ten sons of your body begotten and many wives, like the first one did. Or the concubine neither. That part didn't turn out so good."

Aunt Lillie weakened and her cold turned to pneumonia. The doctor urged her to come to the hospital for treatment, but she refused.

"I'm afraid of hospitals. I don't want to die in no hospital. If it be my time, let me die at home, under my quilts, with Charles and Gideon nearby."

They hired a nurse to stay at the farm and care for her. She was comfortable, but she faded. Three days later Lillian Lincoln, mother, grandmother, great grandmother, great aunt, artist and friend, died in the night.

Aunt Lillie left two of her quilts to Gideon. One was the first he had seen that had so moved him. The other she had made many years earlier, a very traditional pattern, though one she had realized in a deliberately irregular and original way.

"The pattern is called a 'Double Wedding Ring,'" Charles said. "Did she know something you haven't told me?"

"It would be something I don't know myself. Could have more than one meaning, though."

He hugged his friend fiercely. "Good-bye, Charleston. It may be long before we meet again."

99

It was October. Helen stood next to Gideon at Kareem's grave. He looked at the stone, grieving for the brutalized and once brutal man he had come to love.

Helen took his hand for a moment and squeezed it. He returned her squeeze. A small smile crossed her face, then she turned and walked to her car. Gideon lingered, saying a last goodbye to Kareem. Then he turned to his own car and drove away.

The End

DISCLAIMERS

This book is a work of fiction, but not one of which it can be said, "Any resemblances to actual persons, places and events is purely coincidental." Like many novels that lodge fictional characters and stories in historical events, it is a mixed work of imagination, truth and fact.

Gideon Roth and Kareem Jackson are fictional characters, as are Helen, Susan, Joshua Jackson, Fannie Jo, Jason, Mama, Uncle Benjamin, Seth, Charleston, Ezekiel Samson, Lillie Lincoln, Officer Vanderson, Timmie Ray Phelps, Gerard Jeffers and essentially all other characters not specifically identified here as real people. These fictional characters are not based on real individuals.

None of the attorneys at Gideon's law firm is based on any attorney at the firm where I have worked for four decades, Fenwick & West LLP; and Harkin & Lessman is definitely not my firm. For more than twenty years, Fenwick & West in fact gave unstinting and exemplary support to my own work on a real death penalty case, in which our firm (with our brilliant second counsel Richard C. Neuhoff) finally achieved success for our client in 2008. This book is not based on that case.

Stephen Reinhardt is a real judge of the Ninth Circuit Court of Appeals, as was Fifth Circuit Chief Judge Tuttle, all of the other judges in this book are fictitious characters and not based on real individuals. The jurors are also fictitious. However, Lester Maddox was a real individual who did operate the Pickrick Restaurant, and he became Governor of Georgia based on his racist stand. John Doar was a real person, the head of the Civil Rights Division of the U.S. Justice Department in the 1960s. He led the federal government's efforts against segregation in the South, and personally prosecuted the men who murdered Schwerner, Chaney and Goodman, obtaining convictions for civil rights violations.

Kareem Jackson's life history and crime are not based upon and bear no similarities to those of the death row client I represented. Similarly, all the members of Kareem Jackson's family are fictitious characters, and they are not based on and bear no resemblance to family members of the death row client I represented.

Mickey Schwerner, James Chaney and Andy Goodman were real people, and the account of their murder at the hands of Cecil Price and the other individuals identified in this book is factual. Likewise, the novel provides a factual account of the futile efforts of civil rights workers to get the FBI to investigate their disappearance (and perhaps prevent their murders) while they were still alive. Bob Moses, Jim Forman, Hartman Turnbow, Charlie Cobb, Charles McLaurin and Ron Carver were real civil rights workers, engaged in the freedom struggle portrayed in this novel. The other civil rights workers, local people, police and other persons whom Gideon encounters in the South in the 1960s are fictitious.

Further Reading and Reading Group Guide

To learn more about subjects touched on in this novel, including white supremacy, the civil rights struggle, and the death penalty, please go to www.mississippi-reckoning.com. The Mississippi Reckoning website also includes a Reading Group Guide.